Heat Seeking *Missile*

A Black Watch Security Novel

Kristen Casey

GALLANT FOX
PRESS

Content Guidance

I want my readers to always feel comfortable picking up a Kristen Casey romance, and I recognize that certain topics and scenarios can be challenging to encounter when reading for pleasure. As an avid reader myself, I want to give you the tools to keep yourself safe.

If you would like detailed content information for any of my titles, please scan the QR code or follow the link below, and you will be directed to a dedicated page on my website that lists this information.

In addition, if you encounter a situation in any of my titles that is not listed (but you believe should be), I encourage you to reach out to me at *KristenCasey* [dot] *com* to recommend adding it.

Thank you.

https://www.kristencasey.com/content-guidance

The Black Watch Security Series

False Flag

Heat Seeking Missile

Brothers in Arms

Fight or Flight

Search and Destroy

Squared Away

About This Book

When Bennett Shaw joined the Navy, he had every reason in the world to leave Texas behind—but the biggest one of all was Kim Sutherland, his little sister's best friend. Kim was too young and too pure for the likes of him. The prom queen to his juvenile delinquent. The prize in the forbidden candy jar.

The girl he wanted most but could never have.

The Navy gave him the escape he needed, but now Bennett's been kicked out of the SEALs—and he and the rest of his team are on a dangerous path to expose the people who ruined his only chance to make something better of himself.

Even worse, Kim has shown up in the middle of their operation, claiming to have information they need. With the help of his new employer, the shadowy Black Watch Security firm, Bennett must now execute two missions: take down a crooked arms manufacturer with ties to a U.S. senator—and keep his attraction to Kim on lockdown, no matter how she tempts him.

Bennett hasn't gotten this far by being weak, however. Come hell or high water, he'll make the people who stole his future pay—and under no circumstances will he surrender to Kim Sutherland.

For the ones who persevered.

Prologue

Tate

WITH A MIXTURE of concern and resignation, Tate Monroe sat back in his hotel suite armchair and stared at the breaking news report on the TV. Through the open doorway of the bathroom, his wife Lyla was reflected in the big mirror, a contact lens balanced on her fingertip.

She listened for a moment, then called out, "Dan Cox. Why does that name sound familiar?"

"Because he's a mark in one of my cases."

"The one with the SEALs?"

"Yup."

She popped the lens into her eye, blinked it into place, then bustled out of the bathroom and waved Tate out of his seat. "Your brother's party is in an hour. Get moving, soldier."

He pushed to his feet and accepted the tie she held out, tucking it under his collar and beginning to knot it. However, it seemed he couldn't tie a Windsor while trying to think through the ramifications of this newest development.

Tate gave up and looked at her. "Shit."

"What's wrong?"

He massaged his forehead and sighed, "Babe, this job is growing more legs than a tank full of octopuses."

Lyla cocked her head. "Wouldn't that be *octopi*?"

He shot her a look and continued, "I gotta say, though—this twist was one I did not see coming."

His wife glanced between him and the television, her fancy necklace glittering in the overhead light. "What do those women have to do with it?"

"They're saying the dark-haired one is named Shannon Shaw."

"Explain," she said, presenting her back. Tate zipped up her dress and dropped a kiss on her neck, then waited while she found her cosmetic bag on the bureau.

He blew out a long breath as he turned the problem over in his mind. "One of the new hires is named Bennett Shaw. Also, from Texas."

"And you think they're related?"

"I know they are. Shannon's his sister."

Lyla stopped daubing stuff on her cheeks and leveled him with a clear-eyed stare.

"The SEALs I hired think the senator who went after them is dirty. And they're not wrong—Doggett and his family were definitely up to something in Nabarut, and they had to have had help from within the naval chain of command to accomplish it."

His wife didn't utter a word. She simply waited while he stepped through it.

Tate went on, "Now, I've discovered that the sister of one of those SEALs is all over the evening news because her best friend dated Senator Doggett's stepson. A stepson who, I might add, was probably dealing illegal arms to a warlord at the same incident the SEALs ran afoul of the senator. Does that clarify things?"

Lyla snorted delicately. "You left out the part where this was your fight long before those SEALs came to you for help."

"Old news, babe."

"Yeah, okay. But what's your guy Shaw going to do about this? What comes first, right now?" She said it like she was plotting one of her popular mystery novels.

Tate blinked at the calm question and abruptly realized he was wasting critical time. "Where's my phone."

Lyla reached behind her and snagged it off the bureau, then tossed it to him.

Gaines took longer than usual to answer, but once Tate had an open line he barked, "Is he there?"

"Yeah."

"Put him on."

Shaw came on a minute later, mumbling, "Look, I know what you're gonna say, but I've got to go."

"Stand down, Master Chief."

"I'm not—"

"I have a pretty good idea of what you are and what you are not, Shaw," Tate told him. "What you are not going to do is go off half-cocked when you have no idea what you're wading into. You got that?"

"Try and stop me, *Monroe*," Bennett muttered, "From wherever you are right now."

Lyla brushed Tate's hands aside so she could knot his tie while he talked. Tate winked at his wife and let his tone go lower.

"I shouldn't need to remind you that as of last week, you are my problem to handle. So, listen up. We are going to recon, and we are going to put together a sensible plan. *Together.* Is that clear?"

There was a long uneasy pause as Shaw pulled himself together. Eventually, he emitted a grudging, "Yes, sir."

Tate nodded to himself, pleased with how fast the man had gotten with the program. Gaines had said he was smart.

"We're not going to let anything happen to your sister," he assured him. "That I can promise you."

"Or Kim."

Kim Sutherland was the other woman being shown on the broadcast, hurrying arm in arm with Shannon and breathlessly identified as Dan Cox's ex. Tate met his wife's eyes, a fresh tendril of concern winding through him.

"Or Kim. Who is…what to you, exactly?"

Bennett hesitated, a beat longer than necessary. "She's a family friend. My sister's best friend since kindergarten."

Tate rolled his eyes and drawled, "If you say so." He'd heard that tone of voice before, most recently from Shaw's buddy Gaines. Consequently, Tate suspected that this mess was going to get way more complicated than Shaw was banking on.

In his agitation, Bennett didn't take Tate's amusement well. "What's that supposed to mean?"

"Just don't kill anyone before we've had a chance to put our heads together. Okay? Stay put, and if you won't listen to me, listen to your boy Gaines. He won't steer you wrong."

"Your faith might be a tad misplaced," Bennett replied drily, "but I'll hang tight for now."

"Roger that."

Tate disconnected the call and shook his head. Shaw was not hard-wired to play nice. That call had bought Tate precious little time to get this circus under control.

Across the room, Lyla had finished with her makeup and was slipping on her shoes. She didn't even look up when she announced, "Don't even think about skipping out, Mr. Monroe. There will be plenty of time to put out your fire, *after* your brother's party."

Tate chuckled. "You don't know Bennett Shaw."

Chapter One

Bennett

B ENNETT SNAPPED TO attention in his chair, upsetting three of the beer bottles on the table and nearly spitting out the swallow he'd just poured into his mouth.

A ghost had walked into the bar.

Except, it couldn't be her. It really couldn't be. They were thirteen hundred miles from Respite, Texas, and his new boss had emphatically warned him to keep his distance from this woman until a solid plan could be hammered out.

There was no way she could have found him on her own, which made this either an unholy coincidence or an exasperating data leak, courtesy of his one and only sister.

It was like a horrible joke. *A girl walks into a bar...*

What in the *hell* was she doing here?

Bennett shook his head as he watched her.

Kim Sutherland, as he lived and breathed. She was standing, incomprehensibly, in the middle of Skippers, and Bennett couldn't fathom how she hadn't started a stampede yet.

She certainly didn't look like she belonged there. Kim was the equivalent of a museum diamond, glinting in a case full of flea market glass—as glaringly conspicuous as if she had a spotlight trained on her.

Bennett glanced around to see if any of the guys had noticed her. *Not yet.* He'd spotted her in time. Somehow, against all odds, she'd remained invisible to the hounds he kept as friends.

No such luck with the bartender, however, who looked ready to drool into his cocktail olives. Same went for the asshole in the faded Bon Jovi t-shirt at the bar, who drained his highball glass as Bennett watched, then leaned forward to try to catch Kim's eye.

Bennett shot up at the sight, mumbling something about a fresh pitcher before lunging toward his doom.

Peyton swung in from out of nowhere, cutting off his advance. "Now, before you go crazy," she said, "Kim reached out to me. She said she saw me on TV and found me through work. Okay? All I did was tell her where she might run into some SEALs around town. That's it."

Bennett looked at Buck, who was standing beside his fiancée, and getting red in the face. His buddy stammered, "Babe, seriously? *Here?*"

"If half of what she told me is true, they need to talk. And you said it yourself—if Bennett couldn't go home, you'd have to bring those women here." Peyton shrugged. "Well, here's one of them. You can thank me later."

With that, she turned on her heel and headed for the bathroom. Buck stalked after her, then sullenly parked himself outside the lavatory door when she shut the door in his face.

Bennett's throat felt dry as dust, but he managed the last few steps to Kim, who lit up like a beacon when she saw him. God, was it possible that she'd gotten even prettier? Her cheekbones were more defined, somehow, and her mouth looked…made for sin.

Mayday.

"Peyton is good people," he told her by way of greeting. "You shouldn't have used her to find me. After what she's been through, she needs real friends, not phonies."

Kim's perfect eyebrow arched upward. "It wasn't like that. And for the record, she had your back. Even with me sweet-talking her, she wouldn't give me anything more than which bars *might* have some SEALs in them."

"Oh, is that all."

"Look, Bennett, I've been trying to find you for ages now. At the rate I was going, I was liable to turn into San Diego's newest barfly before you actually showed."

"What are you talking about?" Bennett demanded. "How long have you been here?"

"Two weeks," she said. "And let me tell you, I am going to have to do one heck of a juice cleanse to flush all the crappy beer from my system."

Two weeks. Jesus, she'd probably come out to the coast within days of that news program they'd seen. No wonder he'd been walking around feeling like a bomb was about to drop on him.

"You could've told me you were coming," he said.

"And have you wave me off? How's that helpful?" Kim looked around impatiently, then gestured to a booth a couple was vacating. "Look, can we sit down? Let's just talk, okay?"

Bennett followed her numbly and slid in across from her. It took him a hot minute to get his mouth reconnected to his brain, and even then, all he could manage to spit out was, "Kim, why are you *here*?"

She fiddled with her bracelet. "Well, you probably saw on TV what the press has been getting up to back home. I had to get out of Dallas for a bit."

She seemed determined to look everywhere but at him, and Bennett took the opportunity to study her demeanor. She hadn't quite been able to camouflage the circles under her eyes, and she seemed off. Jittery, somehow.

Things were worse than she was letting on.

"Anyway, Shannon and I had a conversation and we decided I should come find you."

Bennett gaped at her. "You never considered a vacation? You could be sipping Mai Tais and working on your tan somewhere, instead of haunting seedy dive bars."

Kim peered around with a frown. "Does this count as a dive? It's a little sticky maybe, but not too bad. It has atmosphere, at least."

"An unfinished basement would be nicer than this joint. Come on."

"That is an exaggeration. Don't you remember the honky-tonks outside Respite?" Her smile was forced, like it was an effort to keep up the positivity.

Bennett was getting more worried by the second. "Kim, *why* are you *here?*"

She blinked and sagged a little. "I was scared, Bennett. Shannon, too. You're the only person we could trust to help."

"God only knows why. Surely, you've heard about the shitshow I am currently embroiled in."

"I know. I'm sorry. This was all we could think of."

"And neither of you thought to ask me first? Make sure it was a good idea?"

"Shannon told me I should surprise you. That you wouldn't let me come, otherwise."

"Well, she was right about that."

Kim looked even more worried. "Look, do you really want me to leave? Those reporters will start bothering her if I go back again, but I could...I could maybe go visit this woman, Meg, I know in Boston. I met her and her husband at a conference a couple of years ago. I bet she wouldn't mind a visit."

At the mention of the husband, Bennett felt his shoulders get inexplicably tight. "What's the husband do?" he scowled.

He'd heard Kim had become some kind of interior designer. Any conference she would've been at would have had more of the same, along with contractors, builders...maybe even architects.

"Edward?" she mused. "I think he's an architect."

Bingo, Bennett thought. He could just picture the asshole's dress shirt and fancy pen.

"He and his brother renovate historic houses all over New England," Kim continued. "They're, like, British aristocrats, too. They have titles and everything."

Bennett groaned and shook his head. "Only you, Kim. I swear to God. Only you would just bump into royalty and make friends with them."

"What? They were nice!"

"I never said they weren't."

She eyed him for a minute. "So, do you want me to leave? Tell the truth."

Bennett snatched the laminated apps menu from its stand and stared at it with blind eyes. "I am not sending you to hide out with some weaselly count. What's he gonna do if there's trouble? Smack someone with his monocle?"

Kim laughed. "He's a viscount," she corrected primly, "and I think you have formed a wildly inaccurate impression of him."

Which could only mean the guy was good-looking. *Awesome.*

"In any case," he retorted testily, "Now that you are here, I can't exactly run you off. I only wish one of you girls had thought to give me a heads-up so I could have had a chance to prepare. Now, we are going to be scrambling to get up to speed before the press finds out where you are."

Kim reached out and squeezed his forearm, her hand warm and so familiar his chest hurt. "We'll come up with something together. Okay? We'll do this together."

Together. Jesus, he hated the way she said that word. It was brimming with confidence and eerily similar to what Tate Monroe had said when he'd called to tell him to stand down a couple of weeks ago.

If Bennett had thought his situation was bad before, it was now turning into the ninth circle of hell—and he was walking straight into it with the prettiest woman on earth by his side.

Naturally, Kim was oblivious to the danger.

"So, how have you been, otherwise? You dating anyone?" she asked, cheerfully switching gears.

Bennett stared at her in surprise. "Not at present, no."

"No one you're interested in?"

"Not at present, no," he smirked. She'd always been a tenacious little thing.

"I asked Peyton, too. She said Buck told her you haven't dated anyone since y'all got back from Qahat," she said carefully. "That's a long time, Bennett. Doesn't seem like you."

Bennett shrugged uncomfortably. How would Kim know? Besides, he'd met plenty of women over the years, many in this very bar, and had occasionally fallen into a regular routine of weekend hookups with them. If he hadn't felt like doing that for a while, who was to say he didn't have good reasons for it?

It wasn't something he needed to explain to Kim Sutherland. Particularly today.

He told her, "Peyton talks too much."

"I don't know," she said gently. "She seems like she cares a lot about you."

Bennett met her eyes briefly. "Those two conditions are not mutually exclusive."

Kim laughed. "Look at you, sounding so brainy. I thought Peyton was the professor, not you."

Bennett chafed at her tone. It seemed petty to point out that he had, in fact, earned a college degree, same as Peyton, same as Kim. He'd simply done it while serving his country, instead of playing division one football on scholarship, like everyone had expected of him.

In any case, her comment was a good reminder of why Bennett had always tried to avoid this particular woman, if not any others. They mixed about as well as oil and water, despite the way his heart thumped an ungainly staccato whenever she was near.

Many years ago, in the dark of long teenage nights, Bennett had wished he was good enough for a girl like Kim. She was beautiful, sure, but also smart, and a smartass—and somehow managed to remain sweet at heart despite those things.

He knew for himself how wholesome Kim was.

More than one Sunday morning, he'd passed her exiting church with her parents, clad in little cardigans and flowered skirts. She'd made quite the contrast to his simmering hangovers from the prior nights' festivities.

He cleared his throat and cast around for something neutral to say. "Shannon mentioned you were dating some guy you went to school with," he said, keeping Kim's topic alive like a fucking masochist. "Before Dan, I mean."

Kim shrugged and looked away. "Didn't work out."

Bennett didn't mention that his sister had told him the guy in question was now a major country music star. What kind of butter-brained fool would mess up a chance with Kim Sutherland? Bennett shook his head. Other than him, that was.

"What happened?"

"He drank too much," she admitted. "What else is new, right?"

Well, hell. Bennett shifted on his side of the booth, the overflowing pitcher of beer he was clutching sloshing into his glass with perfect emphasis. An ancient, familiar mantle of embarrassment settled across his shoulders. *Once again, executing the role of the Village Jackass, our very own Bennett Shaw!*

It'd been years since he felt this way. Years of Navy discipline, years of pride in his role on the Teams. So much time and so many miles separated him from the fucked-up kid he'd been in Respite, Texas, but Kim had brought him roaring back with no effort whatsoever.

The last time he'd laid eyes on her, Bennett had been used to playing his assigned role. Though people in town had only known the barest highlights of his story, they'd sure expected him to perform his part and who was he to let them down?

He'd allowed himself exactly one moment of weakness with Kim, and that was all.

He wasn't dumb, though, then or now. One slipup was all you got, and sometimes not even that.

Unfortunately, he'd been a strapping kid, too good-looking and too clever by half, and for a long time, Bennett had been able to pretend he wasn't the least bit concerned with issues of morality or points of decorum. He couldn't have afforded to be— he'd been too busy trying to keep his head above water.

He'd managed to forget so much, but he'd never forget how that had felt.

And if it had been anyone else on earth sitting across from him, Bennett would've resented the hell out of them barging into his life and bringing the past with them.

Alas, he'd always had an inconvenient soft spot for Kim Sutherland. Once, he'd thought that the hold she had on him would surely lead to his demise.

Turned out, some shit never changed.

Chapter Two

Kim

TWO WEEKS. TECHNICALLY, it'd taken Kim two weeks and a mess of Texas charm to get Peyton to give her the barest hint of where to find Bennett Shaw. But even then, she'd had to keep showing up at these bars, hoping to run into him.

What kind of man didn't give his sister his address? If it had been anyone else, Kim might've assumed that was a Navy SEAL thing, but she knew Bennett, and caginess was like his calling card.

He'd changed in other ways, though. As she sat across from him, Kim found herself cataloging the differences: his face was older, he'd grown a few more inches, and he'd definitely filled out. Bennett had always been a big kid, but he'd become a formidable man, tall and muscular and so much more than he'd been.

She hadn't been ready for it. Sure, his looks had always thrown her for a loop, but now Bennett radiated a sort of icy capability that sent butterflies flitting through her belly.

Kim felt a little unmoored as she stared at him. He was so familiar, and at the same time so alien to her. It hit her rather suddenly that she'd probably been looking for this man for a lot longer than a couple of weeks.

Kim had been trying to recapture his expressions and wry manner ever since he'd left Respite. Not that she'd had much luck—her dating history was littered with a whole lot of nothing special, and now that she was faced with the real deal, she understood why.

Bennett was as rare and unique as a unicorn. She'd never found a substitute because there *was* no substitute. Not for her, anyway.

She had her work cut out for her here in California, much more than she'd thought.

Because officially, she'd come here to get away from the press dogging her every move. She'd told Bennett that. Soon Kim would have to talk to him about Dan, too, so they could figure out if she knew anything that could help him and his friends get reinstated. She'd promised her best friend she would do those things, and she would.

Kim had also come to San Diego with a private motive, however. After spotting Bennett on the news last year, she'd known she had to find out, once and for all, if her memory of him was accurate—or if she'd simply made up the boy who'd crushed her young heart so badly fifteen years ago.

It'd taken five seconds in his presence to discover that. The Bennett Shaw of memory might've had a hold on her all these years, but he was a thin shadow of the man he'd become. Kim knew, without learning anything else about who he was now, that no one else could ever fill his shoes.

He hadn't wanted her back then, though, and it was entirely possible he wouldn't want her now. That didn't mean she couldn't try. Hell, she'd likely never forgive herself if she didn't.

"Listen, it's getting kind of late," she told him after they'd caught up for a bit. "And your friends keep looking over here. I think they're wondering what's going on."

Bennett glanced at the table of equally powerful guys across the room and winced. "Oh, I think they've got a pretty good idea," he muttered.

Kim plowed on. "I should still let you get back to them, though."

He nodded mutely, his eyes skating over her face like he was trying to commit it to memory. Distracted as he was, it took him a minute to pick up on her hint. "Wait, how long are you here for?"

She shrugged yet again. "Indefinitely. I'm staying at the Foundry for now, but depending on how things go, I might move into one of those residence-style places. I'm getting kind of sick of takeout."

Kim didn't miss the way Bennett's eyes flickered at the mention of her luxury hotel, but what was she supposed to say? Her father had offered to pick up the tab, and he wasn't the kind to park his baby girl in some flophouse. *His words.*

Bennett didn't tease her, though. All he said was, "Okay, uh…let me talk to the team and we can help figure out the best landing spot for you. If we're going to look out for you, we'll need wherever you end up to fit certain specifications."

His gaze danced around the space over her shoulder, like he was already visualizing it.

"Bennett," Kim said, then stopped when his piercing blue eyes landed on hers.

"If that's okay," he amended.

"It is," she told him. "But you don't have to—"

He cut her off. "Someone might need to stay with you. Just so you know."

There was only one member of Bennett's team that Kim wanted to stay with her, but it seemed spoiled to point that out. She nodded instead.

Bennett gripped the edge of the table, a wild look shadowing his eyes. "You should probably give me your number. And I guess I need to give you mine."

Access to him. Whenever she wanted. Kim dwelled on that for a long moment, then jumped when he gestured abruptly. She dug her phone out of her purse and called up the contact screen.

"Here. You may as well enter it yourself. I don't want to get something wrong."

Did Bennett hesitate too long when she handed it over? *Hard to say.* He sure froze up once she texted him back, though.

His finger hovered over the screen for an eternity before he began entering Kim's name in his contact list. Like he thought the letters might burn him.

It made her worry, but not so much that she didn't push her luck a little while she ordered herself a car. "Maybe we can grab some dinner tomorrow night, if you're not busy."

Bennett blinked at her, apparently caught off guard. "No. Yeah." He squeezed his eyes shut and shook his head. "Sorry. That would be nice, yes."

"I should probably tell you what I know about Dan Cox," she said.

"Okay, yeah," he mumbled. "We can do that. When do you, uh…" he swallowed awkwardly. "When do you want me to pick you up?"

Kim eyed him quizzically. "How about six? You pick the place. I still haven't figured out my way around."

With that, she got to her feet and smoothed down her blouse, then slipped her purse over her shoulder. Bennett jumped up and stuck out his hand, like he actually expected her to shake the thing—but Kim stepped past it and wrapped her arms around his middle, instead.

He even smelled better than he had before, and Bennett's heady scent had been one of the best things about her adolescence.

"It's really good to see you," she murmured next to his heart.

He rumbled something too low to catch, but Kim felt the words under her cheek, and the moment felt so intimate and so right that she had to push away out of sheer self-preservation.

With a quick jerky wave, she bolted for the door, only remembering to slow her steps and act normal about halfway there.

"Kim!" he called. "Do you need a ride?"

She shut down the fevered image that called up, right quick.

"Nope, I'm good. Ordered one already."

As she pushed her way outside, she risked a look back—and there was Bennett, still gratifyingly frozen in place next to their booth, eyes burning into hers.

BACK AT HER hotel, Kim changed into gym shorts and a sweatshirt, flopped on the bed, and tried to parse what had just happened.

If she'd wondered whether she'd feel the same way about Bennett once she saw him in the flesh, she could put that question to bed now. He'd been worth every second of pining and then some—especially in his grown-up form.

Unfortunately, Bennett also appeared to be just as tortured as ever. The mixed signals he'd once given her were still in evidence—his overprotectiveness, his thinly-veiled curiosity about her love life, and the marked physical reactions if she so much as tapped his shoulder.

Shoot, the way he'd thrown out that question about Billy Aikers? Kim had to shake her head. She hadn't pointed out that she'd only dated Billy for a few weeks before she'd cut him loose. Once he'd shown up at her apartment, drunk off his ass and so mad that she'd missed his gig that he spilled water all over her laptop, she'd had to show him the door.

The fool had obliterated days of work Kim had put in on a design for her drafting class, country music star or no.

However, if she'd cringed at the memory like she normally did, Bennett would've demanded to know what was up, and then he'd have wanted to go looking for Billy like the incident had happened yesterday, not years and years ago.

None of them had time for that goat rodeo.

So, Kim had yanked several napkins from the dispenser and mopped at the spreading puddle of condensation around her glass, so she'd have something to do besides meeting his penetrating gaze. The man had been gripping his beer like it would save him from drowning—even though he was ten times the person Billy ever was.

There had been other guys, before and after Billy and Dan, of course. None of them had held her interest for long and as she'd sat there staring at the one and only Bennett Shaw, Kim had finally gotten an inkling as to why.

The hard truth was she'd spent a lifetime longing for her best friend's big brother. Not one man she'd ever dated had compared to him. It would be funny, perhaps, if it didn't fill Kim with such frustration.

All her life people had wanted things from her, but they'd given Kim nothing in return. What was her reward for all those dance classes and pageants, for singing in the choir when she'd hated every minute, for agreeing to do that commercial for their neighbor's barbecue joint, only to have its tagline—*Mama, when can we eat at the Smoke Shack ag'in*—follow her into adulthood?

To hell with that. She'd only ever wanted one thing in life, and by now she ought to have earned him. Kim was done being set on a pedestal and done living by other people's rules.

She was going to have to pull out all the stops if she intended to win Bennett over, though.

First, she would help the man she adored clear his name. But while she did that, Kim was also going to shoot her shot, swing for the fences, and make her play—once and for all.

And, if Kim needed to be not-so-well-behaved to land Bennett Shaw, then so be it. The payoff would be worth it.

Chapter Three

Bennett

I T TOOK A few minutes for his brain to come back online once Kim left, but when Bennett's lobes began working as a team again, he pointed his boots toward his roommates and headed over.

His world might have been upended, but they were still business as usual, discussing the fact that Senator Doggett's stepson, Dan Cox, had clearly been in Nabarut off the books—up to no damn good and likely dealing illegal arms—and that he was absolutely their next mark.

They'd been talking about it for two weeks straight.

Things had gotten testy in Bennett's absence, however, because right as his butt hit the chair, Joe told Wyatt, "Why are you so weirdly pressed about that army unit? You act like you knew them."

"I didn't need to know them personally," Wyatt fired back, "to know those soldiers were the same as us. The rare few willing to put their lives on the line for their country. Ring a bell? And, not for nothing, most of them were barely in their twenties. Those kids probably never thought they'd end up dead so far from home, before they even got a chance to live a life. So, yeah—I care. Have a little fucking respect."

Joe went gray around the gills, instantly chastened. "You're right. I'm sorry. I'm a dickhead, obviously."

When no one said anything more, Bennett scooted closer and slapped his hand on the table. "Did you all know she was here?" he demanded.

"Who?"

"You know damn well who. I've been going crazy, trying to get you cocksuckers to settle on a plan to help Kim and my sister. And then Kim shows up here. Or should I be asking, how long have you known she was on her way?"

He stared down each of them in turn. As expected, Wyatt crumbled first.

"Okay, look—Noah picked it up when she made her reservations, so Monroe has had eyes on her the whole time she's been here. We didn't drop the ball, I swear."

Bennett turned to Joe, who added, "Bruh, we did not expect her to call Peyton like that. Buck told us to let it play out, though."

"Let it play out," he drawled. "Like this is a game. Why didn't any of you *tell* me? Prepare a man, for fuck's sake."

Bennett was most upset with Buck, who was supposed to be his best friend. His *brother*. Instead of facing the music, however, that coward was lingering at the bar with Peyton, leaving these two to dance. Man did Bennett ever want a piece of their hides.

Wyatt was wearing his placating expression—no surprise there. Bennett had half a mind to plant a fist in the center of it.

He wanted to hear what he had to say, though.

"Listen, you've been a bit jumpy about this," Wyatt murmured. "I mean…have you looked in a mirror recently? You've got a matched set of luggage under your eyes. You're not yourself. You haven't been thinking clearly."

Bennett huffed in exasperation, but his buddy held up a hand. "Look, I get it. It's different when it's family. But just like we made Buck sit some shit out when Peyton was in trouble, you get to take a back seat now. At minimum until you settle down and stop looking so manic."

"Manic," Bennett complained. "Are you fucking kidding me right now?"

"See, this is what we're saying," Joe chided. "Looking at you, I'm thinking you're a flight risk, or that you're about to go dark and start racking up a body count. That ain't you, man. You're usually a team guy all the way."

Bennett crossed his arms over his chest and glared at them. "I am behaving perfectly fine. Y'all are the ones acting stupid."

"Stop being emotional and try to hear us," Wyatt said calmly.

The command was so at odds with Stitch's usual jokey demeanor, and so dissonant in Skippers at happy hour, that Bennett paused.

He took a deep breath. And another.

He realized, eventually, that they were right. When he'd seen Kim and his sister on the news and grasped that they'd somehow gotten caught up in the Doggett investigation, he'd lost his head.

Hell, Bennett hadn't even known that Kim had dated that prick, Cox. He'd been rationing his inquiries about her for years, so Shannon wouldn't think he was a creep, or too interested.

And yes, he admitted to himself, if he'd known ahead of time that Kim had been intending to come to San Diego, and that he'd have to see her face to face—have to act as her protective detail, for God's sake—he might actually have run for the hills.

The worst was over now, though, wasn't it? They'd staged a whole "what a coincidence, fancy meeting you here" reunion, and he'd spoken to her. For the first time in fifteen years, Kim Sutherland had been close enough to touch. She'd…she'd even hugged him, dovetailing into place against his body like she'd been made for it.

Sweat broke out across Bennett's brow, just remembering it. *Fuck.*

Chaos was raging in his chest, but he must've looked calmer because Wyatt piped up, "So…damn. That's your hometown girl, huh? I have to say I'm surprised. She's got that whole uptown princess thing going on. It's not what I expected from you."

Bennett closed his eyes and locked his jaw so he wouldn't toss his cookies. Wyatt was a *bait first, think later* kind of fella, and that was doubly true when he had a buzz on. He didn't mean anything by it and resisting only made it worse.

As civilly as Bennett could muster, he said, "Son, shut your mouth."

Wyatt chuckled merrily and sang, "Oooooh," like Bennett was trying to be scary, and failing.

Bennett's fist shot out and connected with the bastard's biceps like it was on autopilot. Stitch only laughed harder, but the sudden burst of movement must've startled Joe. He jerked back, upsetting his beer and sending a wave of tepid, amber IPA across the table and into Bennett's lap.

Joe bolted up and snapped, "Dude, what the fuck," in his clipped Boston accent—as if Bennett had punched him instead of Wyatt.

"Pretty pissy for a guy who's yet to offer me an apology," he complained, standing to mop at his jeans with a couple of soggy napkins.

Joe's face flushed red. He squared off across the table, spoiling for a fight to cover his embarrassment. "Hey, you wanna go?"

Wyatt popped up next, like a prairie dog that'd been sent to make peace. "Whoa. Whoa," he murmured, glancing around at the folks at the other tables with a "Nothing to see here" expression.

"Y'all sit down," Bennett told them. "I'ma hit the head, and then I'm leaving. Bruiser over here will chill out once I'm gone."

He threw down some cash to cover his share, then strolled through the bar to the restrooms. He ducked into the men's to take a leak, then pushed out the back door, into sunshine that was still going strong though suppertime had come and gone.

Bennett winced at the glare reflecting off the windshields of the cars in the lot and retrieved his hat from his back pocket. As he jammed the thing on his head he winced again. Had he seriously whipped it off when he'd clapped eyes on Kim? What was he, fifteen and trying to put on fancy manners?

With a grunt of disgust, Bennett yanked the frayed brim low over his eyes and stalked toward his truck. Disconcerted, and furious with himself for it.

* * *

BACK IN RESPITE there'd been certain expectations regarding the elder of the Shaw children. Bennett would get rowdy. Bennett would bend, or more likely, break the rules.

Sure, he'd been good-looking and athletic, but he'd also been lousy in school and more likely than not to have a beer in his hand come dark.

Bennett had never hurt for something as prosaic as a date— but the kid had sure gone wanting when it came to opportunity. Select townsfolk had made certain of that.

It'd been a tight box to live in, but Bennett had been excellent at meeting expectations.

What he'd learned about himself since, however, was that he was also very good at *exceeding* expectations.

Some folks had likely scratched their heads when he'd ended up in the military instead of playing football in college, and more than a few had probably wondered about his choice of the Navy over the Army. There was a story to be told about all of that, one that very few knew.

Thanks to their proximity to Fort Sam Houston, the Army gained several Respite residents with each graduating high school class, but not a single soul had known him in the Navy. They hadn't known his family, they hadn't known his history, and Bennett had been free to be only…himself.

Divested of expectation. What a way to live at age eighteen.

He'd also chafed at being told what to do, particularly by no-good bullies like Sheriff Fecteau had been. *Go figure.*

Through sheer defiance, Bennett had managed to break out of his little box, and he'd busted his ass every second of every day, until his baby sister was secure with a college degree and a good-paying job, and until he'd earned his own degree in night school and completed OCS.

Bennett hadn't stopped, either—not until he'd landed a spot on the Teams, an accomplishment that no one could sneer at, not even him. He'd turned himself into a real-life superhero and crushed into the sand the disreputable taint that had clung to him throughout his adolescence.

It was true, some things about him had stayed the same. Ladies still gravitated to him, and Bennett wasn't one to turn down a beer. But he was proud as could be about the rest of it, built single-handedly from his own sweat and blood.

He'd slept soundly for many years, secure in the knowledge that the souls of Respite, Texas could kiss his victorious, cracker-born ass.

At least, he had until one dirty senator with a stick up his butt had decided to take down Bennett's entire SEAL team.

The scaffolding he'd built so carefully around himself had come crashing down in a matter of weeks, but Bennett figured he'd be carrying his grudge against Roy Doggett and the rest of his shady family for eternity.

It figured that Kim Sutherland would choose this moment to sashay back into his life. She was probably the only other person on earth with the ability to destroy Bennett so thoroughly.

He had to hand it to her, though—the woman had always had impeccable timing.

Kim Sutherland, here in San Diego, Bennett thought to himself. *Holy shit.* It was almost as bad as thinking he'd have to go back to Respite, Texas, to get her.

Chapter Four

Kim

W ELL, I FOUND him."

Kim gestured with her toothbrush and smirked at the screen of her phone, propped on the window ledge next to the bathroom sink.

Shannon rolled her eyes. "That only took forever."

"Tell me about it. At the rate I was going, I was gonna have dates lined up into the spring."

Her best friend snorted in exasperation. "That would only happen if you accepted the offers. Besides, you're way more patient than I am—I would've given up and called that lunkhead a week and a half ago."

"I know, but I didn't want to spook him."

"So you said. Anyway, tell me how it went. How'd he look?"

Kim smiled in sympathy. Shannon was as starved for news of Bennett as she was, and probably more. He wasn't just her big brother, after all. As far as Kim knew, he was Shannon's only family—and aside from Kim, her closest friend.

Not that you'd know it with the way he'd played possum all these years. He'd claimed it was to protect Shannon, but Kim suspected that was only partly true.

"Bennett looked good," she told her friend. "Really good. And he was there with a bunch of guys, so at least we know he's not pulling his loner routine."

"Was he too skinny? Or does he look like he's eating enough?"

Kim thought back to Bennett's broad shoulders and solid chest. His thick arms corded with muscle. She cleared her throat, flustered by the heat that flooded her belly.

"Trust me, he's fine. Healthy as a horse, far as I could tell."

Shannon digested that information for a minute. "Good. That's good."

"I'm supposed to see him again tomorrow," Kim offered. "We're planning to grab some dinner. You want me to tell him to call you?"

"No, it's okay. Now that he's seen you, I expect he'll be calling me shortly."

Kim nodded, because Shannon wasn't wrong. But as she set down her toothbrush and leaned against the sink, she watched her friend closely. Shannon sipped at her tea, seemingly lost in thought.

"That reminds me…" Kim said.

Shannon frowned, instantly alert. "What?"

"Your brother and I traded contact info at the end, so I could reach him if I needed to."

"And?"

"The number he gave me is different from the one you have." Kim studied her reaction, but Shannon looked just as suspicious as she'd felt at the time.

"But—" Her friend broke off with a scowl of annoyance. "Then which one of us got the real one?"

"Damned if I know."

Shannon grabbed a pillow, mashed it against her mouth, and growled into it.

"He is so shady," Kim agreed. "But hey, I'm gonna look out for him. I promise."

"I know. I just wish I was there to help."

"Are you still doin' okay? No one's bothering you anymore?"

Her friend shrugged. "So far, so good. Maybe they don't know I'm back in San Antonio."

Kim sighed. The press had been transfixed when they'd figured out that she'd dated Dan, but they'd been doubly intrigued when they learned that her best friend was related to one of the SEALs Dan's stepdad had screwed over.

Whatever reprieve Shannon was enjoying now, Kim suspected it wouldn't last.

"Lay low, okay?" she told her. "I hate the thought of you having to deal with those people by yourself."

Shannon laughed. "Well, if it gets too bad, maybe I'll come out there. Enjoy some sun and fun and flirt with my brother's new friends with you."

Kim smiled. That would be something. "Alright, you. I'm gonna go now. I wanna get up early tomorrow and see if I can get a run in before the treadmills fill up downstairs."

"Okay. Let me know how your dinner goes. And good luck." Shannon blew her a kiss and cut the call.

Kim finished brushing her teeth, then washed her face. She was slathering on moisturizer when her phone started chirping again. She reached for it quickly, figuring Shannon was calling back with some follow-up thought that had occurred to her.

Thankfully, her brain registered the name on the notification a split second before her finger touched the screen. Kim yanked her hand back like she'd been burned.

Alix Hernandez. The lifestyle reporter from The Dallas Sun. She'd met the woman last year at one of her client's parties, and their chat had been friendly—enough so that they'd exchanged numbers at the end of the evening and had planned to meet up for lunch sometime soon.

The lunch had never happened, but an unplanned media onslaught sure had, and to no one's surprise Alix now wanted to leverage their association to snare an exclusive interview.

Kim declined the call and set her phone aside with a sigh. She'd thought the woman might be a friend, but that hope was dying fast.

She had no idea what Alix's connection to her client was, and on the off chance she was a beloved relative or something, Kim was trying to stay polite. Instead of chewing the reporter out, she'd simply ignored each attempt and hoped Alix would eventually get the message.

She didn't think the woman would share her number with anyone else. Alix thought she had an in that no one else did, and Kim doubted she would cede it easily.

She'd clearly underestimated the woman's tenacity, though. Kim considered taking a page from Bennett's book and getting a different number, but it would probably be an exercise in futility. In her business, the new one was bound to get out before long.

Kim picked up her phone, scrolled through her contacts, and bit her lip. Alix had valuable connections, but Kim didn't really need more work in Dallas. Her interior design shop was based in San Antonio, and that was where she had to nurture a professional network.

Enough was enough.

Decision made, she blocked Alix's number with a couple of taps. Kim wandered over to the floor-to-ceiling windows, pressed her fingers against the glass, and watched the cars go by down below.

She needed to check in with her dad and stepmom—and, for that matter, with her own mother, too. She didn't feel like it, though.

All she really wanted was for Bennett to wrap his arms around her and envelop her in his warmth and safety again. Next time, she wouldn't let go so easily. She was tired of being alone.

Kim would have another chance tomorrow, assuming he followed through and didn't bail on her. She needed to come up with a plan for what to say to him, she supposed. *Easier said than done*. Besides, there was one more thing she had to do before she could pack it in for the night.

She slipped her phone out of her hotel robe pocket and found the number she needed. Kim tapped out a quick text, revised it a couple of times, and sent it off.

Thanks again for your help tonight. I hope Bennett isn't too mad at you for it.

Peyton's response popped up in seconds.

Happy to do it. And don't worry—Buck swears Bennett will be fine once he calms down.

Kim shook her head. *Will be*. Not *is*.

Peyton's fiancé Buck might very well be as close to Bennett as she'd said, and for Bennett's sake, Kim hoped that was true. She'd known him a long time, though, and he wasn't one to go splashing his secrets around. Which would be fine, if Kim wasn't so anxious that some of those secrets might come back to bite him soon.

When she'd met with Buck and Peyton last week, they'd explained how Bennett's team was trying to stay squeaky clean while they delved into Senator Doggett's activities and connections. They couldn't afford any hint of trouble—nothing that might hinder the possibility of them getting reinstated by the Navy.

Kim suspected that Bennett might've kept some important things hidden about himself, and a man with secrets was a man who could be hurt by them. When someone like Bennett went down, however, he was liable to bring others with him.

He'd never forgive himself if that happened.

And so—despite that haunted look in Bennett's eye when he'd collared her at Skippers earlier—Kim reassured herself for the umpteenth time that she'd made the right decision to come here.

Between what she knew of the old Bennett and what his teammates knew about him now, surely they'd be able to protect him together. She had to believe it was true.

Bennett was important to her—always had been, always would be.

Now that she'd talked to him, though…*important* seemed like a grievous understatement. Bennett Shaw was etched on Kim's soul, and she had to find a way to make him see it.

Chapter Five

Bennett

B ENNETT HAD BARELY put his truck in drive before he found himself stabbing at the screen on his dashboard to call his sister. He couldn't wait till he got home—he was *that* frustrated.

When she answered, he hollered, "Girl, what were you thinking?"

"Oh, for god's sake," Shannon muttered. "What now?"

"You know good and well what now," he told her. "Never mind the fact that you should've called me long before hatching one of your little schemes—now I've got to worry about you two being in different places. How am I supposed to look out for you when you're hundreds of miles apart?"

"Bennett, I get that you're mad, but I do not have time for this. I'm at work."

He checked his watch. *Damn it.* He'd forgotten about the time difference.

"Staying kind of late, aren't you?"

"Honey, I am very important. I got shit to do."

"Whatever," Bennett snorted.

"Look, I'm sorry I didn't warn you, but we both know you would've been weird about it, and this was the only solution Kim felt comfortable with," Shannon explained. "You'll still take care of my friend, though, right?"

"Of course, I am. And not for nothing, she's my friend, too."

"You got a funny way of showing it. Now, hang up. I'm busy."

"Shan, no joke. There're some bad dudes involved in this mess, and with Kim here now, I worry about you," he said. "Be careful."

"I will. As usual," Shannon muttered, and hung up.

Okay, then.

Bennett pulled into the lot of a coffee shop and parked in the back. He sat there bouncing his knee and thinking through his options, before firing off a secure text to Tate Monroe, his new boss. Buck had undoubtedly apprised him of the situation already, but the man would not be able to ignore a direct request from Bennett himself.

I'm holding you to your promise. My sister better be protected, now that she's out there by herself.

Then he waited until he got a response.

Already done. N can review specs with u and give sitreps.

Bennett sniffed at that. Damn straight he was going to comb through the plan, and Noah—Black Watch's I.T. prodigy—was sure as shit going to give him situation reports. On the hour, if Bennett had his way.

He'd once gone through hell to keep his sister safe, and he did not intend to let the wolves have her now.

With Shannon's protection secured, however, his racing thoughts veered back to Buck. Bennett had thought he could trust a guy who'd taken literal bullets for him but apparently, he'd been mistaken.

After the fiasco he'd helped engineer tonight, Bennett had a few choice words he'd like to share with his supposed best friend, but as far as he knew the man was still back at Skippers, making eyes at Peyton as if he wasn't a total traitor.

That was okay—Buck could have his fun. Bennett would wait, and get his revenge when the time was right.

He put his truck in gear and headed toward home.

BRIGHT AND EARLY the next morning, however, Bennett had parked himself on the front step of Buck and Peyton's cottage to ring their doorbell.

He'd stopped for coffee and donuts on the way, because he wasn't a complete savage, but when Buck finally opened the door on the fourth or fifth ring, all Bennett could do was demand, "*Play it out?*"

"Fucking Wyatt," Buck groaned and reached for the coffee. "Great to see you. Come on in."

Bennett stepped through the door and came face to face with Peyton, her hair still damp from a shower.

"Oh hi, Bennett! I didn't know you were coming." Her eyes cut to her man, curious and a little uneasy.

"Neither did I," Buck told her.

Bennett wasn't going to apologize, not after what they'd pulled last night. He just held out the box of donuts and waited for someone to take them.

Peyton suppressed a smile as she brought the box to the kitchen, then accepted a coffee cup from her fiancé. She peeked under the lid, and twinkled at Bennett a little more warmly.

Like he wasn't going to remember her order? She'd lived at the apartment with all of them for weeks.

"I'm going to finish getting ready," she announced. "Try not to kill each other, okay?"

Then she turned tail and fled into the bedroom, the big chicken.

Bennett considered whether he could get away with chasing her down, but Buck stepped quickly into his line of sight and shut him down.

"Don't even think about it," he warned.

Bennett glared right back. "My entire team thought fit to exclude me from the plan, and Peyton was in on it. I want to know why."

Buck handed Bennett a cup and gestured for him to take a seat on the couch near the windows. His buddy looked tired as he added a few creamers to the remaining coffee, then settled into an adjacent armchair.

"Listen, I need you to hear me," Buck began. "There was no big conspiracy. We were all working the problem together, as you know. But everyone could see how much you were dreading going to Texas, and Monroe was more than a little curious about what the deal was with you and Kim."

"There's no deal," Bennett explained. "She's been my sister's best friend since they were babies. That's it."

Buck eyed him skeptically. "Sure."

"It's true."

"Okay," he said. "Regardless, Monroe already had Noah keeping tabs on your girls, so when Kim booked her flight, he picked up on it right away."

"I know all this," Bennett complained. "What I want to hear is why you all decided to cut me out for the ensuing two weeks."

"Look, Kim didn't waste time. She landed out here in a matter of days. I thought…" Buck hesitated, rubbing his chin. "…I thought if we let her get settled, and we set up a rotation to watch over her, you'd feel better once we told you. That maybe you wouldn't panic so badly, hearing the news."

"This is not panic," Bennett argued. "This is frustration. And worry. Kim might be close and secure, but now my sister's out in San Antonio by herself. She—"

"Shannon is being looked after, too. Monroe told you this."

"You still should've included me. These women are my fucking family. I deserved to know."

Buck simply stared at him, and his sharp eyes seemed to see way more than Bennett was comfortable with. He shot to his feet.

"Am I cut out of the whole operation, then?"

"Of course not. And for Pete's sake, none of us expected Kim to track down Peyton like she did. That's some determination, right there."

"If you had roped me in from the start, I could've warned you what she is capable of."

"Easy, I know Wyatt told you this last night, but I'm going to say it again. Whoever this girl is to you—" Buck held up a hand when Bennett tried to protest again. "—you have not been yourself since her face popped up on that TV screen, and if you can't pull yourself together, you are going to compromise everything we are working toward. So no, we didn't tell you what was happening. We couldn't trust what you'd do. But now you do know, and now you need to man up and find your center. Because otherwise, yes, you *will* sit out this op."

Bennett could feel a hot flush prickling up his neck, and shame tightened his throat, as Buck scolded him.

"I'm fine," he muttered. "I've never let y'all down before now, and I ain't about to start."

"I know. But until you admit that you feel a certain kind of way about your sister's bestie, I'm going to keep sweating this shit."

Bennett scrubbed his hands over his face, feeling about two inches tall. "I did not do this to you when Peyton came to town. I did not force you to confess all your sordid secrets."

"Well, that pretty much tells me everything I need to know," Buck retorted wryly. "And don't worry. Your secret's safe with me."

"I doubt that," Bennett muttered darkly. "It's not even safe with me."

THE CONVERSATION WAS knocking around Bennett's brain when he rolled up to Kim's hotel later that evening, making him sweat like a hooker in church. Not Kim, though. She simply sauntered out of the Foundry's lobby like they went out together every damn day.

He got out of his truck so he could better size up her approach. She was carrying a strange bundle in her arms, and when she got closer Bennett realized it was a folded blanket and a small, soft-sided cooler.

He eyed them warily. He was positive he'd told Kim they had dinner reservations, so why did she look prepared for an outdoor picnic?

She didn't offer any explanation, so he jerked his chin at her bundle and inquired, "What's all that?"

"Howdy to you, too." Kim's words were tough, but she looked guilty.

His heart skittered in alarm, and any charm Bennett had once possessed fled the area.

"Well?"

"Well…to tell the truth," she said, "I can't seem to get enough of the beaches here. They are much prettier than Corpus Christi."

He narrowed his eyes and studied her. Something about her posture was very shifty. She was lying.

"And…?" he prompted.

She didn't answer right away, looking pointedly at his truck, instead.

Bennett managed to unlock her door and hold it open for her, but he still held his breath, adding suffocation to his cardiac worries.

Kim stowed her gear behind the seat, then nimbly hopped up into the cab and buckled herself in. He'd witnessed this divert-and-deflect routine a time or ten before, however, so he didn't move away—he just draped his arm on the doorframe and waited, counting down the seconds until she crumbled.

It took longer than it used to for her to break. "Well?" she demanded. "Don't just stand there gawking. We've got places to be."

Bennett sniffed in amusement. "That's all you got?"

"What?" Kim blinked at him, the very soul of innocence.

He tipped his head at the sketchy pile behind her seat, then searched her angelic face. Lord, how many times had he witnessed this exact expression on her or his sister—usually moments before all hell broke loose? It had to be in the thousands.

Kim huffed in annoyance and turned to squint out the windshield. "*Fine*. If you must know, I was hoping we could go to the beach after we ate." Less certainly, she added, "I haven't gotten brave enough to see it at night yet. I bet it's really nice, though."

Bennett gave her another once-over and decided that was most, if not all, of it.

"It is," he agreed, and shut her inside.

As he rounded the bed of the truck, his heart decided to start working again, settling into a rapid staccato that had everything to do with the notion that he was trash for this girl, and did not possess the stones to upset her little plan.

That meant, in a couple of hours, he would very likely be sitting on a dark, romantic beach next to Kimberley Sutherland, eternal bane of his existence.

Did he have no sense of self-preservation at all?

To buy himself another few seconds, Bennett fiddled with the tailgate and kicked his back tires, then paused with his hand on his door to pray—no, beg—for divine assistance. Or at least some sign that he hadn't lost his ever-loving mind.

Kim was waiting patiently when he wrenched open the door and hauled himself inside.

"So, is this your truck?" she wondered. "It's so snazzy."

She asked it innocently enough, but the question made Bennett bristle. *Wasn't he good enough to drive a nice vehicle?*

"Kimmie, listen," he began, sidestepping the class divide issue and zeroing in on the real problem at hand. "I'm not sure the coastal afterparty is a good idea." Bennett threw the truck in reverse and twisted around so he wouldn't have to look directly at her.

He'd blurted out her childhood nickname without a thought, but it'd caused something to flicker behind her eyes that sent another wash of panic through his system. He did not want to peer too closely at why that was, but suddenly the Italian bistro that Buck and Peyton had suggested for tonight seemed like a terrible choice.

It was way, *way* too romantic for two people who were just old friends. *Only* old friends.

Bennett was too off-balance to come up with another option on the fly, however. With his brain on the fritz, he was liable to find himself in another sushi restaurant like the one Peyton had once dragged him to. No one wanted that.

Reluctantly, he turned in the right direction.

"Why not?" Kim argued, barging into his rioting thoughts and forcing him back on topic. "Peyton told me it's allowed. Besides, it's not like you **need** to worry about me getting frisky—if I tried to jump you, you could probably fight me off blindfolded."

Bennett swallowed thickly. Kim's comment should not have sounded so fucking hot, but the moment the words exited her lips, there he was, jabbing at the dash to jack up the A/C. She tried to help by turning all the vents toward him, but her brow was wrinkled into a cute, curious frown.

"You okay?" she prodded, no doubt wondering if he was having a stroke.

"It ain't you I'm worried about," Bennett muttered grumpily.

That shut her down right quick. Alas, far too soon he was parking in the metered lot of the public beach closest to the restaurant, because he'd failed to come up with a new, utterly platonic strategy for the night, and his goddamn truck was too big to fit in any of the street spots.

Was this how it felt to walk toward your doom? Bennett had always assumed the way would be less picturesque.

He tried like hell to ignore Kim's triumphant expression as she got out and looked around, and realized where they were. Then, as they hoofed it the two blocks to the bistro, Bennett tried not to think too hard about why she felt so smug.

Naturally, the universe hated him, so the restaurant was every bit as cozy and candlelit as he'd feared. It didn't matter that Bennett was wretchedly tongue-tied, tangled in guilt and lecherous fantasies that made him feel like the worst kind of slime. Kim kept up a steady, cheerful patter that only made him feel worse.

She talked about the weather. Her job. His job. His sister. The food. The other diners. The hotel amenities. Her words flowed over Bennett in an indistinct symphony that sounded like nothing so much as home.

The sheer familiarity of her accent and cadence and figures of speech simmered warmly in his chest—but it hurt, too. There were too many stinging wounds, things he'd thought had scarred over years ago.

Bennett recognized what Kim was up to even so, and he had to admire her, just a little, for how good she was at it. The onslaught of cheerful words probably worked like crazy on other guys. He simply knew Kim too damn well to fall for it.

By Bennett's estimation, he'd experienced every last one of her tricks by sophomore year at the latest. He would've been hard-pressed to choose a favorite. Kim possessed professional-grade feminine wiles that had always, without exception, made him weak in the knees.

Case in point, this bright conversation of hers. It was a classic diversionary tactic, and so elegantly delivered that Bennett was becoming increasingly nervous about what exactly she had planned for later. Whatever it was, Kim did not want him to examine it too closely.

Bennett pushed away his steak, unable to swallow another bite. The food that was already in his stomach sat there like a landmine.

Why were they acting as if every commonsense indicator wasn't pointing to *this is a date?* What's more, how could he pretend that the equation of Kim-plus-blanket-plus-moonlit beach wasn't lurking in the wings, scaring him worse than a canyon of crossfire?

Kim had a good chance of prevailing, he knew. Despite Bennett's good intentions, his protests, and his piss-poor conversational ability, she would likely win—and she would do so, he knew, because he was still, under everything, enough of a dirtbag to let her.

Sure, he could sit back and deny it until he was blue in the face, but "Easy" Shaw was not, at his core, the kind of man who would pass up the chance to sit on the sand—under the light of the stars and the moon and the Coronado bridge—with Kim Sutherland under his arm.

Especially when he knew, in his head and his cock, precisely what she was cooking up.

Chapter Six

Bennett

BENNETT STRETCHED HIS legs and eyed Kim suspiciously in the dim light of the moon. Her cooler had a six-pack of Coke and a fifth of whiskey in it—because *of course* it had. She'd even remembered plastic cups and stirrers, like a real girl scout.

As prepared as she was, one might think she'd staged a beachside seduction a time or two before.

While the thought was troubling, it was ultimately immaterial in the face of the bigger issue, which was that Bennett clearly had not prayed hard enough earlier in the night. If he had, the good lord might've seen fit to throw him a bigger bone than making sure they weren't completely alone out here.

Thankfully, two other couples had produced the same genius idea as Kim, along with a handful of late evening dog-walkers. In perhaps the only thing going his way, their presence seemed to give Kim pause.

Her voice shook a little when she announced, "I was right—it sure is pretty out here. Thank you for bringing me."

Then she stalled, laying out her supplies and fussing over mixing the drinks. Bennett tried to set aside his nerves and get a bead on her mood, but studying Kim so closely backfired, and only underlined the fact that moonlight was even more flattering on her than the restaurant's candlelight had been.

As it was, Bennett had been half hard and thoroughly disgusted with himself all through dinner, surreptitiously obsessing over Kim's expressive mouth and the way her pinned-up hair showed off her neck. So much so, he'd begun to wonder if he'd somehow been turned into a vampire without realizing it.

He'd needed to get a grip then, and he needed to get a grip now. If he lunged across the blanket and gave in to his desire to bite her throat, it would only earn him a swift knee to the 'nads, and probably a restraining order.

He'd taught her that much, at least.

Instead of indulging his rapidly weakening resolve, Bennett trained his eyes on the dark horizon and kept them there until Kim finished her bartending. When she finally shoved a drink in front of his face, he grabbed it gratefully and slammed it back in two swallows.

Then he coughed in surprise. *Damn.* She poured heavy, and he was driving. No more cocktails for him.

Somewhere inside himself, Bennett attempted to summon a shred of decency by mentally reciting all the reasons he couldn't let this get further out of hand.

Kim was a good girl, despite her villainous machinations. She was his sister's best friend, nearly family, and therefore off-limits. She was way too good for him in every way that mattered.

What's more, Kim was scared. The media's fascination with her connection to Dan Cox had driven her to seek protection from him and his team, and getting involved with a client—or whatever she'd become when she'd landed in California— undoubtedly violated any number of Black Watch rules and protocols.

When Bennett got home, he probably needed to look up specifically which ones.

Kim giggled suddenly, jarring him from his freak-out. "Are those people *skinny dipping?*" she cried, pointing at the ocean.

He peered at the breakers cutting across the inky water. The couple was hard to decipher, the reflection of the moon glittering just enough to obscure exact details. Even so, they did appear to be quite naked, and quite enamored of each other.

Inspiration. Just what he needed.

Like that, Bennett was thrown back to high school, and a memory he'd tried, and failed, to excise from his brain many times.

It must've been late summer, mere weeks before the start of his senior year. Kim's folks still had their backyard pool open, and blooming vines had been climbing all over the pergola that'd marched down one side of their yard. He remembered the heavy scent of the flowers like it was yesterday.

Bennett had shown up too early to pick up his sister, but he'd already hit the drive-through of the burger place for dinner. If he and Shannon ate it on the drive home, they could go straight to their rooms and avoid conversation with their folks.

No interaction would lessen the likelihood of an argument, and back then, those were a dime a dozen. Bennett hadn't been able to stop pointing out the elder Shaws' shortcomings, both as parents and as adults, but he might as well have been shouting into the wind for all the good it had done. Mama and Daddy had been farther gone every time he'd laid eyes on them.

He wanted to cuss at the memory, even now. They'd only needed to hold their shit together for six more months. Once he'd turned eighteen, they could've scattered to the four winds, for all he cared. Bennett would've been an adult and could've taken legal custody of Shannon, to keep her out of the foster system until she turned of age herself.

That's what the internet had told them anyway. Bennett hadn't ever figured out how to verify it for real, not without tipping their hand to the very people they'd needed to keep out of their business.

Regardless, on that balmy August night, his beat-up car smelling like French fries, Bennett had turned off his radio to coast quietly down the Sutherlands' curving driveway. He'd drifted to a stop and searched the front of the house for signs of activity, but up on the second floor Kim's bedroom window had been dark, and Shannon was nowhere to be found.

Bennett had always hated the embarrassment he'd felt, ringing that doorbell—and that night had been no different. He'd skulked around the side of the house, instead, thinking the girls might be in the kitchen.

No such luck. There'd been no sign of Shannon, Kim, or even Regina, the housekeeper. That part was fine—the less Bennett had been required to interact with adults, the better. They'd asked too many questions, ones he had no answers for.

But he'd been loitering on the porch, deciding whether to slip inside and hunt for them, when he'd heard the girls giggling softly in the darkness behind him.

All the little lights the Sutherlands had hidden in their landscaping were turned off. So were the pool lights. Bennett remembered slinking across the grass with his heart in his throat and ducking under one of the arches of that long pergola like he was ditching the hold of an irritating linebacker.

He'd caught sight of his sister first, hair slicked back and shushing Kim from the dark water. But then, Kim had taken three long strides out of the shadows to dive headfirst into the deep end, her tan skin made pale as she'd arced through the moonlight like a mystical creature.

She'd broken the surface of the water a few beats later, laughing quietly as she swam to the ladder. Kim had scaled it nimbly and paused at the top, and Bennett had been struck by the incomprehensible fact that she didn't have a stitch on.

Kim. Sutherland. Buck naked. Yards away from him.

There'd been no doubt about it—Kim and his sister were skinny dipping in the dark, the only light coming from the moon and the million pinpricks of stars, scattered across a Texas sky that never stopped trying to make Bennett feel small.

In that cursed instant, he'd understood with a jolt that Kim was no longer his kid sister's equally young friend. She'd changed without him realizing it, and his hormonal scumbag of a body had recognized something it wanted with a ferocity that'd dismayed him.

Bennett had been well used to self-loathing by then, but the realization had made his soul want to curl in on itself. It'd taken a minute to regain his wits, but once he'd been able to think clearly, he'd turned his back and edged carefully into their line of sight, pretending to be distracted by his phone until he was certain they'd noticed him.

Once they had, he'd turned to discover that Kim was not, in fact, naked. She'd been wearing a modest, khaki-colored two-piece, close enough to her skin tone that it'd disappeared in the bad lighting.

Thank God for that. She'd been sixteen, and an innocent compared to his experienced seventeen-and-a-half. He felt like a degenerate even accidentally imagining tainting her.

Bennett could no longer remember what he'd said or done next. He could only recall the way Kim's eyes had come alive at the sight of him, and he'd known, deep in his gut, that he'd have to leave Respite soon. If he didn't, his messy life was bound to infect Kim's—and as ever, the blame would definitely fall on him.

Funny how he'd done everything right, but it'd happened anyway.

If was difficult to anchor himself in the present and remember that he wasn't a lost kid in Respite, Texas, anymore. Bennett was a grown man, a Navy SEAL—kind of—and he had resources at his disposal. Backup if he needed it.

He no longer had to panic or flee.

As he sat beside Kim in her prim apple-green cardigan, listening to her laugh about the couple in the waves, he didn't feel very capable, however. He felt like a ravenous wolf sniffing at Little Red Riding Hood—and he wasn't sure he could survive it another time.

Bennett glanced at Kim and found her eyes on him. Her laughter died away and a wary look crept over her face.

Oh, *now* she was worried? This outing had been her big idea, but someone, somewhere had to have warned her not to mess with a bull if she couldn't handle the horns.

Kim cleared her throat, his stormy mood making her nervous. "Bennett…I've been wondering. How has it been for you all this time? How'd you get—" She gestured vaguely around them. "—here?"

"Seriously?" Bennett shifted around, trying to find a position that wouldn't get too much sand in his shoes or press his hip against hers. "That's what you want to talk about?"

Kim shook her head, wide-eyed and at a loss for words for the first time since she'd rolled up in Skippers. Bennett punched his cup into the sand and twisted to the side, intending to give her what-for.

He froze. She was far closer than he'd thought. His gaze snagged on her mouth, lush and pink.

"How'd you end up in Dallas?" he fired back.

"Daddy had a colleague who bought this big old house. I was only intending to stay for a few months while I worked on it, but three months turned into six…and then I met Dan at a party they dragged me to, so…" She trailed off and shrugged daintily.

"Do you like it?"

"It's alright. Not home, but I've got a lot of work coming in, so it's hard to complain."

Kim stopped talking, and seemed to just…freeze. She blinked slowly, and Bennett clocked every millisecond as her lids swept down, blotted out the shine of her irises, and slowly rose again, revealing a gaze heavy with want.

In the space between one heartbeat and the next, he cradled Kim's face between his palms and crashed his mouth against hers. She squeaked on contact and a wet burst soaked the front of his shirt.

Her drink. Bennett didn't care. *Fuck the drinks.*

Kim parted her lips to say something—sorry, most likely. He didn't want her apology. His tongue plunged into her mouth before a single syllable could exit, and he was lost.

Kim. Lord, how was it possible that she still tasted the same after all these years? That was the only thing that was the same, though. She wasn't the inexperienced girl he'd once shocked into retreat any longer—Kim was a grown woman who knew what she was about.

This Kim was not at all afraid to seize what she wanted, and when her graceful hands gripped his thighs, Bennett thanked heaven for small mercies. If he'd worn shorts instead of khakis tonight, he didn't think he'd be able to handle the sensory overload.

As it was, he couldn't stop devouring her. She was perfect. From her soft skin to her lithe limbs to the way her tongue gave as good as it got, she absolutely checked every box in Bennett's erotic logbook. Probably always had.

He felt more dampness, this time on his fingers. Her drink hadn't splashed that high, though, had it? He broke away and grazed her cheekbones with his thumbs, recoiling in horror when he realized what it was.

Tears. *Aw, hell.*

He hadn't meant to attack her—he'd meant to keep his hands off her and his inappropriate wants on lockdown. But true to form, he'd gone and ruined everything.

Kim cried harder as he stared, but she didn't smack him or cuss him out, and Bennett couldn't quite decide what to say. He'd known it was a bad idea to come out here.

Like that made it better.

"Honey, I am so sorry," he finally murmured, flinching when she gulped in a big lungful of air. "I'm such an asshole. I did not mean for that to happen."

"I did," Kim sniffled, trying to stifle her tears, "So, stuff it. *God.* I just knew you would do this."

"I…" Bennett paused. "What?"

"You think I don't know I'm not your speed? This right here proves it. Five minutes in, and you're already trying to do damage control."

He stared at her, trying to catch up. "Kim…I basically assaulted you and you started crying. What else am I supposed to say?"

She whacked him on the arm, hard. "These are *happy* tears, you numbskull! Though I am still annoyed you made me scheme like a soap opera character to get you out here."

Bennett fell back on his ass in surprise. "What is happening right now?"

Kim swiped roughly at her cheeks and started working herself into a real lather. "You know, I can't tell if you're dense, or simply obstinate. Can you *really* not see that I've been sitting here wanting you since grade school? Given your track record and your cute little ESP trick, I doubt that. So that means you really are gonna sit there with your tired old excuses and expect me to swallow them yet again. Just say I don't have a chance, and put me out of my misery, already."

"Kim," Bennett started, without any clue what to follow it up with.

"Kick rocks, Bennett Shaw," she said, then grabbed the whiskey bottle and took a long slug.

Bennett grabbed the bottle out of her hand. "Okay, hold up. Let's not make things worse."

"You know what? You started it. I never asked to be put on some stupid pedestal. I'm out here making a fool of myself, trying to get you to kiss me, only to have you turn around and *apologize* for it! I think I have earned a stiff drink."

He'd never seen her so unhinged. It had to violate every rule of civility she'd been raised on, but unfortunately, if there'd been a page in her etiquette books that had covered this kind of thing, Bennett had not been privy to it.

He was flying blind, and then some. If he acknowledged that he'd been aware of her youthful crush, he'd have to defend why he'd feigned ignorance for so long. And if he admitted to the fact that he'd wanted her just as badly as she'd wanted him all hell was liable to break loose.

"You are a decorated Navy SEAL, are you not?" she demanded. "A literal hero?"

"Disgraced," he clarified, "And discharged." *How was that relevant?*

"Did you get a *dishonorable* discharge? Are you incarcerated for your supposed crimes? Or do you, right this minute, have people trying to clear your good name because they recognize your worth and want to help you?"

"I mean, yeah, but…"

Kim jabbed a manicured finger into his chest so hard it hurt. "Then you're back on your classist bullshit, aren't you?" she demanded. "Well, guess what? Rich people deserve love, too, you dumbass."

A bark of laughter escaped him at that. He couldn't help it. Her words were preposterous to the point of hilarity.

It seemed that was the correct response, however, because Kim finally relented and stopped poking at him. "Do you see how little sense you make?" she wondered, sliding into his airspace and dropping a soft kiss on his lips. "Just give in, already."

A flash lit up his peripheral vision, and Bennett hunched around Kim reflexively, shielding her from…a simple camera flash, from two girls taking photos of each other posing in the surf.

He pulled back sheepishly, but the jolt of adrenaline sent a cold wash of sense through his system. Kim was still off-limits and possibly in danger. *End of story.*

"No surrender," he told her gently. "This will not happen again."

"Why?"

He shook his head and got to his feet, and Kim jumped up, too, indignant. "Bennett—why not? I liked it!"

He had more than liked it, but there was getting caught up in the moment, and there was acting stupid as a choice, and Bennett was not about to go down that rocky road.

"You didn't like it?" Kim pressed. "Is that it? You didn't like kissing me? Because it sure seemed as if—"

He glared at her with enough heat that she snapped her lips together right quick. "It doesn't matter whether I liked it or not. We should not be doing that, and you know it."

"Who says? We're grown, Bennett. And I don't see anyone butting their noses into what we do on our own time." Kim stewed for a minute, then demanded, "Is it because I dated Dan? I'm not, like, spying for him or anything. You know that, right?"

"It's a conflict," Bennett explained. Not to mention an important point of self-preservation. "You came to my employer for protection—"

"No, I came to *you* for protection," she corrected.

"Fine. Then Shannon—"

"What about her? Your sister knows us better than any person on earth. You think she wouldn't be thrilled to see us together? Relieved that she doesn't have to worry about some stranger breaking one of our hearts again?"

Bennett's heart felt like a storm was brewing inside of it. "What about when one of us hurts the other? That's a wound that runs deep, Kim."

She stared at him in disbelief. "What planet are you living on? The wound is already there. You just need to decide whether you're going to heal it or make it fatal."

Bennett had zero answer for that. Out in the water, the skinny-dippers were gone, and he suspected his sanity had fled with them.

Chapter Seven

Kim

IT WAS HARD to believe that somehow, someway, Kim had finally landed on the magic formula that'd made Bennett give in to the heady attraction simmering between them. And yet, sure as shootin' the lunkheaded man had caved at last, and his hunger was just as wonderful as she'd always envisioned it would be.

Who was she kidding, though? Her imagination hadn't been that good. It hadn't even come close to doing him justice. Bennett was a hurricane, and she was a paper heart, along for the ride.

Kim suspected she'd end up mashed and mangled if he ever decided to be done with her, so task number one was making sure Bennett wouldn't run scared and leave her out of panic, or some misguided sense of martyrdom.

Like he was fixing to do any minute now.

She could help him take down Dan's stepdad later—that was only fair. But she had to get to the bottom of why Bennett looked so rattled over one thirsty kiss first.

"I don't get it," she said as she packed the cooler with the liquor and their empty cups and cans. "You're a step away from losing your shit over a smooch, but you're cool as a cucumber when a real crisis hits. What's that about?"

"The Navy trained me well." Bennett's expression didn't change as he took the cooler from her and began picking his way across the sand. Over his shoulder, he added blandly, "I've also heard it can be a trauma response."

Was he really out here dropping bombs like they were discussing the weather?

Kim grabbed the blanket and rushed to catch up, eyeing him with fascination. Shannon had said that their home life had been hard—but Kim hadn't realized it'd been *that* hard. Not trauma hard, certainly.

She bit her lip, contemplating Bennett's stony profile. "There's a lot I don't know about you, isn't there?"

"You know plenty," he muttered.

"Apparently not enough. This might be easier if you shared a thing or two."

He shot her an arch glance. "Your mama teach you to be so nosy?"

"Said the guy who would've run background checks on my every Homecoming date if he'd been able to."

"I was only trying to look out for you."

"Why, though?"

Bennett picked up his pace, and Kim scurried to keep up. "I'm serious. Why?" she asked again.

"You can stop trying to psychoanalyze me anytime now."

"Great, so you're already seeing a therapist?"

He grunted in frustration. "Kim, that's none of your business."

"That's a yes."

"That's not a no or a yes. That's a mind your beeswax."

"If it was really a no," she reasoned, "then you would've rolled your eyes and scoffed at me. Probably would've tacked on a reductive nickname, too. Like *sweetheart.*"

Bennett stared blankly at her, momentarily speechless. "Miss Sutherland, you are tarter than a bag of lemons," he said eventually. "You ain't never been sweet."

"I beg your pardon," she protested, stumbling on a corner of the blanket that caught under her foot. "Just what is that supposed to mean?"

"It means you are contrary. Ornery and argumentative. A complete pain in my ass. Always have been, always will be."

Kim's mouth dropped open in outrage. "Well, don't flatter me too much, Bennett. It might go to my head."

"I think that ship has sailed." And then the infernal man tacked on, "Sweetheart."

"*Excuse me?*" She stopped trying to keep up with him and planted her feet in the cool sand. "Call me crazy, but it sounded like you just said I'm spoiled."

"I did, yes," he agreed. "Why does that come as a shock to you? You have gotten everything you've ever wanted in life, and more besides. What else would you be, with that kind of unbroken boulevard of dreams in your wake?"

Kim couldn't fathom how Bennett had transitioned so quickly from sucking face with her to insulting her so thoroughly.

"You know, for a smart man, I'm beginning to think that you don't know a lick about me either," she sputtered.

Bennett looked nothing like the person who hadn't been able to resist her moments ago. Instead, he looked alarmingly like Shannon's daunting big brother again.

He told her, "I know all I need to, believe me."

What a flaming liar.

"You have known me my entire life," Kim declared. "Your sister is my best friend in this entire world, and I have never been anything but kind to you, too. So, I cannot understand why you are treating me like this. What's the point? Two minutes ago, you were kissing me like you loved it. Why is it so necessary to keep me at arm's length now?"

"There's no point," Bennett sniffed.

"Oh, so you're doing this for the fun of it? Try again, numbskull. Unless you've had a recent personality transplant, you aren't that mean."

Bennett glared at her, then spun and marched away again. Kim frowned at his broad, retreating back, and chased after him. "And now you're fleeing. If you weren't a certified badass, I'd start to wonder if you were scared of me, Bennett Shaw."

He laughed darkly. "A little thing like you? Please. I could take you down in a heartbeat."

Except, Kim heard him swallow and even in the dark of that damn beach he looked a little green.

She scowled harder at his stupidly handsome face. "I am not some five-foot-tall weakling," she spat. "I am five-nine and have taken taekwondo since I was nineteen. You know good and well I would not go down easy—I would give you a run for your money, and that's a fact."

Bennett clenched his jaw and went from green to white, but he didn't say a word. He simply stared over her head, staunchly silent.

Kim wanted to stamp her foot with frustration. "Bennett, you have tried everything from insults to outright flight to push me away, and I still cannot see a dang reason why," she hollered. "What on earth could be so important, that you would go to these lengths to keep it from me?"

As the last syllables left her mouth, it felt like everything on the beach stopped. The seagulls and the waves—even the dog frolicking in the surf seemed to freeze in place.

The air between them grew heavy and slow, and Bennett's glittering eyes flicked down to meet hers. What came next happened so fast, Kim didn't have time to take a breath, much less defend against it.

Bennett hooked a foot around her ankle and swept her clear off her feet, bringing her down to the ground so smoothly she couldn't fathom how she'd ended up with him looming over her, blocking the stars. He used his long limbs to cage her against the sand, and growled into her ear, "One heartbeat."

He dropped his weight onto her, letting Kim feel all the hot places their bodies aligned. "Two heartbeats," he said next.

Then Bennett's mouth landed on hers, claiming her with a kiss that shattered Kim's world into spinning, glistening shards. His tongue laid expert waste to anything she thought she knew about attraction and left an inferno burning in its wake.

She grabbed his hard shoulders and hung on, because she sure wasn't going to miss round two over something as petty as pride. Her eagerness pulled a low moan from him, but far too soon, Bennett pulled away.

"Three heartbeats," he told her, pushing to his knees, and then to his feet. He held out a hand to help her up, then repeated, "Three heartbeats, Kim. That's all it took for me to ruin everything. Your pretty lipstick. Your ironed skirt. Your perfect hair. Imagine what I could do in a month, or a year."

Kim *could* feel sand in her hair—coating her back from neck to heels, actually—but hell would freeze over before she'd let him see her shake it off.

"You think I don't know you're carrying a torch for me?" Bennett continued. "I know. But you have no idea what you are asking for. You never have. Getting mixed up with me would wreck everything good about you, and despite what you may think, I am not enough of a reprobate to be a party to it. So, yeah—I will continue to keep you at arm's length, and it will be for your own dang good." He sniffed in annoyance. "Someday, you'll thank me."

"And I don't I get a say?" Kim demanded.

"What, so you can argue some more? No, thanks."

She glared at him, shaken to the core by the rapid swings their evening had taken. First his customary bullheadedness, followed by his sudden, soul-searing kiss. More inscrutability, then another explosion of passion.

And now this: Bennett's supposedly final, condescending retreat. Kim wanted to strangle him, but she also wanted to kiss him again.

"You're wrong about one thing," she gritted out.

He was wrong about so much more than that, but now didn't feel like the time to list it out. "I haven't gotten everything I've ever wanted. Turns out I'm still chasing the only thing that ever mattered to me."

Then Kim turned and pulled a dramatic exit of her own, charging down the beach in the direction Bennett had just been headed, hoping like hell it was the way back to his truck.

She didn't get far. He caught up with her a few steps later, wrapping a heavy arm around her waist in a hold that would've made his old football coach proud.

"Don't go," he said next to her ear. "I'm sorry."

"You literally did the same thing to me, ten seconds ago. Doesn't feel so hot when someone runs away in the middle of a conversation, does it?"

"No. And I shouldn't have done it. Like I said, I'm sorry."

Kim wriggled around until she was facing all that contrition, gratified when he didn't let go. "Why did you?"

"Because you make me crazy. And I was trying to keep from doing what I ended up doing anyway. So much for my supposed control."

"Don't be too hard on yourself. It took a lot of goading to make you snap."

Bennett snorted—but he also smirked a little.

"Besides, I like it when you lose control." Kim considered a minute, then clarified, "Maybe not all the sand down my neck. But everything else."

"I like it, too," he admitted ruefully. "Too much. Whatever this is between us is…fucking with my head, Kim. It's a lot to take in, after all this time."

She reached up and ran her fingers along the pale gold hair at his brow. "You've made it your life's mission to fight against the inevitable. I imagine it's hard to change gears."

Bennett nodded faintly.

"Am I really that bad?" she wondered, feeling guilty for pushing him. "Is that why you don't want to give me a chance?"

"You know that's not it."

"Pardon me. *It's not you, it's me,* right?"

"It's a classic for a reason," he shrugged.

"It's lame, but I think we've had enough angst for one night. Will you take me back to my hotel now?"

"Of course." Bennett bent to gather up her picnic supplies, but he looked cowed in a way Kim didn't like.

"Bennett…Mama might not have raised me to be nosy," she began.

"Came by that all on your own, did ya?"

She narrowed her eyes.

"Damn girl, give a guy a breather, why don't you?"

"But she didn't raise a quitter," Kim finished. "This ain't over."

Bennett blew out a breath and his anxious eyes met hers. "Don't you think I know that?"

Chapter Eight

Bennett

BENNETT SCRUBBED A hand over his face, completely checked out from the conversation flowing around him. He was still smarting over how the night before had gone. He'd let himself get cocky and he'd paid the price, simple as that.

He'd thought he could hold out against Kim, but she was too pretty, too sweet, and too charming for the likes of him. When her game had come to a head, he'd crumpled faster than a beer can under a tank tread.

Truth be told, he ought to have known better than to set one foot on that beach with her. Every instinct he possessed had been shooting off flares, but apart from their surprise reunion in Skippers, he hadn't seen Kim in years.

Bennett had forgotten the way she so effortlessly turned him stupid—forgotten the hold she had over him, and that it had real-world consequences.

It was not the time to mourn his absence of good sense, however. He had actual work to do, and agonizing over whether Kim was still upset by his meltdown was definitely not on the day's agenda.

Refocusing on the men beside him, Bennett said, "One thing I've been thinking is, what Rohaan meant when he called those girls *lost*. Are we talking about unidentified remains, or kidnapping, or what? Lost can mean a lot of things."

Their young Nabaruti informant was still safely ensconced in his computer science program at UCSD, where Noah was able to discreetly watch over him—but Rohaan had never stopped pushing for them to find the girls who'd gone missing from his village during last year's ambush by a small-time warlord, his girlfriend most of all.

The team tried to meet with him in person as little as possible, hoping to ensure that he stayed under the Doggett family's radar, and that of any Qahati operatives that might be lurking around. They had no intention of dropping the ball, though. In fact, they'd agreed to gather at one of Black Watch's secret warehouse refuges this morning to see what they could hammer out.

"Mr. Monroe agrees with you," Noah said. "First thing he had me do was look into the Nabarut cleanup records to see what I could find."

"And?"

"There were only four unidentified sets of remains by the end, all of them adult males. The surviving villagers had a pretty good idea of who they were generally, if not specifically."

Bennett shook his head. "So definitely not the twelve teenage girls we have to find."

Noah nodded. "Exactly."

The fourteen-and-up students had reportedly been more excited about their school opening than even the littlest girls. They'd certainly been old enough to understand what was at stake—that by reaching for an education, they might anger some of the very men they'd be expected to make lives with soon.

"Well, they didn't just vanish," Wyatt complained. "If they were taken, dead or alive, someone had to have seen it."

"If so, no one's admitting it," Noah shrugged. "Understandable, I guess. For all they know, Kadir could still be breathing down their neck."

Wyatt frowned. "What do you mean, could be?"

"There's drone footage of al Kadir's camp from the days after the ambush. "No, I'm not going to share how I saw it," he told Bennett. "One day it's there, and the next it's gone. And before you ask, the girls seemed to just evaporate once the fighting started. I combed through frame by frame to make sure."

"That's..." Bennett shook his head, not wanting to show his surprise at Black Watch's capabilities—and this kid's in particular. "So Kadir packed up the camp?"

"Yes. Whole thing vanished overnight. No one's figured out where he went yet, so the villages in the area are still pretty jumpy."

"It's nearly been a year. How does a guy like that lay low for a year?" Wyatt wondered.

Noah shrugged. "With help, I imagine."

"And we're supposed to believe the Qahatis have nothing on him? Nothing at all?"

"They've had three bad years of drought. They've got a lot on their plate."

Bennett's knee started jumping as he pondered that intel, so he gripped it with his hand and held it in place—something he'd been doing ever since the time his mother had noticed it and assumed he was as hopped up as her. He'd been fourteen, the same age as some of the missing girls.

"So...they picked up the girls one-by-one in the confusion, and either hid them in the Boshad Pass or trucked them out immediately." Bennett considered the facts for a minute. "They couldn't have flown them out. Command would've made note of any civilian or military aircraft that wasn't ours."

Noah simply nodded, letting Bennett work it out for himself.

Wyatt leaned in, though, planting his elbows on his knees and staring into Bennett's eyes. "That's not a smash-and-grab, bro. It's a preplanned, coordinated maneuver. Kadir *meant* to take those kids. It was his whole reason for being there. That's what you're saying?"

Before Bennett could agree, a muted alarm sounded from Noah's laptop. He wheeled to check the screen, tapped a button, then turned to watch the warehouse door.

Joe ambled in a moment later, looking pale and tragic. His hair was still damp from a shower.

"Rough night?" Wyatt smirked.

Bennett didn't smile along. He could hear the concern lacing Wyatt's words and see for himself the condition Joe was in—undoubtedly due to the night terrors the guy regularly endured.

Joe shoved his hands in his pockets as he approached, only saying, "Sorry I'm late. What'd I miss?"

Bennett wasn't surprised he didn't acknowledge Wyatt's question. It was an open secret amongst the team that Joe sometimes stayed up all night to avoid the nightmares, or slept in his car if he was worried that they might hear too much.

"Well, our techie Boy Wonder is performing his usual magic tricks," Wyatt explained, "And Sherlock here has been busy cracking The Case of the Missing Nabarutis."

He patted the chair next to him. When Joe eased stiffly into it, Wyatt passed him the large tumbler of coffee that he'd brought with him. Joe accepted it with a faint nod, prying off the plastic lid to inhale the aroma of Colombian roast like it might save his life.

Hell, maybe it would. They would have to address the problem of Joe eventually, but he was hanging in there for now. Barely, but Bennett wasn't about to cast stones.

"Where's Buck?" Joe inquired, once he'd taken a long slug of the brew.

"Watching over the agent Monroe sent to meet with Doggett's new PR person."

"Kenya," Noah supplied.

"Right." Bennett checked his watch. "He said he'd meet us here after."

Joe drained some more of his coffee but waved away the breakfast sandwich Wyatt fished from the bag at his feet.

Bennett held up his hand for the pass, but when Wyatt tossed it over, Noah snatched the thing clean out of the air. Fortunately, Stitch knew his audience and was armed with a sufficient supply of bacon-egg-and-cheeses. Before Bennett had a chance to complain, he'd delivered another sandwich to him and pulled a third out for himself.

Bennett unwrapped his breakfast and turned to Joe. "We've been walking through the ambush, trying to nail down how and when the girls were grabbed, and where they might have ended up. It doesn't track that they died. There'd have been some sign by now."

Joe nodded, some color returning to his face as the caffeine took hold. "There had to have been a crew, right? One group of fighters assigned just to that task, while the rest engaged with the villagers and the Army unit."

"Seems likely," Noah agreed.

Wyatt jumped up and paced around with his sandwich, less tense now that Joe had arrived. "This is such bullshit, though. All those girls taken God knows where, and not one person in Nabarut saw anything? Don't they want their daughters back?"

When no one responded, he planted his feet and pointed at them. "I say we go back. Talk to those fucking cowards ourselves."

Noah glanced at Bennett in alarm.

"Hold up," Bennett said calmly. "We're not going back to interrogate a bunch of villagers. And they're not cowards, they're terrified of what will happen if they snitch."

He could understand the guy's frustration, though. If CPS had ever tried to take Shannon away from him, he would've raised holy hell to get her back. But unlike the gentle Nabarutis, he was no pacifist—he was an instrument of war, and always had been.

"But that's what you do when you lose something," Wyatt argued. "Right? You go back to the last place you saw it and retrace your steps."

"Waste of time," Joe commented. "Those girls are far gone from Nabarut. I'd bet they're not even in Qahat anymore."

Wyatt stuffed the last of his sandwich in his mouth and gestured wildly. "None of you feel the slightest bit of urgency, here? It's been ten months! You know what could've happened to them in that time?"

Bennett passed a weary hand over his eyes. He knew better than most how far a kid's life could plummet in the space of a few months.

"Wyatt, sit down," he said bleakly, wishing Buck would hurry up and get there already. "Freaking out isn't going to find them faster."

"No one rips young girls from their homes for altruistic reasons," Wyatt bellowed. "You get that? They're not out there somewhere having book club, while we dick around trading theories."

Like that, something in Bennett snapped. He shot out of his seat and got in Wyatt's face. "Will you shut the fuck up? We get it, okay? We all fucking get it! *Christ.*"

Noah's door alarm chirped again, and soon Buck strolled up, a wry look on his face. Fucking *finally.*

After a long beat of heavy silence, he asked, "You jokers all done, or do you still have things to work out?"

Bennett and Wyatt glared at each other but returned to their seats like good little boys.

"Welcome to the party," Bennett grumbled. Clearly, he wasn't cut out for leadership roles—one look at Noah's wide eyes told him that much.

Buck jingled his keys as he looked them over, then dragged a chair across the stained gray concrete and dropped into it with a sigh. "The meeting went smoothly, thanks for asking," he commented. "Doggett's PR guy handed over the same old media packet and didn't stray one inch from the script they've been following."

"Did Kenya plant the bug?" Noah wondered.

Buck smirked. "Sure did. You weren't kidding about her. She's exceptional."

The kid nodded and looked smug as he turned to his laptop, fingers flying over the keys as he brought up stills from the day of the Nabarut ambush.

Buck eyed Bennett speculatively, then turned to the others. "I take it by your foul moods that you haven't made much headway?"

Wyatt sighed. "We figure they can't be dead. So Kadir had to have hidden them in the pass until things died down or trucked them out during the confusion." He scowled at Bennett, then added, "I think we should go back and talk to some locals. Find out for sure if anyone saw something."

Buck was shaking his head before Wyatt even finished speaking. "No go. You want to start another international incident before our appeal is even heard?"

Joe snorted. "You know that's a pipe dream, right? The inquiry board is never going to reinstate us. Or have you forgotten that there's someone dirty in the chain of command?"

Noah glanced among them. "I haven't."

Buck looked like he was trying hard to keep his cool. "No one's forgotten. But we have a plan, and we're going to see it out. We said we were going to climb our way up the hill of this stinking mess, right? Well, we've already nailed Joely and Tim Stein to the wall. Now we go after Cox."

"And then what?"

"Then we get Doggett. See where he leads us. We're going to find who's infiltrated the brass and we're going to find those girls too. The plan will work."

Joe shook his head, looking tired. "And yet, we have nothing solid on Dan Cox yet. So, what are we even doing here?"

"Interesting you should mention that," Buck said, turning back to Bennett. "If I'm not mistaken, San Diego's newest visitor happens to be the ex-girlfriend of the very man in question. I wonder if she's come bearing information that could help us."

Bennett's heart dropped into his shoes. With all his handwringing about sucking face with Kim, he'd clear forgotten that he was supposed to find that out.

"Did she tell you anything last night?" Wyatt wondered.

Bennett cleared his throat. "No. We mostly got caught up, is all."

"Mostly," Joe snorted. "I'll bet."

Chapter Nine

Kim

WHILE KIM WAITED for Bennett to work up the nerve to call her again, she kept herself busy catching up on work and tweaking the portfolio pictures she had featured on her website.

She didn't need to take on any new projects just yet, but if she stayed in San Diego much longer, she'd have to consider what her next professional steps would be.

What's more, while Shannon had promised to keep an eye on her condo in San Antonio, it was probably time for Kim to step up her search for a more comfortable landing spot out here.

She'd already told Bennett that a residential-style hotel, or even a longer-term vacation rental, would make life easier for her—but she hadn't clarified that it would allow her to take on new commissions.

Why panic him worse?

It wasn't as if she was considering a move already. Kim simply wanted to test the water, to see if her design style translated to southern California enough for her to keep her business afloat. If it even came to that.

She was being practical. That was all.

She was going on three weeks in this room, with no relief in sight. Besides, if she had to stick close to the hotel while Bennett's team got a better handle on what her security measures ought to look like, Kim figured she might as well find someplace where she could cook for herself and spread out more comfortably.

With that in mind, she bookmarked a few real estate websites, set aside her laptop, and wandered onto her room's little balcony.

All this planning sure made it *seem* like she meant to stick around for a while. As Kim tried to get a peek at the ocean between the neighboring buildings, she acknowledged that she didn't hate the idea.

She'd found Bennett and seen for herself what kind of man he'd grown into. It was hard to envision turning around and leaving him behind once more.

She'd left Texas to get away from the reporters, and to offer up whatever dirt she had on Dan.

Reminiscing with Bennett Shaw would not fix anything else wrong with her life. To do that, she had to win him. To keep him.

The task loomed big enough to shoot her right back into self-doubt, though.

Kim went inside and dropped into the leather office chair, spinning around as she contemplated her position. Over the last couple of days, waiting for Bennett to reach out again, she'd managed to distill her whirling thoughts into ten facts she was completely sure about.

She'd listed them on her phone, so she could refer to them whenever Bennett's mixed signals made her wonder if she was doing the right thing by angling for his heart.

Kim slid her phone closer and tapped on the note.

1) The kisses on the beach were the best she'd ever had.

2) They'd been so good, in fact, that Bennett had panicked and fled.

3) His casual reference to trauma responses definitely required further investigation.

4) His oblique admission that he was in therapy, or had been at some point, demonstrated emotional growth and was an unequivocal green flag.

5) Bennett had basically admitted that he'd been trying to take care of her all these years, so he couldn't be *too* concerned about her acting spoiled.

6) He remained absolutely horrified by the notion of corrupting her, and…

7) …he seemed even more appalled by the notion of her packing up and leaving.

8) Bennett had the ability to communicate his feelings (when pushed), but there was room for improvement.

9) He wasn't nearly as cocky as he pretended.

And last, but not least,

10) He knew as well as she that they had unfinished business.

Kim bit her lip as she contemplated each item, searching for a way forward. She hadn't learned a lot about present-day Bennett yet, but she had enough to work with.

The truth was, she'd been fishing when she'd urged him to share his secrets with her. Kim already knew his worst one, and while she had no problem helping him keep it—particularly from the likes of Dan's stepdad and his cronies—she really wanted Bennett to trust her enough to share it with her on his own.

He needed to believe that it didn't change how she felt about him, and the only way that would happen was if they talked about it. Only then would Bennett have no doubt that his adolescent actions had left no damage. On her, anyway.

She'd known going in that Bennett had demons.

That only made it more important to do this the right way. Bennett *had* to share the whole story willingly.

Kim got up and paced around her room, wondering whether he would. Right now, it felt like it'd be easier to pull blood from a stone.

No, that wasn't true.

Bennett had shown her that he could open up when necessary, and the fact that he'd sought out even a little therapy was proof that he'd taken steps to conquer the baggage he'd carted into adulthood.

He'd probably acquired other burdens since then, given his career—but that was a worry for another day. Kim had to clear the biggest hurdle first. She had to convince him they were meant to be.

This thing between them didn't feel like it was only physical. Bennett cared about her feelings, too. About her well-being and happiness.

While that wasn't an outright declaration of eternal love, it was plenty to build on.

Maybe.

She sighed. Bennett had been through a lot in his thirty-one years, and his heart deserved coddling. She had to be careful not to pressure him or back him into a corner. If he was going to be hers forever, she wanted him to choose that with zero reservations.

Kim ran a hand through her hair, restless and nervous. She had to be patient, and that was not always her strong suit.

She'd managed not to call Shannon and demand answers, however, and she hadn't caved and pestered Bennett, either. So far, so good.

He'd reach out when he was ready, and when he did, she'd be ready, too. She'd give him the answers to whatever questions he came up with—and Bennett *would* have questions. Anyone would.

With that in mind, Kim slipped into her chair and cracked open her laptop again, considering what she'd brought him. Once, he'd been at the mercy of powerful, unscrupulous people. They'd been kids then, but she was damned if she was going to let Bennett face the same kind of enemies on his own now.

But what if…?

With shaking hands, she slipped her external hard drive from her computer case and glanced behind her. It felt weird to be so paranoid, but if the fervor of the reporters hounding her back home was anything to go on, Kim couldn't risk one of them finding out what she had.

She got up and shut the sliding door, checked the lock, and pulled the heavy hotel curtains closed, too. Then she went to the hall door and flipped the security lock over the bolt.

The secrecy felt necessary, especially until she was able to turn her stash over to Bennett and his team and wash her hands of it.

So even though her hotel room now felt like a cave, Kim felt safer connecting her backup drive and calling up the files. Soon, she was scrolling through page after page of credit card charges and phone logs.

What if Bennett laughed her off? What if all this wasn't enough to help him?

She hoped that wouldn't be the case. There were so many line items that simply didn't add up, for more reasons than the one she'd been most concerned about when she'd stolen the information.

Bennett would want to know why she had it to begin with, she realized abruptly. He had no idea why she and Dan had split up, because she'd been too embarrassed to bring it up.

Bennett had been too preoccupied with trying not to kiss her to ask, and with how to keep the local media from noticing she was in town.

Since Shannon was a vault and swore she would never share Kim's secrets with her brother, Bennett would have no idea that Kim was normally a pretty easy-going girlfriend. She wasn't suspicious—certainly not enough to go through her boyfriend's mail, trying to catch him in a lie.

That part had happened entirely by accident. What's more, once the photos had served their purpose, Kim had diligently deleted them from her phone and moved on with her life, not thinking about them again until she and Shannon had started planning her exodus to the coast.

Only then did Kim remember the backup service she'd used to protect her project files ever since college, and Billy's spilled beer. She'd known what she had to do. The download to her hard drive had taken less than fifteen minutes, and the pictures were restored.

Two months of Dan's expenditures and calls, all there in black and white.

Kim sighed. She was going to look like a jealous, conniving floozy when she turned the hard drive over to Bennett. Not exactly the enticement she'd been hoping to offer him.

Seriously, though—what was a self-respecting woman supposed to feel when her boyfriend got dinner reservations at the restaurant she'd been dying to try for months, then canceled at the last minute for a work trip?

Disappointment was bound to be an issue. So, when that woman happened to be minding her business in his kitchen some weeks later, drinking a cup of coffee before she left for work…and her eyes fell on the pile of open mail next to her on the counter…?

When she spotted a big charge for that hard-to-get-into restaurant, on the exact date they'd planned to go? Suffice it to say, accidents happened.

Someone had gone out to eat, but it sure hadn't been her.

There'd been other weird charges, too. Clubs in Dallas, florists, boutiques—all for the two weeks when Dan had supposedly been in Hyersville, West Virginia, tending to a crisis at the gun manufacturer he ran for his mother.

Crisis, her ass.

Dan Cox had begun cheating on Kim a mere three months into their relationship, and she'd been exceedingly annoyed by his nerve. How many times had she zoned out while he tooted his own horn over cocktails? How many faked orgasms and dates that'd fallen through?

Trying to date Dan had been a waste of time from the start, due in no small part to his incessant narcissism and penchant for gaslighting. It never should've dragged on as long as it had.

It'd been the gaslighting, in particular, that had sent Kim into an angry lather that morning. She'd taken photos of his bills because she'd wanted to confront him with the receipts when she dumped him—to leave him no way to weasel out of it.

And now? She refused to feel sorry about it, now. If Dan hadn't wanted to be discovered, he should've left those expense reports at his office.

Kim sniffed in derision as she highlighted a sketchy line item that she'd missed on her first few passes of the files. She'd already spent hours matching everything to her calendar for those months, making notes on the discrepancies between where Dan had told her he was, and where his credit card said he'd been.

She might hate his guts something fierce now, but it still smarted to see his betrayal laid out in black and white like this. To wonder how Bennett and his friends might judge her for it.

Shannon had, of course, drilled into her head that Dan's cheating hadn't been her fault. For the most part, Kim believed that was true. She didn't *want* to feel embarrassed when she told Bennett the truth.

She was only ashamed that it'd taken her so long to figure out Dan's lies—that she hadn't pegged him for what he was the moment she met him. Maybe then, she wouldn't have spent one minute on the jerk instead of three months.

She'd let herself be swayed by her dad and stepmom's admonitions, though, and it had gotten her exactly nowhere. Again.

She shouldn't work so much. She should get out there and enjoy life while she could. What was she waiting for, anyway? Prince Charming only existed in fairytales.

There'd been less-direct insinuations, as well—hints that Kim wasn't getting any younger and that her looks would soon fade. Her own mother had taken up that refrain the closer Kim had gotten to thirty, as if hope had already been lost.

Kim let out a sound of disgust, then closed out the files and disconnected the drive. Once she had it stowed safely in its case again, she reopened her room to the beautiful cool breeze and slanting, late afternoon sun.

She felt jumpy now, cooped up in this room. Kim wanted to go find Bennett, but whether that was because she wanted to be rid of the documents once and for all, or because she wanted him to kiss her senseless, and obliterate any trace of Dan's memory and misdeeds, was anyone's guess.

Kim sighed yet again, frustrated with herself. She had to be patient. Bennett would call her soon.

THAT EVENING, SURE enough, a text lit up from him, innocuous and loaded, all at once.

Can we get together tomorrow? We need to talk about your protection, and other things.

It took Kim a minute to realize what Bennett meant by "other things." It couldn't only be the kisses he was so pressed about—he considered those a closed case.

This had to be about Dan. She'd insinuated that she had dirt, after all. She just hadn't had a chance to tell Bennett the specifics, yet.

Another frisson of doubt cascaded through her. What if her information was stuff they already knew? What if Dan's activities made no difference at all to Bennett's case against Senator Doggett?

Would he still let her stick around long enough to see where their relationship might lead? Or would Bennett send her packing back to Texas with a phalanx of nameless guards that would never care about her the way he did?

She'd find out soon enough, she supposed.

I'm free whenever, Kim texted back. *Name the time and place and I'll be there.*

Chapter Ten

Bennett

B ENNETT SAT BEHIND the wheel of his truck, fiddling with the radio so he wouldn't have to back out of his spot and go meet Kim like they'd planned.

He felt weirdly relieved that he'd finally sprung for the gleaming black Ford last year. If he hadn't, he'd have to drive Kim around in the same temperamental old junker he'd nursed along for a decade, and Bennett could only guess what she'd have thought.

It would look like he was *still* the same overgrown hellraiser the people of Respite had always believed him to be—like he hadn't grown up, hadn't changed a lick.

But he had, hadn't he?

"Fuck it," Bennett muttered to himself, finding the country station out of Fresno and turning it up. Some guy was singing about a girl like smoke, one he couldn't hold on to and couldn't let go.

The lyrics fit Kim to a tee. There'd always been a push-and-pull with her—one day she was an ephemeral dream, perpetually on the verge of slipping through his fingers, and the next she was carved so deeply on his soul that even dying wouldn't excise her.

Sort of like his career on the Teams, come to think of it.

Bennett forced himself to start driving, but he was awash in memories. Since Kim had shown up, so much was coming back—shit he hadn't thought about in a decade. After years of relative stability, though, he hated how unsettling it felt.

Just that morning, he'd remembered the time he took Shannon and Kim to watch the late-night freight trains passing on the far outskirts of town. He'd pulled up close to the tracks for them, and stayed behind the wheel when they'd climbed out and parked themselves on his hood to gossip with each other.

Their words had been mostly carried away by the screeching of the wheels, but Bennett had been content to watch Kim through the windshield. She'd been luminous against the black velvet sky, an unattainable angel untouched by the dense fabric of the night.

Even inside the car, Bennett had felt the rattling rush of the boxcars in his bones. When the train had raced away, it'd taken the stolen moment with it, like he'd wished he could.

Shannon and Kim had loved country music back then, and they'd sung along to the radio the whole way home. But no matter how many times he'd rolled his eyes or groaned at their goofy serenades, they'd never changed the channel. Maybe they'd known Bennett would've had to be dead inside to not secretly love their shining eyes and giggling voices, bestowed only on him.

Later, when he'd gone to work and the girls were safe in their beds, he remembered humming their favorite songs to himself and marveling at how everything about Kim had seemed so *normal*—wholesome and pure in a way he'd never been.

It was that unassailable sweetness that he'd clung to, deep in his heart where no one could touch it, for all the impossibly long years he'd been stuck in Respite.

Bennett had once longed to be the man standing between Kim and the ugliness of the world, and he'd assumed her family and privilege would shield her from the things he could not.

It hadn't quite worked out the way he'd expected, but what had?

Bennett was right back to protecting her again, except now, she actually needed it. The irony, of course, was that Kim thought her worst adversaries were the reporters trying to get the scoop on Dan Cox.

Bennett understood that the real enemy was him. The very last thing Kim needed was to be saddled with a partner that had the kind of history Bennett did—no matter what hare-brained notions of compatibility she'd concocted. She thought she knew him, but she had no idea how close he'd come to ruining everything.

Because of that, he was going to have to get much better at keeping his cool when she tried to entice him.

It would be no easy task, given the skill set she was rocking, but Bennett had already survived the fire once. Somehow, he would get through this, too.

WHEN BENNETT FINALLY made it to Kim's upper-level suite at the luxurious Foundry hotel, he didn't knock right away. Instead, he stared down at his boots and stalled. He'd purposefully donned jeans that were old enough to be relics, and nothing better than a worn-out t-shirt and an ancient Longhorns ball cap to see her. As if trying to prove how little Kim meant to him.

It'd been a choice, for sure, but now that he was standing in the posh sophistication of the hotel hallway, it felt a touch disrespectful. A bit…ornery.

Bennett didn't have time to go home and change, however, and it wasn't like Kim hadn't seen him in some version of this uniform a thousand times before. A million times, probably.

So, he knocked lightly and waited. When she didn't answer despite clear sounds of her moving around inside, he resorted to laying hard on the little doorbell set into the jamb.

A bell outside a hotel room, he sniffed. What planet did she live on?

The peephole flashed when she stepped up to it, and next thing Bennett knew, Kim wrenched open the door.

"Really?" she squawked, apparently exasperated by his use of the bell.

Either that, or she was still unhappy with him—which might explain why she'd been incommunicado for the last few days.

"You should put tape over the peephole," he told her.

Kim scowled mightily at him.

Bennett took some time to clock her formfitting tank top and tiny running shorts, and another few seconds to travel down miles of tanned legs to hot-pink running shoes. Then he headed back north again.

However, it wasn't until his gaze settled on Kim's lid that his eyes narrowed in fury.

She wouldn't have. She couldn't have.

She knew immediately that she was in trouble. Her baby blues went round as dinner plates under the frayed and faded brim of that old camo hat, and Kim shuffled back a few steps like she intended to defend herself.

She didn't go far enough. Quick as a cat, Bennett snatched the hat off her head and flipped it over to examine it.

Kim tucked her fine platinum hair behind her ears self-consciously, and when Bennett met her eyes again, her expression was a fascinating mix of outrage and trepidation.

She was a good faker, though—he'd give her that. Kim demanded, "Bennett, what are you doing?" with all the confidence of someone who'd been good and truly wronged.

He'd seen all he needed to see, however. Bennett yanked off his Longhorns hat and stuck it in his back pocket, made a quick adjustment to the camo one, and parked it on his head. It settled there as if it'd never left, belonging on his skull even more than his own hair.

He couldn't believe it. Though it'd been years, the hat was definitely his—the very same one lifted from the gas station where he'd worked, and had worn nonstop in high school. Shannon had insisted it was gone when he'd ghosted into Respite one day after boot camp, to check on her and retrieve the last of his meager possessions.

"Kimberley Jane Sutherland," he demanded now, "Would you care to explain how you are in possession of my favorite hat? Particularly since my baby sister told me it was *lost?*"

While it wouldn't be right to lose his mind here in her entryway, considering she was already unhappy with him—this betrayal was beyond the pale.

Kim cleared her throat, but she hung in there, setting her jaw and not saying a word. With her hip cocked and her hand planted on it, she looked like the very picture of defiance.

In another time and place, Bennett might have drooled at the way her stance set off her long, lean muscles and got his blood pumping.

Not today. He looked her over again, and decided absently that she must have been about to work out, but hadn't yet. No person would still look that pristine after running for more than a few seconds, not even Kimmie.

"Don't be mad at Shannon. I expect she did think it was lost," she finally admitted, albeit reluctantly.

Bennett stared at her. "You rotten little thief," he ground out. "Do you have any idea how much I missed this stupid thing?" He jammed his Longhorns hat deeper into his back pocket to keep her from stealing that one, too, and glared at her. "Once it was gone, I…"

Bennett inhaled quickly, catching himself just in time. He'd had nothing left, nothing to link him to his past life but his sister. Despite everything that'd happened, the unmooring had been brutal—but Kim didn't need to hear that.

"Why didn't you just get a new one?" she squeaked, avoiding his accusatory stare. "Those things are a dime a dozen."

Dumbest question ever. "It wouldn't have been the same, and you know it. This hat and I have history."

To be fair, Bennett also hadn't had a dime to his name for a good ten years, since he'd been sending everything he had to Shannon for her student loans. Yet more information Kim would never understand.

She kicked at invisible lint on the carpet, sulking.

Bennett felt unaccountably irritated by her lack of contrition. "Why would you even want this, anyway?" he wondered. "It didn't mean shit to you, but it did to me."

He took the cap off and checked it over again, worried that she might've washed or sanitized it in the intervening years. It still looked as decrepit as ever, though. It was a wonder she'd allowed it to touch her head.

As she watched him pull it on again, she still didn't try to defend herself.

"Seriously, Kim," he said. "What the hell?"

She swallowed and laced her hands together, knuckles turning white. After way too long, she finally whispered, "It reminded me of you, okay?"

"It—" Bennett shook his head. "What?"

"*Shannon* had your old shirts, and some of your photos, and stuff," she blurted, almost against her will. "But I had nothing. All right? Nothing at all. Not one thing to prove you'd been there for most of my life. You were just *gone*." Her voice cracked, and she took a moment before she went on, "Like you'd never been there at all."

Bennett shook his head again, his mind a mess.

"I missed you, is all," Kim murmured defensively. "Who knew that would be such a big deal."

He gaped at her a full minute before his boots started moving without orders. Bennett wrapped an arm around her waist and pulled her against him, crowding Kim deeper into the swanky room as he kicked the door closed.

Then he kissed her lush, cinnamon-spiced mouth, and filled his lungs with her seductive scent.

Oh. *Oh.*

Kim *had* been running already. This close, he could pick out the subtle notes of sweat, and her delicate floral deodorant, and the warm fragrance of her mama's same old laundry detergent.

It was a heady mix and sexy as all get out. Given his way, he would've licked her all over.

Kim was too perfect for words, but when she moaned into his mouth, husky and wanting, Bennett knew he had to step away.

It was either that or toss her on the big bed standing ready in the alcove off to their right.

"I'm sorry," he mumbled. "I can't…" Bennett swallowed thickly and put a few more inches between them. "I don't know why I did that."

Kim rolled her eyes and stomped to the desk, flopping into the chair with a disgruntled huff. "Would you stop apologizing? You're a grown man, for Pete's sake."

Bennett blinked, startled by the bite in her words. He kept forgetting she was nearly a thirty-year-old woman, and not a naive sixteen-year-old anymore.

She took a long swig from a water bottle on the desk and stared at him. "Well? You said we needed to talk. It doesn't look like we're gonna do much else, so let's talk."

"We, uh…" He scrubbed a hand along his jaw, trying to think. "I need to run through your protection plan with you. And…I reckon we should talk about Dan, too."

"That joker is slicker than a slop jar," she muttered. "You know that, right?"

"Obviously."

"Good. Then I have things I need on this agenda, too."

"Such as?"

"Such as, what really happened the night you left Respite? For real, I mean. Shannon's always acted like you took off out of nowhere, but I know that isn't true. You two were thick as thieves—you'd have never done something like that to her."

Bennett flinched at her unexpected change of direction. "Kim, that's all water under the bridge." He glanced around, then went over to an uncomfortable-looking armchair and perched carefully on the edge of it. "There is zero reason to dredge it up now. And believe me when I say, the less you know, the better."

She shook her head in disgust. "You know, I didn't want to hear it at the time, but Daddy always said you were too proud."

He reared back. "What's that supposed to mean?"

"It means you might've had help if you'd ever tried to ask for it."

"You—you have no idea what you're talking about," Bennett sputtered.

"Don't I? He used to admire you, you know. Said you reminded him of himself when he was younger."

"Then he wasn't as smart as he looked." He frowned at Kim and struggled to get his bearings. Bennett couldn't be sure how much Shannon had really told her, and he had to navigate carefully. "If I'd tried to go to anyone and tell them what was really going on at our house, they would've split us up. Do you understand? Shannon would've been sent to live with strangers, with no one to protect her."

He jumped up and paced around, thinking for a minute before he tacked on, "I might not have been the sharpest knife in the drawer, but I sure as hell knew what happened to pretty girls in foster care."

"Because of you, that never happened." Kim's expression went soft with compassion. "You had a heavy load," she murmured. "I'm sorry you had to carry it alone."

Bennett spun away, unable to look at her. "Don't you dare pity me."

She came right over to him, unwilling to back down. "It's not like that, Bennett. Come on."

He let her stroke his back for a minute, but that was all he could stand. "Please stop."

"What?"

"Stop staring at me like that. You've been doing it our whole lives, and it makes me feel like the man-eating wolf in a zoo."

Kim staggered back, catching her sneaker on the carpet and grabbing at the chair for balance. He felt a flare of guilt for acting like such an ass.

"If you're a wolf, what does that make me?" she wondered.

"Little Red Riding Hood, probably. Too brave and not a lick of sense to back it up."

"I'm pretty sure Little Red Riding Hood killed the wolf, Bennett."

"Wrong. He ate her, but your version certainly goes down easier."

"That's what you think of me?" she demanded. "That I'm trying to hurt you?"

Bennett stomped as far away as he could get, a scant ten feet that felt more like ten inches.

"Don't you turn away from me again," Kim threatened. "We are not done."

He kept quiet, like the stubborn mule he was.

"Stop it!" Kim stamped her foot—actually *stamped her foot* like a petulant child. "God, why are you so obstinate? You never—"

While she hollered, she stalked closer. Bennett spun to face her, and in some hideous miscalculation they ended up nose to nose, instead of that safe ten feet. An epic storm was brewing on her face, her eyes burning like flares and lips set in a furious line.

With her typical disregard for boundaries, Kim set her hands on his chest and slid them up around his neck, obliterating another crucial barrier of molecules between them. Bennett wasn't entirely sure whether she intended to push him away or throttle him.

"Do not do that," he growled, his already tenuous control slipping into the critical zone. "I'm hanging by a thread as it is."

"You have got to stop fleeing when I'm trying to talk to you," she said.

"Careful what you wish for. If I hadn't left Respite, you wouldn't have gotten to do half the shit Shannon says y'all did. And you sure as hell wouldn't have gotten mixed up with an asshole like Dan Cox, I can promise you that."

"I believe it." Her nails pressed into the skin of his nape. "You let us do even less than my daddy did. Always with the *not him* and the *not there*. Like you weren't a kid, too."

"I wasn't. Not in any way that mattered."

"I'm sorry. I didn't know, but I should have."

Kim was breathing hard, her breasts pressing against his chest with every inhale. Her lips were parted, and her necklace glittered against her throat as her lungs worked to draw in air.

Bennett did the only thing he could, despite his vows to avoid it. He dipped his head and kissed her.

Chapter Eleven

Kim

HE WAS KISSING her. Bennett Shaw was kissing her, *again*. If it'd been anyone else, Kim might've thought the boy had it bad for her—because despite his vows to keep away, Bennett couldn't keep his lips to himself.

It *was* Bennett, however, so Kim wasn't amused so much as shocked. It felt like every one of her teenage fantasies unspooling in real time.

Well, except for the arguments that always seemed to precede the smooching, or the lingering awareness that Bennett had once again managed to sidestep giving her any answers about the night he'd left Respite.

If they were going to get past whatever was holding him back from a real relationship with her, Bennett had to tell her sometime soon, though. Sometime…after this flare of desire ran its course.

Kim moved her hands to Bennett's taut waist, but his breath hitched when she did, and his eyes squeezed closed as if it hurt for her to touch him.

She pulled him in anyway, and held him close. Bennett caressed her shoulders with shaking fingers, drifting lightly down her arms before parking his hands carefully on her hips.

His hungry kiss faltered, tapered off…and that was it. Bennett stood inertly in her arms, and Kim wondered for the umpteenth time if this was truly a good idea.

He was supposed to like this, not suffer from it.

She rested her cheek against his galloping heart and when his hand landed on her hair, stroking softly, remembered something Shannon had once told her.

There'd been a boy Kim had dated briefly in college, a fraternity brother she'd met through friends. He'd shown up in the middle of the night once, drunk and pounding on the door of her dorm room, bellowing her name.

It'd taken four campus security officers to wrestle him away, and when Kim related the story to Shannon the following morning, she'd commented that it'd seemed like a stunt Bennett might've pulled.

She could still hear Shannon's chuckle. *"Bennett? God, no. He's gentle at heart, especially when he drinks. He didn't do half the stuff people accused him of."*

Kim had been taken aback at the time. *"But…why take the blame, then? Why not defend himself?"*

Bennett had toted around quite the reputation, after all—a charming delinquent people only wanted to know until the heat was on. Then, he might as well have been steaming trash on the sidewalk with the way everyone bitched about him.

Shannon had been amused by her confusion, of course. *"Kim, I love you, but you don't know the first thing about my brother. Even when we were kids, he was always protecting someone. Just not himself."*

Shannon ought to have known—Bennett had protected her most of all. Kim understood that now, and so much more. It made her worry about what he'd gotten himself into with Senator Doggett.

"Bennett?" She squeezed his sides a little, hoping to jog him out of whatever fugue he'd retreated into.

He opened his eyes and looked down at her, his expression troubled.

"What's wrong?" she wondered.

"I don't want to taint you," he admitted. "This…us. You deserve someone worthy. Someone who can give you the things you deserve."

Lord, it was almost word for word what he'd told her the night everything had fallen apart. One minute, he'd been fulfilling her every wild hope, kissing her desperately in a dark corner of that stupid prom—and the next, he'd skipped town forever.

"There's no better man than you," she told him. "Not for me, anyhow." Kim went up on her toes and dropped a soft kiss on his jaw, all she dared in his current mood. "Trust me, I've checked."

Bennett grunted quietly, but his hands squeezed her hips to steady her and miraculously stayed put. His stunning blue eyes traveled over Kim's face, hungrily devouring her features.

He patted her and stepped back.

"Kim…" His voice was unsteady. He spread his fingers wide, clenched them, then shook them out like he was trying to erase the feel of her, or to not grab her again. "I know your dad could've hired you a bodyguard back in Dallas, and I know you didn't come here just to get manhandled by me at every turn. So, what is this about? Why are you really here?"

And there it was—Bennett's infamous sixth sense. Kim had been expecting the moment when it would rear its head and she'd have to fess up, but somehow it still felt like it'd arrived too soon.

She went to her desk and retrieved the drive, then handed it to him. "It's password-protected, but that's it. No encryption or anything."

Bennett frowned. "What's on it?"

"Dan's credit card and phone statements. I thought they might help y'all with whatever his dad is pulling."

He went silent, contemplating her words. After a tense minute, he growled, "That fucker *cheated* on you?"

"Yep." There was his ESP, again. Guess she wouldn't have to explain, after all.

"With Joely Spitz?"

"No, I think she came later. Literally." Kim winced awkwardly.

Angry red flags flared to life on his cheeks. "I hate that pecker. I really do."

She could relate. "Same."

"I'm sorry he did that to you, Kimmie. You don't deserve to be treated like that."

"I'm mostly over it," she shrugged. "The password is *RattlerPride*, by the way. Capital R, capital P, no spaces."

Bennett grinned at the reference to their high school mascot, then tucked the drive in the waistband of his jeans, under his t-shirt. "Thanks, darlin'. We'll check this out right quick, and get it back to you, okay?"

"Keep it. I hope it helps," Kim told him.

"Is there anything else I need to know?" he asked, eyeing her running clothes with a little less angst now. "Anything that's not on the drive?"

In for a penny, in for a pound, she figured.

"Yeah," Kim told him. "I reckon I would like to be manhandled at every turn, long as you're the one doing it. What's a girl gotta do to make that happen?"

Bennett smiled again, relaxing even more. "How did I forget how tenacious you can be? You're like a dog with a bone."

"Look in the mirror, Big Ben. Can you blame me for trying?"

He barked out a laugh and hooked his arm around her waist, yanking her close once more.

"Did you make that nickname up just now?" he murmured against her lips.

Kim dismissed it with a shrug. "Oh, you know—it's something I've been working on."

"Well…keep plugging away. It needs work," he chuckled. "And now, I'm sorry to kiss and run, but I have to cut out for a bit."

Kim pouted. That wasn't what she'd expected, but maybe her hard drive had changed things. "When can I see you again?"

"How about seven? Wear something nice, and I'll take you out to dinner again." He smiled. "Sound good?"

Kim grinned right back at him. "Now we're talking."

BENNETT WAS SHEEPISH when he returned that evening, and explained that he hadn't been able to get a reservation on short notice for the place he'd wanted to take her.

And so, as he inched out of his parking spot, trying to see around a delivery truck unloading a succession of flower arrangements, he asked Kim, "What do you think about picking up some tacos and bringing them back here? There's a great place nearby called Luisa's."

"I'm down for that, but where else could we go?" Kim wondered. "I'm sick of my room. I haven't gone anywhere without you, like you asked, but I'm so bored."

Bennett shot her a sympathetic look. "I know. But you do need to lay low for now—especially in broad daylight. You're a little too eye-catching to stay anonymous for long. Someone's bound to recognize you sooner or later."

"But I was out looking for you for two whole weeks and no one did," she reasoned. "I can wear a hat and sunglasses and stuff. It'll be fine."

"Like Dallas was fine?"

Dallas had been a melee. Kim did not want to do that again.

She pondered for a minute, but came up blank, "Seriously, where else could we go? Let me have a change of scenery, at least."

Bennett was too focused on steering his truck down the narrow side street to pay much mind to her question. He only murmured, "Uh…" and even that sounded distracted.

"What about your place?" Kim prodded. "That's got to be safe, right?" As soon as the idea hit her, she was stuck on it. It would give her such a tantalizing window into his world.

Bennett's head whipped around, attentive as hell, all of a sudden. "My place? Why?"

"Because it's safe?"

He looked at her like she'd gone around the bend. "For *who*?"

KIM WON OUT, eventually. After they picked up their dinner, Bennett called ahead and browbeat his roommates into leaving so they'd have the place to themselves.

The apartment itself didn't have a ton of personality, but it was neat as a pin and clean enough to be a hospital.

The food was another story. Kim worked her way through a stellar margarita and a pile of carnitas nachos, as she relaxed on the comfortable sofa. Bennett turned on a rerun of that year's Aggies bowl game and made no mention of the hard drive.

Kim didn't bring it up either. He probably needed time to comb through what she'd given him, anyway, and pestering him wouldn't make the process go faster.

Still, she couldn't sit there all night and pretend like nothing was up in the air between them. *Everything* was up in the air. Kim set aside her plate and got to her feet.

A little too quickly, as it happened. That margarita had been stronger than she'd thought.

"May I use your bathroom?" she asked him, needing a quiet minute to collect her thoughts before she made any bold moves.

Bennett pointed her down a short hall. "Last door on the left is my room," he said. "The head's a far sight more tolerable than the one in the hall. Wyatt and Joe share that one."

Kim smoothed down her clothes and tried to act casual. No need for Bennett to see how eager she was to get a peek at his private space. If he caught on, he was liable to drag her back to her hotel before she could start some fun.

She murmured, "Gotcha," and sauntered off.

Bennett didn't stop her, so she must've been convincing. And moments later she found herself standing in his bare-bones room, looking around at a whole lot of *Spartan Bachelor Living*. She'd never set foot in his personal space before.

It smelled like him, but it was a little depressing to think of Bennett spending any time there. There was an awful lot of gray. Gray-on-gray. Gray for days.

As she headed for the ensuite bathroom, Kim trailed her fingers along the side of his bed and was surprised by how soft his covers were. They might look ascetic, but the material was high quality, and would feel great to sleep on.

Not that she'd want to sleep, per se. Not at first.

Kim snorted at her shamelessness and made her way into the lavatory. It was an unfortunate study in builder-grade finishes and frequent cleaning. Bennett appeared to only use three products, at most, to keep up his brain-melting looks, but that was forgivable because the bathroom smelled even more like him than his bedroom had.

She inhaled deeply, took care of business, and stopped herself from snooping in his medicine cabinet after she washed her hands.

She was here with him. That was good enough for now.

Kim believed that lie for a whole five seconds, until she opened the bathroom door to find Bennett lingering in the gloom, his body in shadow as he leaned against the bureau.

His face was illuminated clearly by the light slanting in from the hall, though, his eyes heavy-lidded and his gaze direct and scorching.

Kim knew she was a little tipsy, but only a little. There was no way he'd outpaced her without her noticing, and consumed enough tequila to forget all his inhibitions.

Frankly, that was a crying shame, but it did beg the question— what was he up to?

"Howdy sailor," she drawled. "Looking for a good time?"

"Just looking for you."

"Well, you found me. Now what?"

He chuckled, low and shy. "Hell, if I know."

He'd followed her in here, though. Kim could read that signal well enough, whether Bennett meant for her to, or not.

She said, "In that case, I might have an idea or twelve."

Bennett pushed off the dresser and met her next to his bed, slipping an arm around Kim's waist and pulling her against him in a move she was rapidly getting addicted to. His lips brushed her ear.

"I'm trying, but I can't stay away," he said. "Are you sure this is—"

Kim glared at him. "Oh no you don't. I've given you about a hundred signals that I want you. If anyone is going to chicken out here, it sure ain't me."

His fingers touched her hair so gently, she might've missed it if she hadn't been watching. "I don't…" His bright eyes turned dangerous. "Damn it, I…"

Bennett clamped his lips together and stared at the divot at the base of her neck, no doubt stuck in the weeds of his misplaced honor.

Kim huffed in frustration. "I know that look. What is it this time? Don't want to sully the princess, aren't worthy of such a paragon, or some new excuse? Honestly, Bennett, this is getting—"

He clapped a hand over her mouth, lips twitching. "I was going to say that I have no idea how to get this cute thing off you. I'd rip it down the middle, but it probably cost you more than my truck."

Kim felt her face flush. "First of all, I got this romper at Target. And second, it has a hidden zipper, you numbskull."

Rather than lose more momentum with the rash of pointless questions she could see forming on his lips, she untied the matching belt and dropped it beside her feet before dragging that zipper down. She wriggled out of the straps and pushed the garment past her hips, then stepped out of it and handed it to Bennett.

"There." *Let him chew on that.*

Bennett barely glanced down before he tossed it aside. "We need to work on you finishing my sentences, impatient little thing. You've got about a 40% accuracy rate."

"If I waited for you to finish a thought," Kim snapped, "we'd be here all day."

He chuckled ruefully. "I can work with that." His rough palms drifted down her throat and skimmed a line straight to her belly button.

Kim was happy she'd chosen nice underwear earlier, just in case. It probably wasn't what her old Girl Scout leader had meant by *always be prepared,* but she wasn't about to split hairs when the results had this kind of payoff.

"Now don't go trying to pass off some pale imitation of yourself," she warned Bennett softly. "I expect you're worrying about hurting me or shocking me or something, but I've known you a long ass time, boy. When I tell you I want you, I mean the real you. Not some redacted robot you think won't offend."

His eyebrows shot up at the scolding. "Guess someone won't be beating around the bush tonight."

"Aren't we past that?"

He nodded, laughing, "I reckon we are. Any other demands?"

"You could get nekkid, already. I'm out here peddling my wiles like it's a fire sale, but you'd never know it to look at you. Standing there cool as a cucumber while I shiver in my panties."

"Kimmie," he grinned, "How much have you had to drink?"

Possibly more than she'd thought, given the stream of nonsense coming out of her mouth. She wasn't fixing to give Bennett any more reasons to back out, though—not when he was making so many strides.

"Less than you, I imagine," she said. Then she leaned up and kissed him, and poured every ounce of seduction she could into it.

Lest there be any mistaking her intentions.

Bennett broke off with another laugh. "You seem to have a goal in mind, darlin'. Should I be letting you lead?"

"If you insist." Kim dragged her nails up his sides, then giggled at the shiver that ran through him. "Ticklish? Don't worry—your secret's safe with me."

Bennett smiled wolfishly, then grabbed her hands and held them behind her back. "That what you said to your senator's son? Or country phenom Billy Aikers?" He laughed when she nipped at his lip. "What's he got now that you dumped him? Three platinum records?"

Kim pulled her wrists free, but he batted her hands away when she tried to go for his belt.

"I'm an excellent muse, but I don't have any idea how Billy got so famous," she complained with a huff. "That boy drank like a fish and his lyrics were nothing special. I *was* glad when his folks got him into rehab, though. He was awful young to have a problem like that."

Bennett shook his head in exasperation. "Girl, you are too much. Acting like you're no big whoop and missing the point, as usual."

"I beg your pardon. I am exactly the right amount," Kim protested, "and I was missing your stupid point on purpose." She grabbed the hem of his t-shirt and worked it over his head when he obligingly raised his arms. "Now pipe down and hold still while I defile you."

Bennett's gaze was blistering as it traveled over her lace-framed breasts. "Nah, I don't think so. I've got a better idea."

Chapter Twelve

Bennett

BEFORE HE QUITE knew what he was doing, Bennett crowded Kim toward his bed. He'd already decided not to do this, but having her here had done something to him—changed some vital barrier under his skin that had helped him hold back.

He stopped her when her legs hit the mattress. Kim's skin felt hot under his hands as he took her mouth, and he gripped her hips hard, like she'd disappear if he let go.

She might anyway, but he couldn't seem to worry about it now.

He hated to break away from Kim's eager, marauding tongue, but Bennett wanted to feel her body under his—to cage her in with his limbs and to pin her with his weight. He needed…he needed to possess her.

Kim seemed to agree. She smiled as she pulled her hands free and let herself fall backward.

As she shifted up toward the wall, he worked to keep himself in check and not go feral. He dropped his pants and kicked them away before Kim could ask, then set a knee on the foot of the bed and crawled over her.

Bennett nipped and licked his way from her warm belly to her ear. "You still good?" he murmured.

"Yes. Are you?"

"I'm all right. Thought I might go on a little scavenger hunt, see what I can find."

When he flicked his gaze down to her breasts, Kim folded her arms behind her head and chuckled. *Offering herself up like a buffet.*

"That sounds interesting. Let me know if you need a hand," she told him mildly.

Bennett left open-mouthed kisses down her throat, glancing back at her face once he reached her cleavage. "I think I can manage."

He sucked her nipple into his mouth through the lace of her bra. Kim relaxed into his pillows with a moan. "Done this a time or two before, have you?"

Bennett hummed against her in agreement, grinning at the goosebumps that broke out across her skin. He toyed with her other breast with shaking fingers, working the tip into a hard point before he switched sides and went to town again.

Was he really doing this? Yes. Yes, he was.

All the lace was pretty, but it was in his way, so Bennett pushed his hands under Kim's back to pop the hooks of her bra free. Once he'd peeled it off her, Bennett cupped her firmly and spent some more time teasing her—until he had her writhing and begging beneath him.

The sounds she made were like nothing he'd ever imagined. Deeper. Sexier. Bennett was addicted and then some.

Kim had to be ready. He braced himself above her, mouth watering as she ran fervent hands over his pecs and shoulders.

"I want to taste you," he told her. "Can I?"

"Baby, you can do whatever you want with me," she drawled. She was trying to be seductive, he could tell—but her elation was a palpable thing, shimmering in the air around her.

Bennett chuckled darkly. "I don't think you want to give me that kind of leeway."

"Oh, I think I do," Kim countered. "Consider this my blanket consent to whatever you have in mind. Have at it, Tex."

"Tried to tell you."

Bennett gave into the hunger that had been beating like a drum inside him for days, and inched his way south on her body. He deposited kisses here and there and brushed his lips over velvety skin, taking his time.

Kim squeezed her eyes shut, like she was savoring every sensation. Bennett wanted her to see his head between her thighs, though. In case this was their one and only shot, he didn't want her to ever forget it.

He sure as hell wouldn't.

"Look at me." He dragged his fingers along her folds and growled deep in his chest when he felt how wet she was. "Damn girl. This all for me?"

A shudder ran down her spine, as if Kim had felt his words deep inside her. "Oh, hell yes," she agreed.

Bennett gave her a long lick, then pressed his lips against her clit, sucking hard. His throat vibrated with another euphoric hum and Kim moaned louder, raising her hips to meet him, chasing the arousal he was delivering with fierce determination.

He clamped a hand around her thigh and another on her hip, holding her in place. The sight of Kim, utterly focused on careening over the edge because of what *he* was doing to her, was hotter than Brownsville in July.

He tried to think of something to say, something to get Kim talking again. His usual words were nowhere to be found, though, his head lost in a tangle of velvet flesh and sweetness on his tongue.

Kim was getting close, though, her limbs tense and gasps growing sharper. Bennett changed his angle, learning her, sucking and licking faster as he slid a finger inside her.

Her sudden inhale was overly loud in the quiet room, but it goaded him on. Now that he'd tasted some, he wanted more. *All.*

Bennett groaned against her, adding a second finger to the first and feeling for the spot he hoped would drive her wild. He worked his fingers in and out in time with his tongue, his senses prickling with awareness of each tiny shift in her tone and body.

Kim was straining for release, suspended on a razor's edge for impossible minutes as she worked for it. For him.

Bennett glanced up. Her platinum hair was spread across his pillow like a halo. Her whimpers of approval were sending ravenous shockwaves through his veins. Her cunt was hot and tight, insistent and delectable.

He wanted the moment to go on forever. He wanted her to cross the goal line so he could sink into her with his cock. He wanted to live in this bubble for all eternity.

Kim tumbled into bliss with a surprised cry. Bennett kept going, though, dragging out her orgasm until she pushed him away.

He set a few careful kisses on her thigh, then pushed up so he could lay alongside her. Bennett watched her blank profile, and a tendril of nervousness threaded through him.

Kim blinked at the ceiling for a few seconds longer, then managed a shaky, "Damn, boy. Go ahead and wreck me, why don't you?"

He turned her face toward his, waiting until their eyes locked before sucking his fingers clean. "Probably shouldn't have let me do that," he told her with a searching grin. "Now you'll never get rid of me."

If she only knew.

Kim arched a single brow. "If that's supposed to worry me, you might want to try again."

Bennett kissed her shoulder softly. "You want anything? Glass of water or a washcloth or something?"

Kim shook her head, snuggling closer to his chest. "I wouldn't mind returning the favor."

He'd been afraid of that. There was the inescapable bond that came from giving, and then there was the one from receiving. If he stopped now, maybe, just maybe, he could stave off the chains settling around his heart a little longer.

"Maybe in a bit. Let me just hold you for a while, okay?"

"Okay," she mumbled softly.

As he'd hoped, Kim was asleep within minutes. *Thank Christ.*

With the way Bennett's mind was blown to fragments by what they'd just done, he didn't think he'd survive getting blown in other places.

He needed time for his whirling emotions to catch up with his body, which was still screaming *full speed ahead*. Bennett untangled himself carefully and slipped into the bathroom. He hesitated briefly before giving in, taking the edge off as efficiently as possible and guiltily avoiding his eyes in the mirror while he washed his hands.

Then Bennett went back and curled around the one person in the world who was able to reach inside him and make these acts mean something more than the sum of their sensations.

He watched Kim sleep long into the night, afraid to move, afraid to drift off. Afraid that he would wake at dawn and discover it had all been a dream.

HOWEVER, KIM HAD still been there in the morning, still beautiful beyond all common sense, still… fine as hell. She'd been smiling in her sleep, for fuck's sake. How was that even real?

Bennett had left her sleeping in his wrecked bed, softly unaware of the fan clicking overhead or the way the numbers on the bedside clock ticked later and later.

He'd dozed off and on for hours, but once the sun rose his muscles had twitched with the urge to move. He'd been starving in more than one way, and the longer he'd laid there, restless and unfulfilled, the more he'd craved sustenance.

Kim needed sleep, though. So there Bennett was, nursing his second cup of coffee and flipping through Wyatt's discarded newspaper, knee bouncing as he tried to decide whether he was supposed to go climb back into bed or proceed with his day.

Should he let Kim sleep in, and if so, for how long? Should he wake her, make her breakfast in bed, *wake her* with breakfast in bed? Bennett did not make a habit of sleepovers and was lost as to the protocol.

He very much wanted to get this right. However, given his agitation, he wondered if he'd be doing both of them a favor if he went for a long run. He probably ought to her a note, though.

Bennett glanced down the hallway yet again, and Kim appeared like an apparition, leaning on the wall with a faintly sheepish look on her face.

That hint of embarrassment snapped his spine straight. He eyed Kim as she padded toward him, trying to get a read on where her head was at.

He got an awkward, "Mornin'," as she pulled out the chair across from him, but that was all.

Bennett's restlessness went abruptly quiet, and he was really fucking glad that Wyatt and Joe had slipped in late and cut out early and thus weren't here to witness his utter lack of chill in the face of Kim Sutherland, The Morning After Edition.

"Good morning to you," he drawled, then raised his eyebrows when her cheeks flushed pink.

Yeah, I'm also remembering what we got up to last night, he thought, *the whole play-by-play.*

Kim fixed her eyes on his mug and cleared her throat.

"Please tell me there's some more of that."

Bennett grinned. She was cute when she was sleepy.

"Coming right up. How do you like it?"

"Lots of milk and no sugar."

Thankful to have a task, he went to pour her a cup, then set it in front of her. As Bennett dropped into his chair again, he tried to figure out why she was throwing him so far off his game.

There were a few obvious issues. He almost never brought women home, preferring to accept what they offered on their turf. It made them feel more comfortable and gave him the option to leave when he needed to.

Bennett rarely saw his hookups in the unfiltered light of dawn, since he was usually long gone by then. Sitting across from Kim now, knowing they'd spent the evening before crossing all kinds of lines…well, there just wasn't any precedence for that.

Kim peeked at him shyly over her mug, and Bennett smiled at her messy hair and overlarge t-shirt. She'd probably grabbed it off his floor—it was the one he'd worn to pick her up yesterday, then shucked off early in the festivities last night. Likewise, his gym shorts might as well have been a skirt with the way she was swimming in them.

He could only imagine how conflicted she must have felt, trying to choose between the walk-of-shame outfit or morning-after man threads.

"Wyatt and Joe are already gone," he reassured her, then asked, "You hungry?"

Kim bit her lip. Tried to smile. "I could eat."

Why was this so all-fired awkward? He had to have banged a dozen women in his life, but here he was, sweating third base.

Bennett's knee started bouncing again, and he considered whether Kim might be regretting what had felt like the culmination of decades of desire for him. Had he come up short? Disappointed her?

Last night, she'd worn that sleek black thing she'd called a romper, with dark makeup on her eyes and a deep red on her lips—and she'd looked erotic and seductive, instead of her usual dauntingly polished style.

Beside him on the couch, Kim's skin had been smooth and luminous in the flickering light of the TV, and warm with an intoxicating perfume Bennett hadn't smelled on her before.

He'd always been a sucker for a nice perfume. Between that and his simmering memories of their recent kisses, he couldn't have resisted Kim if he'd tried.

The margaritas had only served to weaken his resolve. But what if they'd affected his performance, too? Let him think he was making a touchdown when he'd barely passed the thirty-yard line?

All of Kim's siren trappings were gone now, kissed, washed, or slept away. She was less intimidating this way. Bennett could clearly see the hazel of her eyes, like mossy rocks in a streambed. He could almost count the freckles spattered across her nose.

She was unfiltered, unembellished, with shadows under her eyes, fading wrinkles from his pillow on her cheek, and…hell, to him she was still fucking gorgeous.

He knew he had to have seen her like this sometime in their adolescence, given the hundreds of sleepovers his sister had with her.

Except, Kim wasn't a teenager any longer. She was a woman he'd spent the night pleasuring—one he'd abandoned himself to in a way he never did.

Her bare lips looked so…accessible.

She coughed and snatched blindly at a section of the paper, and Bennett realized abruptly that he'd been staring like a lovestruck fool instead of getting up and making her eggs like he should have been doing.

She clearly had no idea what to do with him this morning, either. That made them even, he supposed.

"How'd you sleep?" he wondered, getting to his feet and mentally reviewing what he could offer her for breakfast.

He should probably offer to bring her back to her hotel, but he didn't want to sound like he wanted to be rid of her.

Kim dropped the paper and gave him a wry look. "Sleep?" she asked, "Who slept?"

There she was. All at once, Bennett relaxed. He knew how to do this.

"C'mere, girl," he told her, and damned if she didn't jump right up to wind her arms around him.

Bennett stole a quick, coffee-flavored kiss, then lifted Kim up and hauled her back to his room. He had excess energy to spare, and an excellent idea of how to burn it off.

* * *

BENNETT SUMMONED THE team to Noah's warehouse bunker the following day so he could tell them about Kim's hard drive.

"I doubt it'll be very helpful," he admitted as they pulled up seats. "She said she took pictures of some bank and phone statements that Cox had left out, but it sounds as if they're from the time right before they stopped dating. That might be too early for anything regarding his trip to Qahat."

Buck shrugged and passed the drive to Noah. "We'll still take a look. You never know."

"Let me guess," Joe sneered, rolling his eyes. "The asshole cheated on her."

Wyatt retorted, "Why else would a woman take photos like that?"

Bennett shrugged and dragged his chair closer to Noah, who was connecting the drive to his bank of computers. "Password is *RattlerPride*. One word, capital R, capital P."

Noah nodded and called up Kim's files, one for each monitor. Credit card statements, call logs, and a spreadsheet where she'd highlighted certain items and made notes about them.

"Keep in mind, Kim wasn't looking for the same stuff we would be," he pointed out. "This might be a waste of time."

"Let's cross it against Senator Doggett's trip itinerary anyway," Noah murmured, scrolling through her line items. "See if any of the vendors pop."

Buck knocked shoulders with Bennett, acting normal despite Bennett barging into his kitchen all salty last week. "Never hurts to check," he said. "Is this all she has?"

"As far as I know." He'd have to grill Kim a bit more to be sure, but it didn't sound as if she and Cox had dated more than casually for a matter of months—not enough time, he suspected, for her to be privy to many of his secrets.

"Not exactly the breakthrough we were hoping for," Joe commented. Wyatt shoved him in the arm. "What? It's true."

"Just...give the kid a chance. Okay?" Bennett asked.

After several minutes of steady clicking, Noah finally announced, "I'll comb through it more, but I have to be honest. I'm not seeing anything off. Cox probably wouldn't have run Qahat expenses through his personal accounts, anyway. He'd want the tax write-off through *Landry*."

Bennett sighed. He'd known this was likely, but he still felt strangely bad about it. "Don't say anything to Kim yet. She'll be crushed."

"Wait, don't we have Dickhead's account numbers, now?" Wyatt argued, undeterred. "Or at least parts of them? We should try to hack in and look at more recent statements."

Noah rocked in his chair and frowned. "I tried that once before but didn't get very far. I could give it another go, if you want." He looked to Buck for the okay, while the rest of them gave each other impressed side-eyes.

God knew how Tate Monroe had come across him, but he'd certainly uncovered a keeper. The shit Noah could accomplish with a few clicks of his mouse was mind-boggling.

Noah spun back to his monitors, muttering to himself as he typed in fits and spurts. Bennett folded his arms across his chest and tried to be patient. To not make this about Kim's feelings.

Buck asked him, "Have you had a chance to go over her protection plan with her yet?"

Bennett blinked. "Uh—"

"Maybe over the tacos and margaritas you guys had?" Joe prodded.

Wyatt shook his head. "Come on, dude. My guy was too busy knocking boots to talk business."

Bennett scowled at his tone. "We didn't do that."

"My bad," Wyatt scoffed, cutting eyes at Joe. "Can't imagine why I thought that."

"You said you came home late," Bennett barked. "You said—"

Buck looked between the three of them and cut him off, "Is Easy getting busy with that woman *already*?"

Noah smacked his table with a resounding thud, silencing them instantly. "Shit. Shit. Shit," he chanted, punctuating the curses with more frenetic tapping on the keyboard.

"Sitrep," Buck ordered.

Noah lifted his hands and sat back suddenly, the glow from the monitors reflecting off his glasses and making it impossible to decode his expression. "No go," he said. "Sorry guys. Bank security bumped me out again."

Joe jerked his chin at the kid's high-tech setup. "They gonna be able to track you?"

"Nah, we're good," Noah said calmly. "Cox might get a security alert from the bank, but he'll have no reason to think it's anything other than a run-of-the-mill breach."

"Unless…that fucker has reason to suspect Kim," Bennett mused. "Which he does, because she confronted him with this stuff when she broke things off."

Wyatt cursed softly.

"After what the Doggetts did to Peyton," Buck said, "I'm concerned that Kim could now be in danger."

He and Bennett stared at each other for a while, and Bennett could see his buddy thinking about the meatheads that'd shown up more than once at his fiancée's door.

Buck's hand shot out and landed heavily on Noah's shoulder, and the command in his voice was nothing anyone would want to argue with.

"Call up Kim Sutherland's security plan. We need to go over that shit again," he announced. He pointed at Bennett and added, "And you need to fill her in as soon as we are done here. Forewarned is forearmed."

Chapter Thirteen

Kim

WHEN SHE ASKED Bennett about the hard drive a couple of days later, he hedged, telling her, "It'll take us more time to go over everything." His eyes wouldn't quite meet hers.

That made sense, Kim supposed. There was a lot of information on there, and they'd only had it for a short time. Time would tell if she'd brought them anything useful in their fight against Dan's dad and she'd have to be patient.

"Do you have any questions about the security detail?" Bennett asked, pulling her from her thoughts.

He'd shown up this morning bearing coffee and pastries but so far, his mood had been all business. *Sadly.*

"I don't think so. The team's keeping an eye on my hotel, I should call them if I have to go anywhere, and I shouldn't go anywhere." Kim wanted to crawl back into bed and hide just thinking about it.

Bennett's eyes twinkled, like she was funny. "Exactly."

"How long will this last?" she whined, looking around her suite with despair. "I'm already going stir-crazy."

"I know, darlin', but I promise it's for the best. You got lucky those first couple weeks. We'd know by now if anyone had figured out who you are, but we can't count on that continuing.

From now on, we'll make sure you're safe—especially with the hard drive in play. If Cox suspects for even a second that you're sharing dirt on him…"

Bennett was purposefully not giving her an end date and for what? A whole lot of nothing, probably.

"Dan's a big baby," Kim scoffed. "All hat and no cattle."

Bennett's expression flattened quickly. "I wouldn't say that. Cox has a few cows we need to worry about." He hesitated, wandering over to the windows before adding, "You said yourself you thought he was shifty."

"He is a manipulative gaslighter," she agreed. "And shady, too. I'm just embarrassed that your company is making such a fuss over me."

He glanced over his shoulder, fighting back a smile. "What did you think was gonna happen when you came to me for help?"

Kim shrugged. What *had* she expected? A massive kiss-fest with some bodyguarding thrown in?

"I was hoping you'd get all growly and protective and that we'd get to hold hands a lot," she admitted.

"Mission accomplished," Bennett laughed ruefully. "Now what's our game plan for getting you out of this hotel and into a more secure hidey-hole?"

She flopped onto her bed, groaning in frustration. "I need your help. I've been looking for days, but I don't know anything about the neighborhoods, and everything seems so expensive. My father said he wants to foot the bill, but that doesn't mean I want to take him for a ride, you know?"

Bennett sat next to her and slung a heavy arm around her shoulders. "I get it. Let me find the place. I'll make sure you won't have to rough it too bad."

"We have to do it together," Kim countered. "I'll need to weigh in on what kind of space would work long term. There are some ins and outs to consider if I'm going to get any work done."

Bennett hung his head and laughed at that.

"What?"

"You want ins and outs, huh? I can give you ins and outs." He pulled her down and pressed her to the mattress, nuzzling into her neck with a sexy little moan. "Mmmm. I like this neck."

"Bennett Shaw! Quit horsing around," Kim cried. "This is not the time!"

He raised his head and pretended to look around. "No horses here. One stallion, though. Lucky you." He kissed a line down her throat.

That move was her new weakness. She tilted her head to give him better access and shivered as his warm breath skated over the sensitive skin. "You are incorrigible."

He chuckled, low and dark. "You know what they say about headstrong stallions, right? Probably have to ride me to break me."

"Will you—" Kim wrestled out of his grasp and managed to brace a forearm against his throat, fighting back a giggle as she tried to shove him off. "—get off! What has gotten into you, you big horny ape?"

Bennett grinned at her, unperturbed by her protests. "Hey, are you wearing those beige panties again today? Those sure were pretty."

Kim blinked at all the hotness looming over her, and tried to steel herself against it. It was a losing battle, though. *What else was new.*

"They're in the wash," she finally admitted. "But I have other colors that might interest you."

"Show me."

She was sorely tempted to comply. Instead, she shook her head, exasperated by what absolute trash she was for this man. "Please try to focus," she said primly.

If possible, Bennett's grin grew even wider, all white teeth and avid eyes. "Trust me, I am focused. So, so focused."

"On the wrong thing!"

"Says you. Need I remind you, you're the one who came gunning for my attentions." He winked, and it was devastating.

"Well, you got me now, darlin'. Congratulations—I've got a shitty return policy and there's no takebacks."

Kim held up her hands, like that would hold off the fine man smiling down at her. "Okay, you need to leave." She felt along the bed for a pillow, so she could whack him if he got any friskier. "And I need to find a new place to stay."

"I could leave," Bennett agreed, cheerfully bracing his hands on either side of her head. "Or—hear me out, now—I could stay, and we could work on this together."

He followed that up with a blinding smile that'd probably turned many a brain to mush.

Kim hadn't developed full immunity yet, but she did have experience with his bag of tricks. Bennett was doing his damnedest to distract her, and while his effectiveness was cute, it was also quite annoying.

She narrowed her eyes and told him, "You're too pretty for your own good. You know that, right?"

"Aw," he drawled, "you think I'm pretty?"

"That is not what I said," she retorted peevishly. "I said *you* think you're pretty."

He paused, looking away as he rewound the conversation in his head. "No, you didn't. You said, and I quote—"

"*Not my point, Bennett.*"

"Okay, fine. You win," he grumbled, climbing to his feet and straightening out his clothes. "Give me a list of must-haves for your new digs, or text me links to some places. I'll let you know if we can make any of them work."

Kim sat up and attempted to get her brain back on track. "Okay. I can—"

Her phone's insistent ringtone cut her off. Bennett grabbed it off the desk, glanced at the screen, and handed it to her. "It's my sister."

Kim snatched it from him, scowling at his nosiness. "Hey, friend!" she called once she connected the call.

Shannon launched right in. "Hey, do you know some woman named Alice? She showed up outside my building the other day, acting like y'all are friends."

Her heart dropped into her shoes. "It's *Alix*. You didn't say anything did you?"

"Hell, no. She was persistent, though. I had to get salty before she'd leave me alone."

Bennett chuckled softly.

Kim was just relieved. "Good," she said. "You did good."

"So, who is she?"

"No one you want to talk to." She glanced at Bennett, whose smile had faded at her tone. "I'll text you the details, but if she shows up again, call the cops."

"And here I thought you ran with a swanky crowd," Shannon snorted.

Kim wasn't amused. She was still smarting over the way she'd been duped by Alix. She'd thought she was making a new friend, but the woman had only been chasing a story, and the thought of having to explain to Bennett how doubly pathetic she'd been back in Dallas chafed.

To redirect her friend's curiosity before it got even more uncomfortable, Kim sang out, "Never mind that—guess who I'm with?"

Shannon guessed right, of course. "Is it an overgrown lunkhead whose golden hair and magnetic charisma are wasted on him?"

"Yup. Say hi."

"Hey loser," she muttered.

"Loser?" Bennett complained. "That ain't right."

"Oh really?" Shannon demanded. "After you gave your own sister a bum phone number?"

Kim stifled a laugh. Her best friend could act like a porcupine covered in quills at times, but it'd taught Kim a few priceless lessons over the years.

Bennett, on the other hand, did not seem similarly appreciative. He puffed up with indignation, protesting, "What are you talking about? That number is the only way you can get a hold of me no matter where I am in the world or what I'm doing. You're the only person I gave it to!"

"Yeah?" Shannon wasn't having it. "And you think it'll work now that you've been discharged?"

"I…oh." he tucked his head and gripped the back of his neck, turning red. "Maybe not. I didn't think of that. Dang, my bad."

She clicked her tongue testily. "I see how it is. But hey, don't worry—Kimmie gave me your real digits. Since she actually cares about me."

He blew out a disgruntled breath, and shot Kim a sheepish look. "Awesome. Thanks."

"So, when can I visit?" Shannon wondered. "I want to meet your hot friends and work on my tan like the other cool kids."

"Hot friends, huh?" Bennett cut eyes at Kim again. "Where'd you hear that, I wonder?"

Scorn dripped from Shannon's every word. "I watch the news, dumbass."

He shook his head, tutting with disapproval. "Anyway, you can't visit yet," he told his sister. "We need to let stuff die down before you come stirring up trouble. You read me?"

"Fine," Shannon sighed dramatically. "But when did you become such a stick in the mud?"

"At birth," Bennett retorted. "Like you don't know."

Kim was well aware that the Shaw siblings could go around in circles like this for hours, so she interjected quickly, "This is a heartwarming family moment. Really. It's like a Hallmark movie in here, but I'm afraid I have other stuff to do."

Bennett winked at her and called to his sister, "And there's our cue. Stop emailing me goofy owl videos or I'll change my number again."

"You're dipping out already?" his sister squawked. "Come on, guys. I feel left out."

"What?" Bennett hollered. "I think we have a bad connection! Can't hear you! Bye!"

Shannon growled, "You ass—" and he hung up.

"That was not nice," Kim told him. "She'll make you pay for that."

"Like you aren't going to call her again in an hour," he pointed out. "Besides, she should keep clear of me. It's better that way."

"For whom?"

Bennett scowled and shot back, "Who's Alice?"

Shoot. She'd been hoping he wouldn't catch that. "Alix," she clarified again. "She's a—" Her phone started ringing again, so she glanced at the screen. "Hang on, it's my stepmom."

Kim tapped the notification before the call could roll to voicemail. "Hey, Kara!"

"Hey girl," the woman chirped. "I'm so glad I caught you! I never know what I'm doing with the time difference, and all now."

Her stepmother was not dumb. When she acted like she was, it was a good sign that she was nervous.

"I mean…we're only two hours apart," Kim commented. "And I'm not working or anything so it's not like I'm busy."

Kara didn't address that, she only inquired, "Are you seeing all the fun things? Did you go to Rodeo Drive yet?"

Shopping had been the least of Kim's concerns, and this was not a vacation. "No, I'm in San Diego, remember? Rodeo Drive is like three hours from here."

"*At least*," Bennett whispered.

"It'd be worth the hike, though, right?" Kara prodded. "I heard they have Dior."

Kim frowned. There was a Dior boutique in Dallas. "Maybe?"

"Okay, sugar. Well, I won't keep you," her stepmom said suddenly. "I just wanted to check in and make sure your phone was still working. If you're having trouble, your daddy says he can have a new one sent, though."

Kim and Bennett locked gazes, and he looked as confused as she felt.

"My phone is working fine," she said carefully. "What makes you think it isn't?"

"Because I ran into that nice little Alix Hernandez at the nail place the other day. She said y'all were supposed to get together, but she hadn't been able to reach you—said her calls kept dropping out. Me and your daddy wondered if maybe your bills got misplaced during your trip, or something."

Kim clenched her jaw so hard it hurt. "Kara, I can pay for my own phones, and I've never missed a bill in my life. I had to block Alix because she would not leave me alone. That's why her calls won't go through."

"I'm sorry, you did *what?*" Her stepmother's voice was tight. "You do remember that she works the society page, right?"

"Yes, and that makes her a reporter. Alix was harassing me." Kim emphasized each word. "I had to block her, because nothing else was getting through."

"Oh, shoot." Kara fell silent for a spell, then murmured, "Well, now I just feel dumb."

"*Why?*" Kim demanded, brushing off the quelling hand Bennett set on her arm. He wouldn't be nearly so calm once she explained what was going on.

Her stepmother cleared her throat, starting and stopping a couple of times before managing, "I sure wish you'd told me and your daddy that."

"Why?" Kim reiterated.

"Because I told Alix she was probably having trouble since you're on a different network out there. She said she'd been trying to set up a lunch with you and her girls, but she didn't even know you were in San Diego."

Kim sat down, stunned that her stepmom had been so obtuse. "Kara, why did you tell her that? You *know* the media has been giving me trouble. That's the whole reason I had to come out here!"

"But Alix is just the society gal," Kara argued. "She doesn't care about—"

"She's a *reporter*!" Kim fired back. Bennett squeezed her arm and gave her a reassuring nod.

He didn't look worried. That probably should've made Kim feel better, but it didn't.

The luxury of anonymity she'd enjoyed out here had well and truly gone down the tubes, and with a sinking feeling, Kim realized she was going to have to commit to Bennett's protection plans even more now.

"Kimberley I am so sorry," Kara murmured eventually. "I had no idea you two weren't on good terms. I feel terrible."

"Don't worry," Kim told her numbly. "My friend out here can help me. Just…don't say anything to *anyone* else, okay? No matter who they are or what they tell you."

"I won't. I promise."

"Give Daddy my love, alright? Tell him I'll call this weekend."

"I will, honey. You be safe out there, okay?"

"I will."

Kim hung up and looked into Bennett's steady eyes.

"Don't panic," he said immediately. "We've got this under control. You're gonna be okay."

Chapter Fourteen

Kim

BENNETT HAD QUICKLY swung into action after Kara's call. Kim had only felt capable of sitting still and freaking out, but not him. He'd gotten busy by calling Buck and warning him that Kim's location had been leaked, and announced in no uncertain terms that moving her into a random vacation rental was off the table.

Bennett had always been good under pressure. Kim knew that.

What had taken her by surprise was how rapidly he'd whisked her away from her suite at the Foundry and installed her in his own bedroom instead.

He'd insisted they leave the hotel separately, but he'd met her in a nearby garage where he'd stashed his truck and they made their roundabout way to his apartment together. A brisk woman named Kenya checked Kim out of the Foundry and brought her luggage over a few hours later, and the move was done.

Every step had been executed smoothly, as if the group had spirited away a hundred people before her. Perhaps they had.

It hadn't felt as if one lovelorn debutante merited such stealth, not until Bennett had sternly reminded Kim of what had happened to Peyton—the professor engaged to his friend Buck—only a few months earlier.

Kim wasn't nearly as important as Peyton, but Bennett didn't seem to agree. So, here she was.

She sighed softly and looked around at Bennett's bedroom walls, every one of them bare. She ought to be feeling grateful for how seriously everyone was taking her situation. To an extent, she was.

In this apartment, she'd be protected around the clock by not one, but three, former Navy SEALs, and could retain a little normalcy. What's more, the team wouldn't have to devote extra manpower to staking out some random location.

Kim certainly wasn't upset about sleeping in Bennett's bed or having access to a kitchen. It was the part where the guys had asked her to keep the blinds mostly closed—like she was a vampire and not a woman starved for air and light—that made her want to cry.

She supposed she could understand their reasoning, though. None of them wanted the media to find her, but they especially didn't want Dan to discover that she'd shacked up with the very men his dad was trying so hard to discredit.

As Kim sat with her legs crossed on Bennett's bed, watching him make space for her clothes in his closet, she reckoned that point, in particular, merited further discussion.

"Given the way this day has gone," she commented, "I'm going to assume you've met Dan and his dad in person."

Bennett glanced back at her. "Roy, yes. Dan, no." He hesitated, then added, "Did you know we were the ones who extracted Senator Doggett and his wife from Nabarut last year?" When she nodded, he went on, "They turned it into a whole entire shitshow, believe me. We were lucky to get them out in time."

Kim sat back, surprised. She'd known that the senator had attended the opening of a Qahati girl's school as a publicity stunt for his presidential campaign—Dan had talked about that a lot. But the event had taken place months after she and Dan had split, so what little she knew about the fighting had been garnered solely from scattered news reports.

Those had made it sound as if the SEALs had been the obstructionists, not the Doggetts. It hadn't rung true at the time, but now it made more sense why that was.

Dan's parents had turned on the very people they owed their lives to. They wanted to cover up their mistake.

Like stepfather, like son, she supposed. *Bless their hearts.*

"Don't trust him," she said abruptly, staring at Bennett's back. "Dan's a liar and a cheat, just like Roy. If he acts like he has something to tell you about his folks, you shouldn't believe him."

Bennett froze and turned, a neat stack of t-shirts in his hands. "Don't worry," he said slowly. "After the way his stepdad has conducted himself, suffice it to say we're confident we've got both their numbers."

"Promise me you'll be careful, though. Dan comes off real slick, but underneath he's…"

He frowned when Kim didn't continue. "What?"

"He's a real snake," Kim said after a while. "He only cares about himself."

What had she ever seen in him?

Bennett set down his shirts and sat next to her, carefully taking her hand in his. "Kimmie, I'm sorry you had to deal with that. You deserve better."

"Easy for you to say," she shrugged. "You haven't seen the dating pool I've had to pick from."

"True." Bennett looked down at their linked hands, nodding to himself. "I think it's hard for you because you have this…this light inside. One you don't dim for anyone."

"Must be a bug zapper. It seems to attract an awful lot of insects."

Bennett chuckled. "Easy now. Guys can be intimidated by lights like yours." Then he added thoughtfully, "I used to think of it as the afterglow of all that money y'all had. Like it was glow-in-the-dark privilege, or something."

That hurt. It must've shown, because Bennett gently kissed Kim's knuckles before he barreled on, "Eventually, I came to realize that you really are that special. That light shines right out of you, and you don't even realize."

"Bennett," Kim whispered.

"Lesser mortals get scared off, you know? The ones that aren't are drawn to it, though, and not always for the best reasons."

"Were you one of those guys?" she wondered, despite the nervous pulse fluttering at the side of her throat.

Bennett peeked at her from under long lashes. "Maybe. But there was no way in hell I was gonna reach for all that heavenly gold with my grubby fingers. It was for the best that I stayed away from you."

He'd expressed that sentiment before. Kim squeezed his hands, willing him to look at her. *Really* look at her.

"Bennett, I wish you would've tried. I couldn't help my circumstances any more than you could help yours. And I worked really hard to not be a jerk about what I had. I still do."

"See, this is what I'm saying. Who thinks like that? Not most grown folks, and certainly not many kids. People can't help but love you, because you never give them a chance not to."

She stared at him, breathless with the notion that he'd revealed more than he'd intended to. "People? Or you?"

Bennett dropped her hand like a hot coal and shot up, muttering, "Don't do that," as he paced away.

Kim blinked at his sudden pivot. "Do what?"

"Humiliate me." He stalked to the far side of the room, his shoulders stiff.

She reared back, confused by how quickly his open demeanor had clamped shut. "Admitting you feel something for me is humiliating? Bennett, do you even hear yourself? If you never let yourself feel, how are you supposed to relate to anyone? How do you make any kind of connections at all?"

"I don't," he retorted. "Keeps everything simple."

Well, that was just sad. "There's not one person you trust with your heart?" Kim demanded. "With your story?"

"No," he shrugged. "Don't get me wrong, pieces have slipped out here and there. With Buck and Wyatt, mostly. Joe, once in a while. But those guys have taken bullets for me, so I reckon they've earned it."

"You don't think your sister's earned it? Shannon loves you like crazy."

"Shannon crawled through the fire with me," he said. "She doesn't need my burdens on top of her own."

"Except, you are not a burden." Kim bit her lip, wondering if she was about to push too far. "I've been friends with you a long time, too," she said finally. "Where do I rate?"

Bennett spun to face her, his turquoise eyes glittering. "I am not going to answer that, and you know why? Because you've only ever known a small part of me. You mean well, Kimmie, and you assume you understand, but you…" He shrugged uncomfortably, looking away. "You don't. Not like you think."

"So, enlighten me."

"And be the asshole who sullies that golden glow? I'll pass."

Kim clenched her hands together in her lap. Bennett was circling his wagons again. She didn't know what to say to convince him she was a safe harbor.

"Bennett, please stop doing that. I am not some statue in a museum. I'm human, and I'm as imperfect as everyone else. Don't treat me like a piece of expensive crystal and just…meet me on level ground for once."

"And what then?" he demanded. "What happens when you finally get what you want and solve the eternal mystery of Bennett Shaw? What happens when you turn your sights to the next shiny challenge and move on?"

Kim stared at him in shock. "You think I would do that? You *actually* think I would take your heart, and just…walk away. Like it means nothing."

Bennett seemed to realize that he'd struck a nerve, because he blinked uncertainly for a minute before focusing resolutely on the wall over her shoulder. Like if he ignored her, she would disappear.

Tough luck, sailor. You're the one who brought me here.

"You know, I ought to be offended that you think so little of me," she said quietly.

He stretched his neck from side to side and commented, "You idealize me, too, for the record. Back in the day, you looked at me like I was a hero, just for carrying my sister and grabbing for whatever scraps the world tossed our way. You don't know that I was willing to do *anything* to keep Shannon and me together— to keep us safe. I did things that—"

Bennett's voice broke, and he turned a little green.

He swallowed a couple of times, trying to compose himself before finishing with, "I did it all."

Kim's heart felt like a jumble of torn-up shreds as she watched him try to keep his armor intact. Bennett was right about one thing—she couldn't imagine the roadmap of bruises he had hidden under that impenetrable shield. She was starting to get some idea, though.

"I'm sorry," she said softly. "You were a scared kid trying to do grownup things. Instead of blaming yourself for that, maybe try giving yourself a little grace."

A choked sound escaped his throat. "You wouldn't say that if—"

"If I knew what a horrible person you are?" Kim waved him off. "Yeah, you keep mentioning that. Are you trying to convince me, or yourself?"

Bennett flinched at her exasperation but didn't try to argue.

"I'm not buying it, Tex," she continued. "Maybe let yourself off the mat, for once."

He ran a shaky hand across his mouth and looked away, unable to keep eye contact.

Kim went on, "How long have you been out here protecting everyone else, already? You'd think you could manage a care for yourself once in a while, too."

"That is not part of my job description," he mumbled.

"Oh, is that so?" She arched a brow at him. "Why do I bet that's not an accident?"

Bennett snorted, but at least he didn't seem quite as brittle anymore. Kim risked going closer, resting her hands on his chest until he looked down and met her eyes.

"Stop punishing yourself, Bennett. Stop denying yourself happiness now, because your parents forced you into survival mode fifteen years ago. You deserve to leave the past in the past, like Shannon has. You deserve a full life, surrounded by people who cherish you."

"It's not that easy," he whispered, his gaze so haunted, it crushed her soul all over again.

"And yet, it kind of is, if you make the choice."

With that, Kim turned and went to the door to leave him in peace.

When she reached the threshold, however, she couldn't resist one last question. "Just out of curiosity, what do you think would happen if you let yourself have me?"

Bennett stared at her, long enough that she thought he might actually be considering his answer. Like all the other times Kim had tried to challenge him, however, he gathered his defenses around himself like a cloak, shook his head, and turned away.

She narrowed her eyes at his back. If she were a different person, she might be inclined to make him pay for the way he kept reeling her in, then dismissing her. The problem was, she was a fool for Bennett, through and through. She was going to keep giving Bennett chances until the cows came home.

A knock sounded on the door behind her, making her jump.

Bennett rushed over to yank it open, revealing a grim-faced Wyatt on the other side.

"Hey, man. Sorry to interrupt. Just learned something I thought you'd want to hear." He glanced nervously at Kim.

"About me?" she asked.

Bennett motioned for his roommate to spit it out.

"Monroe's been keeping an eye on that person we talked about, and Noah just called to tell us they booked a flight here this morning."

Bennett looked at Kim, and she swallowed back the knot trying to climb her throat. "Alix?" she wondered.

He nodded grimly. "That sure didn't take long. Mind if I go see what's what?"

"No, go ahead," she told him. "I'll, uh…I'll be out in a minute."

"Take your time." With that, he slipped out the door and followed Wyatt down the hall.

Kim sank to the trunk Bennett kept at the end of his bed, troubled by their conversation and the old memories it stirred up, but also epically irritated with her stepmother.

She couldn't believe Kara had forgotten that she wasn't supposed to talk about Kim. She didn't think the slip had been intentional but, honestly—the obsession with gossip knew no bounds. Thanks to her, Bennett was liable to demote Kim to virtual house arrest out here.

As for Alix, why *was* she so all-fired fixated on her? Kim simply wasn't that interesting, and she'd only dated Dan casually for a few months. Why lose her ever-loving mind over it?

Kim had assumed that if she kept quiet and laid low, Alix would eventually lose interest, but that plan hadn't worked. It didn't make any sense why.

Whatever the reasons, Kim had to figure out how to make them all go away. The longer reporters poked at her story, the greater the chances that one of them would discover her and Bennett's shared history in Respite. And if they dug too deep, they were bound to unearth skeletons that were best kept buried.

What Bennett had done on his way out of Respite fifteen years ago was no one's business but his own. Kim needed to figure out the right course of action to keep it that way.

However, with Alix headed to California, would Kim have the time she required? *Perhaps not.*

Still, if her mama had taught her anything, it was that sometimes you had to fake confidence before you felt it for real— and Kim had accrued plenty of experience doing that.

With that in mind, she closed her eyes and practiced a few breathing exercises, then got up and combed her hair. In the bathroom, she found her makeup bag and reapplied her lip gloss, and then Kim walked out to the living room.

Bennett looked up from his sprawl on the couch, turning away from the football game on the TV as if nothing at all was amiss. As if her presence in his home was the most natural thing in the world.

If she had her way at the end of all this, it would be.

Chapter Fifteen

Bennett

HALF AN HOUR passed before Kim finally emerged from his room, looking as if nothing at all was amiss.

Bennett couldn't say he felt the same. He and Wyatt had sorted out the particulars of the Alix Hernandez situation on a call with Buck, but once the basic framework was in place, they'd tabled further discussion until they could meet without the potential for Kim to overhear something she shouldn't.

But the new development had him on edge.

Kim had no idea that he and the team were hunting her ex-boyfriend like bird dogs on a pheasant, and Bennett could not figure out how to tell her in a manner that wouldn't jeopardize everything they'd been working toward for months now.

The mission dictated that he had to keep her somewhat in the dark, for her own safety as well as that of the team. However, Buck had instructed him to "give her context." What did that even mean? How much detail was enough?

Until Bennett got clarification, his dilemma would keep making things awkward between them—though not as much as Kim's refusal to understand why Bennett couldn't let himself fall for her the way she so clearly wanted him to.

He was at a loss, and the college football game Wyatt turned on had been a welcome distraction, to say the least.

His roommate had fifty bucks riding on the Sooners thumping Bennett's beloved Longhorns, but the score was already 21-3 at the end of the quarter, with Texas in the lead. Bennett didn't have to worry about that outcome, at least.

Which left Kim. She hovered at the edge of the room when she reappeared, only darting past the TV between plays, and burrowing in beside Bennett on the couch. He was acutely aware that they hadn't settled things before Wyatt had interrupted, so he bent close to her ear and whispered, "Sorry about before. Are we good?"

"Of course," she murmured back.

Then, for the next few downs, she pretended to watch the game while sneaking looks at something she was reading on her phone.

At the next commercial break, Bennett leaned over to get a peek at what could possibly be more interesting than their home team handing their biggest rivals their hats. It took three seconds for him to get an eyeful of "*wet cock*" and "*good fucking girl*."

"What the hell is that?" he cried, scandalized.

Kim flipped her phone over in an uncharacteristically awkward spasm and flushed an intriguing shade of rose. "Boys can't hang on to the ball today, can they?"

"Nice try," Bennett laughed. "It's a commercial break. You are not watching that game at all." He poked at her phone. "Not that I blame you. *Lawd.* Talk about lady in the streets—"

Kim sat up straight and hissed, "Don't you dare finish that sentence, Bennett Shaw. Besides, give me some credit. At least I'm not bothering anybody. Y'all are talking over the game so much I'd be surprised if you even knew the score."

"It's 21-3," he told her.

"21-9!" Wyatt whooped, then groaned when the Sooners missed the extra point.

"Game's getting closer now," Bennett smiled. "Don't you want to see what happens?"

Kim rolled her eyes. "Please. Oklahoma doesn't stand a chance."

"Hey!" Wyatt cried, offended. "They're just getting warmed up. Give them a goddamn minute. *Geez.*"

Kim shot Bennett a loaded look and subtly shook her head. Wyatt noticed, but he didn't call her on it—instead, he wondered, "Hey Kim, you play any sports?"

"Nope," she responded cheerfully, "And I'm not sorry about it, either."

Bennett shook his head. "Now hold up a minute. Don't get too cocky. Cheerleading counts. You did gymnastics for years before that, and I reckon the dance stuff rates, too."

"Oh yeah?" Wyatt looked her over with interest. "My cousins dance. What kind did you do?"

Kim elbowed Bennett hard. "My mother put me in ballet. Some tap, later on—but I hated that."

He grinned and elbowed her back. "Tell him what you did like."

"Seriously? You're just going to roll me under the bus with your friend. Like it's nothing."

Bennett smiled wider, irrationally loving how he was getting under her skin. Then, since he knew she wouldn't, he turned to Wyatt and explained, "Kim *also* did hip-hop dance in high school."

Wyatt eyed her and chuckled. "Not gonna lie—that's hard to picture."

She sniffed in disdain, but Bennett pointed at him. "You'd be surprised," he said.

He pictured those recitals, and those sequins, and it was like he was seventeen all over again, the music thumping through his chest and the blood roaring in his ears with the unexpected knowledge that Kim could move her body in ways he hadn't imagined.

"I can still see those costumes like it was yesterday," he mused aloud. "Remember those baggy, low-rise pants y'all had? And the little cropped tank tops? Middle of January and you girls were sauntering around like it was May."

Kim dropped her head into her hands, rubbing her skull with a pained groan.

With no small amount of glee, Bennett told Wyatt, "They had these fishnet arm sleeve thingies. You have no idea."

"I'm getting one," Wyatt retorted, looking between them with a bemused smirk.

Bennett shook his head, kissed his fingertips like an Italian chef, and raised them to the ceiling. After another moment of reflection, he nudged Kim again.

"Shannon still has pictures. You know that?"

Kim jerked her head up and glared daggers at him. "She told me she threw those out."

Rookie mistake. He shrugged happily, "Guess she's got a taste for blackmail." *Boy, did she ever.*

Kim didn't dispute it—she'd been best friends with his sister since kindergarten. She knew as well as Bennett the kind of perfidy Shannon was capable of, so instead of arguing, she snatched her phone off her thigh and started texting with a vengeance.

"I am going to destroy her," she muttered after a moment.

Bennett spotted a blurry image of the exact costume he'd been describing on Kim's screen and laughed harder. "I wish you luck," he told her. "Shannon is scrappy as hell. She's got tricks up her sleeve you will never see coming."

"Wonder who taught her that," Kim grumbled sullenly, but her expression went soft as she studied that old photo.

They'd had some good times, Bennett reflected, among all the bad. Funny how often he forgot that.

All at once, he remembered. *Middle of January.* Kim's final hip-hop recital had been a week before her birthday, and Shannon had borrowed money from him to get her friend an extra gift for it.

Their folks had skipped town just after Christmas, though, and Bennett had been forced to pawn their dad's old guitar to make ends meet. It'd been the first of many such transactions over the next six months.

That part was unimportant. What mattered was that Kim's birthday had to be coming any day now, and if Bennett's math was correct, it would be her thirtieth. A milestone.

He surreptitiously texted Shannon for the exact date, then sat back and stared at a football game he could no longer follow. His sister's reply came swiftly, followed by a stern threat to *"do something fun since I'm not there. Or else."*

Bennett chewed his lip, thinking. Kim would hate to be stuck inside with nothing to do on her birthday. She was also guaranteed to not say a peep about it.

There had to be some way to take her out and still preserve her anonymity, and there was only one person who would know how to pull it off.

Buck. He was the man with the plan, always.

Without giving himself time to agonize over it, Bennett asked Kim, "Hey, your birthday's coming up, isn't it? Anything special you'd like to do for it?"

Kim gave him a cheeky grin. "Y'all got any tall blonde Texans 'round here?"

Wyatt choked on his beer, the fucker.

His face felt hot as blue blazes as he warned Kim, "You can't go meeting new folks. I told you. You're stuck with—"

His roommate was still coughing and laughing, though, waving his arms around like a church elder. "Oh, no you don't! She answered you loud and clear. No saving it now."

Kim's sly smile never wavered and neither did her gaze, boring into Bennett like a promise and a threat all at once.

He swallowed back a wave of nervousness. He had no idea what he was doing.

He had game, normally. He operated at his best when his body and brain were working together in pursuit of a solid goal. With

Kim, however, Bennett's body had careened ahead without authorization, and his heart had been left to stumble forward through the wreckage, struggling to catch up.

Lord only knew where his brain had gone, but it sure wasn't in his skull.

The situation felt chaotic and out of control, his least favorite state of being.

"Never mind. Leave this to me," he told her, with a bravado he did not feel. "I'll take care of everything."

IT'D TAKEN SOME convincing, but Bennett had eventually wrangled Buck on board the Birthday Express—and the plan he'd come up with had most of them rolling up to a shabby honkytonk called The Wagon Wheel out past Idyllwild a few days later.

The joint was as anachronistic as it was remote, and seemed to be the only game in town. Plenty of the local populace had still seen fit to partake of its pool tables and half-off pitchers of beer that night, and it wasn't even the weekend.

Joe took point as they escorted Kim inside, surging through the loose crowd to claim the only empty pool table, tucked in the back. It was clear why it wasn't already in use. A certain aroma wafted from the nearby bathrooms, and one of the lights hanging over the felt was out, giving it an eerie look.

The booth against the wall also looked worse for wear, spewing stuffing from the fake leather seats, and sporting a stain Bennett really didn't want to know the origin of.

Wyatt brought up the rear, assessing the area with a quick sweep of his eyes before making the nook even dimmer by taking out another light. While Joe took his time choosing a stick from the rack, Wyatt unscrewed the bulb in the flickering lantern on the wall and tossed it aside.

Work of a moment, and twice as much coverage. *So far, so good.*

Still, Bennett wanted to cringe bringing Kim to a shithole like this. Every flat surface was some version of grubby or sticky, and whenever the front door opened a new miasma of unpleasant odors drifted around them. Beer. Piss. Stuff he didn't want to put a name to.

It was precisely the sort of place Kim might expect him to frequent, and the last place she would.

She wasn't Kim tonight, however. She was "Beth," outfitted in a long, wavy brown wig and a backwards baseball cap. They hadn't had a ton of time to come up with a truly imperceptible disguise, but they'd done their best to obscure her shape with ill-fitting clothes pulled from their own closets.

Kim was swimming in a ragged pair of jeans from Wyatt that she'd had to cinch tight with a belt and roll up a couple of times, and a faded flannel shirt from Joe that flapped around as she moved.

She'd gotten into the spirit of things and ordered herself a clunky pair of sandals off the internet and removed the polish from her fingers and toes.

She hadn't worn a speck of makeup, jewelry, or perfume. She looked laid-back and uncontrived.

It was jarring, however, watching her inhabit a persona so unlike her own. Bennett could still spot the echoes of her true self—there'd been no obscuring her cultured voice or the graceful way she held herself. Kim had not been trained for deep deception, so her attempts to mask her posture or upper-crust accent had only made the disguise ring false.

As long as they kept her in the shadows and far enough away from prying eyes, the charade should hold, though. Bennett didn't hate that idea—the caveman in him wanted to keep her all to himself, anyway.

Somehow, even when she looked like a completely different person, he still found Kim irresistible. The tomboy look suited her and she was more bubbly than usual tonight, gleeful at having been sprung, even temporarily, from her confinement. Kim was tipsy and flirty and handsy and he wanted nothing more than to carry her off and have his way with her.

Unfortunately, the anxiety that they hadn't done enough to protect her, or shouldn't have brought her out to begin with, kept riding him. It must've shown.

"We're fine," Joe murmured as he edged past to line up his shot. "If the wasp leaves its nest, we'll know."

Buck and Noah were running surveillance on Alix Hernandez tonight, at her hotel back in San Diego. With Noah hacked into the hotel cameras and Buck on the ground, there was no way the reporter could get by them. They'd sound the alert the instant the woman tried to go anywhere and if they did, Bennett would ghost Kim right out of here.

In the meantime, Kim had a few hours reprieve to celebrate her thirtieth birthday—and would have a funny story to tell someday, when this whole mess was over.

Bennett leaned against the side of the booth and watched her mouth the words to the country song blaring from the TV screens mounted near the bar, shimmying in place as she waited for her turn to shoot. Even drowning in menswear, she looked sweet. Sexy. A flame he couldn't help touching, over and over again.

Kim took a minute to warm up to her impromptu performance. Bennett knew from experience that her voice was nothing earth-shattering, but she could hold a note—and her facial expressions were spot-on, flawlessly mimicking those of the singer in the video. Soon, she had the moves down, too, and by the time the song had wrapped up, she'd managed to lock down the whole two-stepping routine, right there next to the pool table.

Still a quick study, he noted.

Wyatt said something that Bennett couldn't make out, but it had Kim glowing with happiness.

He had to smile. It'd been a long time since Kim had let her mom put her through her paces with all that pageant nonsense, but the girl still remembered how to work a stage.

On one level, it was funny—there couldn't be a more useless thing for her to be good at—but it also made Bennett feel weird. They'd grown up in the same small town and had known each other most of their lives. However, flashes like this just emphasized the differences in their upbringings.

Kim might as well have lived on a totally different planet. It was a wonder they'd had anything to say to each other at all.

She sidled over to him, draping herself against his side like she intended to take a sailor home if it was the last thing she did, so Bennett did what any red-blooded man looking to expunge his demons would do.

He slid a hand around the back of her neck, pulled her face to his, and kissed her until she was breathless.

Christ, he was stupid.

Wyatt whistled like a fucking construction worker on the street, and even Joe, dour as he'd been the last several months, collapsed with laughter.

Bennett scowled at his roommates and handed Kim his stick.

"You know what? All y'all can kiss my redneck ass," he told them. He slapped his back pocket to emphasize the point. "Right here, assholes. Right here."

It didn't have the effect he'd hoped for—it only made them laugh harder. He shook his head at them.

"Don't let me hear you treating…" he paused, swallowing back Kim's real name in his annoyance. "…*Beth* like that. You got me? Have some respect."

With a glare aimed at each of them in turn, he stalked off, trying not to let their smirks get under his skin. He hadn't gone four paces before Kim burst into giggles too, her clear voice mingling with the deeper tones of his friends like she was one of them already.

Bennett bit his lip to hide the smile that broke through his irritation and stepped into the men's room. They were supposed to be laying low, not cutting up and attracting attention. He needed to pull himself together, but Kim's taste was fresh on his lips, and the feel of her lithe body was branded on his palms.

There were a thousand reasons why he ought to keep away from her but at that moment, he couldn't think of one.

Chapter Sixteen

Kim

BENNETT'S GRUMPINESS HAD passed by the time he returned from the restroom—but in its place was a friskiness Kim felt far less equipped to manage.

Before he'd stomped off, she'd been standing there with her arm around his taut waist, hand tucked into his back pocket like a high school girlfriend. Yet, soon after he returned, she found herself getting mercilessly heckled about their pool game.

Bennett had always been competitive, but it seemed that in her thrill at unexpectedly being sprung from the apartment, she'd gotten a little too full of herself for his taste. And so, true to form, Bennett took it upon himself to knock her down a peg.

He broke out every trick in the book in his efforts to rattle her, from trash-talking to lounging sexily at the edge of the table, close enough that Kim could smell his aftershave and feel the warmth of his body.

His success was infuriating. Kim had wholeheartedly believed that she'd picked up a few tricks in the years since he'd been infamous for this infernal game, but no one would ever know it to look at her.

Bennett had it mastered.

Particularly now that Kim knew he could use his tongue in ways she'd never imagined.

Bennett had nerves of steel, and Kim…

"Stop crowding me," she griped as he shifted closer. She hated that he was getting the best of her.

"Sure thing," Bennett grinned easily.

Too easily, as it happened. Kim lined up her next shot and Bennett was there, caging her against the table with long, muscled limbs, his cheek hot against hers.

She could feel his erection pressing against her. Kim's heart stuttered to a stop, stunned into paralysis that Bennett would do something so overtly sexual in the middle of a crowded bar. In front of his friends.

He must have her surprise. Just as Kim began to melt into him, as her vision went a little dark around the edges, he chuckled low and dirty in her ear, reached forward to tap her stick an inch to the left, and stepped away.

That cheater.

Before she could chew him out, his roommate Wyatt arrived, carrying a pitcher of beer that sloshed onto the table when he set it down. Kim tried to regroup and take her shot, but she was too shaken to follow through. Though Bennett had lined her up perfectly, her hands shook, and the ball went wide.

His blue eyes glittered as he *tsk*ed at the errant ball. "Come on, girl. Don't lose focus. You're gonna make us lose."

"Kiss my ass," she muttered. Bennett had probably taught her that line, too.

Joe stepped up to take his turn, ignoring Kim when she shoved away from the table, and Bennett when he pulled her close.

"Don't think I won't," Bennett drawled in Kim's ear, his breath warm against her sensitive skin.

The flush that hit her was like walking out of a cold grocery store on a hot August afternoon—just a wall of heat in the face, that had nothing to do with the shots of bourbon she'd had earlier.

"Bennett, could you please dial it down a thousand?" she scolded. "Literally everyone in this bar can tell what you're doing."

"If you could manage to keep a straight face, they'd have no idea," he retorted. "And for the record, that's a riot, coming from you. You've been pulling out every big gun you have this week. I warned you I was trouble, but you wanted things your way. Now you're in for it."

"Is that any way to treat the birthday girl?"

"You've been asking for it. Now, suck it up and take your medicine like a good girl."

"Stop making everything sound so dirty!" Kim cried.

Joe tossed his stick on the table with a growl. She didn't know what *he* was so pressed about—he and Wyatt could've been pushing balls into the pockets with their bare hands this whole time, for all she cared.

"You two need to bow out?" Wyatt asked, corralling his stick from against the wall. He didn't attempt a shot, he just waited for Bennett to answer him.

Bennett grinned and shook his head. "I'm no quitter. What about you, Kim? You a quitter?"

Wyatt smirked at her, trying not to laugh despite his exasperation.

In a different situation she might've given in, if only so she could drag Bennett out to his truck and take advantage of him. Bennett knew her too well, though.

She said, "No sir. Never quit a thing in my life."

"Except those pageants," Bennett clarified, leaning down to drop a kiss on her cheek.

"Right. But those were terrible."

Joe had been staring into space, not paying much attention to the exchange, but all at once, he inserted himself between them and muttered, "Yo, cool it with the PDA. People are beginning to notice."

Bennett frowned. "People, who?"

"Dude over there in the plaid shirt. I'm not positive, but he might've taken her picture and texted it to someone just now."

"You think Kim's been made?" Wyatt murmured.

Bennett angled himself between Kim and the guy, and asked her softly, "You ever seen that guy before?"

She stole a peek as she hugged him. "No. Who is he?"

"No idea, but we ain't sticking around to find out." Bennett slung his arm around her shoulders and pulled her against his side. "Bruiser, what's the play?"

Joe smoothly grabbed the pitcher and guffawed at a joke no one had made. "Stitch and I will take care of shit here. You get Kim out the back, and we'll meet you outside." He grinned and jostled Wyatt, who also roared with incongruous laughter.

"Stitch?" Kim wondered, as the two bumbled toward the bar.

"Like the little blue guy from that old Disney movie. Remember? Dude loves food," Bennett explained, handing Kim her purse. "And he'll eat anything that doesn't eat him first. Now, I need you to go in the ladies' room. Once you're sure you're alone, lock the door behind you. Find the stall with the window and open it up, and I'll be on the other side to help you out."

"How do you know there's a window?" she murmured, glancing over her shoulder as a ruckus erupted behind them.

The guy in the plaid shirt was soaked with beer, fending off Wyatt and Joe as they tried to mop at him with napkins.

"Giddy up, darlin'," Bennett told her, propelling Kim into the little hallway near their table. "We don't have much time."

"You swear you'll be outside?" she asked, stepping into the women's restroom.

"Cross my heart. Go on now." Bennett peeked into the main room, then motioned her on.

Kim checked in all the stalls, then shot the bolt on the main door. Sure enough, one of the toilets had a window behind it, so she climbed on the seat to push it open.

It wouldn't budge. The frame looked as old as the hills and was sealed shut with about ten layers of aging paint. Kim struggled for a bit, getting more anxious by the minute.

If she had to go back out there and find one of the guys, would it mess up their plan? Were they even still there?

She cursed under her breath and tried again, then dug through her purse for her keys, so she could scrape around the edges and try to dislodge things. *No luck.*

Kim banged on the glass in frustration. Now what?

An answering thump sounded from the other side. She knocked again, harder this time, beating out a silly rhythm that Bennett couldn't possibly mistake for anything else.

Her phone dinged with an incoming text. "Seriously?" she demanded, yanking the thing out of her purse to glare at it.

Get back, Bennett had texted. *I'll break it.*

Kim scrambled off the toilet and out of the stall, and a minute later the bottom panes shattered inward. Bennett punched out the rest of the glass with his t-shirt wrapped around his fist, then beckoned her over.

"I'm sorry," she whispered. "It was painted shut. I couldn't get it open."

"No worries. Put your arms around my neck and let me help you out." He quickly checked behind him, then added, "Be careful of the sides. I don't want you to get cut."

Once he'd lifted her free, Bennett checked Kim over for broken glass, then grabbed her hand and dragged her to Wyatt's idling car. His roommates were already inside. Bennett yanked open the back door and protected Kim's head so she wouldn't hit it getting in.

She tensed when he didn't follow. "Aren't you coming?"

"I'll be right behind you." He thumped the roof of the muscle car. "Be good, now."

Before Kim could protest, Bennett stepped back and shut her door, and darted for his truck a few paces away.

The road was dark as they tore away from the honkytonk. Wyatt's car wound through the canyon like it was a rollercoaster ride, hugging the road and taking the turns with ease, but Kim had had too much to drink, and she was scared.

Up front, Wyatt and Joe hadn't said a word.

She fought down the faint queasiness rising in her throat, and spoke into the silence, "This seems like a lot of fuss over a guy that was probably minding his own business."

Joe's voice was low, and meant for Wyatt, not her. "Buck says Alix is on the move." He showed his friend his phone.

"Shocker," Wyatt muttered.

Kim blinked at the back of their heads. "What?"

Wyatt's gaze met hers in the rearview mirror. "The rest of our team was watching your reporter friend tonight. She just ran out of her hotel and jumped into a rideshare. Still think it's a lot of fuss over nothing?"

Joe intoned, "She's heading for the 15. Take 79, instead."

The interior of the car lit up as a pickup truck fell in behind them, flashing its high beams a few times before dimming them to a normal level.

"Easy up," Wyatt announced.

Kim twisted around to peer out the back windshield, but it was hard to make anything out with the headlights shining in her eyes. "That's Bennett?"

"Yup."

She exhaled in relief and closed her eyes, trying to shake off the adrenaline from fleeing the bar. It was a two-hour drive home, but at least now Bennett was close by and everything would be okay.

THEY WERE MINUTES from home when Buck texted again, reporting that Alix had arrived at The Wagon Wheel and was chatting up the plaid shirt guy in the parking lot.

"Okay, so maybe it wasn't nothing," Kim admitted sheepishly. "But isn't the cat out of the bag now? That guy's just gonna give her whatever else he has on his phone."

Wyatt and Joe glanced at each other and grinned. "You mean this phone?" Joe asked, holding one up between them.

"You stole his phone?" she cried.

"Can't do much about what he already did," Wyatt explained, "but at least now we can find out who he is, what he got, and who he sent it to."

"But it's locked. How are you going to get into it?"

Joe tucked the phone away and smirked. "We have a guy."

Kim shook her head and turned to watch the outskirts of San Diego pass by. "Of course, you do."

Any trace of the buzz she'd been sporting earlier in the evening was long gone now. She was sober as a preacher, and she needed to talk to Bennett alone.

However, as they crowded into the apartment, the guys were in crisis mode, their rapid-fire words and all-business demeanors shutting her out and exhausting her.

All Kim wanted to do was get out of her dumb disguise, cry under a hot shower, and crawl into bed. She'd managed to do just that by the time Bennett came to find her.

"So, our friend Noah did a quick facial recognition on what we sent him," he explained, as Kim curled up in her pajamas. "We think the guy's name is Ron Cruz. Ring any bells?"

She shook her head. "Never heard of him. Who is he?"

"He's the LA-based entertainment reporter for the Dallas Examiner. Isn't that where Alix Hernandez works?"

"Yes. But…" Kim bit her lip. "Bennett, how did they know where we were going to be? I thought none of us was supposed to tell anyone."

"None of us did, far as I know."

"So, a lucky coincidence, then?"

"Hell of a coincidence," Bennett said. "You were in disguise, and we were no where near L.A. or San Diego."

"I wish they would just leave me alone," she complained. "They ought to be more worried about Dan's jailbird fiancée than some random ex like me. Move on, already."

"Listen, honey—we *don't* think it's a coincidence," Bennett said gently. "We think they might be tracking your movements."

Kim crossed her arms and scowled at him. "How could they do that? The last time I saw Alix, I didn't even know I was coming out here yet."

Bennett perched beside her on the bed. "I'm not sure," he said, then reached for her purse on the night table and offered it to her. "I have a good idea of where the tracker might be, though. Mind dumping this out so I can look?"

She stared at him. "I think I would know if there was something odd in my handbag."

Bennett was totally serious, however. He simply shrugged and tipped his chin at her bag, urging her on.

Kim upended it with a huff, watching as her lip balm, wallet, keys, and sunglasses fell across the comforter between them. Bennett carefully picked through the menstrual products, makeup, and more, his expression intent as he examined each item before setting it aside.

The pile grew until the only thing left was her purse itself. His long fingers caressed the leather, searching along the straps and pockets.

Kim couldn't peel her eyes away. "Boy, you never touch me like that," she tried to joke.

Bennett froze, his expression shifting into one of triumph. Pulling his hand from the outside pocket, he showed her a small silver dot held between his fingers.

"Bingo," he said softly.

"What is that!" Kim gaped at the device. She'd never seen it before.

"This is how they've been tracking you." Bennett dropped it on the floor and crushed it beneath his boot. "Dime a dozen on the internet. All they had to do was drop it in your bag when you weren't looking."

She stared at the metal fragments on the ground. "Again—why go to so much trouble over someone's meaningless ex? What is Alix's *deal?*"

Bennett's eyes were soft as he studied her. "I have to ask this, and I hope you don't take it the wrong way, but…do you think Dan might be directing her behind the scenes? Could he know that you brought us that drive?"

"No way," Kim said quickly.

She thought about the periodic texts and voicemails Dan had sent since they'd broken up and faltered, though. She'd always deleted them without reading, but…

"I don't know," she amended. "Maybe."

Bennett nodded. "We're gonna figure this out," he assured her. "Don't you worry."

"Thanks."

Kim scooped up the contents of her purse, but hesitated before shoveling it all back in. "Can I still use this?"

"Should be fine now," he agreed.

She set it aside and sighed, scooting closer so she could lay her head on his shoulder.

"Thanks for the rescue earlier," she told him. "You're making quite a habit of saving Sutherland women, aren't you?"

Bennett went stiff. "What?"

"Well, tonight, obviously. And back in the day with prom. Plus, my mom—"

He looked like a cornered cat for the briefest moment before his expression went blank. "Don't dredge that up. It's not the same thing. You don't know—"

Was she really going to do this now? Her night was already shot. *Hell, why not.*

She forged ahead, "Bennett, I know how you saved my mom that night."

He shook his head, emphatically denying it.

She should've let him be. Instead, her words came tumbling out too loud—probably because she'd kept them to herself for so long. "You did, Bennett. I know all about what happened. I know what you did for her."

His face leached of color, and he shook his head frantically again. "I didn't do shit to your mama, Kim. I swear to God."

She frowned at his distress, not understanding why he'd be so upset when he'd been such a hero. "You saved her life," she said carefully. "I know that much. Mama didn't realize how far gone she was. It doesn't matter what you were doing out there yourself. If you hadn't talked her down, she could've hurt someone. She could've gotten a DUI or ended up in jail. Worse, even."

His blue eyes snapped to hers. "What?"

"You didn't have to hide it from me all this time," Kim said. "I know getting in the car wasn't the smartest thing for her to do, but…we all have our dark moments. Thank god you were there to talk some sense into her. After that, there was nothing for it but to learn from her mistakes and move on."

Bennett swallowed thickly and looked like he might be sick. "How did you…where did you hear that story?"

"Mama told me. I must've pestered her one too many times, because she finally broke down a few years ago."

Kim had felt such a rush of victory at the time. Her mother's tale hadn't explained everything about the night that had soon driven Bennett from Respite, but it'd told her enough.

"Okay. Well…" His words faded away and his eyes skittered around the room.

"It's okay. You don't have to go over it all again. I only wanted to say thank you. For that night, as well as tonight. I really appreciate you looking out for me. For us."

His gaze landed on her face, and Bennett looked as earnest as she'd ever seen him when he said, "I will always watch out for you, Kimmie. No matter what."

"I know you will. Now, come on. Let's hit the hay. I'm tuckered out."

Bennett nodded, but his distraction was clear. "You go ahead. I need to talk to the guys about that tracker, but I'll be along shortly."

"And there go my big plans for a birthday seduction."

That got a small smile out of him, at least. "Hang on to those. With that to look forward to, I'll be back before you know it."

Chapter Seventeen

T HE TEAM HEADED back to the Black Watch warehouse the following day, where Noah had been tasked with decimating the meager defenses on Ron Cruz's phone so they could examine his actions at the Wagon Wheel the night before.

While Noah worked, Bennett tried to burn off some of his frustration by pacing around the nondescript space that made up the kid's favorite lair, but it took several circuits before Joe finally summoned him back over with a curt, "We're in."

The pertinent contents of the pilfered phone were displayed on three big monitors. Cruz's camera roll came first, with a disguised Kim—and less frequently, an undisguised Bennett—arranged in an organized, chronological grid.

Bennett saw their mistake immediately. Anyone recognizing him or the rest of the team would absolutely have paid attention to the woman hanging out with them. That was simply human nature.

He cursed to himself. They should've anticipated that—planned for it—but there was no saving it now.

Stepping closer and peering over Joe's shoulder, Bennett focused on the middle screen, which featured Cruz's contact list. There were a few unnamed numbers highlighted. He guessed those would be the reporter's secret sources—hardly unusual for a guy who made his living trawling for gossip about notable people, but a small obstacle in their current situation.

However, Noah and Buck were intent on the third screen, where they were digging into who Ron Cruz was outside of his professional gig. They were muttering between themselves, for the moment not sharing whatever rabbit hole they were diving down with the rest of them.

Bennett tapped Wyatt's shoulder and tipped his chin at the monitors. "What's going on?"

"The kid's doing some skip-tracing, trying to cross-reference those burner numbers. Two of them were copied on the text he sent to Alix with the pictures of Kim."

The rapid clicking ceased and Noah pulled his fingers from the keyboard.

He didn't turn around, but his words carried when he said, "That's getting really old, man. I told you before I'm not a kid."

Wyatt smirked as he looked Noah over. "Oh, yeah? Then how old are you? Because you don't look a day over twenty to me."

Joe huffed in amusement as Noah swiveled in his chair, serious as a heart attack behind his tortoiseshell glasses.

"For the record, I'm 27. I served four years in the Corps between undergrad and grad school, so you can fuck all the way off with that bullshit. I'm over it."

Joe looked dubious. "Not sure that math is mathing, son."

Noah spun in Bruiser's direction, and Bennett marked the subtle change that flowed over him. The four-eyed nerd faded away, and an actual threat bubbled to the surface. *Well, hell.*

"I skipped sixth grade. Try me."

Even coming from a jarhead, it was a hell of a threat to make to a SEAL. Leveling it at Joe, who at the moment was not perhaps the most stable he'd ever been, was akin to choosing violence.

Bennett put his hand on Joe's shoulder, pinning him in place before he got any big ideas. Then he looked to Buck and silently encouraged him to intervene in the brewing problem.

"Easy there, sailor," Buck murmured. "We had it wrong. No harm, no foul."

Joe sat stiffly for a second or two, but eventually he nodded, and took a long swig of his coffee while he worked on settling himself down.

Buck leaned in to clap him on the back, then urged Noah back on task. "Our mistake. Won't happen again."

Wyatt sprawled back, hiding the face he made at Bennett. Bennett pulled a spare chair close to his roommate and wedged himself into it.

"Christ," Stitch whispered once he was settled, "Talk about baby faces. Can you believe that shit?"

"Monroe should've warned us," Joe snapped.

Bennett shook his head, smiling a little. "Appearances are deceiving. That's not news."

Bennett knew that more than most—he'd made an art form out of giving people what they expected to see, instead of what was.

Noah's background did explain more about how Monroe had come across the guy and Bennett felt better having him on their team, knowing that he had actual life experience, and not just a ferociously capable brain, under his belt.

The Corps would've trained Noah up right and depending on his post, he undoubtedly would've experienced some shit or another while he'd been active. If or when the time came, the guy would know what to do.

He was still a kid, though.

At a lull in the frenetic typing, Bennett spoke up. "Question. Was Cruz in place when we arrived at The Wagon Wheel? Or did he slip in after us?"

He turned to Joe, with his eerie recall for faces. Bruiser stared into space for a time, then shook his head. "He wasn't there when we rolled in. Must've gotten there soon after us, but I didn't notice. Why?"

"Because I'm trying to square the timing in my mind. If the tracker in Kim's purse was his, and transmitting at regular intervals, Cruz must have gotten on the road soon after we did."

"Okay," Buck said, drawing out the word.

Wyatt picked up Bennett's thought process, though. "It's a two-hour drive and a dark road. We would've seen him if he was trailing us."

"So, he was waiting somewhere outside?" Buck frowned. "How'd he know where to be?"

Bennett shook his head thoughtfully and caught Noah's eye. The kid knew right where he was headed—the tracking dot was a red herring.

"Bring me her phone as soon as possible," Noah told him. "I'll make sure it's clean."

BY THE TIME Bennett made his way back to the apartment it was late afternoon, and he was still frustrated and on edge. They'd gone in circles all day, but if there was a way to prove that Dan Cox was corrupt, they were having a hell of a time finding it.

They couldn't even figure out who Ron Cruz's anonymous contacts were, and Kim's hard drive was looking like a dead end, too.

Wyatt and Joe had given up long before Bennett and were already settled in front of another football game with beer and plates of nachos when he came through the door.

Surprisingly, Kim was there as well—legs curled under her on the armchair and daintily snacking from a bowl in her lap.

Her face lit up when Bennett walked in, and damn if that didn't do weird things to his chest. "There you are! Guess what?" She hopped up and darted over. "I placed a grocery order this morning and look at what they had. Pimiento cheese!" With that, she held a cracker in front of his mouth until he let her pop it in.

The taste bloomed on his tongue as he chewed and swallowed. "That's actually…really good." Bennett hadn't known he could find that stuff out here. Not any he'd want to eat, anyway.

"Right?" Kim agreed. "I won't tell Mama if you don't."

Mrs. Sutherland's formal white living room flashed through his mind, neat as a pin and reserved for guests only. He'd sat on that couch only once, terrified that he'd foul it up in the minutes it took Regina, the Sutherlands' housekeeper, to fetch Shannon and bring her down.

He'd just spent two hours at football practice in the withering Texas heat and though Bennett had made a point to change before arriving, he'd still felt the sweat and grime coating his skin.

He'd been starving, and not terribly confident there'd be food waiting for them at home, but there'd been a silver tray of hors d'oeuvres on the coffee table in front of him, presumably for one of Mrs. Sutherland's club meetings.

Once Regina had left him alone, Bennett hadn't been able to resist the lure of the small rounds of bread slathered with Rayann Sutherland's locally famous pimiento cheese dip.

He'd eaten one, and then two more, before quickly rearranging the plate to hide his theft.

He'd been so fucking hungry. That day, for some forgotten reason, had been worse than usual.

Kim gently called his attention back to the present. "You look tired. Do you want some iced tea? Or a beer?" She hesitated as she searched his face. "We can order in, if you want, but Joe and Wyatt said they'll grill later. There're enough burgers for all of us."

"I'm good for now. Thanks, though." He glanced at the TV, and at his roommates.

It was so like Kim to try to nurture him with refreshments. The hospitality instinct ran strong where they were from, and had probably been drilled into her from birth.

But Bennett didn't need food right now, and he sure didn't want booze. If he was going to take the edge off his mood, he wanted to do it with Kim, spread out beneath him and calling his name.

He couldn't drag her into his bedroom without being obvious, however, and he'd rather not embarrass her if he could help it.

While he stood there dithering, Wyatt set his plate in the kitchen and headed to the hall bathroom, where Bennett soon heard the shower running.

Joe moved to the kitchen, too, barking criticisms at the game while he put together a salad and prepped burgers for the grill.

They'd ignored him and Kim, but it still felt untenably crowded in the apartment.

Bennett estimated he had ten minutes before his roommates started trying to entertain Kim again. He knew they wanted her to feel comfortable, but she was also just that kind of woman.

Knowing her, she'd probably already promised to make them brownies for dessert. They'd be insufferable if Bennett let that happen, though.

On a lark, he held out his hand. "Hey. Come with me."

Kim smiled and he looked her over. She was pretty as a picture in a soft gray skirt that brushed the tops of her knees and swished around when she moved. *Perfect.*

She asked him, "Where to?" but she was already hauling Bennett toward the door—as if she was itching to get out of there, too.

"For a ride. That okay?"

His face flushed hot. There were guilty consciences, and there was this: every word exiting his mouth sounding like a double entendre. He felt like a caricature of himself.

"You bet." Kim let go of his hand and hurriedly put her sandals on. "Let me grab my bag and we are good to go."

HE TOOK A roundabout route out of town, winding up the coast until he hit a canyon road that cut inland. Soon enough, he found the park he remembered and followed the access lane to a remote lot in the back, nestled in a stand of eucalyptus trees that almost no one but the rangers visited.

While Kim checked out the scenery, Bennett opened the windows, hit the button to maneuver his seat as far back as it would go, and turned off the truck. Then he fixed her with a look that he hoped would be well received.

"Kimmie, I'll be honest," he told her. "It's been a long day. I've got no sweet talk left, but I'd be much obliged if you wanted to take off your panties and bring your sweet self over here."

Her lips dropped open, but he had to give her credit—she recovered quickly. She glanced around, quickly gauging how alone they were, then scrambled to comply. It was yet more evidence that they were in the same boat with this whole situation…ship.

He had an excellent view of Kim's slim, tanned thighs as she slipped out of her skivvies and clambered over the gearshift to straddle him.

In seconds they were necking like teenagers, but Bennett didn't know how long they'd have, and he couldn't wait long.

After a few minutes of hot-and-heavy, he murmured against her lips, "You ready for me, honey?"

He removed his hand from her ass to run his fingers along her cleft. Oh, lord, she was. Bennett could feel it, but he still wanted to give her the chance to back down if he was pushing her too far.

"Sure am," Kim murmured, "but we're not going to get very far with you like this."

Right. Bennett was still buried under two layers of material.

"Hang on. Just have to—" He fumbled a condom out of the door pocket, but before he could do much with it, Kim had him out of his gym shorts and sheathed rather expertly.

He narrowed his eyes. "Girl, just what have you been getting up to while I've been gone?"

"Never you mind," she smiled, cupping his balls for a hot second before positioning his cock so she could slide on down.

Bennett squeezed his eyes shut and held on as long as he could, but Kim was riding him like it was the goddamn rodeo, and instinct was hard to fight. He fisted one hand in her hair, gripped her hip with the other, and drove into her as hard as he dared.

His world fractured suddenly, a release streaking down his spine like napalm, Kim right there with him.

The aftershocks went on for minutes, but when it was all over, Bennett did another perimeter check before dropping his skull against the headrest like the tendons in his neck had snapped. He stared at Kim's flushed face and groaned.

"I needed that," he told her, brushing her hair off her cheeks.

She let out a breathy little laugh. "If I had known that was on offer, I would've needed it too." Kim stroked his shoulders, then his arms. "You've been holding back, Mister."

She didn't sound like she was bullshitting. Didn't look like it, either, but the words were hard to comprehend.

Bennett cleared his throat. "I hope that wasn't too…" He choked on the word *rough,* not quite able to make himself say it. He was still buried inside the woman, for fuck's sake.

"Too what?" Kim wondered with a frown. "Don't tell me these west coast girls can't handle you. Hell has surely frozen over if you're doubting your charms."

Then she winked—full of herself, the impertinent thing.

Bennett snorted. "Now, don't be mean. I was only making sure I delivered the kind of customer service you've been led to expect."

"You are just right," Kim said, serious as could be. "No matter which way you deliver. Don't ever doubt it."

He couldn't think of a thing to say, so he kissed her lightly and lifted her off him, divvying up the coffeehouse napkins stuffed in his door pocket so they could clean themselves up. Not the best aftercare, he knew, but if this corner of the park had a hot shower available, he wasn't seeing it.

Bennett had, however, spotted a portable toilet Kim could use, but before he could point it out, she said, "Why do I feel like you did this a time or ten in high school?"

He squinted at her. She was trying to sound blasé, but her tone was off.

"Now, why would you bring that up?" he wondered.

Kim shrugged, and it was even less convincing than her awkward smile had been.

"I don't suppose you'd like to know if you're just another horse in my stable, or not."

She flushed a vivid pink. "No. I mean… *no.*" Everything about her expression screamed *yes.*

Bennett's skin crawled with the notion that she might remember every one of the parade of girls he'd filled his free time with back in the day, and that she might still know some of them. There were many more she'd never know about, but not one had looked like her.

There'd been brunettes and redheads, petite women and plump ones. None were tall and lithe, though, with a soft fall of white-blonde hair that brushed the top of their collarbone.

Bennett couldn't have endured a faux Kim Sutherland—it would've broken him worse than the real McCoy was likely to.

He rested a gentle finger on her lips. "Darlin', from the moment I set eyes on that little towheaded thing shadowing my baby sister, no other girl could compare. Whoever you're worrying about right now will never hold a candle to you. No one can, not for me."

Bennett forced himself to clam up then, because he'd already handed the woman way more firepower than was wise—and the more he gave her, the deader he was going to be once this, whatever it was, was over.

Still, as he stroked his fingers through her fine flaxen strands, he marveled anew at how impossibly silky her hair was. He shouldn't be allowed to touch it, not with the stains he carried on his soul. He had, however, and he was willing to pay nearly any price to keep doing it.

Any price, but for lying.

There were so many reasons not to tell Kim what really happened that messy night in Respite.

Back then, it'd been better for Kim to believe the worst of him. It'd meant she'd be protected after he was gone, once the really bad gossip started circulating.

He couldn't have risked her trying to Lois Lane the situation and have Sheriff Fecteau turn on her too, so Kim had needed to accept things as they were and move on.

The plan had hurt, but it'd been the plan. Bennett had had to execute the plan.

Besides, Shannon had been stuck in Respite for another two years, and the only way he'd been able to force himself to abandon her was because he knew she'd be safe with Kim.

So, he'd lied, mostly by omission. And it'd gone smoothly. Mostly. Bennett couldn't have anticipated how painful the truth would feel now, however.

He wanted Kim something fierce, and she was making him believe that she wanted him, too—but having to keep lying to her for eternity seemed like an awfully bad way to start a relationship.

Once she learned the truth about what he'd really done—and she would, someday—any prayer of them staying together would die a cold death.

"Do you ever miss it?" Kim asked him softly. "Respite, I mean?"

Bennett missed exactly three things about his hometown, and three things only: the beautiful countryside he'd once escaped into as often as he could, his sister, and Kim.

He offered her a truth that didn't feel too difficult to share. "The sky is different there," he admitted wistfully. "Bigger. And I miss the bluebonnets. That probably sounds kind of dumb."

Kim's eyes were soft as honey as she gazed back at him, though. "No, it doesn't. Not to me."

Chapter Eighteen

Kim

K IM'S PLAN FOR Bennett's birthday had been progressing smoothly all morning. Amazing, but true. Then her father called.

Before that, Kim had managed to dispatch both Bennett and his roommates with a minimum of effort, and soon, she'd intended to get gone, too.

But then her phone lit up with her father's name, and the whole production ground to a standstill. She supposed that was to be expected—every genius plan had a hitch in it somewhere.

So, while Kim normally loved to hear her father's easy baritone drawling things like, "Princess! How's sunny California treating my baby girl," today was just not that day.

She still tried to match his cheerfulness, though. No need for him to get suspicious.

"Hey, Daddy," she said. "It's good! Things are going well."

She checked her watch. *Until his surprise call had slowed her down, anyway.*

"Good. That boy Shaw looking out for you?"

"He is. And not for nothing, Bennett's a Navy SEAL in his thirties. I think you can find something else to call him besides *boy.*"

"Fair enough."

Kim ducked into the closet to grab her purse and spotted the clunky sandals she'd ordered off the internet for her own birthday disguise. With barely a pause, she slipped them on and smiled. *Perfect.*

They were far more comfortable than they'd looked all those times she'd seen them on people with more bohemian aesthetics. She might be a convert, strange as it seemed.

California was already working on her in mysterious ways.

Her father cleared his throat nervously, pulling her out of her reverie and putting her on instant alert. This was no casual social call if her daddy was making noises like that.

"What's going on?" she asked warily.

"Listen, sugar—I wanted to apologize for Kara's misstep with that newspaper woman the other day. I hope you know she meant no harm."

Kim rolled her eyes and glanced around Bennett's room for anything she might've forgotten. "Of course, I do. I only wish she'd thought it through a bit more."

For the briefest moment, she considered telling her father what had happened as a result of Kara's *misstep* but tabled the notion just as quickly. He'd only worry, and her stepmom would feel even more terrible.

"I know. She gets caught up with all the society nonsense sometimes. Just wants folks to like her, is all."

"I understand." Kim checked her watch again. She did not have time for Kara's insecurities. Her taxi was going to be there soon. "Daddy, I'm sorry but I actually have to go. I have a quick errand I need to run, and my ride is supposed to be here any minute."

So much for not rousing his suspicions. She could feel his disapproval through the phone, heavy as a horse blanket.

"I thought you weren't supposed to be going anywhere," he said.

"I'm really not, but it'll be fast. In and out in five minutes, I swear. I just have to pick up something real quick."

"What if someone sees you?" her father demanded.

"No one will," Kim assured him, and prayed that was true. "I'm wearing a hat and sunglasses, and different clothes. No one will even notice me."

"Hat and sunglasses, huh?"

She frowned at his tone. "What's that supposed to mean?"

Her father paused for half a second, then commented, "Didn't exactly work the other day."

Kim sat on the end of the bed with a startled gasp. *How did he know about the Wagon Wheel?*

"Why…why would you say that?"

"Well, it's a funny story," he said drily. "I got a new patient this morning. Young man filled out all the intake forms, sat through BP, got weighed, and whatnot. And then, when I went in the exam room to hear about his bum shoulder, he pulled out his phone to show me sketchy photos of you, dolled up in a brunette wig and ballcap, sucking face and shooting pool in some honkytonk."

"He *what?*" Kim cried.

"Yes, ma'am. And then he wanted to know what my daughter was doing gallivanting around in disguise in Nowheresville, California."

She swallowed down the bile rising in her throat. None of this was normal. Why were these people hunting her like this?

"What did you tell him?"

"Well, I figured you and Shaw had to have a good reason for carrying on in public like that, and it sure wasn't that man's business. So, I told him it wasn't you and that if he'd ever met my baby girl in person, he'd know you wouldn't be caught dead in a place like that."

"Okay. Okay, that's good. Do you think he believed you?"

"Seemed to. But he left in an awful hurry when I threatened to press charges for insurance and identity fraud."

Kim scrubbed her hands over her face and tried to gather her scattered composure. "Good work, Daddy."

"Still want to go on that errand of yours?"

Did she? Ever since she'd come up with this plan, in the hours after her and Bennett's tryst in his truck, Kim had assessed the risks over and over. But with Bennett's colleagues keeping tabs on Alix, and the tracker in her purse destroyed, she'd ultimately decided that she had a more-than-decent chance of slipping in and out of her destination with no one the wiser.

Besides, the incident her father was describing had happened back in Dallas. It didn't really impact what was going on here in San Diego, did it?

Plus, she'd already dispatched the guys on their various "errands," and it was her task that was the crucial linchpin of the entire plan.

"It's kind of important," Kim told her father, "And I'll be careful. I promise."

Her father sighed, knowing from experience that once she'd set her mind on something, arguing was pointless. "Tell that fella of yours where you're going, at least. Or better yet, bring him with you."

Kim was categorically *not* going to do that. It would ruin the surprise.

"Will do," she agreed.

A car honked out front, launching her from the bed and sending her hustling for the door. "And now I have to go," she added. "Can we catch up in a few days?"

"You bet. I want to hear all about your dive-bar birthday. Maybe have a talk with this Shaw character, too."

Kim smiled at the dry-as-dust timbre of his voice. "It's a deal," she said, and cut the call.

IT WAS HARD to ignore her lingering misgivings as she slipped into the back seat of the cab. Kim's father was a sensible man, and Bennett was, too. She respected their opinions.

They would both hate what she was about to do.

That being said, Bennett needed her surprise more than he knew, and neither he nor her father was as familiar with Dan as Kim was.

The idea that Dan was acting like some scheming puppeteer behind a curtain, pulling the strings of random reporters, felt like utter nonsense to her. He was a pretentious narcissist, that was all. He believed everyone was dumber than him, yet was not clever enough himself to be any kind of supervillain.

As for Alix Hernandez, she might have been intrigued to be offered access to the Doggetts—one of Texas's most infamous and powerful families—but she was far too astute to have fallen for Dan's bluster for long.

That didn't rule out Alix going along with something shady to bolster her career, but that still would've been a far less insidious scenario than Bennett and his team suspected.

It didn't change the fact that Bennett would still be angry when he learned that Kim had left the apartment, and she hoped that the eventual payoff when she pulled off his surprise would be enough to counteract it.

She wasn't trying to be stupid, after all. She'd given the taxi company a fake name and was going to pay the fare in cash. She'd also donned another disguise, of sorts.

With her hair tucked under Wyatt's straw beach hat and her figure obscured by a loose shift dress she'd found in a boutique her first week in town. She looked nothing like herself, and combined with her sunglasses and new sandals she reckoned she was good to go.

Fortunately, this wasn't going to be a complicated trip, either. All Kim had to do was duck into the gallery, pick up her package, and slip out again. As long as the cab waited for her, she could be there and back in half an hour. Long before anyone noticed she was gone.

All told, there was nothing to worry about, and so much to be gained. She was determined to see this through.

As she watched the streets roll by, Kim reminded herself that her reasons were good ones. She'd never heard someone sound as forlorn as Bennett had in his truck the other day and her heart had ached for his sorrow.

He'd had to excise himself from everything he'd known, at such a young age. She couldn't fathom how difficult it must've been, and the injustice of the whole thing made her flush with anger, even now.

Kim couldn't undo Bennett's past, but maybe she had the power to soften its sting. Bennett needed a little slice of home, and she was set on giving it to him.

The minute they'd returned to his apartment after their sexy open-air encounter, she'd gone online and started searching.

She'd found the painting of a Hill Country field of bluebonnets at a gallery she knew in San Antonio. It'd been remarkably easy to arrange to have it sent to a local gallery she'd located near The Foundry, downtown, for reframing.

Despite Bennett's depressingly bare bedroom walls, Kim doubted he'd have liked the ornate gilt frame the painting was sporting when she bought it. The new gallery had been kind enough to rush the reframing job, though, and had promised to have it ready today.

Bennett's birthday.

Based on the way he'd been acting this morning, he probably assumed Kim didn't know. His roommates sure hadn't. But the fact that Bennett's birthday fell soon after hers had been burned in Kim's brain decades ago, and she would sooner root for Oklahoma than let the day pass without an appropriate level of fanfare. *Particularly* after the lengths he'd gone to commemorate hers.

Kim sighed, rolling down her window to let in the crisp morning air. She had made an effort to work within Bennett's rules, but sweet-talking the new gallery into delivering the painting hadn't worked and they hadn't been too keen on using a courier given the painting's price tag.

Kim *had* to pick it up herself—there was no one else to ask. Wyatt was going to pick up the cake after he went to the gym, and Joe would be getting balloons at the party store across town.

She'd tasked Bennett with buying dinner ingredients at a gourmet market she'd located in Solana Beach, but it wasn't like Kim could've made him fetch his own birthday present, anyway.

He would have a conniption if he caught wind of how much money she'd spent, and one look at the gallery would be all the hint he'd need to figure that out.

No matter. Kim had it covered. Bennett might think he could ignore his birthday, but when they all got back to the apartment, his best friends were going to give him a little party. Later, Kim would cook him a special dinner, and they could enjoy dessert while they admired his gift. Alone.

A giddy bloom of possibility unfurled in her chest. Bennett might be more skittish than a feral cat, but he'd slowly started to open up to her.

What's more, after they'd gotten busy in that pretty grove of trees, he'd as good as admitted that Kim had a chance to win his heart.

No way was she going to blow it over a tenacious society columnist, or her stupid ex Dan Cox.

"KIM? NO WAY! What are the odds, running into you like this?"

Three steps from the cab, the hairs on the back of her neck stood up at the familiar, mocking cadence.

"Dan? What are you doing here? I thought you were in Dallas." Kim looked over her shoulder at the taxi, gratified it was still idling at the curb.

"Nah…I flew in to meet some folks about the TV program they're doing on me," he said with a smarmy grin. "Trying to see if we can keep it going, you know?"

Kim swallowed and kept her distance. He wasn't supposed to be here. Dan was supposed to be anywhere *but* here.

"Forgive me—do you mean the documentary your new fiancée was supposed to be filming?" she wondered. "Because she's in jail now, buddy. She ain't working anymore."

Dan turned a little red, but didn't appear terribly put out. "We'll figure it out. Anyway, it's great to see you. You look terrific, as always. Except for that bag you're wearing. Is that supposed to be a shirt or a dress?"

Kim scowled. Dan's obsession with her appearance had been outmatched only by his tone-deafness, and her beachy bohemian vibe was clearly lost on him. It figured that she'd bump into him now.

Naturally, he feigned innocence. "What?"

"What do you mean, *what?*" she spat. "You cheated on me, and then got engaged to some random woman a month later. Now you're gonna take shots at my *dress?*"

He rolled his eyes. "Come on, Kim—it wasn't like that."

"It was exactly like that, *Dan.*" She could not believe he was going to stand there baiting her. Not after what he'd done.

Dan shook his head like she was the one off her rocker, then turned and waved off her cab, sending it away.

She wanted to stamp her foot in frustration. She had better things to do than stand here arguing semantics with a dumbass like him, and now he'd dispensed with her getaway car. Her subterfuge might have gone belly up, but she didn't particularly want to hang around for an impromptu reunion, either.

Kim looked around for an escape and found her solution in a sushi place down the block. She'd promised her mother she would try it while she was out here. Mama had seen it on TV and wanted to know if it was really as good as they said—not that the woman would ever put a piece of raw fish in her mouth herself.

Regardless, now was as good a time as any to check it off her list. Kim skirted around Dan and marched toward the entrance, figuring she could grab a quick to-go order and schedule a new car before she picked up Bennett's painting. Thanks to Dan, she had time, though not a ton.

She still had to get back home before the guys did.

The restaurant was light and airy inside, filled with tropical plants like a greenhouse in the middle of the city. Kim pulled off Wyatt's hat and exhaled to a count of five, releasing some of the tension gripping her.

Then Dan sauntered up behind her. *Dang it.*

"I'll be damned. You eating here, too?" To the hostess eyeing them, he instructed, "Table for two. Something private, please."

"I don't think so," Kim announced. "I'm only picking something up, and then I'm leaving." She shied away from Dan's hand on her back with a huff of annoyance.

He tsked at her. "Don't be like that. Seriously. Let me buy you lunch, at least. We haven't talked in ages. We should catch up."

"I doubt that very much," Kim muttered. How could she outwait him, though?

She couldn't stand the thought of Dan finding out about Bennett's painting. He would mock her for it, and then she'd have to strangle him.

He wasn't even supposed to know she'd reached out to Bennett, to begin with. It would make his snobby head explode.

However, the thought did make Kim realize something. She probably needed more information before she bailed on him. Her secret mission was a bust, but Bennett would want answers about Dan's sudden appearance in San Diego. A lot of them.

Fortunately, Dan didn't try to put his hands on her again, but he did use his body to propel her along behind the hostess. Kim went along to avoid making a scene. She didn't want to risk more people recognizing her, so she kept quiet and imagined painful daggers shooting into Dan's back.

The snake was apparently never going to stop ruining things for her, but two could play that game. Despite her growling stomach, Kim knew she'd only have to order the most expensive dishes on the menu and leave them uneaten to drive Dan crazy.

Ironic, given the way he could make a woman lose her appetite.

And what the hell—while Kim was sticking it to the cheap sonofabitch, she ought to be really evil and have the hostess take a photo of them "for old times' sake." She could turn off location sharing and send it to Dan's fiancée.

Could people receive that sort of mail in the pokey? *Probably not.*

She wasn't that person, in any case, and Bennett would be furious about it.

Besides, there were better ways to hurt the man sliding into the booth across from her. She could give his secrets to the people working to deliver his family their comeuppance.

She could give them to Bennett, on a convenient little hard drive.

Kim smiled to herself, and Dan sighed happily.

"See, now isn't this better?" he asked her. "We don't need to fight, Miss Priss."

Kim ground her teeth together at the old nickname. Dan Cox had never understood a single thing about her. How had she stayed with him as long as she had? He was a walking red flag, and she ought to have known better.

"Don't call me that," she snapped, then immediately wanted to kick herself at his smug expression. She'd taken the bait, all right. *Curses.*

"Sweetheart, say the word and I'll call you whatever you want."

"Gross."

"If you say so."

Kim checked her watch, calculating how much time she still had to get home. Dan's attempts at flirting were annoying and her window of opportunity was closing.

She told him, "Let's get this over with. I have places to be."

A ripple of anger passed over Dan's face, but he marshaled his expression quickly. "Hold your horses. With that kind of attitude, you'll give yourself heartburn."

"Then start telling the truth," Kim fired back. "I know we didn't run into each other by accident just now. How did you know where I was?"

He shrugged. "One of Roy's campaign workers saw you in the hotel gym. Gave me a heads-up you were here."

Kim frowned at him, trying to piece that together. "Your stepdad's campaign flamed out weeks ago. Why would he have anyone still working out here?"

"You never did understand politics," Dan retorted sourly.

"But…how did you know I'd be *here*. Today?"

"I have my ways."

Kim clutched a menu in her hands and fought the urge to slap him across the face with it. Bennett was going to have to wait in line for a crack at Dan. She'd have to finish with him, first.

"Don't be a jerk," she told him levelly. "How did you find me just now?"

Dan smirked and beckoned over their server, ordering for himself and Kim before she could get a word in edgewise. Once the woman marched stiffly away, Kim tried again.

"Dan. Tell me how you knew I'd be here."

He sat back with an oily grin. "Okay. So, remember that time when we went to the Violet Room? For Rick's engagement party?"

Kim nodded. Dan's friends had been just as shitty as he was. Two of them had hit on her by the end of that night, alone.

"You drove me home," he said, as if that explained everything.

"Because you got too drunk," she reminded him.

"You gave me your cloud password," Dan went on, "so I could download that song on the radio for you. But I kept it."

"So?" Kim regretted the slip but could not fathom how his story was pertinent.

She was wasting vital time trying to get him to tell her anything of value, too. She stood up in a huff. This was a mistake. It was time to go home.

"*So*," Dan said slowly, "it turns out that when you log into the cloud, you can use someone's password to find their device. And that worked out great, because I know damn well you don't go anywhere without your phone."

Kim's knees went out and she folded back into her chair.

"You look a little pale, Miss Priss," Dan said. "Here, have some tea."

Chapter Nineteen

Bennett

IT TOOK LONGER than Bennett would've liked to drive to Solana Beach and pick up the order Kim had placed at the specialty market, and given that it was technically his birthday, he probably ought to have spent that time doing other things.

He'd gotten used to laying low on the anniversary of his birth, though, so why should this year be any different?

A better person might have wiled away the morning at brunch with friends, trading jokes and stories instead of running errands. It wasn't that Bennett would mind something like that—if any of his buddies knew when his birthday was.

He'd never shared the date, however, and therefore no one had known to plan anything.

It didn't matter. That was the expected consequence of not making a fuss about yourself. Bennett lived with it, because making noise created vulnerability, and vulnerability led directly to the exposure of things best left buried. It was easier to move through life giving folks the absolute minimum so they wouldn't know where to strike at him. He therefore could not whine when they gave him nothing in return.

Consequently, the only other people who knew that today was his birthday were his sister and, perhaps…Kim. Could that be what all the fancy groceries and the odd zinging of his nerves were about?

As Bennett pulled into his parking spot in front of the apartment, he took a minute to assess what was potentially about to happen. Knowing Kim, he'd be accosted with balloons and confetti once he breached the threshold.

He eyed the front door, calculating the likelihood.

Eighty percent, he reckoned, getting out and going around to the passenger side to grab a couple of the market bags.

His heart rate ticked up, readying for the onslaught. Kim had definitely been scheming yesterday, and sending him out of the house this morning had clearly been part of her plan.

So, now what?

Bennett set the bags down beside the door and went back for the other two, took a deep breath, and turned his key in the bolt. He swung the panel wide, and…

…was met with chilling silence.

Dead air.

Not a molecule of movement or life.

He didn't need to yell for her. He knew in his gut that if Kim was there, she was in no position to answer him.

He lurched forward, palming his sidearm as he hit the wall and made his way through the apartment, clearing room after room. The place was empty, however—no sign of Kim, Wyatt, or Joe.

Maybe he was overreacting, and they'd simply gone somewhere together? It didn't feel like that, though.

Bennett brought the bags inside and locked his truck, then carried the groceries to the kitchen and put away the cold stuff. He looked around again, frowning at the quiet.

Terror was squirming its way up and down his spine. Something was very wrong. Kim wasn't supposed to be out and about. She knew that, and so did Wyatt and Joe.

She hadn't been sick, and she hadn't been antsy—she'd been biding her time. Up to something. Kim had quite pointedly sent him on a mission to get him out of the house, which meant there had to be a good explanation for why she was gone now.

Where are you? he texted her.

Nothing.

Kim with you? he asked Wyatt next.

At the gym. She's home.

No she isn't, Bennett fired back.

On my way, Wyatt promised, but his gym was a good fifteen minutes away.

Bennett tried Joe and Noah next: *Kim with either of you?*

Negative, Noah replied instantly. *What's up?*

It took a while longer for Joe to respond but once he did, he was characteristically blunt: *WTF now?*

Bennett considered the possibilities and decided he didn't like any of them. Kim hadn't gone more than four daylight hours without contact since she'd washed up at Skippers—and it was exceedingly unlikely she hadn't remembered that his birthday was so close to hers.

Even if she'd forgotten, Shannon would've reminded her.

Therefore, Bennett should've been met with cake, not chilling silence. Not a deserted apartment. While his skin crawled with foreboding, he reassured himself that he'd destroyed that stupid little tracker in her purse.

Noah had checked out her phone, too. No one could've found her.

Bennett scanned his texts again and started when he remembered the apartment complex's gym, across the courtyard from their patio. Kim was bored and stir-crazy. Maybe she'd gone there to blow off steam?

He hauled the sliding door open and charged across the flagstones to peek inside but came up empty. Same deal for the inground pool around the corner.

He wanted to hit something. Tension boiled in his chest as he stepped back into the apartment, only to be met with the sight of Joe scowling in the foyer, surrounded by colorful balloons.

No wonder he'd been so cranky.

"Did she send you out for those?" Bennett demanded.

"No, I thought the place needed some flair," Joe snapped back.

Wyatt batted a few of the balloons out of the way as he let himself in next, then leaned back to hold the door for Noah.

"A party? Guys, you shouldn't have," Stitch cooed.

"We didn't," Joe retorted. "Kim's not with you?"

"No. She asked me to swing by some bakery on my way back from the gym, but I came straight here after I saw Easy's text."

All eyes turned to Noah, who'd quietly moved to the kitchen table and booted up his laptop. Bennett took in his jumpsuit and the toolbox the kid had set on a chair, and cocked his head.

"You're an electrician now?"

Noah chuckled darkly. "No, dude. But no one knows I work for Mr. Monroe, and I'd like to keep it that way." His fingers went flying over his keyboard. "At least until I graduate," he amended a moment later. "Then all bets are off."

Wyatt met Bennett's gaze and shrugged.

Bennett told the kid, "Appreciate you coming, man."

He shrugged. "I was told to trust your gut."

"By who?"

"Better question might be who didn't tell me that. And that would be, no one who knows you."

Bennett paused, but he could deal with that later. "Listen, Kim is smart. She knows she can't be seen anywhere. If she went somewhere, I'm sure it was against her will."

Noah stopped typing and looked at him. "Kim *is* smart. She also thinks the focus on her safety is overkill, because she's been kept in the dark about what we're really doing here. So, I expect she took what she thought was a calculated risk, because it is clearly your birthday, and she is in love with you."

Bennett choked on his own saliva. He coughed for way too long, and eventually managed to sputter, "What…where did you…that's fucking bullshit."

Noah looked at his roommates. "Am I wrong?"

They shot back in concert, emphatically, "*Nope.*"

Like a bad joke, Bennett's phone buzzed in his pocket, making him jump. It wasn't Kim, though.

"Hey, Shan."

"Happy birthday, loser."

"I have to call you back. Shit's hitting the fan right about now."

"Let me guess, Kim is MIA," his sister drawled.

"What?" Bennett snarled. "How did you know?"

"Because Dr. Sutherland just called me, wondering if I'd heard from her. He said he and Kim talked this morning and that she told him she was running a quick, important errand."

"Ah, fuck," he muttered.

"Yep. I know he's not the mellowest guy in the world, but he sounded worried, Bennett. Said he tried to call and make sure she got home okay, but he couldn't get ahold of her. He then asked *me* to check for him, which he never does."

Bennett stretched his neck from side to side, trying to reign in his burgeoning temper. When he got his hands on that infernal woman, he was going to wring her stubborn, beautiful neck.

"We, uh…we're trying to locate her right now," he admitted grudgingly. "Did she happen to mention what was so all-fired important that she had to disobey direct orders to stay at home?"

"No, she did not. She was apparently in a hurry, though. She told her father that her ride was going to be there any minute."

"Kim had a *ride?*" he hollered, risking a glance at his friends. When he saw their thunderous expressions, he looked away.

"She sure did," his sister agreed. "But there's more. Dr. Sutherland said he had someone come into his office the other day, asking questions about why Kim was up in some dive bar, gallivanting around in a bad costume. You know anything about that?"

"I do, yeah," Bennett sighed. "It's under control."

"Let me guess. That was her birthday extravaganza?"

"Options were in short supply, kiddo."

"Got it," Shannon retorted drily. She paused a minute, then wondered, "So, this is you looking out for her, huh? Maybe I should've kept her here with me."

"Don't start with me," he warned.

"You're right—I'll wait to chew your ass out until you *find my best friend*. What the hell, Bennett?"

"Look, Kim knew not to go anywhere, but she still found a way to get rid of all of us this morning so she could leave. None of us know where she went, though."

"She probably went to get you a present, dummy. Did you tell her you wanted anything? Start there."

Bennett shook his head, then covered the mic on his phone so he could quickly debrief the others.

"We should pull in Mr. Monroe," Noah whispered.

Bennett nodded. *Big guns. Absolutely required.*

"Shannon, can you hang on a minute? I need to make a call."

"If you hang up on me, I will come there myself and kill you," his sister hissed.

Bennett pulled his work phone from his pocket and pointed it at Wyatt. "Call Buck and bring him up to speed," he said, then dialed the secure line to reach his new boss.

Tate answered with a curt, "Whatcha got?"

"We need an exact location on Dan Cox. Immediately," Bennett told him. "Kim is in the wind and my money's on him."

As he debriefed Monroe, Bennett knew he had to stay calm. If he lost his shit now, it would only take that much longer to find her.

In his other ear, Shannon squawked, "Bennett, you cannot go fighting Kim's ex-boyfriend. She probably went shopping. Please be serious."

"On it," Tate said, either not hearing the side chatter, or ignoring it. "Is Noah with you?"

"Affirmative."

"Talk him through what you need, and he'll get it for you."

"Roger that."

The line cut out.

Bennett took a deep, steadying breath while Wyatt and Joe got into a heated debate over near Noah. "This is so much bigger than…than fucking jealousy," he told his sister. "Okay? Give me some fucking credit."

She scoffed, but he could hear the worry underlying the sound. "I have to agree with Kim, here. Don't y'all think there is too much fuss over her being Dan's ex? He and Kim weren't even that serious and his new woman makes for far more interesting copy. Why do these people even care?"

"Good question. And you just made my point for me."

"You said you would keep her safe, Bennett."

"I was! But I assumed she wouldn't go haring off on her own when she was under strict orders to stay out of sight!"

"For Christ's sake," Shannon sneered, "You act like you've never met the woman. Kim's nearly as ungovernable as you are."

Why did that thought fill Bennett with equal measures of pride and panic? "God damn it. I've gotta go, hun."

"This is probably a lot of noise over nothing. But please tell me as soon as you find her."

"You got it. And keep your head on a swivel, you hear me?"

"I will. Don't you worry about me."

"Does not compute," Bennett said, then hung up.

He stalked over to the table where Noah was glued to his laptop and asked the gathered men, "Okay, think this through. Where'd Kim go?"

"She had you on food, me on balloons, and Wyatt on the cake," Joe began.

"Yeah, not for nothing," Stitch interjected, "why'd you keep your birthday a secret all this time? I'm kind of hurt, bruh."

Bennett stared at him. "Are you kidding me right now?"

"The present," Noah interjected. "Kim went to get your present."

He couldn't argue with that logic. The gift was the one thing she would've been adamant about getting right and wouldn't have left to anyone else. Bennett nodded numbly.

Surprise, surprise—this was all his fault.

"Let's start with her bank records," Noah murmured absently, as his fingers began another staccato dance across his keyboard. "Maybe she paid in advance."

Chapter Twenty

Kim

KIM STALLED, TAKING a long sip of the proffered genmaicha to cover her shock. "Did you…were you the one who put the tracker in my purse?" she asked.

Dan smirked. "Insurance, nothing more."

"When?"

"A friend took care of it," he shrugged. "Work of a moment."

Kim shook her head, trying to understand. "But *when?*"

"Doesn't matter."

"It does to me."

Dan snorted in exasperation, like she was the one who was being unreasonable. "Okay, fine. It was a few days after we broke up. Happy?"

Kim gaped at him. "Dan, that was months ago! No, I'm not happy. Why would you do that?"

Her stomach somersaulted as she reviewed everywhere she'd been since then. Her mom's house. Shannon's. Those two weeks at the Foundry, and the subsequent time at Bennett's.

Shit. The night at the Wagon Wheel.

Dan knew it all.

Kim had been waltzing around town thinking she was so mysterious, and all that time he'd been marking her every move.

She took another drink of tea, but instead of settling her nerves, it just made her feel queasier.

He hadn't answered yet, but Dan was watching her like a hawk. "Why?" she whispered again.

His eyes narrowed coldly. "Because any bitch that's willing to go through my shit and take pictures of what she finds shouldn't be trusted. And hey, look—I was right. First chance you had, you went running right to those assholes trying to ruin my dad's life. Hell, you probably had that planned all along."

Their server approached cautiously, setting plates in front of them and inquiring, "Can I get you guys anything else?"

Kim met her eyes and tried to broadcast her distress, but Dan pulled the other woman's attention away too soon. "More tea for her," he said tersely. "I'll have a beer."

Once the woman left, Kim told Dan, "I've known Bennett my whole life. He's an old, dear friend. Whatever is happening between him and your dad has nothing to do with me."

Dan's smirk was cruel. "Nice try, Miss Priss, but I'm on to you now. Your helpless maiden routine ain't gonna cut it anymore."

Kim blinked at the venom lacing his words. Something more was going on here. Something she did not understand.

She clutched her purse to her chest and stood, fear and worry crowding out her confusion and turning her stomach. "I don't have to sit here for this. I'm leaving."

His eyes were hard when they flicked up to meet hers. "Stay," he ordered. "Finish your food. We haven't even gotten to the best part yet."

Kim swallowed, trying to think through the sludge bogging down her brain. Dan was scaring her, but she was hardly a shrinking violet. She knew how to defend herself if he pulled something stupid, and she wouldn't hesitate if it came down to that.

Plus, if Dan knew more about his stepfather's feud with the SEALs than anyone suspected—something important, something that would exonerate Bennett and his friends and help them get their careers back—then she had to find out what that was.

Kim needed to get Dan to stop speaking in such vague, threatening terms, and start dishing the real dirt. How she was going to do that when she was close to freaking out was anyone's guess, but she choked back the bile climbing her throat and slowly sat down again.

As uncomfortable as this was, Kim had to see it through. And she had to believe that Bennett would eventually understand.

WHEN SHE FOLLOWED Dan to the exit an hour later, Kim noticed that he still hadn't told her anything. His rotten-slick mask had slipped back into place, too—that same demeanor that had turned her off so much those last few weeks in Dallas.

At the time, she'd thought he'd changed. Now she wondered. Maybe Dan had always been this skeevy. Perhaps she'd been too self-absorbed, too caught up in who he was on paper to see him as he really was.

It didn't matter now, she supposed. After today, Kim didn't intend to spend five minutes in his obnoxious orbit ever again.

As they approached the hostess stand, Dan ducked his head into the bar area off to the side, like he'd spotted someone interesting. *On the make again, no doubt.*

She rolled her eyes and pushed through the door, gratefully taking a gulp of fresh air. As lunch had wound down, it'd grown suffocatingly warm in the booth, and her head was buzzing with frustration. Stupid Dan had dragged things out longer than she'd expected and had given her absolutely nothing she could relay to Bennett.

By now, the guys would've beaten her home, and she was going to have to fess up about where she'd been. Bennett was going to chew her out, but there was no help for that. Kim had to come clean.

She rooted in her purse for her phone.

Dang it. Where was that thing?

She looked back at the restaurant as Dan came out, his face wreathed in an oily grin. He was flanked by a few men she didn't know, but they immediately peeled off and sauntered away, in no hurry to get wherever they were going.

"Rushing off already?" Dan wondered.

Kim backed up a few steps in case he tried to kiss her goodbye. "In a minute, yeah. I think I left my phone inside, though. I've got to run in and grab it."

The way she was feeling, she might need to splash some cold water on her face or ask Bennett to come pick her up. What the heck was wrong with her? Why was she so dizzy?

Kim pressed a hand against her stomach, beginning to wonder if she'd eaten something that didn't agree with her instead of simply losing her appetite in the presence of a horrible man.

When she tried to take a step toward the door her knees buckled, sending her careening backward in space. Her body never connected with the sidewalk, though.

Instead, Kim found herself sprawled across the back seat of a limo, half in the lap of a guy who didn't seem the least bit surprised to find her there. In fact, he'd been ready for her.

Quick as a cat, he wrapped a thick arm around her waist and pressed a sweaty hand against her mouth, dragging her farther into the car so Dan could lean forward and close her in.

Dan blithely ignored Kim's struggles as he waved from the sidewalk, stepping aside as a beefy guy slid into the front passenger seat and another got behind the wheel.

He flashed Kim's phone at her and slipped it into his pocket, looking smug at his sleight of hand.

That *bastard.*

A second later, the car glided into the afternoon traffic with Kim sealed inside its private cocoon of luxury. The dark tinted windows made the outside world seem farther away than it was.

They weren't going very fast yet, and even though she was getting more tired by the second, she knew she had to get out before they hit a freeway. If she could get a door open, she didn't think she'd be hurt too badly if she hurled herself onto a downtown sidewalk.

They'd been lucky, getting Kim into the car the first time. No one seemed to have noticed, but she doubted people would ignore it if they saw her fighting to get away again.

The guy holding her seemed to sense the direction of her thoughts. His grip tightened, giving her no room to breathe, much less work her way free.

She struggled to think. What was the correct move? Jerk her skull backward and break the guy's nose? Figure out how to kick him in the groin?

Kim couldn't make anything work. Her limbs felt heavy and unmanageable and wouldn't obey her commands.

She growled in frustration and kicked at the back of the passenger seat. She could not believe Dan had kidnapped her. *Kidnapped* her! He'd played her like a fiddle, and she had only herself to blame.

And why? Because she'd embarrassed him by dumping him, and happened to know a guy he had beef with?

Dan was an asshole. He had beef with countless people. Bennett was hardly unique in that respect.

Kim slumped in despair at the thought. *Oh, God. Bennett.*

Bennett was going to blow a gasket when he found out what she'd done.

She tried to blink away a sudden wash of tears, but it was an effort. She was worried about how heavy her lids felt—by how heavy everything felt.

How *was* Bennett going to find out, though? The whole thing had happened so fast, and Dan had stolen her phone. What's more, because Kim had been so intent on surprising him, Bennett had no idea where she'd gone or why, and would lose critical time assuming all the worst, wrong things. Doubting himself, or her.

Something was very wrong with her. This was not food poisoning.

"Did you drug me?" she tried to ask, but her mouth was still covered by the guy's hand.

The passenger up front turned around and motioned for him to let her talk.

"Did you drug me?" Kim demanded again. It came out garbled, as blurry as her spiraling thoughts.

He seemed to understand, however. "Of course," he agreed, like that was obvious. "We heard all about that taekwondo of yours. On the off chance it was true, we couldn't risk you putting up a fight."

Then he grinned, nearly as condescending as his boss. "What would people say, princess?"

Kim tried to kick the seat again, but her limbs felt leaden. Too heavy to move. Her sandal slipped off and thumped to the floor.

It could be hours before Bennett realized she'd been taken, and wasn't simply lollygagging in some boutique like the spoiled brat she apparently was.

It might be days before he could take action, if he even did at all. The way Bennett's mind worked, he was liable to assume she'd done him a favor and hied clear back to Texas.

He wouldn't think twice about her leaving all her stuff at his place, either. He'd probably assume she'd discarded it, as easily as he expected Kim to toss him aside someday.

That was not going to do, not at all.

Whatever else happened, Kim could not let Bennett think she'd left him willingly. She'd simply have to watch these meatheads closely, wait for her moment, and get away.

With any luck, Dan had hired henchmen as utterly thick in the head as he was, and she wouldn't even have to try too hard.

In the meantime, it was pointless to keep fighting the inevitable. Kim was going nowhere in her current condition, and she didn't know the surrounding area well enough to make sense of the few landmarks she was able to spot whizzing by.

Who was she going to tell, anyway? Dan had stolen her freaking phone.

She might as well give in to the blanketing darkness looming over her. She was going to need her wits about her when they got where they were going, and whatever they'd doped her with wore off.

Chapter Twenty-One

Bennett

OKAY, BANK RECORDS," Wyatt agreed. "If Kim sent all of us out for party supplies, then she definitely would've bought stuff too. That's a good place to start."

"Yeah, except hacking into a bank didn't go so well with Cox's accounts," Joe noted.

"That was different," Noah explained. "I'm going to give it a try."

Bennett nodded but he couldn't keep still. He paced in tight loops as Noah got to work, but the kid was nervous, and it didn't fill him with a ton of confidence.

Who wouldn't be concerned, though? Noah might've been a Marine, but that didn't necessarily mean he'd ever worked a rescue op. The distinction between finding random data in cyberspace and finding a missing person who might be in harm's way was like the difference between a sidewalk crack and a canyon.

Hell, Bennett, Wyatt, and Joe were used to this kind of thing, and they were jumpy, too.

That was because everything, absolutely everything, changed when you were looking for someone you knew—when the mission was personal.

After a few minutes, the kid slammed his palms on the table in frustration and Bennett's anxiety ramped up.

"No go. I need the setup at the warehouse. We have to relocate. Now."

Bennett looked at his roommates. They didn't care—tools were tools. You used the best one you had to get a job done, and if you didn't have it, you went and got it.

"Fine. We going to the one we met at last week?"

Noah nodded as he gathered up his gear.

Bennett waved everyone toward the door. "Roll out, y'all. Time's a-wastin'."

ONCE THEY'D RECONVENED, the kid settled in front of his boggling array of monitors and drives and wasted no time getting back to work. He set up some code to run on one screen, and began calling up downtown security feeds on another.

Kim still hadn't responded to any of Bennett's texts or voice messages, so he took a moment to step away and call Buck.

"Where we at?" his buddy answered, by way of a greeting.

"Nothing yet. We moved to the war room off of Vine. Kid wanted to play with better toys."

"Fine by me. If it gets the job done…"

"Yeah," Bennett interjected. "Listen, is Monroe up to speed? If we had a location on Cox, it would definitely help."

"Roger that. He's on it, don't worry—but he has to be careful who he hits up. We don't want to tip our hand and give Cox a reason to move Kim somewhere new."

The thought made Bennett blindingly angry. All he could think about was that cluster of incongruently cheerful balloons, drifting around the entryway of the apartment. He wanted to go back and put a bullet in each one of them.

Immediately, remorse swamped him.

Kim had only tried to be nice. If he'd done his job and made her understand the gravity of her situation, she would never have been so cavalier about leaving the house, especially alone.

It occurred to him that they had no idea whether she'd been alone.

Christ. This was on him. His fault.

Bennett would never forgive himself if something happened to her.

Buck had rattled off a few sentences while Bennett had been castigating himself, but now his buddy asked, "Okay? I should be there in fifteen minutes, at most."

He frowned in confusion. "Where?"

"Dude. *There.* I'll be there, as soon as I can."

"Right." Bennett hung up, all out of words.

This was good. Bennett's brain felt like a nest of bees, but Buck would help. He would know what to do next.

Bennett was at a loss. If this day had gone the way it was supposed to, he should be pulling Kim into his arms to hide his embarrassment over her little surprise party. He'd try not to be too obvious about ogling her legs in front of the others, and his buddies would lounge around eating cake and whatever else Kim had planned to make with those overpriced groceries.

Instead, they were huddled around Noah's techie wet dream, waiting for the kid to explain what he was doing and where they could find Kim.

Bennett didn't particularly care where that was, so long as he could get to her fast. By his estimation, she'd been gone for at least three hours already, and he shuddered to think of what could've happened to her in that time.

There was no doubt in his mind who was responsible, however. *Dan-fucking-Cox.* The guy didn't have to share blood with his stepfather to be cut from the same cloth—Bennett was certain that Cox and Roy Doggett were exactly the same kind of wrong.

Wyatt hovered over Noah's shoulder, pointing out some of the camera feeds. "Kim probably already explored the Gaslamp Quarter. What about Seaport Village? I dated a girl who worked over there. There's a lot of shops and stuff."

Bennett moved closer, watching the street scenes play out for a moment before shrugging helplessly. "Maybe? Wherever she went, it wouldn't have been far. She would've known how upset we'd be that she went out. Dollars to donuts she intended to be back before any of us got there."

"She was staying at the Foundry before, right?" Joe pointed out. "I feel like if she was rushing, she would've stuck to the area she knew. Navigating somewhere unfamiliar takes time she didn't have."

Black Watch's boy genius nodded and typed rapidly, and the feeds from the area surrounding Kim's old hotel winked into life on his bank of monitors.

"We'll start at eleven and step forward," he said.

"That's too much to sift through," Buck announced, striding up behind them like he'd been there all along. "That's hours of footage and too large a footprint. We have to narrow it down."

Curiously, the door alarm hadn't broadcast his arrival. However, the relief of having his best friend there jogged Bennett's thoughts into better functioning order.

"We need Kim's phone logs," he told the group. "We need to see who she called this morning besides her dad."

"On it." Noah's fingers flew over his keyboard.

Bennett's stomach surprised him with a loud growl. He rubbed it absently, trying to ignore the hollow sensation gnawing through his abdomen as he had so many times before.

Unfortunately, Buck caught on, as he often did. "You okay?"

"Fine," Bennett shrugged.

His friend scowled, and turned to Wyatt and Joe for the truth. "When was the last time you all ate?"

They studied each other, in sync as Bennett and Buck often were. "Seven?" Wyatt offered.

Joe shrugged. "Close enough."

"I figured," Buck sighed. "You two head out and pick up some food. It's going to take a while to find what we need."

"Hallelujah," Joe muttered. "Don't have to ask me twice." He grabbed Wyatt's arm and hauled him toward the door.

After they'd left, Bennett and Buck dragged chairs to either side of Noah and watched him in silence, until he suddenly proclaimed, "Got the phone logs. Here we go. This morning. Few outgoing calls, cross them against the directories, and…*bingo*. Call to Downtown Cabs at 11. Before that, we've got… *huh*."

The kid sat back. "This one is to the Gabriel Garza Gallery, in San Antonio. Right after that, she phoned…Birnbaum Fine Art. Where's that?"

He opened a new window, called up a map and zoomed in on the address he wanted. "Five blocks from The Foundry."

"See?" Bennett said, his pulse ticking up. *They were closing in.* "Call them," he told Noah.

The kid slipped on a headset and clicked on the listed number, routing the audio through the speakers so Bennett and Buck could listen in.

"Birnbaum Fine Art. This is Sherri."

"Sherri, hi. This is Dr. Sutherland. I think my daughter and I had a schedule mix-up this morning," Noah intoned, pitching the timbre of his voice lower and affecting the slightest upper crust drawl. "Might I ask if Kim has stopped by yet today?"

"I'm sorry, sir. I spoke to her this morning, and she said she'd be here at 12, but she never showed."

"Well, I reckon that's my fault. I do apologize. I'll round her up and get this straightened out right away."

"No rush," Sherri assured him. "We can hold on to the painting for another few days, but after that we'll need to make room for some pieces arriving for a show later this month. Ms. Sutherland would have to pick it up before then."

"Understood. I'll give you a call later today and set something up. Will that work?"

"Absolutely. I'll talk to you then."

"Wonderful."

Noah disconnected the call with a few taps, but before Bennett could ask what could possibly have been so all-fired important about a goddamn painting, Buck wondered, "Can you get us a dispatch log for the cab company?"

"Gimme a sec." And then, a scant two minutes later, he said, "Yeah, here it is. And...yep. Kim gave a fake name, but they picked her up at the apartment at 11:30. Dropoff on the 600 block of J Street."

"Does that match the gallery address?"

"Pretty much."

Bennett felt oddly numb as he directed, "Now the camera feeds. That block only. No way in hell did she make it there before 11:45, so start then and step through frame by frame."

Noah got rid of a few feeds on his monitor, and enlarged the remaining four. He scrolled back to late morning and set the videos to run in excruciatingly slow motion.

Buck clapped a hand on Bennett's shoulder. "Steady. We're almost there."

"I should've told her more," Bennett said morosely. "She didn't believe Cox was dangerous. If he fucks with her, it's on my head."

"It's on all of us. We underestimated Kim *and* that jackwad Cox, but we're going to get her back. Just keep your head on straight. We need you 100 percent and so does she."

"I'm good," Bennett protested. "Dialed in like a motherfucker."

"Sure you are." His expression, however, communicated the exact opposite sentiment.

Noah's first screen let out a chime, and the kid spun toward it eagerly. "*Yes.* I'm in her bank account. How far back am I going?"

"A week," Buck said, impressed.

"Two," Bennett countered. That was when he'd crumbled like dried-up dung and things had gotten physical between him and Kim. It felt like a pertinent milestone, somehow.

Wyatt and Joe returned with bags of burgers just as Noah lasered in on the astronomical sums Kim had paid to the galleries. As they settled in behind him, Bennett shifted uncomfortably.

He'd had a vague idea that art was expensive—but he hadn't realized it was *that* expensive. And while he'd known that Kim's family was wealthy, the indisputable proof that she had *that* kind of loose change to throw around made him feel faintly ill.

Wyatt lurched into his airspace, peered at Noah's screen, and crowed, "Leave it to Easy to reel in a trust fund baby! Dude, your girl spent more on your birthday present than I paid for my car."

"That—that's not for me. I don't know what that's for, but that isn't for me," he sputtered.

"Better hope not. All you got her was some shitty beer at the Wagon Wheel," Joe countered.

The blood drained from Bennett's head as he realized Bruiser was right. *This* was why he'd tried to keep his distance from Kim. Stuff exactly like this.

Buck snatched one of the bags from Joe and dug through it, then pressed a paper-wrapped burger into Bennett's hand. "Don't listen to them. Eat that."

He unwrapped the sandwich with trembling fingers, but he couldn't seem to do more than stare at the sesame seed bun. Biting and chewing felt impossible—doubly so when he looked up and caught sight of Kim's bottom line again.

Buck leaned in and murmured in his ear, "Stop freaking out. She's a hard-working, educated person with a well-paying career. But you are too, okay? There's no—"

"Stop," Bennett begged him. "Please stop."

Wyatt and Joe got busy distributing the rest of the food and handing out drinks. The screen with Kim's banking details went dark, but Bennett couldn't tell whether Noah had put it to sleep intentionally, or it had happened organically.

His face burned with an old, old shame. He lifted the burger, caught a whiff of the stale lettuce topping it, and put it down again.

Noah jerked forward in his space-age chair. "Got her," he barked.

With a few quick taps, he enlarged one of the security feeds and reversed the video a few seconds. Sure enough, there was Kim, stepping out of a car with the Downtown Cabs logo on its hood.

She was wearing a straw hat and a baggy dress, but there was no mistaking those long tan legs, or the elegant way she carried herself.

She didn't get more than a few steps before someone brought her up short, though. Even with the distance and the crappy video quality, Bennett could tell she'd been surprised.

Was it a man? He couldn't be sure with the light pole in the way.

"Zoom in," he demanded. "Who's that?"

Behind him, Joe snorted in disgust. "You don't recognize that fucker? Cause I sure do."

Bennett held his breath as Noah enlarged the image and stepped forward frame by frame. Kim and her companion passed beyond the scope of the first camera, and it took the kid a minute to find another angle that picked them up again.

Eventually he said, "There."

Definitely a guy. They watched in silence as he followed Kim into a restaurant, turning back once to speak to a trio of men that drifted up behind him.

"Hey, that's Moonflower. I've been there," Wyatt said.

"Pause it," Joe cried suddenly. "Those are the jerks who were harassing Peyton. Look."

Bruiser had an incredible recall for faces, but the notion that the same collection of goons who'd stalked and threatened Buck's fiancée mere weeks ago had been bold enough to show up again was too much to believe.

It was also damning. The men had been inextricably linked to Joely Spitz, the woman Cox had taken up with after Kim had dumped him—and the same woman who'd tanked her own career to help Cox's stepfather ruin the lives of every SEAL in this war room.

The woman who was, as far as they knew, still scheduled to marry Dan Cox upon her release from prison.

"You sure?" Buck demanded. "Like, really sure?"

"What am I, an amateur?" Joe asked, taking umbrage. "We were close enough to kiss the bastards last month. Yes, I'm sure."

Noah took a few screenshots, then sped ahead, until they saw Kim exit the restaurant and stumble unsteadily across the sidewalk. Her companion edged her back and back, until quick as lightning she fell into the back seat of a sleek limo idling at the curb.

One of the thugs must've already been in there waiting, because the other two quickly fanned out and got in the front seat when Kim's kidnapper strolled forward to shut her inside.

He stepped back and smiled, brandishing a phone at the dark glossy windows.

Dan Cox. No doubt about it. Bennett's heart felt like it was going to pound clear out of his chest.

"It's him." He surged forward and stabbed a finger at that smug face. "I *knew* it. So help me, I am going to murder that fucker with my bare hands."

Chapter Twenty-Two

Kim

KIM JOLTED AWAKE in a cold sweat, her body protesting the move with every signal it had. She had a wicked headache, and her stomach churned with the sudden change in position.

As she blinked at her surroundings, it gradually registered that she wasn't in the back of the limo anymore, occasionally fighting free of unconsciousness only to be lulled back under by the steady hum of the wheels on the freeway.

She was in a bed, but not Bennett's.

Kim had no memory of arriving there, wherever it was. The ride had seemed to take forever, but there was no way to know how accurate that was. Judging by the angle of the sun slanting through the blinds, she could've been out for two hours, or twenty-two.

Kim moved slowly, letting the swimming in her head subside before getting to her feet. Her sandals had been dropped haphazardly beside the bed, and it took more effort than it should have for her to get them lined up and on her feet.

It was chilly in the room, but she found her cardigan on the nightstand and pulled it on gratefully.

There was no sign of Wyatt's hat, but that didn't matter. It was of no use to her anymore, anyway. Her "disguise," such as it was, had shielded her for less than thirty minutes.

Kim sniffed, absolutely disgusted with herself. Bennett had tried to warn her, but did she listen? No. Her ego had tripped her up once again, and this time she'd managed to go and get herself abducted. Would she never learn?

This was no time for self-pity, however. She'd gotten herself into this fix, and now she had to find her way out of it.

Kim spun in a slow circle, taking in her surroundings with a critical eye. Wherever she'd landed was modern and luxurious, if cold. It didn't feel like a hotel, though—it was more like a vacation home that people rarely visited.

She'd designed more than a few of those.

This one had big windows that looked out on a lush, gorgeously landscaped yard, where the sun shined harsh and hazy. Before she could face whatever else was out there, she was going to need a hot shower and some strong coffee.

Kim edged away from the view and headed for the set of doors on the far wall. Inside was an elegant, airy bathroom. She made sure she was alone, then locked herself in to use the facilities.

There'd be time enough for bathing later—*after* she figured out what this place was, why she was here, and who else was with her.

There would be others, she decided. No way would Dan dump her here alone. He might be stupid, but he knew her better than that.

Kim smoothed out her wrinkled dress and straightened her hair, then ventured into the bedroom again. Just as she cracked the door to the hall, movement outside the back windows caught her eye.

A burly character strolled past, seemingly unaware of her as he moved along the patio with a phone to his ear. She ducked out of her room before he could spot her, then quickly turned in the opposite direction of the TV sounds filtering down the hall.

As Kim tiptoed around her virtual jail, she tried to master her dizziness and nausea so she could get a sense of the owner. There wasn't much to go on, and back in Dallas, the Doggett family had cultivated an odd collection of acquaintances. They'd moved in some of the same social circles as her parents but had also been seen with folks no one seemed to know.

Daddy had always said it was because of the politics, but after dating the senator's stepson, Kim had her doubts. Dan's philandering aside, there'd been something shady about those people.

Something shadier than politics, in any case.

She was admittedly biased by the knowledge that her home state's senator had done his level best to destroy the careers of Bennett and his team, SEALs who had risked their lives to rescue him and his wife from danger.

On top of that, Kim had often wondered whether Dan's company was benefiting from back-door dealing, thanks to his stepfather's connections and position on certain congressional committees.

She wished now that she and Bennett had found more time to discuss her certainty that there was rot under the surface of the family's careful public façade, but they'd been too busy figuring out their relationship these last few weeks to delve into much else.

Stupid her. She'd wasted weeks last spring getting to know Dan, simply because her Dallas friends had insisted that he was a great guy.

But what if it'd been Dan, and not his folks, who'd been the real problem all along? All the more reason to find out what she could now, before she got out of here.

With that in mind, Kim swallowed hard and refocused on her surroundings. *Whose home was she in?*

Whoever it was, they were clearly in tall cotton. The furnishings were of excellent quality, classic, custom pieces that weren't showing any wear and tear. The style was modern and sophisticated. A recent, professional redecoration, by all appearances.

Kim ran a finger along the slat of a window blind in one of the bedrooms. *No dust.* She looked around. Not a speck of dust anywhere.

The place was huge, and it was spotless. A cleaning crew had to be coming regularly.

Peering outside, Kim cataloged the pool and the chaise lounges arranged under umbrellas, the big planters full of flowers and carefully cultivated landscaping in the sprawling yard beyond. Maintaining all that didn't come cheap.

Someone was paying attention to this place, even though they didn't seem to live here full-time. They hadn't left any personal items around, but they had bucks, at least on the surface.

So who were they?

Kim checked the hall again, then tiptoed to the owner suite at the far end. In the expansive bathroom, there were a few rolls of toilet paper under the sink, and a box of men's hair dye. *Interesting.*

The medicine cabinet held nothing more than a travel pack of ear swabs and an old box of dental floss. No E.D. pills, but maybe the fella wanted to keep those close at hand.

The place reeked of rich old man, but only rich old man. There was a certain lack of warmth, both literal and figurative, that spoke to the absence of a softer touch.

That didn't exactly narrow the field of candidates, unfortunately. It described a goodly number of residents in southern California, and countless people she'd seen the Doggetts with.

Kim turned to go, but froze when she realized her exit was now blocked by one of her abductors. In the limo, the others had called him Gordo. Or was it Gordy? She couldn't remember.

"What are you doing?" he demanded.

"Funny story," she said. "Your dumb boss didn't warn me ahead of time that he was going to kidnap me. So, I didn't have a chance to pack an overnight bag."

"Sounds like a you problem," the jerk commented.

"And yet," Kim retorted, "I could still use a toothbrush and some soap. Deodorant, too."

He shrugged, unconcerned, and grabbed for her arm. Kim flinched and her head gave a nauseating throb.

The meathead recoiled when she retched.

"Seriously," she told him when she could speak safely again. "I have a really bad headache. I need aspirin, too."

After a long suspicious look, he tapped a device clipped to his collar. "Princess needs some Tylenol. You got any in the kitchen?"

He listened to his earpiece, then stepped aside and jerked his chin, herding Kim to the living room without trying to take hold of her again. "Wait here and we'll look for something," he told her when they got there.

Kim slumped on the couch and glared. "It better be in a sealed bottle because I am not taking any loose pills from you people."

His jaw flexed in annoyance, but Gordo didn't take the bait. He only turned and left, muttering darkly to himself.

Along with the guy she'd seen out in the yard—who might or might not be the one Gordo was conferring with in the kitchen— her captor count was now up to two. Possibly three.

She shouldn't antagonize them, she knew. There was no way she'd be able to fight off that many big men at once—not if they wanted to force a couple of sketchy pills down her throat, and not if they wanted to do worse.

Fortunately, "worse" didn't seem to be on the agenda so far. Kim only hoped that would last.

She wished she knew what this was about. It couldn't be her hard drive—if what Dan had said was true, he'd had ample opportunity to punish her for that, and hadn't.

No, it wasn't until Kim had moved in with Bennett and his roommates that Dan had made his move. So, was he holding her for ransom? Preventing her from revealing something he wanted to keep hidden?

Or worse—luring Bennett and his friends into some kind of trap? Kim pulled her sweater tighter around herself and scowled.

It still didn't make sense. She hadn't dated Dan for long, and he'd rarely talked about work, or his parents. He'd only ever been interested in who had the most money, where the parties were, and whether Kim was the prettiest woman in the room.

Her value to Dan had mainly been as arm candy, though he couldn't have kept his eyes off other women if he'd tried.

With another churn of her gut, Kim recalled his fixation on her modeling history, and shuddered. She'd stopped in her early teens—around the time she'd also refused to do any more pageants—but Dan had still been fascinated and brought it up often. Like it was a feather in his cap, instead of just a thing she'd once attempted.

Once, he'd even asked her to weigh in on the headshots of some models, younger girls who'd supposedly been vying for spots at an agency his mama was starting. Kim had found the exercise odd at the time, but it felt even more peculiar now.

She had no idea if the agency was up and running yet, or if Dan had been involved in hiring. Would he have had access to the girls in person?

The thought made her shift uncomfortably again. Models sometimes started their careers as young as eleven or twelve and had to be protected rigorously from an industry rife with predators.

Kim jumped up and paced around the living room. She shouldn't be dwelling on that memory now. Dan had never given her any indication that he liked underage girls, and Kim had her own safety to worry about first.

Still, she resolved to tell Bennett about the agency too, in case he and the guys wanted to look into it. Yet another reason why she had to get free soon.

As he stepped into the kitchen, a guy ordered her, "Sit down."

Kim spun to face the new arrival. With the long bar blocking her view, it was hard to assess how tall he was, or how fit. He seemed bigger than Gordo, but she couldn't decide whether she had a chance of taking him down one-on-one.

"Or what?" she wondered mildly.

"Or I make you," he told her, then added, "Feel free to shut the fuck up, too."

Kim sat, and the quick change in position made her head throb again. She clutched her sweater tight and shivered as her legs connected with the couch. It was even chillier here in the main room, with its open floor plan and two-story ceiling.

"Can we turn on the heat?"

"No."

"Did y'all find any aspirin?" she asked.

"No."

She needed her purse. She had a whole first aid kit in there.

Kim stared at her sandals, trying to think. She'd stuffed her sweater in her purse at the end of lunch, because whatever Dan had given her had made her feel feverish. Her purse was definitely on her shoulder when she left the restaurant, because she remembered knocking it against the doorframe when she stumbled on the threshold.

The rest was kind of a blur, but if her sweater had made it into the limo, and from there, into this house, Kim was willing to bet her purse had, too.

"If you give me my purse," she told the guy, "I have ibuprofen in there."

His eyes narrowed suspiciously. "We don't have it."

"I bet you do," she wheedled. "It probably just fell under the seat of the car."

"Didn't I tell you to shut up?"

"Please look. I promise I'll go back to my room and stop bothering you if you just let me get a couple of things out of my bag."

"So you can make trouble?" he scoffed. "Nice try, but no."

Kim shook her head. *Who did he think she was? Bennett?*

"You're giving me too much credit. I'm not going to bust out of here with some old hair ties and a tube of lipstick."

He pressed his lips together and looked away, but now that she'd seized on the idea, she couldn't let it go.

"Look, just go through it before you give it to me, or dump it out on the table so I can pick out a few things where you can see. I don't care."

The goon held up his hand and walked away, murmuring into his little collar mic.

Kim watched him go and sighed in frustration. *So much for that.*

Ten minutes ticked by. The outside guard made a pass around the far edge of the patio, then turned back and headed along the perimeter of the house.

Kim kicked off a shoe and tested the softness of the shaggy rug under her feet.

Real lambswool. *Nice.*

But then, Gordo marched into the room with her purse clutched in his hand. Kim didn't have time to gloat. He stopped next to the big glass coffee table with a deadly glower on his mug, and upended her handbag without so much as a how-do-you-do.

The contents spilled out and scattered across the table and floor. Tissues, tampons, pens, and receipts went every which way, and Kim shot forward to corral the weirdly embarrassing ephemera of her daily life.

Gordo stopped her with a harsh, "Hey. Don't go grabbing shit. Point and I'll decide whether you can have it."

She rolled her eyes. "Okay, but I think it's pretty obvious there's nothing dangerous here."

He shrugged. "Have it your way, but I don't have all day."

Kim bit back the retort that rose to her lips. In all likelihood, Gordo *did* have all day, since she suspected he was as stuck here as she was. Instead of mentioning that, however, she got to work negotiating on anything she thought she could use.

Chapter Twenty-Three

Bennett

A S MILD AS a spring morning, Buck said, "Easy, sit your ass down." It was the mildness, for whatever reason, that broke through Bennett's rage.

He sat. He fumed.

"Noah, see if you can zoom in on the limo's plate," Buck continued in the same sedate tone. "If you can pull a partial off it, we can start crossing it against the registration database at Motor Vehicles."

Noah nodded and got to work, homing in on the tiny license plate and trying to fix the video resolution.

Buck watched him for a beat, then turned to Wyatt and Joe, whispering amongst themselves over Bennett's shoulder. "Go to Moonflower," he instructed. "See if anyone remembers what went down while Kim and Dan were inside. This is going to take a while."

Bennett held his breath as the others left, waiting to see what his assignment would be. Buck only bumped his shoulder and reiterated his prior instructions, though.

"Eat that food," his buddy said. "No kidding around. You might not have a chance later."

"Hey," Noah chimed in, "I've got four digits. Running them against the DMV now. But what about…"

He trailed off with a thoughtful grunt.

Bennett swallowed a mouthful of food that tasted like cardboard. "What?"

With his mouse, the kid drew a square around Cox, expanding the image bit by bit as he played the clip on a loop.

Buck frowned, catching on fast. "Why is he waving that phone?"

"Is he telling her to call him?" Noah played with the resolution and zoomed in more. "Look at the way it's catching the light. The case is glittery. A gun runner has a glittery phone case?"

"It's Kim's," Bennett told him, recognizing it with dismay. "It's gold."

Buck smiled faintly. "So, Cox isn't telling Kim to get in touch—he's gloating that he took her phone. *Shit.* Guess we can't expect her to reach out and give us her coordinates."

Bennett crumpled up his empty burger wrapper and pitched it into the can under Noah's desk. "If Cox needs something from Kim badly enough to snatch her off the street in broad daylight, then he's gonna stay close to her. If we find him, we find her. Although…Noah, I don't suppose you put your own tracker on her phone when you—"

The kid cut him off. "No need. There are other ways to find it. Does she use cloud backup for her business?"

"Probably? Kim has one of those pro models. Takes a lot of photos for work with it."

"Awesome." Noah spun back to his bank of monitors. "I'll find her cloud account, and search for the device from there."

Buck locked his hands behind his neck and stretched his back, then snagged the second bag of food. He tossed a burger at the kid and lobbed another at Bennett before unwrapping one for himself.

Noah pushed the offering aside and pulled up a login screen. "Good for her. This outfit is rock solid. It won't be easy to bust down the doors, but I do like a challenge." He cracked his knuckles and set his fingers on the keys. "And now…"

"Wait." Bennett gestured at the monitor with his food. "What if the password's the same as that drive she gave us? Lots of people reuse passwords, right? Even though they're not supposed to?"

Buck scowled and muttered, "That sentence is an act of fratricide."

"I'm serious." Bennett tapped Noah on the shoulder. "Before you get all crazy, try *RattlerPride*."

The kid attempted a few variations, adding capitalizations and number strings when the core word didn't work. "No dice."

Bennett bounced his knee a minute, thinking. "Try…try a hashtag in front. Kim does that in texts sometimes. Like a joke."

"Mmmm…no. What else you got?"

Bennett didn't know. How could he have spent so long obsessed with the woman and not know?

Buck tilted his head and studied him with a frown, considering. "Hey, what was your number? On your football jersey in high school—what was it?"

"Thirteen. Why?"

The kid snorted. "Not exactly lucky."

Bennett scoffed right back. "I made it work."

"By which he means, he made that number his bitch," Buck clarified. "Now try it with *RattlerPride*."

Fortunately, the system bounced it like it had all their other attempts. Bennett wasn't sure what it would've meant if it hadn't.

"Add an exclamation point," Buck suggested. "That girl is all kinds of extra."

"I beg your pardon?" he snapped. True, Kim was the type to take on Hell with a bucket of ice water, but that didn't give Buck the right to—

Noah exclaimed, "That did it! We're in!"

Buck leveled Bennett with a sly smirk. "Told ya. Didn't I tell ya?"

"Fuck off," he told him. "Now, where's Kim?"

"Kim's *phone* is…" Noah turned to the third monitor, scooting closer as he entered an address on the screen. "…at the Mariposa Ranch Inn, up in Montecito. Whether she is also there remains to be seen."

"Saddle up," Bennett said, shooting to his feet.

"Dude, that's like four hours up the coast," the kid protested. "Lemme stop for gas, at least."

Buck stared at the pulsing dot at the center of the map, then slowly pushed to his feet, too. "Stay put. Both of you. I need to make a call."

BENNETT DID NOT want to stay put—now that they had a bead on Kim's possible location, he was desperate to *move*. Instead, he had to sit there in excruciating silence with Noah.

The forced patience went against every instinct he had to unleash hell.

Buck was right, though. There was no telling what Cox was up to with the escalation. Bennett had the sickening feeling that Kim was in real danger—not least because she didn't know it and was liable to keep popping off at the mouth until she got herself killed.

It would be up to him to save her life, because out of all the team, he knew her best. Only after she was safe would he kill her himself, for going out alone when he'd specifically told her not to.

Kim would be counting on him, Bennett knew. For some bizarre reason, she'd convinced herself he was a paragon of virtue, a white knight destined to ride to her, and everyone else's rescue.

Lord, if she only knew.

It wasn't like he'd never saved a life before, but the first time was the one that still haunted him. The first was the only one that would matter to Kim, too.

BENNETT HADN'T BEEN a SEAL when it happened, or even a sailor yet. He'd still been reckless and no stranger to a good time, but on the night in question he'd been uncharacteristically sober. That was saying something, especially considering he'd been celebrating his eighteenth birthday.

There'd been drama among his friends earlier in the week, however, and as a result Bennett had agreed to be the designated driver for his teammate Travis and Travis's girlfriend Sue. They'd taken Sue's old Corolla to the party, because Bennett had been low on gas, and would have no money for more until payday.

Playing mother hen hadn't bothered him, though. It'd kept Bennett's mind off the thing he was both supposed to—and categorically *not* supposed to—do later that night.

The three of them had left his party when Sue got too hammered. They snuck her into her house through the laundry room door. Bennett had driven Travis home next and spent an awkward few minutes idling in the guy's driveway, listening to his doubts about Sue's long-term potential.

By the time he'd been able to extricate himself, Bennett had been more than ready for a drink or four. He'd still been driving Sue's car, and his mind had been a mess thanks to the mistake he'd nearly made at the party, and the bigger one he'd been heading for.

He hadn't thought about his route.

Or maybe he had.

Either way, Bennett hadn't made it more than halfway home when he'd spotted the silver Mercedes parked by the side of the road. He'd known that particular car like the back of his hand, and it'd had no business whatsoever being out there in the sticks in the wee hours of morning.

He ought not to have been there himself. What's more, he'd had every intention of avoiding the place, despite what he'd promised the Mercedes's driver.

But he'd showed up, because when it came down to it, five hundred dollars was a king's ransom for something he'd normally given away for free. And once Bennett went to college, his sister would have had to make do without him, to keep a roof over her head and pay for essentials.

He'd wished the offer and subsequent meeting could have come from someone else. *Anyone* else. He'd wished he was too drunk to feel anything. He'd wished…a lot of things.

Wishing hadn't made things so, however.

Bennett had crossed the center line and parked on the verge, pointing the Corolla at the other vehicle but keeping a good distance away—like he could've avoided contaminating his real self with the act he'd been about to perform.

After a while, when no one had gotten out of the other car, Bennett had slid from behind the wheel and hovered in the shadows of the underbrush, waiting for a sign of what was supposed to happen next.

Thanks to his birthday, he'd become an adult in the eyes of the law—though he'd already been functioning like one for quite some time. That didn't translate to the act in question, however. Bennett had assumed *she* would know what to do.

He'd worried that he wouldn't be able to get it up, or keep it up. That fear had been yet another reason why he'd forgone any liquid courage earlier in the night. If things didn't go as planned, Shannon would've been left with nothing but her own cleverness once he was gone.

His buyer hadn't made a move. She'd only sat there idling, headlights off and interior dark. For one panicked moment, Bennett had wondered if her husband had found out—wondered if he was about to be shot dead where he stood.

But then a light had gone on in the car, and Bennett had been able to see that she was alone. Slices of light from the dashboard had fallen across her face, and he'd reckoned she was growing irritable as the minutes ticked by, as he picked at the condom in his pocket and tried to steady his galloping nerves.

He had not seen the gun coming, nor the act Mrs. Sutherland had looked like she intended to commit with it.

Instinct alone had made Bennett tumble out of the bushes in a tangle of arms and legs, tripping over roots and fumbling his phone out of his pocket as he'd torn toward her door. His stomach had been in his shoes with dread, and he still had no idea how he'd managed to dial 911.

At first, Mrs. Sutherland had ignored his pounding on her window, pressing the gun to her temple with a blank, watery stare. Bennett had hoped to die right alongside her, if only so he wouldn't have to be the one to tell her daughter about it later.

Eventually, Rayann had eased up her shaking and crying long enough to unlock the doors, but she'd looked like holy hell.

The ambulance had pulled up moments after, and as skinny as she'd been back then, it hadn't taken much for the paramedics to haul her out and strap her to the gurney, even with her struggling.

Bennett hadn't wanted to look, knowing even then that people would find a way to use it against him. There'd been no chance of another soul driving by to bear witness, not on that road, and not at that hour. It was likely why she'd picked it to begin with.

It wasn't until he'd heard the sheriff's sirens approaching that Bennett had been able to move his feet, hustling to Sue's sedan and turning it straight into the woods. He'd plowed in as far as he'd dared in the dark, thinking the whole time that he'd have to tell Sue it'd been stolen so he wouldn't be asked to pay for the damage to her undercarriage.

While the doctors in the emergency room had no doubt been preparing to pump Mrs. Sutherland's stomach, Bennett had texted Shannon from his crouch in the trees and warned her that all hell was about to break loose.

It's already breaking loose, you freaking idiot.

Bennett could still see her words, ominous on his cracked old phone screen.

It hadn't taken long for Sheriff Fecteau to flush Bennett from his hiding spot. He'd only had to stand near the hood of his cruiser, thumbs hooked in his gun belt as he'd hollered, "I know you're out there. Y'all come on out, now."

The man's ugly baritone had carried in the still air.

Bennett had held his ground—right up until the sheriff had fired a solitary shot into the night sky, and called, "Shaw, you dumb fuck. You think I can't recognize your voice on a goddamn 911 call after all the postgame interviews you've given? Get your ass out of them woods before I send in my dog."

Without even asking the particulars, Sheriff Fecteau had cuffed Bennett and tossed him in the back of the cruiser, then left him to stew in the drunk tank for a full day before a public defender had shown up to inform Bennett that he'd been exonerated of any wrongdoing pertaining to Mrs. Sutherland.

Bennett had only been guilty of the destruction of Sue's property—as long as Rayann continued to hold her tongue—but rumors had grown roots and spread before Mrs. Sutherland had even been released from the hospital for her "overdose."

They'd gotten louder when her husband left her, slinking all the way to Dallas so he wouldn't have to face…well, anything.

Bennett and Shannon had long been accustomed to certain citizens of Respite talking shit about them, but after that it'd reached a whole new level. When he'd pried Kim from her mama's bedside and dragged her to the prom, Bennett hadn't even been sure they'd let him in the hall.

She'd been talking about her dress for weeks, and he hadn't been able to stomach the thought of her missing the dance, on top of everything else. The faces of those old PTA mamas had pinched like prunes to see Respite's unofficial princess on *his* arm, though. They'd always looked at him like he was dirty, but it was like he'd become intolerably filthy overnight.

Kim hadn't understood. Bennett was the high school quarterback in a town that sure loved their Friday night football, and as she understood things, he'd recently saved her mama from a terrible fate through sheer lucky coincidence. In her eyes, the town should've given him a medal.

She might've found a way to do it herself, given enough time, but none of them had guessed how soon he'd have to cut out of there, and taking into account all the things she'd never learn…that had been for the best.

As it happened, Sheriff Fecteau had remained unconvinced that Bennett was only a good Samaritan, fortunate to be in the right place at the right time. Why make a run for it, otherwise?

When Bennett had refused to admit to anything worse, he'd first found a way to get his football scholarship revoked, and then he'd laid down his ultimatum—clear out of Respite or go to jail one way or another.

"Your shady little gene pool has been a stain on this town for far too long," he'd said. "I don't want you here no more."

Later, after Bennett had left for good, Shannon had crossed paths with the old lawman only once, at the annual county fair. According to his sister, Fecteau had simply smiled and told her, "Three down, one to go."

Shannon had had the protection of the venerable Sutherland name behind her, though, along with the money Bennett sent her from his pay each month. She'd made it out of Respite unscathed, but Bennett had lain awake in his bunk many a night before that'd happened, imagining all the ways a well-liked sheriff and pillar of the community could make her life a living hell.

BENNETT SHOOK OFF the memories and tried to reorient himself in the present. As Noah continued to ignore him, busy with his computers, he reminded himself that old worries had no place in his present life.

Shannon was a grown woman with a great job now. Nothing bothered her much. Like him, she had ice running through her veins when the occasion called for it, and unlike him, she was sweet as honey the rest of the time.

Even if Bennett were to vanish without a trace, like their folks had so many years ago, she would find a way to survive. However, much like her eternal advocate, Kim, Bennett wanted so much more for Shannon than that.

As if he'd invoked her spirit simply by thinking her name, Kim's heated words rang out in his head. *Did Shannon deserve a different hand of cards than he did?*

Of course, she did. And anyone who knew what Bennett had nearly done, that long ago night, would absolutely agree.

He forced down his welling panic and kept as still as he could in his stupid rolling office chair.

It was all water under the bridge, now. Bennett *had* saved Kim's mama, after a fashion, and he had eventually managed to save himself. Indirectly, he'd maybe even saved Shannon, too.

But saving Kim now felt bigger than all those things. It was more important, more *necessary*.

There was no room to fail. Bennett told himself he wouldn't and willed it to be true.

Chapter Twenty-Four

Kim

D AN LET KIM stew for another day before he finally showed up, full of himself and entirely unrepentant. As usual, once he arrived, she kind of wished she hadn't demanded his presence quite so stridently. She could have guessed he would saunter in and start baiting her from the jump.

He'd been at it for fifteen minutes, keeping Kim wrong-footed and reacting, presumably to keep her from finding out something—anything—useful.

Though it hadn't gotten her anywhere the first two times she'd asked, she tried one of her primary questions again. "How long do I have to stay here?"

Dan smiled, as he had before. "I figured this place was just your speed. Don't you like it?"

"It's nice enough, I guess," Kim said. "Looks like guns have been treating you well."

Dan shrugged, but then he confirmed one of her suspicions. "It's not mine. It belongs to a friend of my uncle's."

Through the two-story windows beside them, Kim eyed the solid privacy walls surrounding the yard and wondered what sort of friend they were talking about. Had the guards come with the property, too?

She matched his small smile and prodded, "Your stepdad's side or your mama's?"

Dan scoffed at her attempt to pry. "None of your business. What's gotten into you anyway? You never used to be so nosy."

"You never used to be secretive."

"Oh, but now that I've found someone else, I'm suddenly intriguing? Give me a break."

"Kidnapping and holding hostages is not intriguing, it's criminal," Kim pointed out. "And I bet there's a whole mess of folks who'd like to know more about what you've done."

"Let me guess—that side of beef you've been shacking up with?"

"Among others."

Instead of letting Dan see how much it bothered her that he knew about Bennett, she stood and wandered the living room, picking up knickknacks and setting them down again. There was a TV, but no game console. No internet access that she could find. Not much that was small and heavy enough for her to use as a weapon.

There had to be some way she could access the outside world, and once she got this weird visit from Dan out of the way, surely she'd be able to come up with something.

The longer he yammered pointlessly, though, the more brain cells she lost listening to him.

What had she ever seen in him? It was hard to fathom now.

Kim wandered into the kitchen and opened a few drawers, but most of them were empty. *Dang it.*

Dan watched her with a smirk. "Sorry, babe. Looks like you can't throw a whisk at me this time."

She flushed with annoyance. She'd whipped a whisk at Dan's head the day she'd kicked him to the curb. She wasn't sorry she'd done it—she only wished she'd taken a second to aim better. Maybe then she could've taken out an eye.

"Might as well get comfortable, Miss Priss," Dan said. "You're not going anywhere."

Kim sighed and went to sit down again. "A change of clothes would be nice," she told him. "Or, I don't know, some decent food."

His perma-smirk looked strained as he settled deeper into the loveseat across from her. "Stop complaining. You have everything you need."

"I'm cold."

"You said it, not me."

Kim looked away, trying to reign in her temper. Angering Dan would only make him leave again, and she needed information from him before that happened.

And some pants.

"Dan, come on," she pleaded. "If you wanted me to feel like I was in the gulag, you wouldn't have picked someplace so fancy to hold me."

He kept grinning, damn him. "*Gulag* seems extreme. Consider it more of a…gilded cage."

"Semantics won't make a pair of leggings magically appear. And even jail gives people soap and clean underthings," she noted.

Over the last few days, she'd figured out that Dan's muscle would leave her alone if she kept to her room, and Kim was nearly funky enough that she was willing to attempt a shower with them around.

If she was going to risk it, however, she wanted to make it worth her while. She wanted soap, and something warm and clean to change into once she was done.

"God, you are spoiled," Dan sighed. "And as oblivious to your situation as ever."

"So, you'll do it?"

He shrugged. "Maybe, maybe not. Let's see how helpful you're feeling."

She blinked, taken by surprise. Had he finally decided to get to the point of all this?

"What do you want?"

He eyed her speculatively. "I want to know what you've been up to since you got to San Diego."

"Not a lot," she tried. "I did a little shopping downtown. Went to a couple of restaurants and checked out the beach. But you probably know that already."

"So, you're not feeling helpful," he commented. "Noted."

"Dan, if you have something specific to ask me, by all means, get on with it."

He chuckled, "Got somewhere else to be?" After a long beat, he went on, "Okay, how about this? Have you made any new friends recently?"

Kim immediately thought of Bennett's roommates, and Peyton, but it would be a cold day in hell before she would utter their names.

She stared him down and said, "No."

"Not one?"

"Bless your heart, but you're annoying. If you mean Bennett, he's an old family friend, not new."

"If you say so." Dan sat there smiling mirthlessly at her. He was waiting, but for what?

She eyed him and decided he wanted her to admit to something specific—but likely didn't want to give anything away by naming it first.

No, Dan was going to force her to walk into his trap before he sprung it. Kim wracked her brain, searching for where the snare might be.

He was too impatient to wait for her—no surprise there. "So, what did you say about me, Kim? What'd you tell your *old friend*?"

"Dan, I hate to break it to you, but you never came up. We haven't talked a lick about you."

"You're lying."

"I'm not."

For the first time, a flicker of anger crossed his face. That was not good—Kim was still having bouts of wooziness here and there and going toe-to-toe with him could end up badly for her.

She needed to buy herself time to think, and to ensure that the remains of whatever he'd drugged her with had fully worked its way out of her system.

"Stop playing coy. You think I can't put two and two together? My bank alerted me to a security breach just after you popped up in San Diego, and right when my contacts informed me you've been sucking face with one of the assholes messing with my dad."

His disgust was palpable and written all over his face. "So, I want to know what you told those punks, and I want to know now."

"Dan, no one is talking about you," Kim insisted. "Bennett and I grew up together. He's a dear family friend, but I barely met the others." Looking into his pinched, arrogant face, she couldn't resist a jab, though. "Besides, you and I are old news. Why on earth would I go around discussing you when I'd rather pretend like I've never met you?"

Dan laughed cruelly. "You really expect me to believe that *you're* friends with that nobody? *You?* Give me a break. I know Shaw comes from nothing—less than nothing. Hell, I've heard tell that back in the day, the sheriff had to run his whole family out of your quaint little town."

Kim wanted to kick him in his florid face, but she didn't know if she could trust her balance yet. *Alas.*

"I don't know who would say that about him, because Bennett Shaw is a good man," she spat furiously. "He has more honor than ten of you put together. So don't act like you know anything about him at all."

Dan looked startled by her vehemence, but he recovered quickly. He squinted at her, then sneered, "Oh, it's like that, is it? I should've guessed you'd rebound with some dumb ox."

He pitched forward to point in her face, his breath sickly sweet as his eyes dragged over her tangled hair. "Don't worry, babe. Is that what you want me to say? That my door will still be open once you're done slumming with the riffraff?"

"I…beg your pardon?" Kim sputtered.

"No can do, sweetheart. I don't need an icicle back in my bed. I've got a real woman now."

"In jail," she retorted.

"Not for long," Dan promised. "And soon there won't be anywhere far enough for you and your meathead boyfriend to run. This place will seem like the Ritz compared to prison."

Kim rolled her eyes. "Is this supposed to be your villain arc, Dan? Because you sure have some bad writers working on your script. Bennett is a decorated Navy SEAL."

"*Was* a Navy SEAL," he pointed out, his face mottled in anger. "And it won't do him one lick of good once he's behind bars where he belongs."

He stood and headed for the door, but Kim *had* to ask him one more thing before he got away. "Just out of curiosity," she wondered carefully, "Why do you think Bennett left Respite?"

Dan turned another triumphant sneer on her. "I expected you knew. Word is, your boy toy raped some socialite he found on the side of the road, then tried to shoot her so she couldn't tell. I heard the cops got there just in time, but I bet there are more than a few folks left in that podunk town who'd still like to carve a piece out of his hide. They'd probably love to execute a little frontier justice if they could."

He left, and Kim sagged against the pillows in shock. Dan had to be talking about the night her mama had nearly OD'd on pills. *Had* to be.

She'd heard the rumors that'd swirled around town, same as everyone else, and if a second thing of that magnitude had gone down on the same night, everyone would've been talking about that, too.

She and Shannon hadn't discussed it between themselves, though. They'd had their hands full with Bennett leaving and Shannon moving in with Kim, and soon after, Kim's parents had split up. Her father had tucked tail and skedaddled to Dallas to be with Kara, and then there'd been Mama's recovery to deal with.

Kim and Shannon had tried their damnedest to act like typical high school seniors, and after that, normal college students. They'd steadfastly stuck to the only thing that would keep them out of the spotlight—they *never* uttered a word about the night their respective families had imploded.

Never. Not even to each other.

Dwelling on what-ifs was pointless, even then.

Kim and her best friend had been bystanders, at best, and would only ever know what Bennett and her mama chose to tell them.

Except, the facts as they understood them were that her mother had been brought to the ER and Bennett had been thrown in jail in the space of a couple of hours, supposedly for unrelated infractions.

Kim still remembered Bennett's desperate tone when he'd called her from the Respite lockup. *"Promise me you'll go get Shannon,"* he'd begged her. *"She's waiting at the Motel 6. Bring her to your house, and don't let her go back."*

She hadn't understood. *"Why on earth would she be there? That place is the pits."*

His deep voice had cracked, along with her tender teenage heart. *"Kimmie, I'm out of time. Shannon will explain everything. Just promise you'll get her and keep her with you until…until this all gets sorted out."*

Kim hadn't grasped a single thing about that night, but she'd still promised.

"I swear. I just wish you'd left that party when you said you would. No one would've cared, and then you wouldn't have gotten pulled over."

He'd stayed because of her, because Kim had been tipsy and doing her damnedest to goad him into kissing her instead of Cassidy Bernhoff.

"I have to go, kid."

Sure, she would've been disappointed if he'd left early, but she would've understood. It was days before she'd come to understand that Bennett Shaw's kiss was everything the girls had gossiped about, and more.

"They're still going to let you go to training camp, right? Sheriff Fecteau would never get you in trouble with your new coach. Would he?"

Lord, how naïve she'd been.

"I'll be fine. You take care of Shannon, and your mama, too."

"I will. Don't worry." The line had gone dead.

Now, as Kim thought back to the things people had said in the aftermath, she tried to sort truth from speculation. Her mama had definitely been in the hospital—Kim and her father had visited her there. Likewise, Shannon had confirmed that Bennett had been kept in a cell for at least a day or two.

Kim burrowed her feet under a couch cushion to warm them, and asked herself if there'd been *anything* solid linking Bennett to her mother.

By his senior year of high school, he'd been tall and strong and handsome as sin, with a wide grin that could charm the scales off a rattlesnake—but though he'd had a reputation for promiscuity, there'd never been any whiff of him taking an interest in older women or crossing the line when it came to consent.

As far as Kim knew, Bennett happening upon her mama the night of her overdose had been mere coincidence. But maybe…maybe that story hadn't been true. Maybe Kim had been even more clueless and naïve than she'd thought.

When she considered that night now, there were pieces that didn't add up. She could distinctly remember Bennett standing in the front hall of Cassidy's house, sober as a preacher and jingling his keys while he tried to get his friends out the door. He'd been the designated driver on his birthday, an injustice she'd found unsupportable at the time.

Before now, she'd never put together that it would've taken real commitment for a guy Bennett's size to end up in the drunk tank an hour later—less, if she subtracted the time it would've taken him to drop off Travis and Sue.

She'd never questioned the explanations she'd been given, but she'd also been nursing a painful crush on Bennett for most of her adolescence, and he'd been leaving for football training camp in a matter of weeks.

She'd known in her bones that he would not return, and it'd felt like a catastrophe of the highest order, obscuring nearly everything else in her heart and mind.

Kim stroked the soft suede of the sofa cushion as she thought about the past. How hard would Shannon have had to work to mislead her? They'd told each other everything, but…the Shaw siblings had been thick as thieves. No one, but no one, had gotten between them.

But had Mama been in on a deception, too? What about Daddy or Deputy Stahl?

She grabbed one of the throw pillows and pressed it against her face with a groan. She was getting ahead of herself, making trouble where there likely wasn't any.

Just because Dan thought his tale was true, didn't mean it was. After all, he wasn't exactly lighting the world on fire with his honesty and good works these days, and he might be making things up simply to screw with her.

However, the knot in Kim's gut told her there was a kernel of truth in his story somewhere—and if she was going to prevent Dan from using it, Bennett was going to have to tell her what it was.

First things first, though. Kim had to get out of this place and find her way back to him. While she worked on that, she needed to decide, once and for all, whether she knew anything about Dan's family that could help Bennett and his friends get their SEAL careers back.

Eventually, Kim realized that she *did*, in fact, know one thing. For reasons that remained mysterious, Senator Doggett's jerk of a stepson had drugged her and kidnapped her off a city street in broad daylight, then held her hostage for days longer.

That was a crime—more than one, probably. What in the hell could be important enough to make him risk such a thing?

Chapter Twenty-Five

Bennett

I T TURNED OUT that getting an op up and running with Black Watch was a far sight easier than it'd been in the Navy. The intel was obtained, the call was made, and…off they went.

Bennett had never guessed it could be so simple.

It was an encouraging start, but he still hadn't known what to expect when they pulled up to the airfield hangar. It sure wasn't the sleek black helo they saw sitting on the tarmac, gleaming and spit-shined within an inch of its life.

Monroe had told them that the bird had been made available, of course—but he'd assumed that meant borrowed, or rented. *Not so.*

The helicopter scheduled to fly them up the coast bore the crossed swords of the Black Watch logo on its nose and looked lethal as sin. It seemed it was theirs.

"Damn," Wyatt breathed in fascination, "You didn't tell us we'd be arriving in style."

"Didn't know," Buck murmured.

Noah also hadn't mentioned anything. He'd only relayed their ETD and hit the overhead lights in the bunker, revealing a hell of a lot more gear than a few computers and some ergonomic chairs.

They ought to have suspected right there that the "startup outfit" they'd signed on with was expanding operations in real time. It'd been one-stop shopping as they'd kitted out for the rescue mission.

Remembering the array of thoughtfully selected gear quelled some of Bennett's anxiety. There were resources going into this. *Real* resources, and smarts to back them up.

Buck turned into the hangar and parked along the far wall. As the team pulled their packs from the back of the truck, Bennett prodded them yet again, "Y'all brought IFAKs, right?"

Wyatt rolled his eyes. "Dude, would you chill? We've never *not* brought medic kits."

Joe hefted his pack onto his shoulders and punched Bennett lightly in the chest. "No one's letting your girl bleed out, bro. Focus up."

He nodded, willing himself to calm down. There were a couple of guys loitering near the bird, so after a quick glance around the hangar, he started over.

"We don't know what we're walking into," Bennett pointed out for the umpteenth time. "I don't want to take any chances."

"We're not," Buck assured him, as he fell in step at his side. "We'll pull Kim out with no one the wiser, and if that doesn't work, we'll be ready for both a fight and its aftermath."

Bennett swallowed. He knew that, and yet, "This feels different."

"Roger that," Buck said, then frowned and stopped walking.

"That our pilot?" Wyatt wondered from behind them.

"I assume so. Didn't know the boss was planning to ride along, though."

Joe sauntered up and squinted at the pair on the tarmac. "That's not Monroe."

Bennett peered at the guy again, studying his sandy hair and faded tactical pants. He'd only met the head of Black Watch in person a couple of times, but it sure looked like his rangy frame and sly grin.

"Afternoon, gentlemen." Buck promptly closed the distance and stuck out his hand. "Looks like we have decent weather."

The pilot went first, introducing himself as Derrick Graves to each of them in turn. Noah had shared his impressive bio with them earlier, but in person Graves had a steady, capable demeanor that immediately set Bennett at ease.

They turned their attention to his companion, and Graves was right on it. "I believe you ordered a medic," he said.

"Tom Monroe, M.D.," the guy announced, straightening from his casual lean with a grin that was eerily similar to his… "Tate's my brother," he tacked on, before anyone could ask.

When he took off his sunglasses and came closer, the differences between the men were more obvious. Tom looked younger and tanner, for one thing, and was brimming with a simmering energy that Bennett identified with, but Tate did not possess.

Buck clapped him on the arm. "Glad to have you."

Monroe smiled easily. "No sweat. With any luck, you guys will do your thing, and this will be a fun waste of my well-paid time."

Bennett cut eyes at Joe, whose scowl deepened at the guy's flippancy. Graves noticed, and slid closer to murmur, "He acts like a joker, but Tom's legit. Spent two years in South America with the Hendricks Group."

Bennett relaxed a fraction. Hendricks operated in the most dangerous areas south of the border. If Tom had spent two years with them, he could handle this jaunt with his eyes closed.

Graves patted Joe on the back and returned to his preflight routine, so the rest of them locked up the hangar and piled onto the bird, stowing their packs and strapping in for the ride up to Santa Barbara.

Bennett went through the motions numbly. He'd been missing this for months. The rush of adrenaline, the application of skills he'd honed to deadly effect over the years—skills he knew the average person did not possess.

As he'd told Buck, however, today felt different. All he wanted was to bring Kim home.

Bennett closed his eyes and rested his head against the wall of the bird. The activity around him subsided as he reviewed the falling dominoes that had led them to this point.

Back at the warehouse, Buck had made his call and Noah had stayed glued to his monitors, downing energy drinks and tapping on his keyboards. It'd taken several minutes, but eventually he'd let out a shout of triumph. The kid had found a match for the limo's plate, dinged by a red-light camera in Santa Barbara, hours after Kim had been grabbed.

She was up there, too. Had to be.

With zero prompting, Noah had staged a call to the Landry Cox home office.

"*Yeah, hi—this is Kent Clark,*" he'd announced, affecting a nondescript drawl. "*I need to confirm the time of my meeting with Mr. Cox tomorrow. Reached out to him earlier, but I haven't heard back.*"

The receptionist had patched him through to Dan's assistant, who'd been understandably confused. "*I'm sorry sir, but there must be some mistake. Mr. Cox is in Los Angeles this week.*"

"*You're kidding. Maybe I wrote the day down wrong.*" Noah had paused, then asked, "*Y'all know where I can reach him? We gotta get this done—I'm heading overseas shortly, and it needs to happen before I go.*"

"*Of course, sir. If you'd like to leave me your number, I can—*"

"*Ma'am, with all due respect, I do not have time for the go-around. I'll call Dan directly if you don't mind.*"

"*I understand.*" She'd hesitated only a moment before coughing up the number.

The Mariposa Inn. *Bingo.*

Wyatt and Joe had returned shortly after, having found a server at Moonflower who remembered Dan and Kim, because Dan was a dick of memorable proportions, and Kim had seemed miserable and wasted by the time they'd left the restaurant.

The server had told them that anyone would've needed a few drinks to sit through forty minutes with Dan, but the woman hadn't ordered alcohol—only tea. She'd assumed Kim had popped a couple of pills instead, and had asked if she was famous.

Her bodyguards had had to pour her into her limo when they'd all left.

Bennett had seen the footage, but the thought had still made him sick with worry.

Buck had returned, full of plans, and fixed all of that. *"We've got transport. Let's go get her."*

ONCE THEY WERE airborne, Bennett caught Tom Monroe's eye across the aisle of the bird. "They drugged her," he told the doc. "Kim would never have gotten in that car without a fight, otherwise. Cox had to have known that."

Tom nodded, meeting Bennett's anxiety with a commensurate level of concern. "I can handle that," he assured him. "Though given the amount of time that's passed, most, if not all, of the usual suspects will have worn off. Hopefully they haven't re-dosed her, but does she have any underlying conditions? Comorbidities?"

Bennett shook his head. "I don't know. I don't think so. She works out regularly. Martial arts and running. Eats healthy, too."

To him, Kim was perfect no matter what she did. He hated not knowing the important stuff, though. He wanted to know. He *should* know.

"It's all good," Tom said, over the din of the rotors. "Whatever happens, I got her."

"Hooyah," Bennett murmured, but his heart wasn't in it.

Trust was not his strong suit, particularly with new people. He was only going along with the current version of the plan because he was desperate, and he trusted Buck implicitly.

His best friend trusted Monroe, however, and by extension, Monroe's other employees. That would have to do for now.

* * *

FINDING COX WAS easy. So easy, in fact, that he could not possibly have known they were coming.

They simply piled into the luxury SUV that had been left at the airfield for them, blending seamlessly into the tony Montecito streets, and then at the luxurious resort where Cox was hiding.

The Mariposa Ranch Inn sported plenty of vegetation, enabling them to comb the property discreetly. They discovered Dan in short order, getting sunburned on a chaise beside the pretty courtyard pool.

Alone.

They kept watch as he snored for an hour or more, blissfully unaware that he was surrounded by killers who wanted his heart on a platter.

Cox awakened only when a family arrived, and the kids started splashing in the water. He took a short dip in the deep end, then toweled off and meandered up to his room—third floor, overlooking the courtyard.

Based on Kim's stories, Bennett assumed the asshole had wanted a good view of any bikinis that might make an appearance. Otherwise, why not opt for the better ocean view?

There was still no sign of Kim as Tom went downstairs to reserve a room at the other end of the curving third-floor hall. They hunkered down and waited until they could set up inside the posh suite, where they waited some more—for their mark to leave again, or for Kim to make an appearance.

Bennett was seriously considering whether he could charm a maid into going in and looking around when Dan went on the move again, heading to the lobby, then folding himself into a low-slung black Porsche parked in the shady lot out back.

"Stitch and Bruiser, see where he goes," Buck said into his earpiece. When Bennett made to argue, he was met with a steely, "Nope. Not today."

"Fine. Then let me talk to the maid," Bennett said. "It'll be easier for her to poke around with Cox gone, anyway."

Buck only rolled his eyes and sighed. "Hold your horses. We're not bringing some housekeeper into this if we don't have to."

"But what if Kim's in there?" he argued, jabbing a finger toward Cox's room. "We could be in and out in—"

Buck held up a hand as Wyatt's voice crackled over the comm. "*We've got a plate number*," he said, then rattled off the digits for the Porsche.

Buck patched it to Noah, who'd been tasked with monitoring their movements back in his bunker.

So far, everything was progressing exactly according to the established plan. Bennett hated it.

"I don't like this," he complained. "If you weren't going to let me search his room, I should've taken point."

Buck had fielded this argument a few times already. He didn't bother explaining himself again, but he did point out, "It could be worse. You stuck *me* up on a hot roof when we had to babysit Peyton. At least you get A/C and a 50" flat screen."

The rebuke stung, but it was no more than the truth. This suite *was* better than a roof, and leagues better than some of the rocky caves they'd haunted in their day. Plus, if they slept in shifts, no one would even have to carpet surf.

Over the comm, Wyatt announced, "*Bruh. Why am I so hungry.*"

And there it was. Business as usual when Stitch was involved.

Tom chuckled and started poking at his phone. "There's a taco place that gets four and a half stars nearby." He looked at Buck. "You hungry, too?"

"I could eat."

"Shaw?"

Bennett was too antsy to eat, and he had MREs in his pack if that were to change.

He told Tom, "Nah, I'm good," and readjusted his earpiece. It was hard to tell if it was fritzing out or if he was just picking up on road noise.

Joe complained, "*I think this piece of shit already needs a charge. Every time I stop at a light it shuts down.*"

"*It's an energy-saving thing,*" Wyatt explained, "*for when you're idling. The button to turn it off is right there.*"

"So, yea or nay on the tacos?" Tom prodded. "It looks like they have it all. Barbacoa…al pastor…"

No one answered as Noah's voice cut in on the comms. "*Got a match on the plate you sent. It's a rental.*"

"I figured," Buck commented. "If you can, see if Cox rented it, or someone else."

Tom waited to make sure they were done, then continued his genial rambling. "My wife likes a good empanada, but I'm a pupusa man myself. Carnitas and pupusas, all day long."

Buck sighed, resigning himself to the conversation. "You been married long?"

"Couple years. We met at my brother's engagement party. Gunning for the same job," the medic laughed.

Bennett tilted his head, getting sucked in despite himself. "Who won?"

"We tied," Tom shrugged. "We banded together and got hired together. I'm telling you—it was love at first sight, man. She blew me away."

Joe pretended not to hear, griping loudly, "*Would you look at these places? Who the fuck lives like this?*"

"*Actors,*" Wyatt retorted.

"*No, I'm serious. This is some real one-percenter shit. They can't all be actors. What do these people do for a living?*"

"Okay, I'm ordering," Tom said. "Buck, what do you want?"

Buck stared at him for a beat or two, undoubtedly confused by the guy's ability to focus on anything other than the scouting mission unfolding over their comms. He glanced at Bennett, then said, "Uh…how about an al pastor platter? Do they have one with rice?"

"Yes."

"I'll take that."

Bennett focused on the street map glowing from the laptop, tracking the pulsing red dot representing Wyatt and Joe as it moved across town.

After a long, loaded pause, Buck said, "Get the same for him. Add on extra salsa verde and black beans if they have them."

"What about Joe?" Tom asked.

"He'll want anything that has potatoes."

Bruiser finally acknowledged them, warning, "That better not be an Irish joke."

The medic smirked. "Is that it?"

"Yes. Just…just get a bit of everything. It'll get eaten."

Bennett waited, but when that seemed to be the end of their exchange, he reluctantly gritted out, "What about Stitch."

"Shit, yeah," Buck agreed. "Order a carnitas platter and something sweet for Wyatt. Anything with chocolate or cinnamon will do the trick."

"Churros. Roger that." Tom moved deeper into the living area to place his call.

"*Okay, here we go,*" Wyatt announced a few minutes later. "*He's turning into a driveway.*"

Joe whistled in wonder. "*Whoa. That's a helluva nice place.*"

"*Looks like we got ten-foot concrete walls and another two feet of rail on top of that.*"

"*Helpful,*" Joe muttered.

"*Yep.*"

Suddenly, Bruiser blurted, "*And there he goes.*"

"*Remote-operated gate,*" Wyatt explained. "*Entered a code at a keypad on the pole. Visual on one guard as he pulled in.*"

"*Address is… 612 Mercato,*" Joe told them. "*I'm going to head up the block and turn around.*"

Buck pointed at Bennett. "Relay it to Noah. Get us the owner, and whatever surveys and permits have been filed with the city."

"*You want us to wait for Cox to come back out?*" Wyatt wondered.

"Can you get eyes inside the property?"

"Might be tricky. Not a lot of coverage out here. It'll be easier once it gets dark."

"Okay. Then stay on Cox until he leaves. See where else he goes."

"Copy."

Tom waited for a beat, then announced, "The food should be here in about twenty minutes. I'll go down to pick it up."

Bennett glared at him, irritated by his cheerfulness. It wasn't Tom's woman in harm's way, though—why shouldn't he want tacos?

Still, he couldn't help asking, "Aren't people going to wonder why one man needs that much food?"

The medic shrugged, unconcerned. "Maybe I like to entertain." Then he plopped on the couch and turned the TV on mute.

Bennett caught Buck's eye and shook his head. Two years, the man had spent on ops much more dangerous than this one. *Two years*, and none of his former coworkers had killed him yet.

Those Hendricks dudes must have had nerves of steel.

IT FELT LIKE it took forever for Dan to emerge from the estate once more. Wyatt and Joe tailed him to the drive-through of a burger place, then followed him back to the hotel.

In all that time, Bennett didn't think he'd breathed once. He'd somehow powered through his dinner, and had responded when spoken to, but all he could think about was Kim.

Was she truly inside those high walls, and if so, how was she faring? What had Dan said to her? What had he *done*, in the forty-five minutes he'd spent inside?

Or could she be steps away, down the hall in arm's reach, waiting for him to come free her?

Bennett closed his eyes and calmed his breathing. Settled his heart rate. Let all the noise flow away. But that only made room for a bigger question.

Once Kim was free…could Bennett be man enough to do right by her?

He had to try.

Chapter Twenty-Six

Kim

P*OP, TURN, DROP.* When that didn't work, Kim huffed in frustration and shook out her arms. She reset her feet and tried again. *Lock, turn, slide?* No, that wasn't it, either.

Why couldn't she remember the steps to her old recital dance? And why was that suddenly upsetting her so much?

Her deep fatigue wasn't helping her mood, that was for sure. She'd lain awake half the night worrying about Bennett, and what he had to be going through with her disappearance.

At least he had the benefit of friends to help him, though, to talk him through it, and figure out what to do.

He had his freedom, too.

Kim, on the other hand, was going stir-crazy, cooped up in this drafty house with nothing to do but think of ways to escape. If she tried to go outside, or even into the common areas, to break up the monotony, she was under the constant surveillance of Dan's hired lunkheads.

She stuck to her bedroom instead and did her scheming alone…while also trying to remember a dance routine from thirteen years ago.

She snorted at her foolishness, but what else was there? It wasn't like her babysitters would let her go for a run, or would procure a punching bag for her to kick the crap out of. They couldn't even find her a bar of soap. She had to do *something* to stay busy.

And so, here she was breaking and rolling her hips in the mirror over the bureau, as she'd been doing for an hour. She was getting it all wrong, but it felt good to move—to think about something other than Bennett torturing himself over her abduction, or how she was supposed to get out of Dodge without any ideas, resources, or help.

Kim tried another combination of moves that felt like she was on the right track, but before she could build on it, the door to her room swung open and Dan stepped in, bearing his usual arrogant smirk.

"Thinking of a career change?" he wondered. "'Cause you might need to augment a bit up top. If you catch my drift."

"I was doing *yoga*, Dan."

He rolled his eyes and gestured for her to follow him. "Come on. I brought you something."

Kim frowned as she trailed him into the living room. He looked too smug for this to be anything good.

Once she was seated, he dropped a brown bag on the table in front of her. "Open it," Dan said. "There's a salad and a protein smoothie in there."

As Kim unpacked those, he fetched another bag from the kitchen, announcing each thing he pulled from it before tossing them on the couch next to her.

"Soap. Shampoo. Toothbrush. Toothpaste. Socks. *Leggings*," he rattled off.

Kim plucked the pants off the pile and found the tag. They were a size too big for her, but that was better than too small. Wearing them would at minimum give her a chance to rinse out her underthings with the shampoo—ridiculous, lacy lingerie that was well suited to flashing one's lifelong crush on his birthday but, as it turned out, not so great for long-term hostage situations.

"Happy now?" Dan demanded.

"Thank you," Kim told him. "Though, I guess this confirms I'm not going anywhere anytime soon."

The sun was going down outside, marking three days, she thought, that he'd kept her here.

Dan shook his head as he sat across from her. "We've been over this. Tell me the truth and you can go home. To Dallas," he clarified when she looked up.

Kim went back to examining the stickers holding the food containers closed, trying to determine if they'd been tampered with. She really didn't want to be drugged again. She was only just starting to feel more normal.

"You never told me I could go home," she pointed out.

"You can if you start acting right. Fess up to what you told those pricks. Go home and don't contact them again. Easy as pie."

She put down the salad and stared at Dan. "And how do you expect to monitor or confirm any of that?"

"Leave that to me." His smile didn't reach his eyes and sent a chill snaking across her shoulders. Kim wished she hadn't left her sweater in her room.

"Dan," she tried again. "I don't know what you want me to say. I explained that Bennett is an old friend, and that we haven't discussed you. What would I even say? You and I went to a few parties together and that's about it. Be reasonable."

"If you didn't think you knew something, you wouldn't be out here," he countered.

Kim decided the salad looked safer than the shake and broke it open. "I came out here to get away from the reporters. You're being paranoid."

"Well, that's your fault, now isn't it?" he said. "I tried to go easy on you with Alix Hernandez. If you hadn't kept ducking her, I wouldn't have been forced to do this. So, you can blame yourself for your predicament."

Kim stared at him. How could she have missed how unhinged this man was? Had she ever paid attention to him at all? And how long, exactly, had she been going through the motions in her life?

"You want me to just…I don't know, make some stuff up? Because that's the only way I'm going to have anything to tell you," she said.

Dan snapped, smashing a fist on the table so hard it sent a pair of cherry tomatoes tumbling across the glass and Kim's heart stuttering into overdrive.

"Stop fucking around and tell me the goddamn truth!" he bellowed.

She was scared. It took her a minute to gather her composure and keep her voice steady.

"I'd love to know what your endgame is," Kim said. "Just…keep me in this big old house until I cave and say whatever the right thing is? And then put me on a plane so I can go home to my regular life like this never happened? You actually expect me—or my daddy, for that matter—to brush off a little kidnapping between friends?"

"You will if you know what's good for you."

She pinched a slice of cucumber between her fingers as she tried to think it through. If she hit on the secret password and Dan let her go, she could run right to the police. He would be arrested, and unable to follow through on his threats.

She thought. The problem was, Kim had no idea who else might be working with him, or how far his reach extended. Someone had provided this house for him to use, and Dan's stepfather had already managed to get four decorated Navy SEALs discharged on pretty dubious charges.

If Dan thought Kim knew something important enough for him to pull a stunt like this, then that knowledge, whatever it was, must be bigger than she'd imagined.

She had to slip him a partial truth, to buy herself some time.

"I…I had more copies of your bank statements," she told Dan. "The ones from when we broke up. I gave them to Bennett and his friends, but they just laughed at me. They said there were no laws against cheating."

Dan shot to his feet, his face turning even more florid in his anger. "You're lying," he hissed, then turned on his heel and stalked away.

He was gone. Again.

Kim was shaken by Dan's outburst. She bent to retrieve the tomatoes from the floor, so they wouldn't get stepped on and ruin the rug, then went to stand at the French doors, staring into the yard.

She didn't have a lot of options. If she told him the whole truth, Dan would be incensed, and she had no faith that he'd simply let her go without punishing her in some way. However, if she stayed the course she was on, he was likely to go further off the deep end, too.

Her only hope was to get away before things spiraled even more out of hand. But how?

Kim had yet to find a way to reach the outside world. As far as she could tell, her only option was one of the thugs' phones—but the men never appeared to use them, and they certainly never let her get close to one.

Had anyone reported her missing? Was Bennett already searching for her himself?

She bit her lip, remembering his incandescent grin as he'd joked with Wyatt about her stupid hip hop recital. She'd do anything to see that expression on his face again—to feel his arms around her, shielding her from the rest of creation.

Kim felt wooden, as she tried anew to remember those old moves. She probably looked stilted too.

She'd been mortified, she remembered abruptly, standing up on stage with the other girls. As they'd waited to begin, she'd noticed several kids she knew from school in the audience with their families. She'd thought she would never live down the embarrassment.

Her instructor had picked the censored version of a song that was a few years past the peak of popularity and had gone totally over the top with their costumes. Kim's mom had applied her stage makeup with a heavy hand, complaining that Kim would be utterly washed out by the harsh lighting otherwise.

Like she'd cared. Given a choice, she would've preferred to disappear entirely. Instead, she'd been a girl band cartoon, dying a painful social death in full view of all humanity.

But then, Bennett had slipped into the back of the auditorium, and leaned against the wall near the doors with his arms crossed over his chest.

Kim had been pinned in place by the weight of his shadowy gaze, but she would've known those broad shoulders and mop of golden hair anywhere.

Several of the boys in the audience had peeled away from their families and gone to orbit around him, but while they'd horsed around, Bennett had kept still—and his intense gaze had felt like a physical touch over the rows and rows of seats between him and Kim.

The music had begun, and something inside Kim had unlocked.

She'd danced for him and him alone, and no one—not her parents, who'd signed her up for that madness, or her instructor, who'd created that scandalous routine herself—could've accused Kim of indecency.

She'd done precisely what they'd expected of her, and she'd done it to perfection. Bennett's memory of it still remained crystal clear, all these years later.

She smiled to herself, shaking out her shoulders. Suddenly, her memory was spot-on too.

All at once, the opening steps of that long-ago dance came back to her. Kim rolled her shoulders and stretched her neck, humming the first bars of the song as she readjusted her footing.

Pop, lock, slide. Break, break, thrust. She had it now.

Watching her reflection in the tall windows, she ran through the moves of the routine, singing softly so she could keep the beat.

Outside, the sun had set. Aside from a few tiny lights tucked into the landscaping, the back yard was mostly dark, stretching beyond the pool to a rise at the far end.

Last night, from her bedroom window, Kim had noticed a subtle glow emanating from behind that rise—like there was a streetlamp or another house giving off light back there. And where there was civilization, there was help.

It felt like as good a destination to try for as any.

The white stucco wall that surrounded the property was maybe an acre or more away at that point. It was much too high to climb on either side of the house, but back there, next to the hill, it was shorter. Maybe even scalable, if she got a running start and could find something to help propel her up and over.

Kim started over and moved lightly through the steps of the dance a second time, remembering most of them now that the beginning had surfaced in her brain. She faltered only when she noticed a couple of her guards reflected in the glass doors, watching her from the kitchen.

Ew. After her dustup with Dan, Kim was in no mood to challenge them. She simply stopped dancing and pulled open the French doors to let in the cool evening air.

The feel of their eyes on her back was not so easily dispensed with, however. She grabbed the salad and dug a fork out of the bag, then went to sit at the table on the patio outside.

Kim doubted they'd stop her. Even though they couldn't see her as well now, they always had at least one buddy patrolling the yard.

For now, that guy wasn't in sight. Kim stabbed at the romaine and examined what she could see of the back wall. There were a few small trees back there, with low spreading branches. From this distance in the dark, it was hard to estimate whether the branches would hold her, or if she'd be able to get a good foothold.

When the time came, she'd need to allow plenty of time to sprint back there, climb a tree so she could grab the railing at the top of the wall, and swing herself over.

How to get rid of the hired muscle for long enough to do it, though? And who knew what she'd find on the other side? If the drop was too far, she could break a leg on impact.

That would get her exactly nowhere. She needed to be smart and wait for the right moment.

She peeked over her shoulder, but the two men in the kitchen had disappeared. And all at once, a third one burst out of the shadows to her right, not sparing her a glance as he tore full tilt toward the front yard.

There was…a commotion of some kind, drawing her watchers away from her.

There might be more men in the yard around her, but there might not. There was only one way to find out.

Kim shot to her feet and looked between the house and the back wall. Then she stepped out of her sandals and took off.

Chapter Twenty-Seven

Bennett

W E'VE GOT AT least two guards inside," Buck reported, from his position at the front wall. "They're moving toward the back of house now."

"One patrolling the north side," Wyatt responded.

Bennett squinted through his scope at the swanky estate Cox kept visiting. "Another lurking back here. That's four."

"Any sign of Kim?" Buck wondered.

"Not yet," Stitch said softly. "Found the office and going in."

This had been designed as a scouting op, but given the low-grade defenses they'd encountered so far, Bennett wondered if they might be able to grab Kim tonight. He sent a silent plea heavenward and refocused on his part of the job.

Panning his weapon, he sighted Joe through the scope, scaling a drainpipe on the opposite side of the sprawling Mediterranean home.

"Need a minute to get upstairs," Bruiser murmured through the comm. "It's like someone greased this shit."

Bennett had landed the sniper job for the evening—or, more accurately, the spotter job. He was positioned on the small rise overlooking the back of the property, presumably far enough away to not screw shit up.

He'd been tasked only with keeping track of the outside guards, and as he lay there watching events unfold, he reflected that, on nearly any other mission, he might've simply picked those fuckers off. Bennett was on U.S. soil, however, and no longer under the protection of the SEALs.

Not to mention, this wasn't a warzone, and popping a couple of heavies in the chest could land him behind bars. He'd already vowed fifteen years ago to never end up there again, so he eased his finger further from the trigger and swung his sight to the left a few degrees.

Buck was right where he was supposed to be, silently making his way over a section of the front wall shielded by flowering vines, nothing more than a wraith in the green glow of Bennett's scope.

He was scanning the yard again when a burst of motion caught his eye, smaller than a person and moving low to the ground.

"*Shit.* You got dogs," he reported.

He hoped Buck had the tranq darts ready. The animals were streaking through the dark, beelining for the spot where his buddy's boots were about to hit dirt, and Bennett really did not want to have to take out such capable creatures.

"I count two incoming," he murmured into the comm at his shoulder, "In five, four, three…"

Buck jumped free of the vine and whipped the dart gun from his vest, dropping the pups before they could rip into him.

Bennett exhaled and checked on the outside guards. They didn't appear to have heard anything. They were still in position, such as it was, but seemed lazy and inattentive—no better than a couple of bouncers at the end of a long shift.

These weren't professionals. Not even close. *Good.*

His shoulders relaxed a little. As ops went, this was a cake walk. They were sure to find Kim in no time and so far, he'd seen no reason not to pull her out tonight. His heart did a little double step of hope.

Bennett drew in a long, slow breath and let it out even slower. He was getting ahead of himself. He had one job right now, and that was to have eyes on the team's six as they ducked in, got a visual of the house's interior, and ducked out again.

They'd plan for Kim's safe extraction only after they had all the information they needed.

Bennett was right and tight, now. More than Buck had been, certainly, when they'd set up outside Peyton's house a few months ago, hoping to catch the assholes harassing her.

On that mission, Buck had been tasked with the same job Bennett held tonight and had been warned to keep clear if shit hit the fan. Instead, his buddy had jumped into the fray mere moments after go-time.

Bennett rolled his eyes.

That was not going to be him. Emotion had not ruled his actions in a long-ass time, and it would not do so tonight. He was cold and lethal. A finely honed, dependable weapon.

He refused to get stressed as the team's voices ping-ponged back and forth on the comm, coming up empty again and again as they searched for Kim inside those perfect, white-washed walls.

They were beginning to run out of time.

Bennett swept the back of the house with his scope and finally, *finally*, spotted their objective himself. Kim was dancing, popping and locking inside a pair of French doors bordering the large rear patio.

Popping. And locking. *What the fuck?*

"Subject located," he announced, as if the woman in question didn't comprise his entire universe. "Ground floor, in the back. She's in the living room off the kitchen."

It felt oddly illicit, watching her like this, as if Bennett was hidden in a dark theater, and Kim was putting on a peep show. He shifted uncomfortably.

She halted her incongruous routine suddenly, glancing over her shoulder and edging deeper into the room. A moment passed as she fetched something and then she came back, slipping outside to sit at the table, where she proceeded to…

"She's eating…a salad. On the patio," he told the team. Because, sure, that made perfect sense.

Bennett's heart took another weird stutter step, and his traitorous brain told him that maybe Kim was there of her own volition. Maybe she hadn't been taken—maybe she'd left.

Left *him*, for all the obvious reasons.

Tom cut in for the first time, though, to ask, "How is her affect? Does she still look drugged?"

Right. No one drugged themselves so they could go wallow under the watchful eye of four goons, palatial estate or not. Particularly his feisty Kim.

Bennett watched her pick at the food and had the eeriest sense that she was peering right at him. Her expression was sharp. Alert. "She looks okay," he responded with relief.

Kim looked like sunrise and meadows of bluebonnets. Through his scope, she seemed close enough to kiss.

There was a thump over the comm, and then Buck hissed, "*Motherf*—"

A flurry of scuffling. Joe barked, "Sitrep."

"Need some backup here," Wyatt answered, breathing hard.

Bennett swung his scope away from Kim to sweep the yard. The guard closest to him was racing for the front yard.

"Buck, I got a guy heading your way," he reported. "Watch your six."

"Terrific. The more the merrier."

Bennett checked on Kim. She'd gotten to her feet and was looking nervously between his position and the house, like a filly ready to bolt.

A split second before she started moving, he recognized why her clothes were bothering him. She was still wearing the same dress she'd had on when she met Cox, days ago.

No one had given her anything warmer, anything clean, and the thought made him abruptly, incandescently furious.

Bennett didn't have time to dwell on it. With one last look into the house, Kim kicked off her sandals and took off.

Right for him.

"That's right, honey. Come to Daddy," he murmured, urging her on.

Kim was athletic and she was fast, but she was also barefoot, and it was too dark to see well. Once she got past the light spilling from the house, she slowed way down, picking her way across the terrain like a cat burglar when he needed her to sprint.

Bennett didn't want to tip off her captors by telling her that, however.

"Faster, baby," he urged softly.

Joe cut in, with razor-sharp irritation. "Who the fuck are you talking to?"

Bennett jumped, startled out of his hyperfocus on Kim. "Subject on the move. Headed for my position," he replied.

While Kim tiptoed through the grass, Bennett swung his scope across the lawn, covering her escape. One of Cox's jackwad bodybuilders was jogging around the side of the house, on a trajectory that would intersect hers if she didn't pick up the pace.

Oh, hell nah.

He dropped out of his perch in the neighbor's tree and slid down the scree on the side of the hill, hitting the wall between the properties with both boots and levering himself over like this was the goddamn Houston Rodeo.

He tore across the manicured lawn and dove, tackling Cox's thug around the waist and forcing him to the ground. The fucker never saw it coming. Bennett had him facedown with a forearm wrapped around his windpipe before he could form a thought, pressing as hard as he dared to put the dude to sleep.

Once he was out, Bennett looked around for Kim. She'd heard the tussle and redirected—but now she was heading back *toward* the brawl in the house, instead of away from it.

She was running scared, and Bennett's heart stopped in his chest when she ducked and covered a second after an errant shot zinged too close. Yelping, she changed direction again, heading for him once more.

"Hold your fire!" he hollered into his comm.

"Tell that to Popeye over here," Wyatt retorted.

Bennett scrambled for Kim and snatched her off her feet, hauling her toward the small copse of avocado trees in the back corner of the yard. She let out outraged squawk and fought mightily, enough that he was forced to press his palm against her mouth and pin her close to his chest.

She was trembling hard. "Shhh. Calm down, Kimmie," he murmured against her ear. "Okay? It's me, Bennett."

"B…Ben?" her sweet voice quavered.

He pushed back his night-vision goggles long enough to kiss her cheek, then tipped up her chin so he could meet her wild gaze. With a finger to his lips, he led her behind the knot of trees, to the spot where the wall was lowest.

Bennett crouched and urged her onto his shoulders, then lifted Kim so she could grab the railing and haul herself up. As he scaled the wall after her, he licked his lips and noted with a twinge of anxiety that her cheek must've been wet with tears when he'd kissed her.

Except…that wasn't salt he was tasting, he realized. It was copper.

Kim was bleeding.

"You okay, honey?" He scanned the neighbor's yard, then dropped into the flowerbed below. "Here, step down on my shoulders."

Kim set her feet where he showed her, but her knees buckled, and she tumbled hard to the ground.

"I'm fine," she said quickly.

"Okay, you're good," he told her, and hauled her upright. "I gotcha." She blinked up at him, wide-eyed in the faint moonlight.

"You found me," she whispered. "I couldn't tell you where I was. But you still found me."

"Damn straight," he agreed. "I'm sorry it took me so long." Into his comm, Bennett reported, "Subject acquired. Moving to rendezvous."

"B…Bennett. I need to tell you."

"Come on, honey, we gotta move boots. You need me to carry you or are you okay?"

"I can do it."

"That's my girl. Let's go."

He kept to the shadow of the privacy wall, picking through flowerbeds until Kim's hiss of pain stopped him in his tracks.

Shit. She was barefoot.

"Sorry," he whispered in red shame. He quickly shifted his pack to the front and beckoned her, "Here, get on my back. I'll have us out of here before you know it."

Kim clambered on without a word and Bennett took off, jogging toward the opening between the driveway gate and the towering shrubs that bordered it on either side.

With a sigh, Kim sagged heavily against him, her cheek resting against his neck.

Still wet.

"Y'all, we got a situation here," he barked into his comm. "We're gonna need a medic sooner, rather than later. I'm redirecting to Bravo pickup. Doc, meet us there."

To Kim, he instructed, "Hang on tight, girl. Once we squeak through this gap right here, I'm gonna pick up the pace and get you some help, fast as I can."

Kim hunched around his shoulders as Bennett shoved through the break in the landscaping. He hoped the branches wouldn't scrape her exposed skin too badly. She had nothing covering her arms, and her face and legs were bare, too.

"I'm okay," she said, but Bennett would believe that only once Doc Tom had confirmed it.

Tom had stayed at the hotel to keep an eye on Cox but at Bennett's command, the medic cut in, "Heading out. Please confirm."

Buck gasped, like he was running hard. "Roger that. Clear out the room and pick up Easy and his date. We'll meet you at the airfield."

From his warehouse bunker down in San Diego, Noah registered that command loud and clear. "I'll radio Graves," he piped in. "He'll be ready on your say-so."

Bennett tucked his chin and jogged a little faster. He didn't know what Kim had been through these last few days, and he didn't want to jostle her too much—but her silence was troubling.

He'd expected her to come out spitting fire, indignant about Dan holding her hostage and spoiling for the jerk's blood. Instead, she was like a ragdoll draped on his back, loose-limbed and voiceless.

He could feel her blood in his collar, and visions of her fading out before he could get her to safety slithered through his brain like insidious vines, spurring him on.

Tom cut in on the comm, "Room cleared. Heading to the truck. Rendezvous in ten." Quick footsteps rang out on the flagstones of the hotel hallway. And then, in the background a man called, "*Hold the door!*"

Bennett frowned, straining to hear what the man and his female companion were saying. There was some static as the elevator doors slid closed and then, clear as crystal, the woman giggled, "*…come with us?*"

The elevator dinged as it passed a floor. Doc Tom chuckled awkwardly. "*Love to, but I'm afraid I've got a plane to catch.*"

"*Leave him be*," the man chuckled, and Bennett scowled harder at the familiar cadence of that voice. It said to Tom, "*Two drinks, and that one brain cell of hers just ups and leaves.*"

"*You two stay out of trouble*," Tom called as the elevator door opened and his rapid footfalls carried him away.

There was a beat of silence as the team processed the exchange. Noah was the one to break it. "Was that who I—"

"Fucking Dan Cox!" Tom hissed in a rush. "What are the odds? I almost got a tracker on that asshole, too, but his girlfriend was handsy as hell. Guy's got some interesting taste, man."

"*Careful*," Bennett warned.

"Wonder if that one knows how Cox treats his exes," Wyatt commented.

"We'll never know," Buck fired back. "Now focus up. Let's get this shit done so we can get out of here."

After a couple of miles of steady jogging, Bennett finally broke from the darkened side street they'd been hustling down and spotted Tom, pulling into the empty lot behind the gas station they'd earmarked as their secondary rendezvous point. *Right on time.*

Bennett eased Kim to the ground and led her to the truck, but her footing was unsteady. Tom, to his credit, barely had the vehicle in park before he surged from his seat to help bundle her into the back. She didn't utter a word of complaint as the medic climbed in beside her and Bennett got behind the wheel.

He pulled out in a scatter of gravel, glancing into the rearview only long enough to see Kim trying to wipe the blood from her face and smearing it everywhere.

Frantic agitation sizzled along his nerve endings. Bennett clamped down on it and kept going. Getting Kim into the safest hidey-hole he could muster had to supersede his panic.

He routed the comm through the truck's sound system while he drove, so he could hear Tom and Kim murmuring in the back and still listen to what was going on back at the estate.

As Bennett careened around a corner, barreling toward the freeway onramp that would take them to the airfield in Santa Barbara, he heard Buck say, "*Comb the property for the girls.*"

Wyatt retorted, "*No one would be stupid enough to stash them here, but you're the boss.*"

"*Exactly*," Buck fired back, "*and I do not want to be the one to tell Rohaan that we met another dead end if I know we skipped something.*"

"*Listen, if they were stupid enough to grab Kim,*" Joe muttered.

"*That's fair.*"

After that, it was a series of dry, "*Hallway one clear, hallway two clear,*" announcements, but Kim didn't seem to register any of those.

No, as Bennett met her glazed eyes in the rearview once more, he knew it was the missing girl exchange that was going to stick with her, for better or worse.

Chapter Twenty-Eight

Kim

G RAZED BY A bullet."

As Tom, the medic, uttered his diagnosis, Kim tried to force herself to muster up a proper degree of horror. Wasn't that what you were supposed to feel when you were told such a thing?

All Kim felt was a strange, disconnected numbness.

Tom had stayed in the back seat with her while he worked on her cheek. He'd gently cleaned up her face and gotten it to stop bleeding, then cheerfully pronounced the wound shallow and unlikely to scar.

It didn't feel shallow. Before he'd numbed it and applied little adhesive stitches, it'd stung like a stripe of poisonous fire. Not that Kim would ever have admitted that to Bennett. His eyes looked wild enough as it was.

He felt miles away, brooding something fierce behind the wheel of the SUV as they raced hell-for-leather down the freeway. He checked on her frequently in the rearview mirror, but his expression was hard to decipher.

Was he angry? Scared? She had no idea.

Reports had been filtering in steadily from the operatives still at the estate, but he didn't seem to be paying them much attention. Kim tried, but her thoughts were too scattered to follow much of what was going on.

She could only imagine what she looked like. It'd been days since she'd had a shower or slept properly, days in which she'd felt nothing short of vile thanks to Dan's roofie infraction.

She hadn't expected she'd be making a break for it tonight, and certainly hadn't thought a team of SEALs would move in to rescue her at the exact moment she decided to run.

Kim might've donned those leggings and her sweater if she had.

Everything had happened so fast, though, and instead of processing her lucky escape, her brain was skipping around, lighting on this detail and that, and not making links between any of them.

Maybe that was why it took so long to realize something important was going on back at that Montecito estate— something bigger, perhaps, than getting her out of there.

"Dining room clear. No one on this floor. Moving to the lower level."

That one sort of sounded like Wyatt, though Kim hadn't seen anyone but Bennett and Dan's thugs on the grounds.

"Who are they looking for?" she asked.

Bennett's lashes flickered, but he stayed focused on his NASCAR routine and didn't answer her.

Kim turned to Tom. "Was someone else there besides me?"

He ducked his head, digging through his black medical bag to avoid her gaze. "I'm sorry. It's not my place to say."

"Bennett?" she tried again. "Who are they looking for?"

She got a response, just not a truthful one. "No one, honey. You just take it easy and let the doc take care of you."

"I thought I was alone there."

Bennett looked grim. "Looks like you were."

Tom extracted a salve that he carefully dabbed on her cheek, then covered everything with a bandage. He took Kim's vitals and pressed a water bottle into her hands once he was done.

"Drink it slow," he told her. "As much as you can stomach." He watched Kim until she'd downed half of it.

Over the radio Wyatt whistled, *"Damn, that's a lot of bottles."* It was definitely him—Kim was sure of it, now.

After a short pause, Joe's distinctive accent reported, *"Wine cellar clear. That's all of it. Those kids aren't here, man."*

Bennett stared at the road in front of them, a troubled frown marring his brow.

"Bennett Shaw," Kim demanded, her voice cracking a little with concern.

He sighed, a heavy, exhausted sound. "Later, okay? I'll fill you in later. Right now, we got bigger fish to fry."

She swallowed and wondered if he'd really follow through. "I think they still have my purse there somewhere. Can you ask the guys to look for it? I don't want to lose my ID and cards and what not."

Bennett snorted at her rapid pivot, but he relayed the request.

"Thank you," she said.

He nodded. Kim clutched her hands around the bottle in her lap to still their shaking.

After a while, a voice she didn't recognize cut in, *"Monroe is reaching out to his contacts on the force. He wants us to babysit these fools while MPD decides what to do."*

Kim assumed that meant the men who'd been guarding her. Who else could it be?

Joe muttered, presumably to the goons, *"Long time no see. Thought we made it clear last time—we didn't want to bump into you jokers again."*

"Fuck off."

"So is stunt-double work not what it used to be, or are you guys just assholes?" Wyatt prodded.

"Oh, they're definitely assholes," Kim confirmed.

Bennett peeked at her again and shook his head, but a whisper of a smile twitched his lips. The glimmer of emotion—of connection—was enough.

Kim closed her eyes and let the hum of the road lull her to sleep.

IT TOOK A while for the rest of the team to finish with the cops, and longer still when Joe insisted on arranging veterinary care for some dogs they'd apparently encountered during Kim's rescue.

As Bennett exited the freeway and Kim listened to the back and forth on the radio, she wondered where the animals had been kept. She hadn't seen or heard them once.

They followed a series of access roads to a small airfield, then wound through it until they reached the far back corner of the property. Bennett parked in the deep shadow of a hangar and went to check in with a pilot checking over the helicopter on the tarmac.

Tom led Kim to a small office inside the hangar to wait for the others.

The night was cool, and alive with small sounds she couldn't place. She was happy to be inside, under the strong electric lights. She had to press her fingers against the hard metal bench to anchor herself, because nothing seemed quite real.

Tom fussed over her, shining his little flashlight into her eyes and taking Kim's vitals again. Bennett returned with a pack from the truck and switched her water bottle with some kind of sports drink.

Kim felt like she was wrapped in cotton batting, thick enough to filter out sound and sensation. By the time anything reached her, it felt dulled and remote.

She might've slept. Bennett and Tom were watching her strangely, but she was saved from having to ask why by the chaotic, overloud arrival of the rest of the team.

In the ensuing swirl of activity and shouted orders, Wyatt's cheerful face swam into focus in front of hers. "Hey, girl. You ready to get out of here?"

Kim nodded. Wasn't that obvious?

He smiled and backed away, tearing into a protein bar someone tossed him. She grabbed for his arm. "Wait—did you guys find my purse?"

"Of course," he grinned, cocky as ever. "I can't give it to you, though. We've got it sealed up in case they bugged it again. You can have it back once Noah looks it over."

"I lost your hat," she mumbled. "I'm sorry. I meant to have Bennett tell you to look for it while you were going through the house." Kim frowned, trying to think. "I'm not sure it was there, though."

"*Pshh*. Don't worry about it," Wyatt said, waving her off. "Those things are a dime a dozen. I can get another, no sweat." He finished off his snack and tossed the wrapper into the trash can like it was a game-winning dunk.

"I'll replace it," Kim insisted. "You might need it one of these days."

"What I need is some coffee," Joe yawned, stalking past. "What time is it, anyway?"

"It's late," Tom commented, from beside her on the bench. "What you really need is some rest."

Joe stopped in his tracks and fixed the medic with a baleful stare. "Gee, Doc, I'd love that. If only it was that easy."

"You have trouble sleeping?"

Wyatt hefted a pack onto his shoulder and snorted as he headed toward the hangar doors. "That's an affirmative."

Tom looked back to Joe. "Is that true?"

"I do alright," he shrugged.

"Do you have nightmares? Or anxiety?"

"What I have, is shit to do. And so do you," he told Wyatt, pulling him a few more steps toward freedom.

"All I'm saying is, you might be shooting yourself in the foot with so much caffeine," Tom called, getting to his feet. "Have you tried chamomile tea at night, instead?"

"Allergic." Joe bent to grab a pile of gear near the door.

Kim watched in fascination as Tom moved a little closer. "Okay, what about valerian root?"

"Made my tongue itchy."

The doctor was dialed in, intent on his subject. "There's a guy on the other team that crochets to help cope with his PTSD. That and knitting work a lot like meditation for some people."

Joe glared, fed up with Tom's efforts. "Do I look like a fucking grandmother to you?"

"Hey. That's enough of that," Wyatt chided.

"There are apps you can get on your phone," the medic persisted. "For meditation, yoga…even tai chi."

"Thank you, Captain Obvious. I've never heard of those."

"Then I'm sure you know there are also prescriptions that can help you. Do want me to get you information about them?"

Joe glanced toward Kim, then disappeared outside. Wyatt gestured for Tom to back off.

The medic relented graciously, but told him, "Get him to come see me in a few days. I can check him out and help, I promise."

Wyatt peeked at Kim, then nodded. "I'll see what I can do."

She watched him join Joe outside, where they began loading gear into the helicopter with practiced efficiency. The rotors on top began to spin hypnotically.

Round and round and round.

She jumped out of her skin when Bennett popped up beside her and squeezed her shoulder.

"Hey," he murmured, ducking to follow her line of sight. "We're gonna head out soon, okay?"

"Is Joe alright? Everyone seems worried about him."

"Bruiser?" Bennett watched his roommates for a long moment, and admitted, "Probably not. But he will be. We're gonna take care of it."

Buck ducked his head in the doors and let out an ear-splitting whistle. "We're cleared for takeoff. Giddy up."

Bennett helped Kim to her feet, led her outside, and guided her into the helicopter. He directed her to a spot near the front of the craft, on a bench lining the wall, then buckled her into the harness like he would a child.

Once he was strapped in beside her, she rested her head against his solid shoulder and closed her eyes. The helicopter lifted into the air and banked around, and Kim had to press her hand to her mouth as all the water in her stomach threatened to surge up her throat.

Their trajectory smoothed out quickly, however, and soon there was nothing but the steady beat of the rotors, Bennett's team making plans for when they landed, and Bennett's warm and dependable arm around her.

When Kim's eyes opened again, Buck was across from her, checking his phone. "Boss says law enforcement and Dr. Sutherland have now been apprised that Kim has been removed to a secure location with protective detail," he announced.

Careful not to dislodge her, Bennett faced his friend. "I need clearance to disclose our full mission. Enough is enough," he said quietly. "Telling Kim half the story got her kidnapped, and I am not going to wait around for the Doggetts to come up with something worse for next time."

He hadn't divulged everything? Well, that was interesting.

"I agree, and so does Monroe," Buck told him. "Once you have her secure, give her the rundown."

"Thanks, man."

They bumped fists, like she wasn't sitting right there listening.

Kim elbowed Bennett's side. "Did you tell Shannon yet?"

He tilted his head toward her. "We'll do it once we land."

Buck whistled to get everyone's attention. "Noah tracked the Porsche to a rental agency near the airport, but that's as far as he got. Cox hasn't been seen since—no flights, no car rentals, nothing."

Kim thought about the voices from the hotel elevator. "Maybe that woman he was with took him somewhere," she suggested.

Buck nodded. "Could be, but wherever he is, he's laying low. The news outlets are already reporting that law enforcement is seeking him in the alleged kidnapping of his ex-girlfriend, socialite

Kimberley Sutherland. Wanna bet the MPD has a leak at their HQ?"

"Has Senator Doggett made a statement yet?" Tom wondered.

"Yes, and it's a doozy. He and Lena canceled a few events and said that they hadn't spoken to Dan in a couple of weeks, but they're sure this is a misunderstanding. They also have faith that law enforcement will find their son quickly and get him to safety, and bring the true perpetrators to justice."

Everyone sat in stunned silence for a minute or two, until Bennett whistled softly. "A lot to unpack there. Puts a little distance between themselves and Dan, yet manages to leave room for a P.R. spin, too."

"Those fuckers," Joe growled. "Not an ounce of shame."

"Think about it, though. If that's going to be their game with Cox gone to ground, we need an airtight plan to get Kim off the grid," Wyatt said. "Right now."

Bennett peeked at her and nodded. "Done. I'm taking her to a campsite I know in Ojai. I've already reserved it and texted Noah what we'll need."

Across the aisle, Joe leaned his elbows on his knees and drilled them with an intense frown. "Not exactly her speed."

"I beg your pardon," Kim snapped, offended. "Bennett knows exactly what my speed is. And don't talk about me like I'm not right here listening."

Wyatt grinned at her, and Buck's eyes twinkled with amusement.

"First of all, that's why this plan is so perfect. Based on her public persona, no one will think to look for her there. And second of all, Kimmie can handle it. Can't you, darlin'?" Bennett asked with a laugh.

"With my hands tied behind my back," she retorted, mustering bravado she wasn't sure she felt yet.

Bennett saw right through her, but he knocked his shoulder against hers as if he didn't. "That's my girl."

AN ATTRACTIVE YOUNG man met them at the airfield in San Diego, waiting next to a handful of vehicles with his arms full of small parcels and bags arranged around his feet.

Once they'd disembarked and gathered their gear, he rapidly distributed what he had with short bursts of instructions.

Eventually, he came to a stop in front of Kim. Bennett introduced him warmly. "This is Noah. He helped out on your birthday, remember? He's like our one-man command central."

"I remember." Kim stuck out her hand, then retracted it when Noah fumbled his remaining packages, trying to free up his own hand. "It's nice to finally meet you in person."

He adjusted his glasses and took a minute to sort through his things, before smiling and deciding on which one to hand her. "Likewise. Here, you can use this for now. It's secure and I've preloaded it with a few numbers. We'll still have to run through a couple extra steps before we can restore all your contacts and stuff, but it should do for now. Sound good?"

Kim accepted the new phone gratefully. "Yes, thank you." When she realized it was the same model as her stolen phone, she relaxed even more. Someone in the group had been paying attention, and she had a good guess as to who.

"Everything is password protected. Unlock it with *wagoner2*. All lowercase," Noah continued. He smiled again. "Get it? Like that roadhouse you went to for your birthday?"

"Got it," she smiled back. At least he'd picked something memorable.

Noah turned to Bennett. "I tried tracing the property records for the estate, but it's held under a shell company. It might take a minute to dig past that, but I'll keep at it."

"Thanks, man."

He shrugged, then went on, "Next up. Kim, I need you to call Sherri at the Birnbaum gallery and designate Kenya Johnston to pick up your painting. Sherri needs it out of there for an upcoming show, but we can store it safely until you're ready for it."

Kim darted a glance at Bennett, startled that her purchase was apparently open knowledge now. His expression didn't give anything away, however, and Noah was waiting.

"You mean right now?" she hedged.

"If you don't mind. They're closed, but you can leave her a message."

With another peel at Bennett, she dialed the number Noah rattled off, and when Sherri's voicemail picked up, Kim's mouth started babbling on autopilot.

"Hey, Sherri, this is Kim Sutherland. I'm so sorry for missing our appointment the other day. I got bit by a dog on my run that morning and had to go to the ER for a rabies shot and a couple of stitches."

She took a breath, remembered that she had a few *days*—not a few hours—to account for, and added, "I had a bad reaction to the shot, though, so I've been laid up for a bit. Also, I had to get a new phone. Anyway, I know you need that thing out of there, so I'm going to send my friend Kenya Johnston to come pick it up, okay? She can be there, uh—"

Kim looked to Noah, who mouthed, *tomorrow, one o'clock.*

"—tomorrow. Let's say one o'clock. Call me at this number if that doesn't work, all right? And again, thanks for everything." She disconnected the call, a little breathless from the stream-of-consciousness explanation.

Bennett's eyebrows were nearly at his hairline. "A dog bite? Seriously?"

"It was the first thing that came to me!" she protested. "I was going to go with snake, but that seemed a little farfetched for downtown San Diego."

"More accurate, though." He turned her toward the group shuttling gear from the helicopter to the vehicles. "Hey, Tom? Any chance you can look this lovely lady over one more time before we take off?"

Tom smiled and waved her closer, while Noah took Bennett to review the supplies he'd procured for their camping trip.

Soon, Kim and Bennett were splitting off from the group in a clean, comfortable SUV, stocked to the gills with God only knew what. Knowing Bennett, he'd prepared for a zombie apocalypse, and then some.

He was quiet as they followed the roads leading out of town, winding into the dark canyons that would bring them to his super-secret hideaway. It wasn't until they'd left civilization behind that he broke his silence.

"Kim, what were you thinking?" he finally demanded, his voice shaking in his effort to stay calm. "You could've been hurt." His eyes skipped to the bandage on her cheek. "Hurt worse, I mean. Way worse."

Kim sighed, tired to her very bones. "I was thinking that I didn't want to stay at that establishment any longer," she tried to joke. "No Wi-Fi. No TV. And the complimentary breakfast stunk."

"That was not a hotel, darlin', and that was not what I was asking."

"One star," she prattled on, "and that's for the landscaping."

She hated how her voice cracked. Now that they were alone, it was much harder to pretend she hadn't been stretched beyond her limits over the last few days, but especially the last few hours.

Bennett noticed. With the preternatural way he read people, that was to be expected. He lifted her hand and watched her fingers tremble, then pulled it to his mouth to kiss her softly.

"Getting a little shocky there, honey," he murmured. "But don't worry—it's just the adrenaline wearing off. I've got you now, and we'll be there before you know it. You're safe and you're going to stay that way."

Kim leaned her face against the cool glass of the window and tried to laugh. "Even you can't promise me that."

"I can and I do. From now on, I'm not going to let you out of my sight." Bennett squeezed her thigh, then ran his hand back and forth, stroking her leg until her breathing evened out and her eyes got heavy.

"Need to close my eyes," she murmured after a while. "You're not going to pass me off to someone else while I'm sleeping, are you?"

"Not a chance."

Before she let sleep pull her under, Kim admitted quietly, "I wanted to make your birthday special. That's why I did it. That's what I was thinking."

"Special wasn't the half of it," Bennett pointed out. "Next time bake a cake."

Chapter Twenty-Nine

Bennett

KIM SLEPT FITFULLY through the night, but that could've had more to do with sharing a drafty tent with an oversized SEAL than it did trauma from her kidnapping.

In any case, Bennett was relieved that she looked better in the light of day. The soft morning sun diffused the smudges under her eyes, and she seemed to have shaken off the disorientation she'd exhibited after her escape.

While she lingered over her cup of tea, Bennett surveyed their setup and let himself relax the smallest fraction. They'd be set for days out here—maybe longer. In addition to the tent, Noah had procured them a full complement of camping gear and a variety of food that was safely locked in the truck.

There'd be no pressure to leave, and no one would find them before Kim got her feet under her. Once she did, however, Bennett would need to learn what kind of dirt she had on Dan Cox. Whatever it was, it was obviously important enough to drive the guy to kidnapping, and therefore likely to be pertinent to the mission at hand.

After Cox was rounded up by the authorities, Bennett could return Kim to civilization with no one the wiser, and rejoin the team's efforts to unearth the truth behind the Nabarut ambush.

With the plan reaffirmed in his mind, he sat near the fire and urged the flames higher. Kim wandered over to join him.

"You're sure you're okay with this?" he wondered, eyeing her cautiously. "I know I didn't check with you first, and I don't want you to think I took liberties."

Kim quirked a perfect brow at him. "Personal liberties?"

"N…no," he sputtered. "Mission liberties."

She snorted. "Oh, that's so much better."

Yeah, Kim was fine now.

Bennett got comfortable and fired off a salvo of his own. "I'd be careful there, Miss Sleeps-Like-an-Octopus. If I were a different guy, I might accuse you of trying to take a liberty or two, yourself."

"I can appreciate a fine male form academically," she said, full of starch, "Without it having to be sexual."

"Nice try," he scoffed, "But you were wrapped around me like a vine, and two steps from humping my brains out."

"Academically, though."

"Have it your way," Bennett chuckled, rifling through the bag near his feet to find the instant coffee he'd asked Noah to pack. "Just don't run to your daddy and try to tell him I kidnapped you, too."

"I won't." Kim settled into the other chair and watched him as he set about boiling more water.

"Bennett…listen, I can't remember if I said it last night," she said, "but thank you for breaking me out of Posh Prison. I don't know what I would've done without you."

He smiled at her descriptor. "Kimmie, let's be clear—you broke yourself out. I only scooped you up so you wouldn't have to run too far."

She shook her head. "How'd you find me, anyway?"

"We pulled some security footage from downtown and got a partial plate on that limo. Noah was also able to track your phone to Dan, who led us to the estate. We were only supposed to be doing recon last night. Checking to see if you were there."

"Ah." Kim sat back and sipped at her tea, her eyes unfocused as she thought about his explanation. "Dan said he's been tracking my phone, too. Guess I need to change my passwords more often."

"You mean the password with my old football number in it?"

She winced. "Could've let that sleeping dog lie."

"And miss a chance to make you blush?" Bennett grinned. "I think not."

Kim sighed and stretched out her legs, then looked around wistfully. "This is nice. It almost feels like old times, doesn't it?"

"I don't recall you being quite this much trouble back then," he teased. "That must've developed after I left."

She rolled her eyes, but her mood stayed light. "How'd you know about this place? Do you hunt out here?"

He tasted the bitter brew in his cup, grimaced, and chugged the rest for the caffeine hit, if not the taste. "Nah," he told her, absently kicking at the dirt. "I don't do that anymore."

"You used to love it."

Bennett sighed wearily. "Yeah, well—hunting kind of lost its allure. What I did on the Teams was enough to last me a lifetime. Trust me when I say, it's different when it ain't critters."

Kim cupped her tea carefully and searched his face. "I believe that."

He looked away from the sympathy in her eyes and shrugged. He'd made his choices. He didn't regret them. Most, anyway.

She cleared her throat and blurted, "Hey, so—are you ever gonna tell me what really happened to make you leave Respite? Or are you gonna let me keep speculating until the end of time?"

Bennett blew out a long breath, though he shouldn't have been surprised. Kim had always been direct, and that topic was one she seemed exceptionally intent on.

God only knew why.

"Let's have something to eat," he told her, hedging. "I need to fill you in on everything that's gone on with the Doggetts, and what our full mission is. After that..." He got to his feet and headed for the truck, where most of their supplies were stashed. "After that, if you still want to know, I'll tell you."

His stomach lurched at the thought, but who was he kidding? The truth was bound to see the light of day sooner or later, and Bennett would be damned before he let an untidy secret put Kim in jeopardy again.

He just hated knowing how it would dim the light in her pretty eyes, sure as the sun set in the west. But again, like he hadn't known that was coming, too?

"All righty, then," Kim told him, settling into her chair. "You have a deal. Lay it on me."

Bennett grabbed a couple of bags and carried them over to the fire, then set them in the dirt near her feet. As he knelt next to her, he pulled out the fixings for her breakfast.

"Listen. Kimmie," he said carefully, "what I'm about to tell you…you cannot tell a soul. You understand? Not Shannon, not your parents, not even your therapist. No one."

She rolled her eyes in amusement. "I don't have a therapist."

"That's funny, given how obsessed you are with me seeing one."

"Bless your heart," she murmured, shaking her head. "You are salty. Just spit it out, already."

Bennett melted some butter in a pan, then cracked a few eggs in it. She had no idea what she was saying. Once he was done talking, Kim was going to wish she had three shrinks on speed dial.

He started his story anyway. "How much did you follow about what went down with us last year?"

"Read everything I could get my hands on." She pulled a bag closer and found them some bread and a pair of tongs, and began toasting slices over the fire.

"Good. Then you know how Al Kadir—that's the Qahati warlord," he added, checking her face to make sure she understood, "He crashed Senator Doggett's photo op at the girls' school in Nabarut."

"And your team was the one sent in to evacuate Roy and Lena. Right?"

"Right. Now, the part that didn't make the news is how Doggett kept blocking our extraction plan because he was pissed that his photo op was getting ruined. At least, that's what we assumed at the time."

"What do you mean?"

"We think he had more going on than just shaking hands and cutting ribbons. Your ex, too. Dan shows up in some unofficial photos, and in a few background stills of his fiancée's little documentary—but he wasn't on any of the official guest lists or schedules. He wasn't supposed to be there."

Kim pulled her tongs from the fire and frowned. "Maybe it was spur of the moment. To support his parents."

"Maybe. But when you have a gun manufacturer with a new line of automatic weapons that he needs to find a market for, showing up unannounced to a warlord's big regional power play, it sure doesn't look good."

Kim hesitated, then held a new slice of bread over the flames. "That is certainly an unlucky coincidence."

"Perhaps," Bennett nodded, shoving the eggs onto the paper plates she'd set out and adding precooked bacon to the pan to crisp it. "But what if I told you that, while Ole Roy was obstructing our efforts to get him and his entourage to safety…and while a small-time warlord who had previously never held much power was somehow able to overwhelm the Army unit who'd also come to help…while all that was going on, nearly every girl of marriageable age in Nabarut simply vanished?"

Kim's eyes snapped to his. "Excuse me?"

"Gone. Just…gone," Bennett shrugged. "No one is willing to admit they saw it happen, and no one's heard from them since."

Kim tried to set her tongs on the little folding table beside her, missed, and dropped them in the dirt. Her face was wan.

"Bennett, I had no idea. That's horrible. How…how many girls are we talking?"

"Around twelve."

"*Twelve?*"

"Now what if I told you that the women of the Nabarut region are known for their beauty? Men routinely come from all over Qahat to look for brides there, and the girls and their families can pick and choose as they want, negotiating some very lucrative dowries, all things considered."

"I'd say that sounded dangerous. Like it might provoke small-minded…warlords." She swallowed audibly and looked away, asking him, "How do you know all this?"

"Because someone who was also there came and found us. And in exchange for giving us photos and details about each of the girls, they provided us firsthand, unassailable proof that Roy and his camp have been lying about what went down ever since."

Bennett would not tell Kim more about Rohaan than that, however. Rohaan's uncle Mohsin, with whom he now lived in San Diego, was a photojournalist on location in Nepal for the next little while, and the kid's continued security was paramount in everyone's minds.

Not too far away from where they sat now, Rohaan was happily ensconced in his college courses, making friends and working as a busboy in the evenings. If not for his missing girlfriend, he'd be settled. Happy, even.

Bennett intended to keep him that way.

"But if you all had proof," Kim wondered, "why did you still get discharged?"

"Good question. We didn't want to endanger our source, and by that point, Buck had already reached out for some back-channel help. We'd been assured that we had enough allies on the inquiry board to come out on top, except that's not what happened. There was a last-minute change to the lineup. Doggett's golfing buddy was replaced."

"Shouldn't that have worked in your favor?"

"You'd think."

"Who replaced him?"

"Some guy named Colson. I don't think he matters. It was Commander Azevedo, the guy running the board, who showed up at parties with Doggett's brother Leon, and Dan's fiancée Joely."

Kim's eyes went wide. "For real?"

Bennett nodded and handed her one of the plates of food. "We don't know much about him yet. His nephew is a chip off the old block, though. He should be completing BUD/S any day now."

"The SEAL training?"

"Yes. Azevedo was on the Teams, too, before he started climbing the ranks."

Kim's color had returned now that the conversation had moved past the girls, and as she dug into her eggs, she looked deep in thought.

"I think you're onto something with this Azevedo character. Is someone looking into him?"

"Great idea, honey. We'll get right on that," Bennett smiled drily.

"Well, you don't have to get snarky," she huffed, jabbing a corner of toast in his direction. And then, after chewing slowly for another long minute, she added, "You ought to go meet that nephew, though. What's his name?"

"Osmar. Goes by Ozzie."

"Okay. So go talk to him. I know you could get him to tell you if he knows anything—you could charm the feathers off a hoot owl."

Bennett smirked at her, but he needed to get her back on track. There was something he had to learn from her, and it wasn't her thoughts on corruption in the chain of command.

"Let us worry about that, okay?" he said. "We really need you to think about Dan now. There's *got* to be something you haven't thought of—something big enough that he felt justified in taking the crazy step of snatching you."

"Bennett, honestly. I don't—"

He held up a hand. "You said he talked about himself a lot. Try to step through everything he told you. Dan is worried about something he thinks you know, and whatever it is, he doesn't want us to find out. That means it's something that could help us, and we need to know it sooner rather than later."

"He did badger me about what I'd told you," she mused. "But…he also didn't seem too worried about those bank statements. I don't think it was those."

Bennett nodded, hating to break the news to her. "Yeah, we're still following up on a couple of things, but I'm not sure your flash drive is going to be helpful."

"It was worth a try," she sighed. Kim dragged her fork across her plate, etching designs into the paper where the food had made it soggy.

Bennett studied her, trying to get a read on her thoughts. He didn't want to press her too hard on this, but at the same time…the team was counting on him, and he was not going to let them down.

He was also not going to let any of them have a go at her.

"What about the other woman?" he suggested. "The one you said he cheated with?"

She shook her head. "No, I don't think it's her. She was just some woman." Then Kim looked up, and her eyes had an odd shadow in them. "Tell me more about those girls—the ones from the village. Was that who the guys were looking for after we left the estate?"

"Yeah," Bennett nodded. He drew the word out slowly, though, perplexed by her interest. "Why?"

"I'm not sure. I'm thinking."

She bent to search through the bags near her feet, and the sight of her long, elegant fingers pitched him headlong down memory lane again. As always, her nails were short and glossy, pale pink ovals that were stark against her tan.

She had to change them up sometimes, but he'd never seen them painted any other color.

Bennett had found himself transfixed by Kim's nails a time or two before, but if he'd ever envisioned them raking down his back he'd crushed those unholy thoughts with a vengeance, because her hands had epitomized everything wholesome and high-class about her.

Who else but a pampered princess could maintain them so meticulously?

Much like he was doing now, he'd watched them back then—adjusting the dial on a car radio, braiding his sister's hair, playing that fancy piano in her parents' front parlor.

Damn. The piano playing.

Bennett had somehow forgotten how painful it'd been to watch Kim sit at that shining instrument, her posture erect, yet relaxed at the same time. The housekeeper's furniture polish had lent the room an eternal lemony scent, and Kim's pink nails had danced across the ivory keys like something from another world.

There'd been so many things that had pointed to how far out of Bennett's league she'd been, but nothing had delineated the chasm quite like that airless room. The yards of pristine white upholstery. The expensive, impractical instrument. The severe, bespectacled instructor.

And Kim. Sweet Kim, dutifully practicing her sheet music while Shannon and Bennett lounged on her mother's stiff settees, impatient for her to finally be set free.

He'd felt like a ruffian amidst all that opulence. Especially when…Bennett flinched anew at the unwelcome memory.

He'd come straight from football practice, grimy and disheveled, to pick up Shannon, and the frigid air conditioning had turned his sweaty skin clammy within moments. Regina, the housekeeper, had not wanted to let him into the sanctum in his condition.

But even as he'd edged into the room, stinking like a farmyard, Kim had knocked off the Mozart and started picking out the notes to "Happy Birthday." Shannon told him later how he'd turned beet red, but Bennett didn't need her to remind him now of how he'd yanked her off the sofa and hustled her out of there.

Not before he'd barked at Kim to stop fucking around, though. Like the real gentleman he wasn't.

Bennett had mellowed somewhat, since then. Kim hadn't known, couldn't have known, the way that he and Shannon had dreaded their birthdays—or any holiday, really.

While the rest of the world had celebrated, they'd been dismal. There'd been no presents. If their folks happened to be around, Bennett and Shannon had bigger things to worry about, and if they weren't around, well…he and his sister had been lucky just to eat.

When they'd gotten old enough to work, they'd tried to surprise each other with small things—but neither of them had ever had a party, and a silly birthday song played by a girl who seemed to get gifts for simply existing had only broadened Bennett's shame.

He'd been eighteen, and a fraud. A caricature. A stain on humanity.

A mistake.

The notion that it had been Kim, yet again, who'd attempted to brighten his birthday with her cake and balloons and mysterious piece of art that was somehow worth getting kidnapped for, curdled the eggs in his stomach like nothing else could.

Present-day Kim had long since extracted a plastic packet from one of the bags, and had gone to rummage through the truck, sublimely unaware of the direction Bennett's thoughts had wandered.

Teenaged Kim had been equally unaffected. While Bennett had bitten off her head for trying to be nice, she'd simply pulled her hands from the piano keys and gazed at him calmly. Accepting him as he was and making him feel worse.

Back then, he'd known all about anger, and frustration, and fear. He'd had little experience with kindness, however, and he and his sister had fought bitterly over his misstep.

Bennett shuddered, shaking free of the memory. He refocused on Kim's hands, here and now. Not playing a piano, and not holding something from the cooler. He squinted at her and frowned, trying to figure out what she was doing.

"Why do you want to know about those girls, Kim?" he asked again.

"Hush."

She laid two long sticks on the ground, and with a Swiss army knife she'd produced from God only knew where, she began notching the ends. Kim glanced at him and smirked, then refocused on her project.

"Kim…"

"Bennett, I'm not sure yet. Okay? Let me think on it for a bit, and I will let you know when, or if, I've got something. Hammering me with questions will not help me remember."

She ripped open a packet and dumped the contents on the ground, and before long she was stringing filament on the sticks and tying hooks on the ends of the lines.

Well, damn him to hell.

Kim jumped up from her crouch, grabbed her improvised fishing poles, and popped the knife in her pocket. She slapped at a mosquito on her leg, and kicked his boot.

"Come on, Tex. No more brooding for now. Grab the hot dogs and let's catch us some fish for dinner."

She strolled toward the creek that cut past their campsite without a backward glance, utterly confident that Bennett would follow with the bait.

He stared at her, too off kilter to call her back. She was obviously done talking and right about one thing—trout would go for a hot dog as easily as the catfish back home would.

Like that, he was assaulted by another memory—another creek, another Kim, this one kicking her toes in a slow brown stream, teaching Shannon and him the ways of fish and homemade poles.

Even then, she hadn't had a pretentious bone in her body, despite all her advantages. The only one affected had been him— by her delicate hands, by her bare feet, by the downy hairs at the nape of her neck, by the impossible smoothness of Kim's skin.

That Kim had been real, and normal, and loyal as the day was long. *This* Kim was all that and more. This Kim had decided that she wanted him and made no bones about the fact.

He'd never thought of her as stupid, but the sheer ludicrousness of the idea sure made him wonder.

However, Bennett wasn't exactly firing on all cylinders himself. Only a man that was dumb as a post would congratulate himself on how clever a hiding place this was, because bringing Kim out here alone had been a massive error in judgment.

Without the buffer of civilization, there was only her, and him, and a lifetime of memories—and they were bearing down on Bennett like a division of resurrected Panzer tanks. Had he really thought he could mess around with her and never pay a price?

He'd allowed himself to wallow in her sunshine for too long already, and his selfishness had to end. He needed information from her now, but the time had also come to tell Kim everything and finally bear the consequences.

Except, as she parked herself on the grassy bank and peered up at him like he wasn't standing there in crisis, she neatly sidestepped his heavy thoughts. "I hope we see some moon bugs later," she told him.

Bennett ripped open the package of hot dogs and sat next to her, relieved to delay his confession a bit longer, yet hating to quash her redirection. "I wouldn't count on it. It's too dry out here for fireflies. Gotta watch out for chiggers, though. Mind where you sit."

Then Bennett prayed like hell that the law, or the Black Watch guys, or even the Devil himself would find fucking Dan Cox soon, because Kim turned to him, sweet as pie, and demanded, "Fine. Then what's a girl gotta do to get a kiss around here?"

Yep. She was definitely going to hate him when this was over.

Chapter Thirty

BENNETT WASN'T NORMALLY a tentative kisser. Usually, he hooked her around the neck and dove right in—ever since he'd decided they were going to be on kissing terms, at least.

Kim wasn't complaining. Bennett was gratifyingly insatiable, and his hunger had lit a twin flame in her, something that burned brighter than she ever would've thought possible.

It was intoxicating, being wanted so much, and she couldn't think of a single thing that would eradicate the last few days from her brain as efficiently as Bennett's desire.

And so, when she asked Bennett for a kiss and he only leaned over and brushed his lips against hers, it was a bit of a letdown. He could've been her cousin for all the heat that he'd conveyed.

Frustrated, she searched out his tongue with hers and, bless his heart, Bennett tried to put on a good show. He couldn't sell it, though, and before long he was pulling back and fixing her with an apprehensive stare that turned his turquoise eyes a flat slate gray.

She bit her lip and frowned at him. "What is it?"

"You know I love your mouth," he started.

"But?"

"But I can't kiss you when I know what needs to be said, and how you're going to react. I feel like an asshole—like I'm taking advantage."

Kim shook her head. She didn't need to ask what he was talking about, but his reaction didn't track with what she knew of that night, or of Bennett. Only a horrible deed would eat at a man like this, and he was not the horrible deed type.

Fifteen years, Bennett had been agonizing over it. Maybe longer.

Kim watched him as he hunched his shoulders on the bank of that lazy creek, his long legs stretched in front of him as he fiddled with his makeshift pole. He scowled into the water as he stewed, and something about the set of his profile made her set her own pole aside.

"You're right, you know," he said softly. "It does almost feel like home. Sitting out like this."

"A little bit, yeah."

"What ever happened with you and that Ricky Stahl guy? I heard he carried a torch for you for years."

"Bennett, come on," Kim scoffed. "If you know that much, then you know he asked me out and I turned him down. End of story."

He was too morose to make the kind of joke he normally would. He only murmured, "Then tell me something I don't know."

His bleak gaze wandered to hers and stalled there. Kim froze, wondering if he already knew what she had to say about Dan.

"You know everything about me," she whispered shakily, "What you didn't witness firsthand, your big-mouthed sister probably told you."

Bennett searched her face, his expression growing more haunted. "Kim, why do you want to be with me so bad? You could have anyone—someone worthy of you."

"You're worthy," she said.

"I…don't know. I might never be able to give you the life you deserve. Do you understand that? I was born so far behind the curve that I may never catch up."

Kim blinked at the despairing rush of words. "Bennett, when you say *deserve*, do you mean things? Like…cars and houses and what not? Because I know you can't mean a nice life in general—that has nothing to do with money and everyone deserves one of those."

"Y…yeah," he faltered. "I guess I do. You're used to ski trips and stuff. That week in Paris you went on with your mom. Other stuff I've probably never even heard of."

She shifted to face him and touched his leg. "Why do I feel like you're equating love with bank accounts, here? You, who ought to know better?"

"I'm not," he insisted. "But you were raised a certain way, and—"

"Bennett Shane Shaw. Don't you dare insult me or my parents that way. We've been blessed with lives of privilege, but they worked hard for what they have and made sure I would, too. They certainly had enough sense to teach me what is important and what is not."

Bennett turned red, but he stayed quiet and let her talk.

"*Love* is important," Kim went on. "Loyalty is important. Honesty and trust are important. And while manicures and cute shoes are fun and give me joy, in the grand scheme of things they are ultimately *unimportant*."

"Right. True." He nodded a lot, but she wasn't convinced he was really hearing her.

Kim looked him over, contemplating what she knew about him. "Tell me something that's important to you. Something so important you feel scared to talk about out loud."

Bennett's flush deepened as he searched for a response.

"That bad, huh?" she commented.

He kept quiet for so long, she thought he'd keep it to himself. But then, all of a sudden, he whispered, "A safe home. Feeling secure. Knowing for sure that the good thing isn't a trick and won't be snatched away if I let down my guard or slip up."

She stared at him, stunned he'd admitted it that succinctly. He'd earned a big truth in return, and she gifted it to him with barely a second thought.

"Bennett, I have known you my entire life and I have loved you without reservation that whole time. Nothing you have said or done—or will say or do—is going to change that, because you are the best man I have ever met. I will gladly swear on whatever you ask me to. I will tell the world. I will promise it before God and country. And if you let yourself admit that you love me back, I promise on all I hold dear that I will never betray you, and never leave you. And that's a fact."

Kim felt a little breathless putting it all out there like that, but she didn't regret a word. Instead, she felt lighter. He knew, now. *No takebacks.*

Bennett blinked at her in shock. "You can't promise that."

"I can. I did—I do. It's not a trick, and even though I have a big mouth sometimes, you know I don't go off half-cocked, saying things I don't mean."

"But if you knew the truth—"

"Try me," she shrugged. "Just try me. You keep holding this dark truth over my head like some cartoon anvil. It's long past time to drop that sucker and deal with what happens next. Whatever the fallout turns out to be, I expect it will be tame compared to what you've probably built up in your mind."

He sniffed ruefully. "Don't be so sure about that."

"Was anyone murdered?"

"Not yet. But give it time."

Kim rolled her eyes and shoved at his shoulder. "Will you quit being such a drama queen? Just trust me for once. I'm tired of begging for crumbs all the time."

"Don't say I didn't warn you."

"Bennett!"

"All right, all right. It's not like it's a complicated story. It just sucks."

She stared at him, and simply…waited. After another long hesitation, he cleared his throat and began.

"About a week before I turned eighteen, I got a call from a number I didn't know," he said, turning toward the creek again. "It was an older woman. A lot older. She said she'd seen me around and wanted to know…she said maybe we could help each other."

Kim scowled in suspicion, not liking the after-school-special tone he'd adopted. "Help each other do what?"

Bennett swallowed thickly and looked up at the sky. "She wanted me to sleep with her—to help her get over her cheating ex, she said. In exchange, she would pay me money she knew I needed badly. Five hundred dollars, to be exact. A fortune, for something I did all the time for free."

"What!" Kim squawked, unable to stay silent. "Bennett, that's soliciting a minor!"

"No shit. But Kim, you have no idea what those last six months were like. Shannon and I hadn't seen our folks since February. And once we got evicted—"

"Evicted."

"Yeah. When no one pays the bills, they kick you out. We moved into that shitty motel off Route 12, but even that was a stretch for us. I was terrified about what was going to happen to Shannon once I left for school in the fall. She was barely sixteen—I had to do what I could to keep her out of foster care."

"Jesus lord," Kim muttered darkly. *On their own since February.* She'd had no idea. "So, what did you do?"

"The woman said we needed to wait until my birthday, so I'd be of age. She gave me a place, and I told her I'd be there. I wasn't sure if I could go through with it, though. Even up to the last minute, I didn't know."

Her heart broke all over again for the boy he'd been. So tough in some ways, and so bruised in others. "Oh, honey. And then you went and got mixed up with my mama's overdose on top of it."

"What? Kim," Bennett stammered. "What do you—? The woman I'm talking about…" He was white as a sheet, forcing the words past his lips with visible effort. "I'm talking about your mama right now. Who…who the hell else would it be? My God."

"*Rayann*," Kim hissed, uttering her mother's name like a curse. There was no doubt Bennett was telling the truth—it only took one look at his tortured expression to see that. "So, it was not an overdose, then. Not a lucky break that you happened to be driving by."

"No," he agreed. "I mean…yes, she was hopped up on half a pharmacy by the time I got there, but no, not a lucky coincidence. I went there straight from dropping off Travis and Sue. And I sure didn't expect her to start waving around a gun when I took too long to get to it."

"A gun? I don't remember anything about a gun," Kim cried. "Where the heck did she get that? Daddy didn't keep any at the house."

"Beats me. I got rid of it before the sheriff showed up. I don't think anyone else knew about it, but I figured she had enough problems without someone trying to commit her once they pumped her stomach."

"I don't understand. Was my mama threatening to shoot you if you didn't go through with things?" Kim could barely wrap her mind around the propositioning. Trying to envision her haughty mother raping a teen at gunpoint was virtually inconceivable.

"I believe she intended to harm herself," Bennett clarified. "But it was a little hard to tell. I was kind of a wreck, and she was worse."

Kim stared at him for a long time, waiting for some part of his story to make even the tiniest bit of sense. She found herself asking, "Bennett, are you joking right now?" even though she knew he wasn't.

It was something to say, when no words she knew fit the bill.

"No," he muttered, "though I sure wish I was."

Kim fumed, utterly incensed that her mother had pulled such a selfish stunt. There was no question Rayann had had no idea what the ripple effect of her actions would be, but like that was an excuse?

"I am going to wring that woman's skinny little neck," she growled eventually.

Bennett's eyes swung to hers. "You…what? I'm sorry, do you mean your mother?"

"Out here acting like she's the first person to ever get divorced. Lord above."

"Kim—"

"Bennett, hang on," she said, cutting off whatever self-destroying apology he was about to utter. "What you clearly don't know is that my parents always had a bit of a rocky relationship. Long as I can remember, they bickered like cats and dogs. I expect they were trying to hold out until I got through high school, but the second I left, those two were going to be Splitsville."

"Seriously?"

"A blind man could've seen it."

"But…everyone thought they were so perfect. All of you. The perfect family."

"People who didn't know us, maybe. And look, I'm not saying I approve of how Daddy went about things, but Mama sure didn't need to go dragging defenseless children into her soap opera. Honestly."

"I'm sorry—" he squinted at her dangerously, "—did you just refer to me as a defenseless child? Me, who beat Kyle Calhoun's ass for trying to steal your lunch money in fifth grade?"

"Wouldn't you? And look back on this circus with your grown-up eyes, not the ones stuck in the past, please. Those people were throwing around money on garden parties when kids right under their noses were living hand-to-mouth. That's unconscionable."

Bennett looked like he was reeling, but Kim knew she wasn't wrong. She *wasn't*. Her mama was extra and then some, but targeting Bennett had been beyond the pale.

When he could manage to speak, he admitted shakily, "I have to say, this is not how I envisioned this conversation going."

"I'll bet," Kim told him, patting his knee. "But I also suspect you've been out of touch on a number of fronts for a long-ass time."

He shook his head, utterly flummoxed. "I don't know what to say."

Kim shrugged. "You could start with *sorry*. Not for that nonsense with Rayann—but whether you meant to or not, you broke my heart into a thousand pieces when you left Respite without a word of goodbye, and that bastard stayed broken for a good long while."

"I am sorry," he said. "But I had to get gone, and I had to do it fast. Sheriff Fecteau, I'm sure you recall, hated my guts. While I was cooling my heels in the drunk tank, he called and got my scholarship yanked. Then, when he finally let me out, he told me I could either sign up for boot camp in the morning or get my ass thrown in jail for good."

"That didn't exactly work the first time, given you did nothing wrong."

"Well, he was convinced I had. He promised to make it stick next time. I wasn't about to call his bluff."

"So, that's how you ended up in the Navy?" she wondered. "He forced you?"

"No, Fecteau had an Army recruiter lined up. But I figured if I had to do it, I was going to join up on my terms. As for your heart…Kimmie, I hope you know that was the last thing I would have chosen. I never wanted to hurt you."

She groaned, sick to her core that so many adults in a row had failed the man in front of her. "It's fine. I forgive you. Just don't go breaking it again, please."

Bennett smirked at her, a shadow of his usual sass peeking through his destroyed demeanor. "I'll see what I can do."

Kim suspected her bossiness was about the only thing keeping him afloat right now, and that was okay with her. It was time to get this show on the road, anyway.

"Good. Then let's pack up all this stuff and head back to town. The fish aren't biting, and my legs have bug bites on top of bug bites. I would also give my left kidney for a hot shower and a strong mimosa."

"Is that right. All that sentimental talk about how homey this camp is, and you lasted exactly one night," he tutted, shaking his head. "Where, may I ask, do you propose we go next?"

Kim tapped her borrowed phone and showed him the listing she'd found. "Here. I'll book us a room. We can check in by 4."

"The Hotel…del Coronado?" he sputtered. "That might be the most recognizable landmark in town. Have you lost your everloving mind?"

Kim smiled smugly. "Nope. It's called hiding in plain sight, and we're going to do it. It's not like we were going to accomplish much hiding out in the woods anyway."

Bennett dropped his head in his hands and groaned, "Lord, save me from strong drink and fast women."

Kim got to her feet and brushed off her butt. "Might want to hang on to the drink, Tex. You carry a lot of tension in those big shoulders, and I am just getting started."

He kept a wary eye on her as he stood, too—like he expected her to bolt or set off fireworks, or something.

"I just have to say one more thing, Kim. I'm…I'm sorry I stole your credit card. Back then, I mean. I left everything I had with Shannon. I didn't really have a plan other than to get out of there, and I had to move boots pretty fast."

Kim wanted to laugh, but she didn't think he'd take it well, given how long he'd held onto his guilt. "Don't apologize," she said. "I left it out on purpose."

"But…what? How'd you know I'd need it?"

She grabbed her pole and headed back to their little campsite, trying to decide what to pack up first. "Lucky guess, I suppose."

Bennett planted his feet in front of her and frowned mightily. "That's the best you got? A hunch? I used that thing for months before it stopped working."

Kim shrugged. She *had* had a feeling Bennett was going to take off, once word got around that his big football scholarship had been revoked and he'd insisted Shannon stay with her. She hadn't dared to offer him help directly, however—his pride would never have countenanced it.

To be fair, she hadn't really believed he would take the card. The fact that he had was yet more proof of how desperate he'd been.

Kim shrugged, feigning an indifference she didn't feel. "I told Daddy I lent it to a friend in need. I imagine he knew who. He always did like you, Bennett."

"I'm sorry," he said again, looking as forlorn and lost as a ripped, six-foot-two SEAL could manage. "I tried to use it as little as possible."

"Don't fret about it," Kim told him, taking him by the shoulders and planting a gentle kiss on his lips. "I'm happy it helped."

Chapter Thirty-One

Bennett

S HE KNEW ABOUT *the credit card.* Bennett wanted to shrink so far into himself that he blipped clear out of existence with the revelation.

Sadly, though he'd felt this way before, he hadn't yet managed to pull off the disappearing trick. He'd have to tough out this situation, like he had all the others.

Kim brushed off her hands both figuratively and literally and marched to the edge of their campsite, popping the tailgate on the truck, then turning and setting her hands on her hips.

She surveyed the area with a determined frown. "What do you want to stow first?" she wondered. "The chairs or the tent?"

Bennett shook his head. Once the woman set her mind to something she was single-minded in pursuit of her goal. It was impressive, but at the moment also inconvenient and exasperating.

He went over and stopped her from reaching for one of the tent poles.

"Hold up. We can't just pack up and leave on a whim. I have people I report to, and procedures I need to follow. If we are going to do this, we need to take the time to do it right."

Kim wrinkled her nose. "Annoying, but sensible. Will you still ask if it's okay, though?"

"I will. But knowing Monroe, I expect we will have to stay here another night at least, to give the team enough time to put support plans in place."

With a forlorn sigh, Kim stepped up to him and wrapped her arms around his waist. Bennett stroked her silky hair and inhaled deeply, filling his lungs with her light, feminine scent.

"Are you okay?" she wondered softly.

It felt like a novelty to be asked outright, particularly in the way Kim meant it. Bennett took a moment to think about his answer and realized that, strangely, he was.

"I am," he assured her, and relished holding her close.

Her reaction to his confession had been the last thing he'd expected, but it'd made him realize that just as he'd had his secrets, she had hers, too. Everyone did.

He ought to have known nothing was ever quite as black and white as it seemed.

Kim's opinion had always mattered to him, and today her clear-eyed perspective had given him a lot to think about. Though right now, they had more practical matters to take care of.

He disentangled himself and smacked her cute butt. "Grab your pole and come on back to the creek," he told her. "I was promised fish for dinner, and fish I shall have."

AS BENNETT HAD predicted, Tate did, in fact, instruct them to hold in place another night, so that Noah and Buck would have time to facilitate a new strategy.

Kim took the news with reasonably good grace. She sat beside Bennett at the fire, watching him debone the fish they'd caught with a thoughtful look on her face.

"What did you end up studying?" she asked after a bit. "Shannon told me you went to night school through the Navy, but I don't think I ever heard what you got your degree in."

Bennett laid the trout on the foil he'd set out and wiped his hands. "Military history," he told her, proud despite himself. Once everything died down, he was planning to go back and get a graduate degree, too.

Kim paused in surprise. "Seriously?"

"It's interesting," he shrugged. "Why is that strange?"

"I don't know. Maybe because you've always been so practical? I figured you'd end up studying something safe, if that makes sense."

"What, like accounting? Can you really see me as an accountant?"

She smiled. "No, I guess not."

"*Safe* was supposed to be me in the Navy until I was dead in the ground," Bennett said. "Your ex-boyfriend's family stole that from me, though."

"But you've got a new job now. Right? It seems like a good one."

"It is, but only as long as I stay fit and healthy," Bennett pointed out. "I doubt very much that Monroe's got a bunk and a mess for me if shit breaks bad and I'm permanently incapacitated."

"Maybe not, but Bennett—you're grown now. You have good insurance, and probably some kind of severance. You can get a new job if you have to. If you should need a place to crash while that happens, then you have friends who will gladly put you up. You're not going to end up poor and homeless again. I do hope you get that?"

Bennett poked at the fire, because no, he did not get that. Especially not now.

The Navy had been his lifeboat since the age of eighteen, and Doggett had sunk it with a shit-eating grin on his face. *That fucker.* The whole family could rot in hell.

Kim ducked down to catch his eye. "Hell, if I know you, you've probably managed to squirrel away a good chunk of change by now, just like your sister. Invested properly, your rainy-day funds will probably make you millionaires one day."

Bennett shrugged. He'd gotten a good start on a nest egg, that was true—but no matter how much he socked away, it never felt like enough. Kim was right about investing, but he didn't know a thing about it yet, and he'd be damned if he entrusted his hard-won savings to some slick stranger with a finance degree without having the wherewithal to know if he was being robbed.

So, maybe that's what his next degree should be in. How was that for *practical?*

Kim gazed at him with eyes that were soft with understanding. "Bennett, listen to me. No matter what happens, you're going to be okay. You've already accomplished so much. You could use your experiences to become a teacher, or one of those speakers who gives talks at corporate retreats and college graduations. You could even advise movie studios on how realistic their war films are."

She studied him and sighed, no doubt picking up on his skepticism. "Hell, you could model if it came down to it. Not too many agencies would turn down that much pretty."

Bennett set his knife aside and grinned at her. "Did you just tell me I'm pretty? In the middle of a serious discussion?"

"Oh, there you are," she smiled back. "Can't keep Shameless Shaw down for long."

He chuckled, glad for the shift in topic. "That's enough depressing talk for now. Why don't you break out that bag of culinary delights Noah packed us, and pick out something to eat alongside this fish?"

Kim snorted delicately. "Bennett, it is four-thirty in the afternoon. How are you hungry already?"

"It takes a lot of calories to keep all this pretty running smoothly," he explained with a wink he didn't quite feel. "And I gave you the last protein bar at lunch, remember?"

"Oh, I remember. You complained about it for an hour."

He gestured at the bag. "Okay, then. Learn from history. Keep me fed and happy and all will be well."

She rolled her eyes but she went along with it, digging through the bag and weighing their options. Most were lipstick-on-a-pig versions of classic MRE fare—rice pilaf, fettuccine alfredo, potatoes au gratin.

Freeze-dried and dead inside.

Bennett watched Kim as she undertook the preparations, from her bandaged cheek to her clumsy hands and muttered curses as she struggled to prepare the noodles. After a while, a shiver of foreboding drifted through him. No one over ten would need to expend that much brain power on the process, and certainly not an accomplished woman who was accustomed to running her own business.

Add water and stir. Like that was hard? He squinted at her and suddenly, everything from her random question to her culinary confusion became clear.

"All right, honey. Spit it out," he said, when it became obvious that she wasn't planning to do it on her own. "What's on your mind?"

Kim turned wide blue eyes on him, the picture of innocence. "What makes you think I have something on my mind?"

"Because you're about as transparent as that plastic wrap you're holding. When you're stewing about something, you ask me aimless questions to deflect. You play with your hair. You avoid eye contact and pick at your nails."

"I do *not*," she huffed.

Bennett raised his eyebrows, daring her to keep lying.

"Okay, fine," she relented. "But stop being so observant. It's impolite."

"*Kim*," he urged. "Whatever it is, tell me now. My imagination's going into overdrive."

She stared at him. He glared back.

"Fine," she finally admitted. "It's two things. The first is that Dan seems to have gotten his grubby paws on some information about you. It's not accurate, mind you," she rushed to add. "But he could use it to hurt you, nonetheless."

There was so much to choose from, Bennett couldn't even hazard a guess. "What is it?"

"He said he'd heard tell that you raped a socialite on the side of the road and that half of Respite probably still wants to see you hang for it."

Kim's expression was troubled, and why wouldn't it be? She'd been carrying around that little tidbit for two days and hadn't said a word—not even when he'd finally told her the truth.

Bennett frowned, surprised despite himself. "Where would he have heard that? Even Sheriff Fecteau didn't go that far. He only insinuated that I'd sold your mama some bad pills."

"That's just it—I don't know," Kim said. "Dan was trying to use it as leverage, though, to get me to confess what all I'd supposedly told you. He got pretty worked up about it."

Bennett's mind leaped ahead, trying to slot this new information into what he already knew. The Doggetts had clearly looked into the background of the team as part of their smear campaign. In all likelihood, however, Bennett's past had been the only one to yield a motherlode of sin.

He'd need to mitigate its impact on the other guys as soon as he could.

Kim touched his arm. "Dan didn't mention Rayann by name. I don't think he knew that part. I did suspect he was talking about my mama, though," she said, "Who else could it have been? Anyway, I hope you know I never believed him. Not for one instant."

Bennett swallowed back the sudden bile climbing his throat. "I wouldn't have blamed you if you had."

She shook her head. "Stop that. I'm just happy you told me the truth. The more people who know it, the more defenders you'll have, and the less traction Dan's stupid lies will get."

Bennett wasn't so sure about that—people loved good gossip, and the juicier the better. Once that accusation got out, the stain would never be removed for some people. No matter how he got redeemed, they'd always assume there was a kernel of truth beneath the lies.

"You said there were two things?" he prompted Kim, not wanting to go too far down that road.

He needed time to figure out how best to handle this newest crisis—time they didn't have. What was more, he didn't have the right to go it alone. Bennett would have to bring Buck, at the very least, up to speed, and likely all the others, too.

Kim cleared her throat in a way that had nothing to do with spit and a whole lot to do with nerves. Bennett peered at her face and wanted to turn tail at what he saw there. Whatever was coming next was going to be even worse.

"What?" he demanded. "What is it?"

"The…the girls you told me about," she said carefully. "It's possible…I think I might know something about them, too."

Bennett sat back so hard he nearly upended his folding chair. There it was—the reason Dan had gone full lunatic mode. *It had to be.*

"Okay," he murmured.

"Okay, so I've been thinking about it and back when Dan and I were dating, he used to make a big fuss about me being a model," she said quickly. "He didn't seem to care that I was a kid when I'd done it, or that I hadn't done it in a long time."

"Shocker," Bennett drawled.

"Anyway, this one time, he brought me a bunch of head shots. He said his mom was starting up a modeling agency, and he wanted my opinion about some girls she was thinking of hiring. Since I had a background in the industry, he said."

"And?" His whole chest felt tight with apprehension.

"There weren't a ton of them, but they all seemed to be one type. When I commented on it, Dan told me that sometimes the Eastern European girls used modeling to get their green cards. He said the girls wanted his mother to sponsor them."

Bennett rubbed his jaw, unnerved by where this was going. "You think he was lying?"

"Possibly," Kim admitted. "To me, their features looked more Middle Eastern than Russian or Slovak. I don't know why, though. It's not like I'm an expert in phenotypes, or whatever."

Her eyes grew unfocused as she thought about it, and he motioned for her to continue.

"The pictures he had were weird, too," she said after a moment. "They weren't professional headshots, or even semi-professional—they looked like mugshots, or something they'd pulled from an old yearbook."

"So, what did you do?"

"I told him about a hundred times that I wasn't qualified to weigh in, and that presence often counts for more than specific features. But he wouldn't give up, so I pointed out three or four girls who I thought had the most potential. The whole thing was strange, but like I said, Dan had always been weird about the modeling. I wrote it off to that."

"Did he ever talk about it again? Mention his mom's agency or anything?"

Kim shook her head. "No, I never heard another word. And to be honest, I didn't really think about it again—not until you said you were looking for those missing girls."

Bennett stared at her, heart pounding. This had to be a missing piece of the puzzle. It fit perfectly and explained so much.

"Do you think it's important?" Kim asked worriedly.

He couldn't lie. "I think this it the most important thing," he said. "The reason for just about everything."

Bennett raked a hand through his hair in consternation. Naturally, the linchpin would be Lena. She was the one person they hadn't looked at too hard.

"Shit, I—I've got to make some calls," he told Kim. "You did good, baby girl. Plate up those noodles when they're ready—I promise I won't be long. We're gonna need to figure out what to do with this, though."

THE SUN WAS dipping behind the trees by the time he finished debriefing Buck, and Bennett had a sick feeling in his stomach as he ambled back to the fire. He was satisfied that the appropriate parties were working on what Kim had told him, but the thought of all those girls in the wrong hands felt like worrying about Shannon in foster care, all over again.

Kim had a plate ready for him when he parked himself next to her. She'd kept it warm somehow, but the food had long since congealed into unappetizing beige blobs.

Like that mattered, though? If human trafficking was on the table, the whole game had changed.

It wasn't as if none of them had considered the possibility yet—they had. It was just that Kim's story had made it a damn near certainty, and that meant that finding the girls of Nabarut, as soon as possible, had become their primary objective.

Far above resurrecting their SEAL careers, and light years ahead of whatever rehydrated consumable was oozing up next to his trout.

"Everything all right?" Kim asked carefully.

Bennett nodded, though it wasn't. "Swear to God, the way this op keeps growing legs? It's like nothing I've dealt with before."

"I'm starting to see that," she said. "But you guys are going to see it through. Of that, I have no doubt."

He poked at a noodle and chuckled ruefully. "I appreciate your confidence, darlin'. I wish I felt the same."

"No worries." Kim squared her shoulders and smiled widely. "Turns out, I've got enough confidence for both of us."

"I'll be happy if there's still a *both of us* at the end of this." He shook his head. It was more than he'd meant to admit, but the twilight hour did that, sometimes. It pulled truths right out of people, and she had, after all, recently professed her undying devotion to him.

Kim's retort was delivered as stoutly as ever, of course. "There will be, and we will be amazing together. Especially once we right some of the wrongs you've been carrying around for so long."

Her persistence was a force of its own. "I appreciate you looking out for me," Bennett told her, "But what's done is done. There's no fixing it now and wallowing in the past helps nobody."

"Maybe that's true for some things," she agreed. "But say you always wanted a dog, and never got to have one. We are getting you a dog. Same goes if you always wanted to go to Mars, because we are gonna get you there, too."

Bennett smiled, tickled, despite himself, at her vehemence. "Mars, huh?"

"Underestimate me at your peril," she laughed, poking his chest.

"I wouldn't dream of it. And what's more..." he double-checked the incoming message on his phone and confirmed, "...thanks to your outsized attitude, we've been given clearance to roll out. First thing tomorrow, we can pack up and restore you to the lap of luxury."

"Thank you, baby Jesus," Kim breathed. "Luckily, that still gives you plenty of time to kiss me senseless under these stars."

Bennett glanced up to see millions of them winking to life over their heads. "It sure does, honey. And believe me, I plan to."

"THE DEL," BENNETT muttered the following day, eyeing the hotel façade stretching in front of them with a hearty dose of exasperation. "Couldn't you find a place that more people knew about?"

"Come on," Kim protested. "Look at it. It is awash in atmosphere. Besides, when in Rome, right?"

"Except we're not in Rome," he groaned, tugging her back into the shade. "I don't like this, Kimmie. It will be too easy for Cox to find you here. All he needs is one random person to recognize you, and we're toast."

Kim wasn't convinced. "Except, you said yourself that your team prepped for us. Live a little." She turned her brightest smile on him and punched him in the arm. "What happened to being a certified badass, anyway? I thought being stealthy was second nature to you."

Bennett hesitated. *Maybe to him. Not to her.* They'd learned the hard way that Kim couldn't lay low if her life depended on it.

"What we need are some fake names," she announced cheerfully. "How about…. Shawn and Landon…Hill. Those'll work nicely. I don't think we should act like we're celebrating anything special, though—it will only draw attention. Best we pretend it's a work trip. Or no—with this stupid bandage on my face, we'd best act like I'm recovering from surgery. You think you can get us some fake IDs?"

Bennett squinted at her, giving himself time to catch up to the rush of words. While he hated to admit it, Monroe seemed like exactly the kind of guy who would be down with a plan like that—and lord knew Noah was an excellent problem solver. Odds were strong the kid could turn out a fake identity in an afternoon.

Kim did not need to know any of that, however. It would only encourage her. Stalling for time, he asked, "Where'd you come up with those names? Little bougie, don't you think?"

"In case you hadn't noticed, I'm a little bougie," she giggled. "And I'm surprised you don't get it. The first names came from our last names. And Hill because we're from hill country."

Then Kim preened, pleased as punch by her own cleverness.

Bennett *hadn't* gotten it. He'd been snagged on the notion that she'd set them up as married so easily. It made sense safety-wise, but it would not help with keeping either of their heads out of the clouds.

In any case, Kenya had pinged his phone with the message he'd been waiting for, so it was time to shut down Kim's plotting with the reality of the situation.

"Listen, honey. It's good to know you're still as big a schemer as ever, but everything is already taken care of," he told her. "We don't need to hit the front desk—we're going straight to the room."

"Aww, really?" she pouted. "I was looking forward to seeing the fancy lobby."

Bennett shrugged. "The less people see us…"

"…the better. I know, I know." Kim sighed and bumped his shoulder with hers. "Those were good fake names, though. Don't you think?"

He couldn't help smiling at how goofy she was. "The best."

He tugged a ballcap over her hair and helped her tuck her platinum ends under it, but there was no masking how gorgeous she was, even with the dressing on her cheek. Fortunately, the parking lot wasn't too busy. With any luck no one would take much notice of them, since God knew *gorgeous* was nearly run-of-the-mill in these parts.

With Kenya's directions, it didn't take long to find their room. Bennett swung the door wide, Kim waltzed in—and then scampered straight onto the oceanfront balcony with a happy gasp.

He hung back and busied himself with their bags, discomfited by how romantic the room felt. It was one thing to get cozy with his sister's best friend in his stupid bachelor pad. That felt temporary, and deliciously illicit.

This place looked like a goddamn honeymoon suite, and felt just as monumental.

Bennett would have to have a conversation with Buck about the unnecessary upgrade—a simple interior room would've been more than adequate.

The thought evaporated quickly, burned away by Kim's incandescent smile when she came back in.

"Now this is more like it," she purred, sidling closer. She trailed her fingernail lightly down Bennett's forearm, adding, "Bummer we can't hang out by the pool. Guess we'll have to find a way to stay busy up here, huh?"

He dropped his pack and chuckled ruefully. His buddy might've been the one behind this ridiculous suite, playing Cupid even when all hell was breaking loose, but Kim hadn't needed a lick of help.

He dropped a quick kiss on her cheek before backing away and clearing his throat.

"No pool," he managed, trying to keep images of her in a bikini at bay. "They probably got us a nice room because we're going to be stuck in it for a while."

Kim sidled close again. "How long do you think we might have?"

"Until someone puts hands on Cox, I guess." When his words hit the heated air between them, Bennett realized exactly how that sounded. "*Kim*," he warned.

"You said it, not me." Her smile was positively blinding as she slipped the generic track jacket off her shoulders and dropped it on a chair. "No one said we couldn't have a good time while we're stuck here."

He shook his head. "Honey, slow down. We have barely slept a wink the last two nights, and I need to go through this room and make sure it's squared away before we settle in."

"I thought your coworkers already did that."

Undoubtedly, they had. He still liked to do it himself.

Kim raised her eyebrows, amused. "You know what? You're right. I'm tired. We should definitely turn in early."

Bennett couldn't help it—his eyes darted to the big, comfortable bed perched to starboard. Kim absolutely noticed.

"Well, sailor? You got enough gas in the tank to show a girl a good time or are you gonna conk out early on me?"

There was no use fighting it. If Kim Sutherland wanted to get in his pants, Bennett could hem and haw all he wanted, but he knew he wouldn't refuse her.

Himself, maybe—but never her.

Bennett stood in the center of that room, steady as an oak, and held out his hands.

Kim pulled the balcony door closed and stepped toward him. She slid her fingers lightly along his palms and onto the inside of his wrists, and the sensation made him hiss.

Now that he'd made up his mind, Bennett was in no mood to be teased. He closed his hands over Kim's wrists and yanked her against him, diving in for a desperate kiss that went on and on.

Eventually, she pulled free. "Hey. Wait a minute."

"You want me, you got me," Bennett told her, but he kept his hold on her loose, in case she really needed some space. "Don't tell me you've gone soft on me now."

"What if I feel like something different? Something…slow and sensual, maybe."

"Nice try, but I've got your number," he smiled. "You like it dirty, girl. Protest all you want, but I know you like a roll in the hay that's fast and hard and deep."

She gave up and giggled sheepishly. "Damn, no need to expose me like that."

Bennett was a little surprised that she'd admitted it and huffed out a shaky laugh of his own. "You have no idea what you do to me. If you did…"

He laughed again, tipping his head back to search the ceiling for answers, or deliverance. He didn't need them, though. He could probably write a book on Kim Sutherland.

"…if you did, you'd probably keep doing it," he finished wryly.

She closed the inches between them, pressing against his body and smiling wider when he groaned.

"Little tart," Bennett murmured.

"No one calls people that anymore."

"Like I care."

"You like me this way."

"Yes, I do." He kicked his pack aside and walked Kim backward, as if there was a target painted on the center of those pressed white sheets.

There'd be plenty of time to sleep when he was dead. Right now, he had a hardheaded woman to conquer.

Chapter Thirty-Two

Kim

KIM DID NOT want Bennett to doubt her commitment to the cause, so when she felt the bed behind her, she turned and crawled onto it, then peeked over her shoulder and tossed him a saucy wink. She was probably mean to taunt him, but the man clearly needed a reminder of what he'd been missing for the last week.

"See? Isn't this nice?" she asked. "No pebbles poking anyone's knees. No threat of bear attack."

"As much as I appreciate the view," Bennett rumbled, "I like this one even more." He grabbed her hip and urged her onto her back.

He had big, strong hands. Kim flopped over with a smile. "Okay, so no rocks digging into my back and keeping me awake. Still nice."

He leaned close and murmured in her ear, "That pallet I made you was too thick to feel any peas, Princess. You might've gotten more sleep if you hadn't been set on exploring the nearby terrain."

Kim wrapped her arms around his neck, so he couldn't get away. "Mmm, guilty. It was such nice terrain, though." She closed her eyes with a sigh, remembering the sight of his abs laid out next to her in the tent.

"Open your eyes," he demanded immediately. "I want you to see who's fucking you."

"I know it's you. It's always been you."

Bennett paused, and his turquoise eyes flickered with emotion. "Got that right. Now take off these shorts. They're in my way."

He held himself off her while she complied, then cocked an eyebrow when Kim quickly slipped out of her t-shirt, too.

"Just saving some time," she told him with a smirk.

Bennett wedged a strong thigh between hers, letting Kim feel his weight. Her panties were soaked, just with that little bit of dominance.

He surrounded her with his indescribable, delectable scent, his warm mouth pressing kisses on her neck, his muscular arms caging her in.

When Bennett's lips found hers, his tongue was hot and hungry. Before long Kim was straining against his thigh, trying to find the friction she needed.

As always, her need wreaked havoc on his restraint. In a sudden burst of motion, Bennett groaned and pushed off her, his face a mask of determination as he wrestled out of his clothes, then climbed over her once more.

His skin was scorching, and incongruously soft against hers. Kim wanted to drown in him and never come up for air.

He ran his hand up her side to cup her breast, then dipped his head to pull down the lace of her bra and wrap his lips around her nipple.

Kim gasped, the tight sensation streaking to her core like an electric shock.

The sudden sound seemed to spur him on. Bennett growled, "Changed my mind," then rolled her over and pulled up her hips, balancing Kim on her forearms and knees.

His palm landed hot and heavy on her lower back, and when she looked back at him his eyes burned with want.

"Don't move," he instructed, backing off the bed and edging toward his pack.

Kim dropped her forehead to the comforter and tried to hold steady, but every sensitive nerve ending she had came alive as the fan sent a cool breeze wafting across the backs of her thighs.

In seconds, Bennett's weight and heat covered her once more. "You ready, baby?" he whispered next to her ear. "You still want this?"

His erection slid through her folds, thick and hard as marble.

"Oh god, yes." She might die if he didn't give it to her.

He moved back and forth a couple of times, spreading her wetness before he slid in slowly, making her feel every inch.

Kim pushed back, needing more. Needing everything.

Once he'd buried himself, Bennett held still, exhaling unsteadily against her neck, his chest rising and falling against her back, his bicep like iron beside her face.

Kim whimpered, awash in how good he felt. How right.

"Please," she begged, "Please."

A low sound escaped his throat, and Bennett started to move, in hard, steady thrusts that pushed her flat against the sheets. Kim gripped the edge of the mattress and held on.

His face hovered inches from hers. "Tell me you're mine," Bennett snarled, not letting up on his pounding pace. "Tell me."

"Yours," Kim gasped, "Always yours."

"Then come for me," he said. "I can't wait, Kimmie. Come for me now." He shoved a hand under her hips and found her clit, undoubtedly knowing how it would send her over the edge.

His finger rubbed careful circles as he drove into her, until her muscles went rigid, and her release took hold. Kim keened, wave after wave pulsing through her.

"*Fuck*," Bennett breathed, sounding shocked despite his prior demands. His hips slammed into her, harder and faster until suddenly he froze, wordless in his completion.

His chest heaved against her, taking in gulps of air while he pulled himself together.

That was fine. Kim was so wrecked she wasn't sure she could look him in the eye, anyway. It seemed impossible to love someone so much—to want nothing but them, for the rest of your days.

Except here she was, a veritable puddle beneath him. *Probably should've seen it coming.*

Far too soon, Bennett pulled out of her and rolled to the side, chuckling sheepishly. He pulled Kim close, and tenderly stroked the line of her spine. After long minutes of drifting between earth and bliss, he teased, "So. You've loved me your whole life, huh?"

"Don't you dare tease me about that," Kim warned. "I did not make myself vulnerable to give you material for your comedy routine."

"I'm not," Bennett protested. "It's cute. I like it."

"Cute?" Kim smacked his shoulder. "You know what, forget it. I take it back. You're a brat and now you're going to have to earn back my affections."

He laughed as he wrestled her into submission, pinning Kim beneath him and twinkling merrily at her as she squirmed.

Could *anyone* stay mad at that face? She highly doubted it. It might make her the worst kind of simp, but she didn't care. Bennett Shaw was worth it.

His shoulder muscles bunched impressively as he held himself over her, but thankfully he didn't drop his weight this time. She kind of had to pee.

He pressed a kiss to her temple and told her, "It's okay, darlin'. You won't break the spell if you go use the bathroom. I'll still be here when you get back."

Kim chuckled. Of course. *Always so perceptive.*

"Awesome. Be right back."

After she'd taken care of business, Bennett barged into the bathroom and urged her into the shower, washing her like she was made of crystal before quickly rinsing off himself.

Then they climbed back under the covers, content to lounge for a while before they had to think about dinner.

Kim snuggled against Bennett's side and commented, "It really is spooky how you always know what I'm thinking. I wish I would've realized you were reading my mind when we were kids."

"I told you, I don't read minds."

His body felt tense. She'd upset him.

"Then what are you doing?" she wondered. "Because you sure seem to notice things that other people don't."

Bennett sighed heavily and fixed his glittering eyes on her. "It's not magic. I just…read body language, I guess. Subtle changes in tone—that kind of thing. I do it subconsciously and faster than most folks, but there are probably a ton of people who can teach that and do."

"You act like it's no biggie," Kim murmured, "But it's an extraordinary talent, Bennett. Really."

"Why? Because I'm a guy?" he snorted. "Shannon does the same thing, and I've never once heard you mention it."

Kim thought back. He wasn't wrong. It was only that she was used to the women in her life having a certain amount of emotional intuition. Perhaps that *was* why Bennett's gift seemed so unusual.

"Bennett, I meant it as a compliment," she said gently. "Why does it upset you?"

He stared at the ceiling and pressed the side of his fist against his lips, as if he could hold the answer in.

It came out anyway. He was making progress, even if he didn't see it that way.

"Have you ever stopped to wonder *why* I would have such a skill?" he said eventually. "Honed to perfection over years and years? It wasn't a choice, Kim. It isn't something the Teams taught me, or something I learned in class."

"Where, then?"

"My parents. Who else? Who else in my life was so volatile, so fucking unpredictable at any given moment, that a baby had to learn to predict what was coming next or else? Carving out an extra few seconds to prepare is a survival mechanism, and every single *fucking* time someone brings it up, I am reminded of what a trash upbringing I had, and what a total fraud I remain."

Bennett rolled to his side so he could search her face. "People act like I'm some kind of marvel, Kimmie, but I'm not. I'm a stray dog that has managed to exist, undetected among purebreds, for a really long-ass time. They're bound to find out eventually. Then what?"

She blinked at him, stunned. "Or *maybe*, you're actually a survivor. An extraordinary human being who overcame huge challenges, and managed to triumph—to succeed in a profession that most people can't even fathom, while still hanging onto your moral compass."

Kim reached out slowly and caressed his cheek. "You're not a cuckoo in the nest, Bennett. You belong where you are."

He flopped onto his back, breaking their intense eye contact. "Assuming I get reinstated. The Navy might not accept our appeal. They've got some new committee that's supposed to rule on whether our appeal can even move forward."

"It will," she assured him. "If they uphold your discharges, they have to know they'd be cutting off their nose to spite their face."

"We'll see, I guess." Bennett's voice was grim, all traces of his prior mischief long gone.

Kim frowned at him. "Is your new job so bad?"

"No." He shook his head and glanced over. "But we haven't done anything except investigate the Doggetts yet. And on that note, I'm not a person as good as you think, because I want to *end* those people. Round them all up and throw away the key, so they can't destroy anyone else."

Kim watched him levelly. "Bennett, I'm sorry I brought up bad memories for you. I didn't make the connection, and that's on me. Mainly, though, I'm sorry you have so many bad memories to begin with. I wish I could've done more to help."

He shook his head. "You didn't know. Shannon and I…we made sure no one knew how bad it was."

"Why?"

"I told you before—so CPS wouldn't take us. No way was I going to let them send Shannon someplace without me. We were better off on our own."

Kim slid her hand across his chest, until she could feel his heart beating wildly under her palm. "Bennett, I might be out of place asking this, and if so, I hope you'll say so. But I'm wondering if you have any contact with your folks now?"

"No."

"When was the last time you spoke to them?"

"February 10th of senior year. They said they were going out for cigarettes and never came back. So long, farewell, have a nice life, kids."

"Dear god."

"Yeah, well. All things considered, we were better off."

"Maybe."

Bennett turned toward her and searched Kim's expression before gingerly touching her cheek. "Definitely," he corrected. "Now, would you like to order some dinner or just get some sleep? With any luck, by tomorrow someone will have found your bastard ex, and we can get you home and back to normal."

"I don't want to go back to how things were," Kim told him firmly. "Not anymore. I thought that was obvious."

"We can talk about that tomorrow, too," he demurred, kissing her gently.

Kim wished she could believe him.

* * *

THE NEWS REPORT was pulling no punches. As Kim sat cross-legged on the end of the bed and watched in amazement, the anchor read out,

"A manhunt is underway for Daniel James Cox, stepson of Texas senator and failed presidential candidate Roy Doggett. Mr. Cox allegedly drugged and kidnapped Kimberley Sutherland, the Dallas socialite he dated briefly

last year, holding her hostage for days before authorities located her at a Montecito estate last week. During the rescue, Mr. Cox escaped capture and was initially thought to have fled to the home of his factory manager in Hyersville, West Virginia. Those reports have proven false, and Cox remains at large. No motive has been released. Authorities say the abduction took place in San Diego's historic Gaslamp Quarter, moments after the victim dined with Cox at a local eatery. However, sources we spoke to…"

Kim shut off the TV and grabbed her chirping phone from the pillow beside her, not surprised in the least to see that her mother was calling again. She connected the call and put it on speaker.

"Mama? What is it now?"

"Sugar, I saw the news and I am calling to check on you. You do not have to be so snippy," Rayann huffed.

"Well, I don't know what you think might've changed since yesterday. I already told you I feel better and I'm safe."

Kim winked at the hunky source of all that safety, fresh from his shower and looking particularly devastating as he leaned on the doorframe of the bathroom in his low-slung towel.

"Yes, but where are you?" her mother pressed. "I don't understand why it has to be such a big secret."

Kim rolled her eyes. "Just gonna have to trust me, I guess."

It was hard to treat her mother the same, knowing what she'd done. That would hopefully get easier with time, but for now, Kim was happy to be several states away and out of murdering range.

Rayann fell silent for a long beat, then switched tactics. "Kimberley, enough of this shady nonsense with that Shaw boy. You need to come home. You should be where people know you and can look out for you."

"Mama, I said I'm fine."

"And I'm telling you I won't believe it until I can see my baby with my own two eyes."

Bennett's shadowed expression turned into a frown as he listened in. Her mother had been singing a similar refrain for three days now, and it was entirely out of character for her.

The real Rayann loved nothing more than a whirlwind romance on a good vacation. Under normal circumstances, she'd be lobbying to come to San Diego and play matchmaker herself, not trying to drag Kim back to Respite.

Something was off and it had nothing to do with her history with Bennett.

Bennett could sense it, too. He'd been talking to his work friends about Rayann ever since her first call. Now he gave Kim a grim nod, clearly hating to go through with what they'd planned but, like her, seeing no choice.

Kim sighed loudly. "Alright, Mama. You win. I'll come see you. Just give me a couple hours to make some plans, okay?"

"Okay, baby." The relief in her voice was hard to miss. "That's good. You let me know as soon as you have the details."

"I will. Bye now."

Once she hung up, Bennett blew out a breath and paced toward the windows, rubbing his wet hair with another towel. Kim watched the divots at the base of his spine flex and gave in to the disappointment that their little getaway had come to an end.

"So, this is the trap, huh?" she asked him. "You think it's Dan?"

"I do," he muttered bleakly. "But like I said, there's no way you're going alone. Let me get dressed and we'll give the guys a call. Hammer out the best way to execute this."

Kim scowled. "I'm fixin' to execute him. How dare he involve my mother like this? Is there no limit to how far he'll sink?"

"Apparently not," Bennett commented. "Which is further proof that whatever he's so ginned up about is no small misunderstanding."

"You mean those models."

He studied her moodily. "Honey, I know we've been over it, but I can't help feeling like we're missing something important. Is there anything you left out? Any little detail? It might not seem like a big deal to you, but it could explain why this guy's gone completely feral, thinking you hold the keys to his destruction."

Kim went to the balcony door, watching the waves while she combed through her memories yet again. After a while, she gave up and shook her head. "There's nothing, Bennett. Just the photos he showed me and his mom's new agency. I'm sorry."

He wrapped an arm around her, lending her comfort. "It's okay. I imagine we're going to hear all about it soon enough. No way is Cox going to drag you up there just to keep his trap shut and brood, right? He's probably practicing his villain monologue as we speak."

"Here's hoping," Kim agreed.

She wasn't worried about what Dan did or didn't have to say, or even about who might try to record him. Kim was dreading the damage Dan could inflict once he got Bennett in the same room with her and her mother.

As far as she knew, Bennett had not set foot in Respite since he'd left in the dead of night fifteen years ago, and his return was going to feature at least two people who could force him to relive that trauma all over again.

He could pretend not to care, but he had to be terrified.

She leaned back against his chest and told him, "Bennett, no matter what happens out there, I'll be with you. Alright? You're not going to be alone."

He nodded, but he didn't offer any words of reassurance back.

It was just as well.

If this whole thing went sideways, Kim wouldn't care…but Bennett would never forgive himself for making another promise he hadn't been able to keep.

Chapter Thirty-Three

Bennett

ALL TOO SOON, Bennett's boots were standing on Texas soil, and his soul was threatening to seep out the bottom of them.

Driving through Respite felt both achingly familiar and disturbingly strange, and he hated how he could still love a place that had done its damnedest to destroy him.

At least Shannon was safe in San Antonio—that was something. Bennett could not have gone through with this crazy plan if he'd had to worry about his sister and Kim, too.

As it was, he'd had to grit his teeth the entire way to Mrs. Sutherland's house, nestled on a cul-de-sac in a swanky new development that sure hadn't been there the last time he'd set foot in town.

Naturally, Kim had seemed fine. The wound on her cheek was healing nicely, but she'd covered the lingering evidence with an expert application of makeup. She was calm and poised, and her demure black turtleneck and tweed skirt looked painfully sexy with the addition of tall suede boots. Under different circumstances, Bennett would have been contemplating how soon he could divest her of them—she had quite a collection of lingerie and for weeks he'd been enjoying discovering each new set beneath her clothes.

Unfortunately, today Bennett had to allow Kim to saunter directly into a trap, and then leave her there for who-knew how long. It didn't inspire the same kind of feelings as a lingerie scavenger hunt, that was for damn sure.

Topping things off, he'd been forced to leave the scouting of Rayann's house and yard to the others, though it went against every territorial instinct he had. It was too late to do anything about it, however. The plan was already in motion and if Buck said he trusted the operatives assigned to this job, then Bennett would, too.

He stood tall in Mrs. Sutherland's driveway, avoided eye contact with the woman hovering nervously on the porch, and delivered his assigned line to Kim like nothing was amiss. "Why don't I go get some gas and run to the store so y'all can catch up for a bit?"

"That would be nice, thanks," Kim said, then lowered her voice so only he could hear. "I know being here is hard. Just…be safe. Don't do anything dumb, okay?"

Bennett managed to smile for her, though her mother's avid gaze made his skin crawl. "And disappoint you? Never."

Kim's eyes were wide and blue, and full of something he didn't dare name. "I guess it's time for you to skedaddle," she whispered.

"Be careful," he reminded her. "Don't go instigating things, you hear?"

"We'll see," she shrugged. "I'm not too happy with these people."

Bennett sighed. He'd tried to drill it into his teammates that Kim was liable to go off half-cocked if she got angry enough, and that they'd better factor it in if they expected to pull this sham off. He only hoped they'd believed him because odds were high that Kim was halfway there already.

She'd been certifiably frosty when she'd greeted her mother, and he'd bet his right arm that ice would turn to fireworks the minute he hit the bricks, or Dan Cox arrived.

Cox could be waiting inside the house, even now.

Bennett stole a glance at the front windows and forced himself to take a deep breath. They'd developed a response for every possible twist of this worm, and the plan was strong—it was his own weakness he was worried about.

Bennett could feel the changes already, like pepper under his skin. Time and space made no difference to the truth—he was a different person in Respite, and always would be.

Still, Buck trusted him, and he'd assured him of that fact repeatedly. Bennett would remember that when he inevitably wanted to tackle Cox later in these proceedings.

All he needed to do was plaster a smile on his face and not snap while the chips landed where they fell. Bennett would no sooner disappoint his best friend than he would Kim.

"Okay, darlin'. I'll see ya soon," he said, and turned on his heel—as if Rayann, up on that porch, was no more significant than a shadow.

Then Bennett got in the rental truck, stole one last peek at Kim, and pulled away.

SOME THINGS HAD changed on the way through town, but not many. The gas station was still in the same place as always, sporting a new sign and the same couple of pumps as ever. It was a little surprising they were still operational, since they had to be older than dirt.

Though he'd worked countless shifts there in high school, the angles seemed all wrong looking at it now. As if the building had shrunk in the intervening years.

Bennett had no time for memories, however, good or bad. He had a role to play here. As he filled his tank, he could only think about the next step.

He went inside to pay, and the clerk behind the counter was a high school kid, as Bennett had been before him and likely countless others. He eyed Bennett up and down, but waited until he'd taken his receipt and put away his wallet before asking, "You Ben?"

Bennett let his face twitch with just a hint of surprise. "Yep. Do I know you?"

"No, but a fella come in here a little while ago. Said if you stopped by, I should give you this." The kid slid a burner phone across the weathered Formica counter. "He said you left it in his truck."

"Dang. So, that's where that went." Bennett clucked his tongue. "Thanks, man."

"You bet." The kid turned back to his own phone, tapping the screen to bring it back to life.

The burner itself was nothing shocking—there'd been a chance that Bennett would get frisked at Mrs. Sutherland's, and they'd factored that possibility in. It was the kid's lack of curiosity that was unexpected.

Back in the day, so little had happened in Respite that any stranger coming through would've merited some suspicion. Bennett had worried over that with every step of the planning.

Maybe he shouldn't have. Maybe more had changed than just him.

He wandered out to the truck, fired up the burner, and saw that there was a new voice mail waiting from "Dad." With a reluctant smile, he played it.

"Perimeter secured. Proceed to the site."

Every molecule of his being was tugging him back to Mrs. Sutherland's, but Bennett pulled onto Route 12 and dutifully headed in the opposite direction. It took about twenty minutes to find the turnoff, but the cabin Ricky Stahl had described was right where he'd said it would be.

It looked like it'd been there for a hundred years. In contrast, Ricky's police cruiser gleamed white and new in the sun. Bennett parked behind it and shook his head.

The 5-0 sure hadn't driven Dodge Chargers when he'd been around. Someone's budget had gotten a boost. He wondered why.

Ricky didn't bother coming out to greet him, though Bennett wouldn't have either. He still paused on the stoop before going in, searching the trees to see if their meeting styles had anything else in common.

Nope, they did not. The woods were empty, far as he could tell.

Inside the cabin, all was as Bennett had expected. Rick was cooling his heels near the ancient kitchenette, and the back room was closed off and hiding an unknown number of occupants. A couple of beaten-down pieces of furniture littered the floor, but not much else.

"Damn, you are predictable," the sheriff said, smug as the day was long. "Just couldn't stay away, could you?"

"Guess not," Bennett shrugged. "I missed you."

"Like hell you did."

Hours after Mrs. Sutherland's call to Kim, Ricky had delivered an ultimatum to Bennett. If he came to the cabin with her, Cox would share the details of Bennett's past with press and the Navy appeal board, putting to rest any chance of him getting reinstated and possibly getting his pension yanked, too.

It was Kim they wanted. And only Kim. He was supposed to get her here, then stay out of it.

Bennett had neglected to tell her that part. She would've flipped her lid, and there would've been no reasoning with her afterward. He'd have to ask for her forgiveness later.

Rick peered around Bennett and turned mad quick when no one else followed him in. "Where's. Kim?" he barked.

"Not here."

"That wasn't what you agreed to."

"And yet," Bennett shrugged.

Rick took a couple of steps away, his boots echoing through the empty room. "Then I guess you're cool with us spilling your secrets." He turned and smirked, "Tired of carrying them skeletons around, Shaw? Or have you figured out that time's finally up on the long con you've been running?"

"Last I checked, food and home insecurity aren't illegal, Rick," Bennett gritted out, hazarding a guess on what he might know. "They're not even uncommon,"

"Prostitution is, though." Ricky smiled slyly.

Bennett covered his shock and tried to buy himself time to process the bomb that had exploded in the room. He had told no one. Not one person knew what had really happened, except for him, Kim, and Mrs. Sutherland.

If Kim's memory of what Cox had told her in Montecito was accurate, then...

"Who you got stashed in that back room, Rick?"

"None of your business."

"Well, I'm gonna respectfully disagree. I'm also going to tell you what I hope you were smart enough to figure out on your own. The guy's using you, Rick. Whatever Cox promised you, he will not deliver. Whatever he's up to, it flies in the face of the laws you swore to uphold. He's a suspected arms dealer, a possible human trafficker, a definite kidnapper—and God only knows what else. So you must believe there is something big in this for you. What is it?"

Ricky flushed, but he held his ground. "You're as full of shit as ever, ain't you?"

"Lie down with dogs and you're bound to catch fleas," Bennett commented.

"You ought to know. Now shut your trap while I get this wagon back on track."

Ricky pulled out his radio and curtly reported to whoever was on the other end that Kim was not with Bennett. Then his eyes drilled into Bennett's for a long moment before he came to a decision.

"Go check her mother's house," the sheriff instructed.

As Bennett watched him, he scoured his memory for any connection that would explain the man's involvement.

He and Rick had played football together in high school, along with nearly every other able boy in town. They'd briefly vied for the QB spot freshman year, but it hadn't been much of a contest. Rick had been a decent player, but Bennett had been an All-Star from the moment he could run.

Back then, Rick's dad had been a good guy, the deputy counterbalancing Sheriff Fecteau's malice with real concern for the Shaw family's well-being. Bennett had not trusted him, but he'd maybe liked him a bit, as far as that was possible for any adult he'd known.

Something else had to link Cox to Rick, and Rick to him. What wasn't he seeing?

Chapter Thirty-Four

Kim

BENNETT HADN'T WANTED to leave Kim with her mother any more than Kim had wanted to stay, but those positions stemmed from very different fears.

He'd been worried that Dan would pull something stupid and put her and Rayann in danger, and rightly so.

He'd wanted her to wear something more practical, just in case, but Kim had overruled him. Dealing with her mother's commentary on outfits that didn't meet Rayann's standards would only fray her patience more, and she had so little to spare as it was.

She'd been in real danger of killing Rayann, particularly once she'd seen the hawkish look on Rayann's face when she spotted Bennett.

Bennett was counting on her, however, so while he backed out of the driveway under her mother's watchful gaze, Kim steeled her spine and stomped toward the stairs, resolved to see this charade through.

Rayann didn't greet her when she reached the top step. Instead, her gaze remained fixed on Bennett's tailgate until it disappeared from view.

That only set Kim's teeth on edge all over again.

"Let's get you inside," she snapped, yanking the screen door open. "You're gonna catch a chill if you stand in this shade too long."

Her mother nodded and followed her in, looking dazed. She trailed Kim through the fastidiously decorated rooms, quiet as a wraith. It was a preposterous amount of space for one person, just as the house Kim had grown up in had been too much for three people.

She looked around and thanked her lucky stars she had something her mother never had—and that was Shannon and Bennett to check her worst impulses. All this excess would never be her. *Never.*

In the kitchen, Rayann settled herself in a sunny spot at the table, watching her expectantly. Kim stood on the terra cotta tile and waited for her mother to drop a bomb.

Any bomb.

Anything at all that would explain why she'd been so desperate for Kim to come home.

When nothing happened, she asked, "You want some tea, Mama?"

"Sure, darlin'. That would be nice."

Kim filled the kettle and set it to boil, then crossed her arms and leaned on the counter, a little piqued that Rayann still wouldn't lift a finger when there was someone else to do it for her.

So much for Texas hospitality. Apparently, daughters—grown or otherwise—counted as help and not guests.

"So…anything interesting going on this week?" she wondered.

"Well, I'm glad you're finally here," Rayann shrugged. "But apart from that, nothing outside the usual."

As far as Kim knew, *the usual* didn't vary much. Every Monday, her mother visited her hairdresser Tammy, to have her roots touched up and her hair blown out. Tammy's daughter did her nails the same neutral pink, unless there was a party.

Tuesdays her mother played cards with ladies in the neighborhood, rotating houses each time. On Wednesdays her mother drove to San Antonio for shopping and lunch, and Thursdays the housekeeper came and cleaned.

Occasionally, Rayann found herself a casual date, and somewhere in the schedule, Kim figured she also found time to make trouble.

She turned to get the teacups, but her mother's lazy drawl stopped her cold.

"Imagine seeing that Shaw boy in Respite again," Rayann commented absently. "Never thought I'd see the day."

Kim turned slowly on her heel and stared at the woman. She'd expected to have this out later, after Dan made his move and Bennett annihilated him for it—but she ought to have known Rayann would be a pot stirrer to the bitter end.

"He's not a boy, though I'm sure you noticed that," Kim said stiffly. "And, with the way y'all ran him out of town back in the day, I expect it took some real bravery for him to come back here," she said.

Rayann gave her the barest frown of confusion, no doubt hampered by her "calming pills" and latest round of Botox.

"Oh, I'm sorry," Kim continued, "You weren't in that posse, were you? You had other irons in the fire."

Her mother's eyes dropped to the table, where she brushed at nonexistent crumbs. "It took me a long time to get well, especially after your Daddy left. You were such a good girl, though, taking care of your mama like you did."

"Yeah well, consider my eyes opened now."

Rayann frowned harder at her. "Kimberley Jane. Just what are you implying?"

It was the reproach lacing her voice that did Kim in. "Mama, how could you?" she snapped. "Bennett was barely keeping his head above water back then and instead of helping him, you went and tied an anvil to his foot!"

Her mother gaped at her as the water began to boil, but Rayann didn't make a move to get it—not when her daughter was there to wait on her.

Kim huffed in frustration and moved the screaming kettle off the burner, then went to get the teabags from the pantry.

Once her back was turned, Rayann claimed, "I did no such thing," but her voice wasn't quite as confident as it could have been. "He happened to be driving by in my moment of trial. That is all."

Kim moved the saucers to the table, dropping them in front of Rayann with enough force to make her jump. Somehow, nothing broke.

Nothing but her composure, that was.

"Oh, is that all?" Kim demanded. "How'd Bennett land in jail, then?"

"How would I know? I was unconscious, if you recall."

"Like I wasn't there," she hissed, crushing the box of tea in her hand.

With one short phone call, one of the best nights of her life had turned into the worst. Until now, she'd never had someone to blame.

Years of helpless fury burbled to the surface, and Kim trembled as she stood there, wondering if her relationship with her mother would ever survive this.

Rayann tutted serenely. "I know you were, honey. And I'm sorry I gave you such a hard time with everything."

Her mother gestured for the box and delicately extracted a couple of bags, then waited for Kim to fetch the cups and the kettle. She waited for her to sit, then poured the water as elegantly as a queen.

"Here's some other things you ought to be sorry for," Kim told her. "You knew I was carrying a torch for that boy. You *knew*. But if your little plan had worked, Bennett would have left his own birthday party—where I'd spent half the night trying to get him to kiss me—to go service my evil mother. If your plan had worked, he would've then escorted me to prom—where I finally *did* get him to kiss me—knowing that he had slept with my mother for money only a few days before."

Rayann winced and looked away.

Her lack of remorse made Kim want to throw something through the plate glass window. "And yet, you said nothing. Can you even imagine what that must've been like for him, Mama? Sheriff Fecteau put Bennett in jail, and you stayed silent. What I had to deal with was nothing compared to him. He and Shannon had no one—*no one*—looking out for them."

Her mother's smile was faint as she blinked at her. "Nonsense, darlin'. They had you."

Kim would never know what violence she might've committed then, because in the next moment, the front and back doors of her mother's house crashed in at once, and three very large men barreled in and cornered them.

Rayann let out a horror movie scream, but Kim only froze, heart hammering like a cornered rabbit. There was no way Bennett had expected *this*. Something had to be wrong.

"Who are you? What do you want?" her mother cried.

Kim couldn't decide whether it was all an act. That was unnerving, too.

"Get up. You're coming with us," one of the men told them, waving his gun.

His *very large* gun.

Kim didn't budge. "Leave us alone."

The others grabbed for her and her mother in unison, yanking them out of their chairs and dragging them toward the back door.

"Wait!" Rayann hollered. "The stove is still on. You'll burn my house down."

Kim's eyes snapped to the stove. Had she forgotten that?

The man who'd spoken first rolled his eyes, but he turned off the burner and glanced around the room, looking for other problems. Satisfied, he herded them outside, where a dark SUV idled next to the garage.

Kim stumbled down the creaky back steps, fighting to get enough air into her lungs. This felt nothing like the first time Dan had kidnapped her, when she'd been too out of it to realize what was happening before it was too late.

Now, she understood what was going on. It was highly unlikely she and her mother would end up in another luxurious holding pen. Worse was the realization that somewhere in Respite, Bennett would soon figure out that all his careful planning had gone terribly awry.

Maybe he already knew. He had to be on the wrong track or incapacitated in some way, or he never would've allowed this to happen.

Kim tried to tamp down her trepidation as the jacked-up thugs corralled them into the back of the SUV. How was she supposed to rescue herself and Rayann, plus a stubborn SEAL, too?

As if to echo her reeling thoughts, her mother hissed in her ear, "Kimberley! Why did I pay for all those kung-fu lessons if you're not even going to try to fight them off?"

"I'd love to, Mama, but it turns out three-to-one odds are not my strong suit. Not to mention the fact that *taekwondo* is not terribly effective against automatic weapons."

"Y'all pipe down," the man next to them growled.

With that, the truck rolled out, winding sedately through her mother's exclusive community before pulling onto the main road, and after a few more minutes, turning west onto Route 12.

They rode in tense silence for a time, before Rayann nudged her arm again.

"Everything alright?" Kim murmured.

"Sugar, I need to tell you something. It's important."

Kim glanced at the men in the front seat, then cut her eyes to the one on the other side of her mother. He didn't react in the slightest.

"Can't it wait?" she whispered back.

"No, I don't think it can. And I just want to say I'm…I'm sorry I waited so long to tell you. I feel truly awful about it. It's…downright shameful, is what it is."

Kim shifted so she could see her mother's face properly and *knew*. She cut off whatever sob story Rayann had been gearing up for and asked, "Is this about the night you went to the hospital?"

"I…yes. How did you—?"

Kim waved her hand, wanting to stop everything. Her mother's too-little-too-late confession, the abduction they were currently embroiled in, all of it. It was too much.

She said, "I already know all that."

"No, you don't," Rayann retorted sadly. "But you need to, now."

"Mama, I *know*. Bennett told me everything." *She hoped.*

Her mother looked startled, but she recovered quickly. "That surprises me," she said eventually. "Given the way he looks at you, I reckoned he'd take that story to his grave."

Kim stared at the back of the driver's head, excruciatingly aware that their captors had to be hanging on every word. "Believe me, I was awfully surprised, too."

"I didn't mean to hurt you," Rayann said.

"Oh, no? You knew how I felt about him. And yet, of all the boys in town, you just had to pick him."

"I meant to hurt your daddy. You know how he loved to watch that kid play ball." Her mother pressed her lips together, still perfectly lined and glistening in flattering peach gloss. "But we can discuss that part later. What's important right now is that Barton Stahl knew the truth, too. Okay?"

Kim shook her head, not getting it. "So?"

Rayann stared at her, willing her to understand. "I dated him for a bit, a couple years before he died." She waved her hand when Kim reared back. "*After* he left his wife. Obviously."

Given the other shenanigans her mother had pulled, Kim wasn't so sure that *was* obvious. "How is that relevant, Mama?"

"Kim, if Barton knew, then Ricky might, too. And if Ricky knows…"

"Again, I don't see how…"

"Ricky made a new friend recently," Rayann said. "Slick fella from Dallas, with a father in politics. 'Course, I'd heard the name before. Some months ago, he didn't treat my baby too well."

Suddenly, it all made sense. "And Ricky could've told Dan everything. Oh, shoot. Mama, you know exactly what is going on right now, don't you?"

Rayann nodded quickly.

"We need to get where we're going, and we need to get there fast," Kim told her.

Bennett was going to be there, she guessed. Dan and Sheriff Stahl, too.

She called out to the heavies in the front, "Hey. *Hey!*"

The guy in the passenger seat turned around with a scowl. "What?" he snarled.

Kim took a deep breath, and hoped like hell she wasn't about to goad them too much. "Since when do kidnappers drive like a bunch of grannies? Can't y'all go any faster?"

Chapter Thirty-Five

Bennett

B ENNETT KEPT QUIET while Ricky instructed his compatriots to round up Kim and Rayann and bring them to the cabin, but he couldn't keep the scowl off his face.

He'd suspected this might happen, so they'd factored it into their projections. Now, Black Watch operatives would track the women's every move, ensuring they got there safely.

They weren't in danger, but that didn't mean he had to like it.

The good sheriff of Respite did not give one hot damn about Bennett's feelings, however. He simply leaned against the kitchen counter, ignoring his guest in stony silence while he waited for the ladies to arrive.

Rick cut a different figure than his father had. Back in the day, Deputy Stahl had been a big, genial man, though perpetually sweaty and disheveled. The buttons of his uniform had strained across a prodigious beer belly, yet somehow always held fast. Sort of like the guy's temper, which Bennett had never seen him lose.

His son, on the other hand, was a trim 5'9, and every inch of his sheriff's uniform was pressed and starched to neurotic perfection. To complement the spanking new Charger out front, he had a hat like a Statey, resting on the end of the counter looking as immaculate as the day he'd bought it.

Unlike his dad, Rick was ambitious. Trying to run with the big dogs.

But though he looked like a new breed, Bennett had spent his entire childhood with the man, and he suspected there was still a whole lot of good-old-boy under that shiny exterior.

There'd better be, anyway. He was counting on it.

The tires of a heavy vehicle crunched on the gravel outside, and soon Kim and her mother were led in and to the dilapidated couch at the side of the room.

Bennett scanned them quickly, but they hardly looked ruffled. That was the Sutherland women, though—a tornado would've had trouble mussing either one of them.

He locked eyes with Kim, searching for signs of trouble. She gave him a reassuring nod as Ricky strode to the bedroom door and swung it wide, revealing Dan and a fourth meathead training their AR-15's on Bennett.

"Well, look who it is," Kim snarked immediately. "*Dan*. You just keep turning up like a bad penny, don't you?"

Dan shot back, "Miss Priss. Fancy meeting you here."

To Bennett, he wondered, "How'd you find us in Montecito?"

"You ain't so slick," Bennett sniffed. *What a tool.*

The dudes in the corners didn't like his attitude, and rattled their guns in warning.

"Whoa fellas," Bennett murmured, raising his hands and keeping an eye on those muzzles. "No need for all that. You asked me to come unarmed and I did."

As if suddenly reminded of his duty, Ricky tore his eyes from Kim, hitched up his gun belt, and came over to pat down Bennett efficiently, though a little rougher than necessary.

Still salty about that QB spot, Bennett supposed.

As the sheriff did his thing, Kim shot out of her seat and glared at Bennett. "Are you drunk?" she wondered. "Why would you come unarmed to what was obviously a set-up?"

Bennett grinned at her as Ricky yanked him toward a support beam and zip-tied his hands behind it. "*To blave*," he told her.

Kim tossed her hands in the air in exasperation, then grunted when Cox pushed her back down beside her mom. If looks could kill, Bennett figured his glare ought to have dropped the man right there in his boots.

Mrs. Sutherland leaned into her daughter. "*To blave?* What does that mean?"

"Never mind. It's from a movie," Kim explained impatiently.

"Which one? Or was it one of those foreign films you used to like?"

"This is not the time, Mama. I can tell you later."

"Don't you worry, honey," Bennett said, catching Kim's eye again. "I'll be fine. These jokers are gonna have to knock me out if they want to get one over on me."

"Ooh," Ricky sneered. "I'm so scared." Then he punched the air near Bennett's chest a couple of times, like Ali warming up at a punching bag.

"Ricky, stop acting the fool," Kim muttered.

The sheriff spun on her. "I'm the fool? Your boyfriend's tied to a post, if you haven't noticed. Not much of a badass now, is he?"

Kim sniffed and tossed her hair, every inch the queen bee.

Bennett smiled fondly at her. He hadn't been joking—he could easily get free and lay out a few of these dummies, but Buck and the others were depending on him to play his part. They'd trusted him, and Bennett refused to be the weakest link.

He plastered a smile on his face and resolved to stay put, though if one of them decided to put another hand on Kim, all bets were off.

"Break it up," Cox spat, striding forward and nudging Rick aside.

To Bennett, he added, "And stop tempting people to knock you out. I need you alert for this part."

"Oh, here we go," Kim complained loudly. "Best get comfortable, Bennett. Dan's gearing up for one of his soliloquies, and he tends to run long."

Cox swung toward her, assault rifle and all, and Bennett's breath seized in his lungs. The man didn't retaliate, though. He only inhaled deeply and squeezed his eyes closed, like he was trying to stave off a tantrum.

The fucker was damn lucky he was successful. Bennett didn't want to kill him and miss the big reason they'd all been dragged there.

"Quick tip, fella," Kim went on. "Best keep your mouth shut and seem like a fool, then open it and remove all doubt."

Lord. That girl could start a fight in an empty house. She was doing beautifully, though—the more off-balance they kept the situation, the less likely it would be that Ricky or the heavies in the corners would guess what was coming.

"Just…shut the hell up," Cox said. "For once in your life."

He added bitterly, "*Jesus.* I do not know what I ever saw in you."

Mrs. Sutherland eyed him haughtily. "Probably hoping one ounce of her class would rub off on you. Lotta good that did."

Cox ignored the jibe, turning to Bennett instead. "You know, she's cute, but a lamp probably has a better sex drive. Feels like fucking a dead fish half the time, am I right?"

Bennett blinked through the red haze of anger that threatened to swamp him. He would not think about Dan Cox's hands anywhere near Kim. He could not.

Instead, he drawled, "Must not have read the manual, Cowboy."

Out of the corner of his eye, he kept track of Ricky. The sheriff looked way too antsy, back behind Kim's mama. If Bennett made any sudden moves, he was liable to pop off a wild shot.

"And I'm supposed to believe you have?" Cox laughed. "Fucking redneck. You've probably never cracked a book in your life."

"Hey!" Kim hollered, indignant.

"Shut up," Cox told her. "Forever, if possible."

To Bennett, he continued, "Now, then. As of right now, you and your friends are going to stop digging into my family. Our business is none of your concern. If you don't—"

He wheeled around and fixed his glittering gaze on Kim. "If you don't, we are going to tell the whole world about you and this little gal's mama. All that dirty laundry, hung out for the world to see. You want to hear about it first, Miss Priss? Maybe next time, they'll let you join in. Like a buy-one-get-one deal."

Cox glanced at Bennett over his shoulder. "Good luck getting reinstated with that kind of mark on your character. No amount of heroics can wipe away a class A felony—hell, you'd be lucky if you could hang on to your benefits."

His gun dropped a bit lower at his side as he mused, "I wonder what the statute of limitations is on rape and attempted murder? The law's gotten pretty hazy in recent years."

Ricky came around the couch to slouch near Bennett's pole at the center of the room. "Bet you didn't think anyone was left who knew about you two, huh? Probably thought you got off scot-free once my dad died," he scoffed. "Never did know your proper place."

Kim's face went dark with fury. "Ricky, put a sock in it," she snapped. "You don't know what the hell you are talking about. And what are you doing, getting mixed up with this jackass, anyhow?"

"That's rich, coming from you," Rick fired back. "I seem to recall plenty of talk about you and him and them fancy parties y'all were always going to."

Kim gasped in outrage and looked at Bennett, no doubt wondering what he was dragging his heels for. He bit his lip and shrugged. He'd get free when it was time.

"Anyway, contrary to you, I know exactly what I'm talking about," Ricky continued. "As it happens, there are three people in this room that were there that night. You, you—" He pointed at Mrs. Sutherland, then at Bennett, before letting his finger wave through the air.

It finally landed on the center of his bullet-proof vest. "—and me."

"You?" Rayann scoffed. "I don't think so."

"Like you were in any shape to register details," he sneered.

Kim's mom flinched and looked away, but Bennett couldn't worry about that. Next to her, Kim was looking positively murderous. He needed to get Ricky to focus back on him before she did something to screw up this ridiculous roleplay.

"Where were you?" he wondered.

In his mind, he went over the scene, and landed on only one real possibility. "No, wait—I know. The duck blind, right? Where you and Darby Decker used to hide out and smoke weed."

Sheriff Stahl looked smug. "I heard that shitty muffler coming from a mile away. When it cut out, I figured someone had broken down…but as it turns out, the truth was so much better."

Cox clearly didn't appreciate getting upstaged, because he quickly inserted himself between Rick and Bennett. "Awfully suspicious how these small-town crimes get swept under the rug, isn't it? And so inconvenient when the maggots come crawling back out to ruin your day."

He straightened his *Landry Cox* polo shirt. "Say it—say you'll call off your little shadow investigation and leave my family alone." Then he pointed his gun at Kim's face.

The dumbass really thought Bennett had the power to do such a thing? *That was a laugh.* He was merely one of many who wanted to see the Doggetts get what they had coming.

"Why Dan," Bennett drawled, swallowing back his anxiety over Kim's safety. "It's almost like you think your parents have something to hide. And here I thought y'all were innocent."

Rick hadn't left him much room with the zip ties, but the wood beam Bennett was strapped to was soft with age. He could snap it, if it came to that. If Cox kept that gun trained on Kim's beautiful face much longer, it was *going* to come to that.

"We are," Cox insisted, his face turning florid. "But your harassment needs to stop. You degenerates already cost my dad the presidential nomination. I won't let you take Texas from us, too."

"That scoundrel does not represent one inch of Texas," Rayann muttered.

"*Hush*," Kim whispered back, her eyes never leaving the gun muzzle staring back at her.

"But what about you, Dan?" Bennett asked. "What are you hiding?"

"I already said. Nothing at all."

"They why go through all this? Why drug and kidnap Kim, then hold her hostage at your buddy's place in Montecito? Why drag all of us here now? You've got an officer of the law doing your bidding, and for what? A whole lotta nothin', sounds like."

The room fell so quiet, he could hear the crickets outside in the weeds. The hired goons didn't move a muscle, but Ricky looked between Cox and Bennett, his brow pinched in confusion.

"You said that Montecito story was a lie."

"What!" Kim shrieked. "Ricky Stahl, this man *roofied* me! I'll have you know I was barfing my guts out for two days."

Bennett smiled. "Did he forget to mention that? Huh. Probably didn't tell you he's been running guns to a nutjob warlord in the Middle East, either."

The sheriff stared hard at Cox, trying to get a bead on him. "Mr. Cox, I hope you have not misrepresented the nature of this little gathering."

"The dude's as corrupt as they come, Rick. Come on," Bennett urged. "Don't let those fancy slacks sway you. You know better."

Rick looked to Bennett. "And why should I believe you? You put Kim's mama in the hospital back in the day. Wasn't pretty, neither. I found the pictures in my daddy's study after he passed."

There'd been photos? Bennett should've expected as much, but the thought still sent a ribbon of nausea through his belly.

But then Rayann got to her feet, and her voice cut through the room.

"Stop. All of you stop," she said. Her command held the authority of a mother who was far past her limit of patience, but it held something else, too. Something that made everyone go quiet.

She scanned the men gathered in front of her, until her eyes settled on Bennett and stayed there. "You thought no one knew what was going on with you and your sister, but you weren't so clever, sugar. We knew. We all knew. None of us did much, excepting Ricky's daddy. I suppose we were all wrapped up in our own problems."

She filled her lungs with air and glanced at Kim. "I've realized…I could've made a real difference for you two, though. I tried to do right by your sister, eventually. With you, I only made things worse."

Bennett froze, not sure he liked where this was going—but what was he supposed to do? Run up and gag her in front of the Respite sheriff, who, much like the one before him, hated Bennett's guts?

His eyes skated to Kim, but she looked calm. Strangely so.

He was abruptly thankful that she'd ridden his ass so hard to tell her the truth for all those weeks, and that he'd finally pulled off the bandage and done it.

At least she wouldn't be hearing anything damning for the first time, now. At least she'd heard his side first.

Assuming that was where her mom was headed. You never could tell with the woman. Rayann was a loose cannon, if ever there was one. She and Kim were about as similar as cats and cows.

"I didn't understand it at the time, of course," Rayann rambled. "Back then, I was a real hot mess. All up in my own head." She shrugged. "The path I chose seemed like the only one available to me. But what I did to you, Bennett—what I allowed to happen to you after? That was unforgivable. I know that now."

Mrs. Sutherland swallowed and looked around the room. "And look where it's gotten us. All this fuss, for a rejected housewife's bruised ego."

Cox laughed uncomfortably. "Why am I suddenly standing in the middle of a hillbilly soap opera? I thought this was a business negotiation."

"Dan, shut up," Kim snapped.

Ricky edged forward, glancing at Bennett before he looked back to Rayann, dignified as an empress beside the rickety sofa. Her hair had faded in the intervening years and there were lines around her eyes, but the woman was still as high-class as ever.

Bennett swallowed reflexively and stiffened his spine, reminding himself that these people were not his betters. They had no power over him anymore, despite how he'd once felt.

"Rayann, what are you talking about?" Ricky wondered.

She smiled gently at him, even as he held a gun next to his thigh. "Did you know your daddy arranged the motel room where Bennett and Shannon stayed after their folks took off? He paid half the rate every week, if I'm not mistaken, to make sure the kids could afford it."

The sheriff flushed, but he nodded warily. "My mother thought he was having an affair. He told me he'd set her straight, but I never could understand why she believed him. I thought maybe that's what broke them up in the end."

"He would've never. He was a good man, your father. Not so much Sheriff Fecteau, unfortunately. But that's a tale for another time."

No one said anything, and Bennett thought that might be the end of it. That his greatest shame might not see the light of day, after all.

But Kim set a hand on her mother's arm, urging her on. "Mama, where are you going with all this? What are you trying to tell us?"

Well, shoot.

He hadn't known about Deputy Stahl's generosity. Bennett's stomach knotted at the thought of what other revelations might be left to discover.

"I always knew it would be hard to hang on to my husband," Rayann told the room. "For years, it felt like a *not if, but when* situation. I'd thought the waiting was the worst part, too, but it turned out that learning it had finally come to pass was worse. I did the only thing I could think of," she shrugged. "I struck at his vanity with the one person he admired almost as much as himself. I chose the all-American boy—the football star. The son he'd never had."

"*Mama*," Kim whispered.

Rayann nodded, like she'd decided right then and there to set it all free. "The night I had my…my breakdown, the sheriff threw Bennett in jail. Everyone thought it was because he'd tried to assault me, out there in the dark, or that he'd given me some bad drugs. The stories people told! *Lord.* They would set your hair on fire. And not once did I correct them." Rayann's lips pursed, thinking it over. "Any of them."

Bennett watched that little movement and thought, he could do a lot of things—hold his breath longer than God intended, haul a grown sailor across a beach under fire, swim for an eternity—but he could not love his girlfriend's mother in that moment.

He couldn't even like her. Dan Cox and Ricky Stahl might be actively trying to ruin his life right now, but Rayann Sutherland had actually done it, and she'd never uttered one peep of an apology, since.

"Go on," Ricky said.

"I'd found out my husband was in love with someone else," she explained. "A couple weeks before. And as I said, everyone knew what kind of dire straits those Shaw kids were in. So, I came up with the perfect solution. Get some real money into the hands of the boy who was likely too proud to accept it outright, and stick it to my cheating man at the same time. It made so much sense to me."

Rayann chuckled ruefully. "What kind of person does that to a desperate kid? Hmm? What kind of monster am I?"

Dan Cox was not a patient man. He'd fidgeted and paced throughout Rayann's recitation, but now he scrambled over. "You know what, Shaw? I set this thing up with my friend Ricky, here, thinking you might be more amenable if you had your girl and her mother to consider. But I'm beginning to realize that Sheriff Stahl wasn't exaggerating when he said there was more to this story. Something even better to hold over your stubborn head. So, please—"

With that, he raised his gun to Rayann's temple and held the muzzle there. "Do go on, Mrs. Sutherland. Tell us *everything*."

Kim gasped, but Bennett disconnected from the emotion of the moment and did a quick assessment. For some reason, Rayann wasn't scared. Kim was, but she trusted him, and was the only person besides him who likely knew there was a team outside, just waiting for his signal.

The goons in the corners were holding steady, like silent sentinels waiting for a signal to get involved. Their tactical gear, he'd already decided, was a misdirection. To a man, they were more motorcycle club than mercenary, in it for a few bucks and nothing more.

Ricky, on the other hand, was wavering. He'd begun this little farce as Cox's henchman, but he was, at heart, a small-town man. He'd grown up in Respite, right alongside Kim and Bennett.

Once Rayann had begun her tale and invoked his father's good name, his loyalty had begun to shift from Cox, an outsider, to his own people. Even to Bennett, who was supposedly his childhood nemesis.

Hard to believe, and yet there it was, plain as day on the sheriff's face.

Bennett would've liked to tell him that he'd never hated him back. He'd had far bigger demons to slay at age seventeen than a wide receiver who thought trash belonged in the dumpster and not on the football field.

But Bennett wouldn't have to say anything now, he realized. If Rayann finished her story, Ricky was going to turn on Cox so fast the man's head would spin. He knew that like he knew his own name.

Which left Cox, the only real problem in the room. He wasn't dumb enough to add murder to his resumé but letting him hear the end of Rayann's tale could create big problems for the team, right as they were starting to make inroads with their investigation. If Bennett was blackmailed, he'd become a liability to them. He could not let that happen.

He didn't know what to do about it, though. He wished Buck was here.

Across the room, Kim caught his eye. She nodded, reassuring him with big blue eyes that had never once doubted him.

"Put the gun down," Bennett said. "And let the woman finish."

"You're not the one in charge here," Cox smirked, but sure enough, he stepped back. He thought he'd won already. Bennett wasn't so sure he hadn't.

Ricky told Kim's mom, "Go ahead, Rayann."

Mrs. Sutherland fluttered a little, and Bennett saw a flash of her younger self, a pretty, brittle woman who'd lit up around men. "It's hard. I'm not proud of it."

"Whenever you're ready."

Cox muttered, "*Jesus.* Can we wrap this up before breakfast, please?"

Finally, Rayann shrugged. "Isn't it obvious what happened? You all know how Bennett was. The whole town knew it. That boy was a hound, for all he was poor as a church mouse. Besotted with my daughter from the age of five, yet humping any other girl he could, the moment he hit puberty."

Dan turned pale. "Explain as if it's not obvious," he snarled, and the gun shook in his hand.

Ricky stepped to his side, put his palm on the muzzle, and forced it down. Bennett relaxed slightly. If the gun went off now, the only thing with a hole in it would be a shitty cabin's floorboards, and not Mrs. Sutherland.

He wondered—was she even Mrs. Sutherland anymore? Dr. Sutherland had decamped to Dallas soon after the incident they were discussing, divorcing his first wife and marrying the new woman a few years later. Maybe Rayann had changed her name by now.

"I offered Bennett five hundred dollars," she explained grimly. "To sleep with me. I waited to meet until his birthday, but Lord knew he did it all the time, and back then I wasn't so hard on the eyes. He was no innocent, so what was the harm? Once it was done, I was going to rub my husband's nose in it like there was no tomorrow."

"*Mama*," Kim hissed again, like the rough words were the final straw.

"I wasn't so brave, in the end. No surprise there. I kept popping pills while I waited for him, and I'd brought my husband's pistol to keep order…but when Bennett pulled up and just…cowered next to that car, shaking in his shoes trying to make himself come closer, I nearly gave up and ended…" she hesitated for a moment, her eyes far away. "Anyway, those bruises you saw in the pictures, Ricky—they weren't from Bennett. I was so hopped up, I fought the paramedics when they tried to get me out of the car and onto their stretcher. Bennett was the one who called 911. Thank heaven for that."

And there it was. Laid bare for all and sundry. For Ricky Stahl, who had apparently never forgiven Bennett for taking the QB spot freshman year, or his dad's attention a couple of years later. For Dan Cox, a senator's stepson with unimaginable resources at his disposal, all aimed at crushing Bennett and his brothers-in-arms.

And last but definitely not least, for Bennett's friends and coworkers, arrayed outside and listening in, ready to come to his aid when the time was right.

Everyone now knew that Bennett had nearly prostituted himself as a teen, and that word "nearly" barely rated in the grand scheme of things.

He'd spent every minute since despising himself, knowing he would eventually have found a way to go through with it. If not that night, then sometime soon after. He'd thought, these last fifteen years, that if anyone ever learned the truth, he wouldn't be able to endure being skinned alive for the world's perusal. The shame had felt like a poison, and if it was ever exposed, it would consume him where he stood.

Except…right now, Bennett didn't feel so bad. Not great, but not horrible, either, because the way Kim's mom had told the story, she'd made it seem like…like *she* was the bad guy. Not him.

Memory was a crazy thing.

As Kim had said, Rayann Sutherland had been a grownup, one with wealth and social position, and she'd propositioned a struggling kid thirty years her junior—then let the kid take the fall when her accidental overdose sent her whole scheme south.

Hearing the story told so dispassionately by someone else, Bennett was shocked by what a different spin it took on.

Perhaps Kim had been right. And, with the worst thing he could imagine over with, he felt…lighter, somehow. Like he could breathe.

Bennett said, "This isn't some big misunderstanding, Rick. Dan Cox is a wanted fugitive, and he's been trying to put one over on the sheriff of Respite. I know we didn't see eye to eye when we were kids, but I also know you're not the kind to let an insult like that slide."

"Rayann, I am going to assume there is some kind of *statute of limitations* on the books for soliciting a minor," Ricky began, sounding so much like a pearl-clutching schoolmarm as he cut eyes at Cox that Bennett wanted to smile. "And so, we are not ever going to discuss this again, you hear?"

"No, no," Cox sneered gleefully, gesturing with his gun, "she said he was of age. Shaw was an adult engaged in a very sordid, very illegal activity. Conduct unbecoming, am I right, Master Chief?"

Ricky flipped switches in the blink of an eye, spinning from Rayann to train his service weapon on Cox. He told him, "Shaw was seventeen when she solicited him. He did not go through with the act. He received no money. He did, however, act quickly to obtain help for a person in crisis, and good Samaritans are not guilty of crimes in this great state."

Rick took a step closer and told Cox, "And you will drop that gun right now, or I will make you."

Cox narrowed his eyes in fury. "We had a deal, Sheriff Stahl."

"Deal's off," Ricky said. "Put the gun on the floor and get your hands behind your back. You are under arrest for the kidnapping of Kimberley Sutherland—twice, I might add—and now for Rayann Sutherland, too. You have the right to remain silent. Anything—"

Cox sputtered, "Are you fucking trying to Mirandize me? You were in on this plan, you goddamn moron. You said, in no uncertain terms, that you would help me snare Bennett Shaw and get him to stop harassing my family. You *said* he was a dirtbag and you would love to see him finally get his comeuppance."

Ricky smiled thinly. "Prove it."

Chapter Thirty-Six

Kim

LISTENING TO RICKY and Dan argue was a bit like watching a heated tennis match, but Bennett didn't intervene, so Kim didn't either.

She'd been watching him carefully from the moment she and Rayann had arrived in this sorry cabin, but Bennett hadn't done much more than send her worried looks and poke at Ricky's ego, even when Dan started waving his gun around like the color guard in a halftime show.

Bennett had clearly hated her mother's trip down memory lane, but it'd been necessary—and Kim hoped that it'd given him more than just his skewed recollections and her admittedly-biased opinions to judge the past with.

That being said, she probably should have gotten more upset when Dan pointed his gun at her mama, but honestly—neither Rick nor Bennett would've let him do anything, and Rayann could use a dose of reality now and then.

She'd parroted Kim nearly word-for-word in her confession, but there was no telling if her mother actually believed what she'd said, if she truly got that her actions had changed literal lives, or if she was only plying the room for sympathy.

Whatever it'd been, Kim didn't know what else Bennett could be waiting for. Dan had been running his mouth like he was running for office, so they had to have enough to nail him to the wall by now.

He'd covered the kidnappings—plural—the guns, the…

The girls. Oh, Jesus. Bennett wanted him to say something about those girls.

Right as Kim realized that, Bennett threw the game-winning pass. He eyed Dan up and down and called out, "Hey, Cox. Whatever happened to those girls from Nabarut?"

He delivered it as casually as someone asking the location of the nearest hardware store, but even the guys in the corners tensed at his words. Kim could hear the ancient floorboards creak as their weight shifted.

Dan, asshole that he was, didn't see the trap. Of course, he didn't—he was thick as a turkey, no matter what his mama told him.

He sneered, "Wouldn't you like to know," and Bennett's eyes shone with triumph.

Kim wanted to gloat, but this wasn't the time. Not by a long shot.

Ricky spun to Bennett, stymied yet again by the rapid change in topic, but Bennett simply locked eyes with him and announced, clear as a bell, *"Blitz."*

A long time had passed since Kim was last a cheerleader, but she still knew a football play when she heard one. It only took a moment for recognition to dawn on the sheriff's face, too, but it did a split second before all hell broke loose.

Ricky dove for her mother and carried Rayann to the floor in the same breath that Bennett snapped free of the pole and tackled Kim, the two men shielding them with their bodies as operatives swarmed the room from every direction.

They cuffed Dan and read him his rights, and the hired thugs set their weapons on the floor and raised their hands without one peep of protest.

Bennett's team swiftly combed the rest of the cabin, but the four of them stayed put on the floor, breathing in the decades-old dust kicked up by many pairs of boots.

Ricky called in the raid on his radio, then looked over at Bennett and muttered wryly, "Golden boy to the end, ain't ya, Shaw? God, I *still* can't stand you." He shook his head fondly.

Bennett smiled. "You woulda been a great QB, Rick. Not state champion great, mind you. But still darn good."

Ricky rolled his eyes, but he didn't throw a punch, so Kim figured there was space for her to get in a dig of her own.

"Mama, don't get any ideas over there. Ricky looks young, but he's a law-abiding citizen and he's got a wife and kid at home. No funny business, you hear?"

Kim might never forgive the woman for what she'd done, and she was damned if she was going to let Rayann's secrets crawl back into the dark to fester again. Still, the strangled silence that met her jibe was a little unnerving.

"Too soon?" she wondered.

"*Yes,*" Ricky protested, but she could see that he was fighting back a smile.

Kim couldn't see Bennett's face at all. He'd buried it in her neck and was hiding there like a big old chicken. She patted his back, giving him another moment to recover.

Rayann blinked at her like a glamorous owl. Once she'd collected herself, she snapped, "Young lady, that is not a joking matter, and you are grounded for the rest of your life."

"Clear," someone barked above them.

Bennett got to his feet and helped Kim stand while Ricky hauled her mother up beside them. He murmured in her ear, "Don't worry, darlin'. If you get collared for deep sixing her, I'll break you out."

Kim snorted. "Mr. Shaw, you taught me how to pick a lock in middle school. I'll break my own self out."

Wyatt and Joe walked by, decked out in tactical gear. As they passed, Joe wondered absently, "What kind of henchmen use blanks in their weapons?"

"Honestly, you get what you pay for," Wyatt mused. "Cox is probably too cheap to supply ammo he can sell somewhere else."

Bennett leaned over to catch the sheriff's eye, but Ricky just shrugged. "Wasn't my idea," he drawled, "But now I kind of wish it had been."

The gaggle of goons in the corner finished up with the assortment of operatives and Texas Rangers questioning them, then conferred with each other for a time. Eventually, they came to some agreement and sent two men over to Kim and Bennett.

Bennett stiffened and edged her behind him.

"Master Chief Shaw?" asked the one who'd been in charge at her mother's house.

"Yes," Bennett answered slowly.

"Clayton Bickford. This here is Keith Hobbes." They stuck out meaty hands, each shaking Bennett's in turn.

Bickford indicated himself and Hobbes and jerked his chin at Bennett. "Foxtrot Platoon, Operation Just Cause," he announced.

Bennett's shock was clear. "No shit? Foxtrot—that's our..." he gestured vaguely after Wyatt and Joe.

Bickford smirked. "Yeah. We been following your case ever since it hit the company listserv. When Rick asked us to pitch in and help him take down a dirty SEAL, we figured we'd see for ourselves what all the fuss was about. Maybe lend you a hand if need be."

"I..." Bennett blinked, at a loss for words. "Thank you. What are the odds? I mean—"

Kim slid her arm through his as an operative led her mother away and Ricky was called outside by one of his deputies.

"The odds are what we make the odds," Bickford said, giving her a wink.

"Hey, you like bikes?" Hobbes inquired suddenly, fishing in his vest and withdrawing a patch to hand to Bennett. "We got a good-sized club here in town and we'd be pleased to have you if you decide to come back."

"That is not likely," Bennett admitted, but he accepted the motorcycle club patch and examined it in silence before showing Kim the glowering embroidered frog, replete with helmet and gold trident.

She took it from him and grinned at the men. "Heck, I'll wear this. It's really cute."

Bickford chuckled as he slipped Bennett a business card.

"Sorry we gave you and your mama a hard time earlier," he told Kim smoothly. "We didn't want to clue you in and have y'all let something slip by accident."

"Kim?" Bennett scoffed, as he pocketed the card. "Never. She's ice cold. Her mother, on the other hand—"

Kim waved her hands, cutting off that topic. "No harm, no foul. And we are not going to talk about my mother."

Hobbes nudged her shoulder with a smile. "Nice looking lady, though. Don't suppose she's single and ready to mingle?"

Kim stared at him. "I am leaving, Mr. Hobbes. *We*," she pulled at Bennett, "are leaving. And I do not want to know about anything that comes after what you just said."

"Y'all have at her," Bennett chuckled, "and good riddance." He shook their hands and accepted their commendations again. Then he let Kim drag him outside, where cops and operatives were teeming across the scrub grass yard.

Ricky appeared out of the fray and took them aside. "Bennett. Quick question. Do you happen to know whatever happened to your folks?"

"Uh, no," Bennett admitted with a frown. "Far as we know, they went out one night and never came back. Why?"

"Want me to see if I can find anything in the archives?" the sheriff offered. "When that joker Cox first came sniffing around, I looked them up real quick. I found a few citations for panhandling and harassing tourists during bluebonnet season, but I can dig deeper if you want. See if there's anything else?"

"Nope," Bennett shook his head quickly. "Thanks, but no thanks. Best to let sleeping dogs lie. Shannon and I have long since moved on."

"Fair enough." Ricky glanced down at his boots, then tipped his hat back so he could gaze straight into Bennett's eyes. "I just want to say, I'm sorry for giving you and your sister such a hard time back then. Clearly, I was an idiot, but I sure do wish you'd said something and saved me from making such a horse's ass out of myself."

"Water under the bridge," Bennett told him. "I was hardly a genius myself, thinking it'd be easier to deal with the rumors than it would be to admit the truth. Sometimes that's how it goes."

"Yep. Still wish you'd let one of us take this gal to prom, though. Shit or get off the pot, know what I mean?" Rick looked between them, then awkwardly cleared his throat, and squinted across the yard. "Pardon my French. Anyway, guess I'd better go do my thing."

He pulled his trooper hat low on his forehead again and told Kim wryly, "Ma'am. I'll keep an eye on your mama, okay? You don't gotta worry about her."

"I appreciate that Ricky, but Rayann's a handful," Kim laughed. "You'll be better off leaving her to those bikers."

"Yeah, well—I've seen a 'handful' or two in my time." He puffed out his chest and strode away. "Don't be strangers, you two."

Bickford and Hobbes caught up with him a few steps away. "Sheriff, if you're about done with us, we're fixin' to head out."

"Is that so?" Ricky eyed them dubiously. "And when were y'all planning mention you were bringing knives to a gunfight?"

Roy turned to Bickford. "Dang, Clayton. Did you forget to tell the sheriff what the score was?"

Bickford shrugged, "Guess I did." A small smile peeked through his gray beard. "Not sure I'd complain too much, though. You ain't seen what Roy can do with a knife."

"I did not hear that," Rick snapped. "Next time tell me what you're up to."

Clayton smiled wider. "Sure thing, Cowboy. Long as you figure out who the bad guy is before the hoedown starts."

With that, they sauntered away to join their companions, and headed for the big truck they'd transported Kim and her mother in.

Rick's face was flushed when he turned back to her and Bennett. "I had a plan," he insisted. "A good one."

"Yeah, you and every other clown out here," Kim murmured.

Rick squinted at her, but he didn't refute it. He just spun on his heel and strode off.

Bennett watched him go, then turned to her with a funny expression on his face. "This has been one weird day," he told her.

"You think?"

"I do. What do you say we get you out of here, Calamity Jane? You need to change out of those dusty clothes, and I need to get out of this. As soon as possible, if you please."

Kim grabbed his hand and squeezed it. "I have no problem with that, but you're the hotshot with the cool friends. Who here do we need to talk to?"

Bennett scanned the yard, brightening when his eyes landed on a tall man with eye-catching silver hair several feet away. His best friend Buck.

"That's the guy right there," Bennett told her. "The man with the plan. He'll know what to do."

Chapter Thirty-Seven

Bennett

THE TRIP BACK to the coast wasn't nearly as uncomfortable as Bennett had feared it would be. Buck had been first out of the gate with a peptalk, naturally, but Wyatt and Joe had also found quiet moments to assure Bennett they had his six, and that nothing had changed between them thanks to the revelations about his past.

He'd worried about being a liability, or a pariah. Instead, Bennett had been given grace by the men who'd gone through fire beside him and emerged his brothers.

Having his whole tawdry history flapping out in the wind would still take some getting used to, but at least his team had seemed to understand that it was off-limits for jokes.

They'd used all of those on his relationship with Kim, and on the photos of Shannon she'd insisted on showing them.

Bennett wanted to groan all over again, remembering it.

He turned his head to the side, where Kim had a book propped in her lap so she could read a bit before bed.

"You can't keep showing pictures of my sister to the guys," he said. "At this rate, they're liable to sneak out to San Antonio just to meet her."

"They enjoy learning more about you," Kim demurred primly, but she kept guilty eyes glued to her book. "Besides, would introducing them be so bad?"

"Yes," Bennett argued. "Do you have any idea where their mouths have been?"

She wrinkled her nose. "TMI, Bennett. TMI." She snapped her book closed and whacked him lightly on the arm with it. "Anyway, I think you're missing the real danger."

"Which is?"

"You ought to be more worried about Shannon showing up here. She mentions visiting every time I talk to her now."

Bennett folded his arms behind his head and sighed. "I know. She's doing it to me, too. I told her she has to hold off until all the media crap dies down, though."

Kim laughed at that. "And you think she'll listen?"

"Probably not. But I'm hoping it'll buy us a little time, at least."

"Fair enough." She rolled to her side and slid her hand across his pecs, until her palm rested lightly over his heart. "How are you holding up? I know you said you're fine, but…having my mother recite chapter and verse in front of everyone couldn't have been easy for you. Are you sure you're okay?"

Bennett covered Kim's hand with his and held it in place. "It's…you know, it's a thing I've kept buried for so long. It feels odd to think that people know the truth now. It's hard to believe they don't judge me for it. So…getting comfortable with that is going to take some getting used to, and in the meantime, I feel like so much old stuff is getting dredged up in my mind. Stuff I thought I'd long since forgotten."

"You think it's because you were back in Respite, seeing everything again?"

"Maybe."

Kim frowned, her expression laced with concern. "Anything we need to worry about?"

"Nah. Just flotsam. Little details drifting to the surface and floating aimlessly on the tide."

There'd been a bit more than random memory debris, but Bennett wasn't going to tell Kim that—not right now, anyway. What had come to him that afternoon was still too fresh in his mind.

He'd been on his way home from the gas station, where he'd worked a double shift, when he learned about the eviction.

Bennett had known the calm couldn't last forever—hell, it had already gone on longer than either he or Shannon had expected. They hadn't known how or when the hammer would drop, only that it would, eventually.

As it turned out, it came in the form of Deputy Stahl, pulling Bennett over on his way home from work, for no damn reason whatsoever.

"Don't worry, son," Stahl had said as he strolled up to Bennett's window. "I ain't gonna ticket you. I just saw you going by and thought you might could use a heads up."

"Yessir. For what?"

He'd looked uncomfortable, but his genial smile never wavered. "Afraid your folks haven't been keeping up with the bills. My boys are fixing to come to your place tomorrow to put y'all out."

Times up, *Bennett had thought.*

"You know what that means, son?"

"Not really." He'd had his suspicions, though.

"They're going to drag all your stuff out to the curb. The landlord wants to rent the place to someone who's actually going to pay, so y'all gotta leave."

"Okay."

"They're going to change the locks on you, too. Don't think you can slip back in."

"No sir."

Stahl had watched him for another minute or two, maybe waiting for Bennett to break. He hadn't. The last thing he'd needed was for the deputy to go home and tell his son Ricky he'd cried or some shit. Ricky would've told the whole damn football team, and from there it was as good as broadcast on the morning announcements at school.

"How're your folks, anyway? Haven't seen them around in a while."

"I guess they're alright," Bennett had hedged. It'd been his standard response, one he'd presumed was reasonably true.

How long had they been gone by then? Three months? Four? Could two junkies die in a ditch in that amount of time? Hell, probably.

"Anyway, I thought you and your family might like to get some things together tonight, before my boys roll up on you."

"Thank you, sir. We'll take care of it."

"Y'all got someplace to go?"

"Yessir. We can rent a room for now. We'll be alright."

Bennett had looked up the rates for four motels in the area. He and Shannon could maybe scrape by for a while at the cheapest one, if they both picked up some extra hours.

"All right, then," Deputy Stahl had drawled. "Take care now, you hear?"

Bennett had thanked him and pulled away, but he'd dreaded having to tell Shannon. They'd needed to come up with some excuse, in case anyone saw their crap on the street and asked about it.

They hadn't yet decided what Shannon was going to do once he graduated. She'd been salty at him for not applying to any out-of-state colleges like she and Coach had wanted, but Bennett hadn't been able to bear the thought of being too far away from her.

What if she'd needed him?

They'd already discussed whether Kim's family would take her in, if it came to that. Mr. Sutherland, they'd thought, would agree in a heartbeat— but the mother was a wild card.

He'd needed to lock that down even sooner, it'd appeared.

Once he'd gotten well out of sight of the deputy, Bennett had pulled over and rested his head on the steering wheel, trying to breathe through the suffocating worry. There'd been so much to think about. So much to do, and he hadn't known how to go about any of it.

"Bennett?" Kim asked softly, nudging his side. "You still here?"

"Yeah, sorry. Just thinking."

"Okay, well—speaking of thinking, I think I still have one bone left to pick with you."

Bennett glanced at her and smiled. "This ought to be good."

"What was with the *Princess Bride* reference in the middle of Standoff Junction? Roomful of men armed to the gills and pointing guns at each other's heads, and you're out there winking and quoting Miracle Max!"

"I was trying to reassure you," he explained with a laugh.

"By telling me *to blave?*" Kim complained, jabbing at him again. "Do you even remember what that means?"

"Of course," Bennett shrugged. "It means *true love.*"

"Exactly! And you didn't see a problem with insinuating that you love me for the first time in a room full of degenerate criminals?"

"One degenerate criminal," he protested. "The rest were supposedly helping us."

"You did not know that at the time."

"You looked a little nervous," Bennett told her, "And I wanted to you to know that I wouldn't let anything happen to you. Despite how things probably looked."

"So, you knew all those people were outside," she accused. "You knew and didn't tell me."

"Maybe," he chuckled. "It was safer that way."

Kim gaped at him in betrayal, but what was he going to do? Lie to her? As hotheaded as she could get, God only knew what she might've blurted out in the heat of the moment. She'd been skating pretty close to the edge, as it was.

Eventually, Kim pulled herself together. "Is life ever going to be the slightest bit normal around you?" she demanded.

Bennett snorted, "Nah. Where's the fun in that?"

She barely hesitated before admitting, "True."

"Forewarned is forearmed, sugar."

"Duly noted. Now, one more question."

"Shoot."

"Have you given any more thought to what Ricky offered? About trying to look up your parents, I mean."

"No," he said, "I haven't. As I've told you before, they were not the most nurturing people on the planet. Having them out of the picture complicated things in some ways, but…it also simplified things, if that makes sense. And now that I've managed to claw my way into a life of stability, dragging two addicts back into the picture sounds like the exact opposite of sensible."

"But maybe they're not like that anymore. Maybe they've gotten sober and want to make amends," Kim insisted.

Bennett tested out the idea and wasn't surprised when it fell flat in his heart. "If that's the case, they sure haven't gone out of their way to find either of us. I imagine a couple of quick internet searches is all it would've taken them."

She eyed him suspiciously, doubting his resolve.

"I'm serious, Kimmie. Ask Shannon, too. I'll bet you ten bucks she feels the same way."

After a protracted silence, she sighed and flopped onto her back. "Well, that makes this next part awfully awkward."

"I don't love the sound of that."

She didn't beat around the bush, at least. She only told him, "It seems my ornery mother had Rick go looking for your folks on her own, as some kind of penance for what she did to you."

"I told him I didn't want that. You heard me say it, right? *Don't go looking*, I said."

"You did," Kim agreed. "Unfortunately, Mama doesn't give a flying fig what other people want, and she can be inconveniently persistent."

"Well, that sucks."

"Listen, if you don't want to know, I respect that, and I understand why. Mama thought she was doing the right thing, getting you some closure, but I refuse to be a party to retraumatizing you."

Bennett stared at the side of her face until she turned to look at him. "So, Ricky found something."

"Yes. As a matter of fact, it's all in that packet that got delivered earlier. Mama had it overnighted to me."

"Did you read it?"

"No. I just wanted you to know that the information is available if you choose to look at it. Take as long as you need or just scrap it. It's up to you, whatever you decide."

Bennett wanted to tell Kim to burn it—to simply incinerate the whole file and good riddance. But the notion of learning once and for all why his parents had never come back…he couldn't quite make himself do it. Nor could he take that closure away from Shannon.

"Would you…" he stopped, ran an unsteady hand through his hair, and tried again. "Would you hang onto it for me? Just for a bit?"

Kim pushed forward and pressed a kiss to his lips. "I sure will. For as long as you want."

IT TOOK BENNETT a week. Seven days of knowing and sitting with that knowledge, before he could bring himself to ask Kim about it again.

"Alright," he said one afternoon, when it was just the two of them at the apartment. "Go ahead and tell me what Ricky discovered. How bad is it?"

"You're sure?"

"Yep."

Kim went to the bedroom to fetch the packet from wherever she'd hidden it and laid out the pages on the kitchen table. She scanned through them quickly and didn't mince words.

"You father died about ten years ago, in an encampment beneath an overpass in Oklahoma City. Looks like he was killed in some kind of drug altercation, along with two other men. The guy who did it went to jail. Ricky says he's still sitting in the federal lockup out there."

Bennett swallowed. It was hardly surprising, given the way his folks had conducted themselves throughout his childhood. There was little reason for the information to sting like it did.

"And…my mom?" he wondered carefully.

Kim's baby blues flicked up to meet his. "Still alive, but barely. She's in a hospice facility in Amarillo. Sounds as if her liver is giving out on her."

"Ah." Bennett tried to picture his mother's face. Tried to imagine her older. Sicker.

He couldn't. All he could see was her gaunt young face in one of the only family photos they'd had. He'd gone back to rescue it, after the sheriff's men had cleaned out the house. The frame had been sticking out of a box, in the jumbled mess of their shabby possessions, piled next to the curb.

Shannon had refused to take it when they'd packed up the night before, but Bennett had thought one of them might want it someday. To show their future children, if nothing else.

With a sudden flare of alarm, he realized that he had no idea what had become of it.

"You don't have to see her," Kim assured him. "But Ricky sent the name of the place where she is, in case you change your mind."

Bennett nodded, but he needed to think on it for a while before he could be sure he was making a sound decision. "Does Shannon know?"

"Not yet. I can tell her if you want me to, but I thought you might want to handle it. Or not. Whichever you think is best."

He nodded again, unsure how the conversation would go. Shannon was as likely to sob as to clock him, he figured.

He told Kim, "I'll do it. You stay out of range in case she blows a gasket."

"You mean when," she smiled gently.

"Either way."

"Bennett…" She shifted closer and pulled him into her arms. "Please. I don't want either of you to feel guilty if you can't bring yourselves to see your mama. You need to protect yourselves."

"I know, darlin'," he replied. "But I suspect it won't be that simple. Heck, at the rate we're going, I might need that shrink after all."

Kim kissed him softly. "If you do, you do. I'll be here for you no matter what."

"I know. And I appreciate that."

Bennett traced the faint scar on her cheek and let the rest of it go. Once he and his sister had a chance to put their heads together, they'd know better how to proceed. And with Kim by their side, it was going to be okay.

"Kim," he said quietly. "What did I ever do to—"

She pressed her hand against his mouth, silencing him. "Don't you dare say you don't deserve me. You hear? We're not doing that anymore."

"If you say so. You're the boss."

She smiled again, like a lovely sunrise breaking through the rain. "So, it's true love, huh? You fought it for twenty years and now you're going straight to soul mates?"

"Guess I am." Bennett nuzzled her neck and pulled her closer. "That going to be a problem?"

"Now what do you think?"

He kissed her and hoped that would cover it.

Chapter Thirty-Eight

Bennett

N O OFFENSE TO your boys," Kim announced a couple of weeks later, "but I need to look for a new place to live. Bachelor living has officially worn thin."

As if to punctuate her words, a deafening explosion from the living room TV vibrated through the wall, replete with squealing tires and machine gun fire.

Bennett muttered, "Change bad," and buried his head under a pillow.

She peeled away his shield and gave him a gentle smile.

"I shouldn't be surprised," he added, "You're a trooper for lasting as long as you have."

He might see his roommates as brothers, but that didn't mean she had to. Not yet, anyway.

The real problem was that in the short time Kim had been crashing with him, Bennett had gotten used to sleeping beside her and waking up to her soft expressions. Having to go without it was going to royally suck, even if he understood her need for space. Shared history or not, they'd jumped straight into the deep end of a relationship and probably ought to slow things down.

At least she wasn't talking about going back to Texas. There was that.

Kim patted him absently, not picking up on his disquiet. "I can transition my business to San Diego gradually, but I'll need to put my place in Dallas up for sale fast. I thought about asking your sister if she wanted to take it over, but I suspect if she's going to move anywhere, it'll be where we are."

"Lord, save us if she does," Bennett said darkly. "When that girl hits town, she's liable to start a feeding frenzy in Skippers."

"Bennett, it'll be fine," Kim chided. "You'll love having Shannon nearby, and you know it."

"So you two can gang up on me again? I don't think so." He flung his pillow aside and wrapped his arms around her waist instead. "I only want you. You and me and no one else."

Kim must've thought he was joking, because she laughed. "That's fine. I'll still have to go home a few times to get everything squared away, though."

"Permission denied."

"I'll time it for when you have to work. How's that? You can even send someone with me, to fend off the reporters." She kissed him lightly, like moving out of his home and his bed was a perfectly lovely thing to plan on a Saturday evening.

Bennett couldn't be mad about minor setbacks, though. He'd already won the bigger war. He'd won her.

"You drive a hard bargain," he grumbled.

"Get used to it."

Studying her carefully, he wondered, "You're really gonna stay in San Diego? Just…pull up stakes and relocate your entire life?"

"You bet," Kim shrugged. "Now that I've got you, I'm not inclined to give you up again. How do you feel about that?"

"Well…having you nearby will certainly make it easier to cling to you like grim death. So, there's that."

She shook her head, but then she ran her fingers through his hair, and the light touch grounded him as it always did. "Bennett, you are a true romantic."

"What can I say? I've got a long and storied reputation to uphold."

"More like the death of a bachelor to announce."

"Nice." He kissed her, then drew back so he could see Kim's expression clearly. "And what am I supposed to do once you realize you can do better? When some guy who's actually worth your while decides to take a crack at you?"

"Bennett, if some other man decides to try his hand with me you can sleep easy, because I will ignore him. I know good and well who holds my heart and it sure ain't a fella who doesn't respect boundaries and thinks any woman he meets is fair game, whether she's single or not."

She shoved his shoulder, adding, "Besides, do you really think I'm shallow enough to leave the best man I've ever known for a slick talker with a fat wallet?"

"You know I don't."

"Is my judgement suspect?" she prodded.

"Of course not. You're excruciatingly practical." The only question he had was, how long would it take to convince that practical nature to move back in with him.

"That's right, mister. I am. And my excellent judgment tells me that we are meant to be. Anyone says different, and I will start cracking heads—including yours."

Bennett grinned and pulled her on top of him. "You're kind of a hardass, you know that?"

Kim braced her arms on his chest and winked. "Learned from the best. At least I'm cute, right?"

"Very cute." He grabbed her hand and laced their fingers together, then kissed each one of her fingertips. "The cutest, in fact."

"Smart man," she grinned. "I think you'll go far."

SHE WORKED FAST, he'd give her that. It was less than a week before Kim was spamming his phone, begging him to meet her at a condo she'd gone to view downtown.

The real estate agent had stepped out to take a few calls when Bennett got there, so rather than waste time on pleasantries, he pulled Kim in for a sizzling kiss.

Never got old. He couldn't believe he'd spent so much time avoiding it.

All too soon, Kim pushed him away and pointed a threatening finger at his chest. "No fair," she accused. "That is not why I called you here."

Bennett just grinned at her.

"Stop that," she warned. Then she stepped back, waved an arm around the entryway, and demanded, "Well? What do you think?"

She led him past the kitchen and into an airy living area, where everything was bright white and smelled like fresh paint. The details screamed big bucks. Fancy marble counters, high-tech light switches—hell, even the view across the harbor had to be worth several extra grand.

"It was gutted and redone recently."

"It's real nice," Bennett managed. "What are they asking?"

As soon the words escaped him, he wished he could take them back. Kim quoted the price, the air rushed clear out of his lungs, and his heart might've stopped for a beat or three.

"Okay, just relax," she rushed to say. "That's not the final amount. The agent thinks there's room to negotiate, and I'll have money to put down from selling my place in Dallas. Plus, Daddy is talking about throwing a few more bucks my way. He feels bad about introducing me to Dan."

Bennett blinked at the rapid-fire words, but he didn't take many of them in. There were simply too many digits floating in his brain to register anything other than horror.

"Bennett," Kim said softly, moving closer and winding her arms around his waist, "I know the price is up there, but I really like this one. It feels peaceful, right?"

He anchored himself in her wide eyes and nodded numbly. She was right, somehow. Despite this being the home of some other, elevated kind of human, the condo did have a quiet serenity to it. Even empty, it felt oddly comfortable.

Safe, even.

"If I were to go for it," she whispered, running her hands up and down his back, "Do you think you'd consider living here with me?"

Bennett swallowed. Maybe.

He'd been thinking of buying an investment property sometime soon himself—between the money he had saved, and his new-and-improved salary at Black Watch, he'd thought he could swing it, and that it made good financial sense.

He'd been considering a small fixer-upper, however, one that he could get for a song and upgrade in his spare time—not some luxury high-rise that could double as a movie set.

"Would you rather keep looking? Or…" Kim paused and looked uncertain for the first time since he'd gotten there. "…or maybe you want to live apart for a bit? I have to admit I've kind of gotten used to you hogging the sheets. I just assumed…"

Bennett shook off his initial panic and ran some quick numbers in his head, before Kim could get too far down that road—he knew it well, and it led nowhere pleasant.

"I'm not going to lie," he told her. "Having coffee with Joe every morning doesn't hit like it used to. Not when I can have it in bed with you, instead."

She smiled tentatively.

What was the money he'd saved *for*, he asked himself, if not for building a future that was light years different from his past? It wasn't like he spent recklessly otherwise, and God knew he couldn't take it with him when he died.

Why *not* buy a permanent home base? One that wouldn't be another headache he had to fix, and one he wouldn't be embarrassed to share with Kim.

If they split the down payment and monthly mortgage, he'd still have a solid chunk of change leftover. With the help of a decent investment firm, he could probably grow it into a healthy nest egg.

Bennett had been too paralyzed by the hurdle of finding a firm he could trust to attempt it yet, and too afraid that if he got it wrong, he'd lose it all. However, Kim might know someone he could use—she probably invested all the time.

In light of all that, the price of the condo didn't seem quite so much like a financial hemorrhage. It seemed more like an opportunity.

Bennett sighed and dropped a kiss on Kim's head. "Show me the other rooms," he told her, "If we're gonna do this, I'm paying half. So, we better figure out whether my bed's gonna fit."

Kim lit up like the fourth of July and danced her way through the rest of the tour, her eyes vivid blue with excitement.

The real estate agent returned at some point, answered some of Bennett's questions, and promised to look into the rest. They threw around some figures, and the ball started rolling.

When she stepped onto the balcony to call her counterpart on the seller's side, Kim and Bennett were left alone once more.

She jumped in place and squealed with delight. "This is so exciting!"

It was something all right. Before Bennett could come up with a suitable response, a text pinged on his phone.

He glanced at it and frowned. "Damn it."

"What's wrong? Cold feet, already?"

"It's not that," he said, pulling Kim away from the sliding doors so they wouldn't be overheard. "Monroe says Cox has hired a phalanx of lawyers to fight the charges. We were hoping we could keep you out of court, but you might end up having to testify. At minimum, get deposed."

Kim didn't look nearly as unhappy as he felt. "I figured that would happen. Luckily, Daddy's introduced me to legions of attorneys in the last couple of years," she winked. "Doctors, too."

"Shame none of them took," he needled back. What wasn't a shame was that her jibe no longer made him feel two inches tall.

He was the one standing here buying property with the woman, not them.

"Well…one of them kind of did," Kim clarified. "I ended up making friends with this guy TJ. He's a killer. I know he'd be happy to help."

Bennett's eyebrows skated up. "TJ, huh."

"Don't look at me like that. TJ is as likely to make a move on you as he is me. Besides, we are both crystal clear on the fact that we're better as friends."

"Did you have to date him to figure that out?"

"I went on a few dates with him. There's a difference," Kim retorted. "If you don't know that, you're welcome to tell me about the ladies you've dated in the last fifteen years."

"Hard pass," he chuckled ruefully.

"That's what I thought."

"Alright, well…do what you think is best," Bennett relented grudgingly. "But you better warn this TJ fella that Cox and his parents fight dirty. He ought to be ready for that, though Monroe said he has someone who can help out if need be."

"I think we'll be okay," Kim grinned. "TJ used to be a divorce attorney. He knows from dirty."

"Used to be?"

"Well, he said if he ever wanted to settle down, he had to leave before he got too jaded. He does wills and trusts and stuff now. Although, it turns out that's just a different kind of messy."

"Love and money, Kimmie," Bennett laughed. "People start wars over them."

"That's the truth." She hesitated, just long enough for his internal alarms to start ringing. "Hey, while we're sharing, here…I guess I've got some news."

"Oh?"

Bennett couldn't help it—his eyes flicked down to her belly, still taut as ever under her clingy t-shirt. Had they been careful? He suddenly couldn't remember.

Kim whacked him hard on the arm. "Not that kind of news!" she snapped. "And it's more like an idea that a newsflash, anyway."

He rubbed his arm and scowled at her. "You're kind of violent, you know that?"

"Buck up and listen. Now, with Dan in the pokey I imagine the media nonsense is going to get more insufferable. I don't think me hiding out is the answer anymore. It's just going to drive the reporters to more invasive tactics."

Bennett squinted at her and recognized all the signs that she was up to something. "What are you planning, you little schemer?"

Kim bit her lip, allowing herself two seconds of conflict before barreling on. "What if I get out in front of it? I could reach out to Alix Hernandez back in Dallas and arrange an exclusive interview with her. She'd lose her mind."

She quickly held up her hands to forestall Bennett's protest. "Hang on. We can work out what I should say with your boss or whatever, but think about it. Maybe that would stop people from following me around all the time and trying to get me to comment. If the story's already out there in my own words, there won't be anything to add, right?"

Bennett took a deep breath and studied her. Kim was absolutely serious, and she wasn't the least bit scared. She also wasn't wrong.

"I can't believe I'm saying this," he admitted, "but that might not be the worst idea in the world. Peyton pulled off something similar a few months ago, too. She and Buck might have some tips."

Kim clapped her hands together, as if all her agenda items for the day had fallen neatly into line. "Great. With that settled, this seems like as good a time as any to finally give you your birthday present. I had Kenya drop it off before you got here, so we could bring it home in your truck."

"What?"

"You do remember the gift that got me kidnapped, don't you?"

"Don't remind me," Bennett growled, narrowing his eyes at her. "Though I have to be honest, I already know what it is. You were a very bad girl, spending that kind of money on me."

"You can punish me later," Kim huffed. "Aren't you the least bit curious to see it, though?"

She tipped her head toward a big package wrapped in brown paper leaning against the living room wall. Bennett had assumed when he'd come in that it was renovation materials, or something the owner hadn't moved out yet.

"Open it," Kim urged him softly.

He carefully lifted the masking tape holding the parcel together and spread the folds of paper wide, revealing a rolling field of bluebonnets, pretty as Kim's eyes. An ache of homesickness hit him right beneath his ribcage, making his eyes sting.

He could see why she'd gone to such lengths to get it. It was perfect.

"Kim," he breathed. "That's…"

"Home," she finished for him. "We might be west coasters now, Bennett Shaw, but hill country will always be our home."

Bennett swallowed down the emotion choking him and turned away from the painting. "You're wrong," he said. "You're my home. Wherever you are, that's where I'll stay."

She blinked rapidly, but the sheen of tears threatening to fall was more beautiful to Bennett than any rectangle of paint and canvas.

"Keep talking like that and we'll end up christening this place before the papers even get signed," she said shakily.

Bennett shrugged. "These things happen. And thank you, darlin', for the amazing gift. It is now officially the nicest thing I own."

"Think of it as your first investment," Kim smiled.

Then she looked at the painting. A calculating gleam crept into her eyes as she glanced around the room, and he could almost see the wheels start spinning.

"Oh no you don't," Bennett told her. "That is where the flat screen is going. You want to hang this baby, you'd better find another wall."

Before she could argue, the real estate agent pulled open the slider and stepped back inside. "I think we're in business," the woman crowed. "You two ready to call this place home?"

Bennett looked at Kim, who was trying not to laugh. "Hooyah," he said, and meant it.

Chapter Thirty-Nine

Kim

B Y THE TIME they returned home, Bennett was oddly agitated. He bypassed the kitchen, marched straight to his room, and flopped on his bed. His body vibrated with what looked like fury but was probably, knowing him, stark terror.

They were moving in together. No, even more than that—they were *buying* a place together. It was a lot, and yet somehow not nearly enough.

Kim sat on the edge of the mattress and watched him for a minute, then gingerly smoothed back his hair.

"Bennett, are you sure you're okay with this? There's still plenty of time to change your mind."

"I need to know how this is going to work," he said abruptly. "Are we just two people dating? A couple living together until some indefinable point in the future when we magically decide it's time to level up?"

"More or less," Kim nodded, bemused by the sharp edge in his tone.

"And then what? I get fed up and decide I'm done fucking around, so I put a diamond on your finger?"

She held back her smile and nodded again. "As I understand it, that's generally the way it happens."

"The problem is, I'm going to be an overbearing, overprotective, arrogant ass. You might start wondering if I'm more trouble than I'm worth, and because I'm impatient, I'm liable to screw up and propose at the wrong time. Like when you no longer want it."

Kim couldn't help laughing at that, and Bennett relaxed a bit. She understood his anxiety. Somehow, despite all the disparities between them, she got him. Always had.

"After everything that's gone on since I've arrived, do you really think I'm going to change my mind now? I have invested years and years of pining in you, Mr. Shaw."

"Never were too bright," he smiled.

She retorted, "My loss, your gain, I guess."

Bennett stared into her face, and Kim could see him trying to decide if she was for real or not. Then, as she'd known he would, he started to make a case for himself.

"I'm good at fixing stuff around the house. I could probably even build you some of that DIY furniture you're always showing me."

Kim tilted her head and considered that. While it was unnecessary, he sure was starting off strong. *Forward march,* as Bennett liked to say.

"You'd probably have to learn to knit to make things even. I've always wanted one of those fisherman sweaters with all the cables on it. Think you could manage that?" he asked.

"*Pssh.* With my eyes closed."

She thought she sounded confident enough, but Bennett was accustomed to playing hard ball. God only knew what kind of concessions he intended to wring out of her next.

The thought made her a teeny bit nervous, but Kim was no quitter. Fortunately, Bennett loved that about her.

"I could take you shopping. And we could go on trips or whatever." He wove his fingers through hers and held on tight.

"Sure could," she agreed, squeezing him back.

Bennett's eyes took on a remote look. "You're the type to do up birthday gifts in fancy paper and bows. You'll agonize over the perfect Valentine's Day card."

"I surely will," Kim murmured. He'd never had those things before, and Bennett Shaw deserved to have someone spoil him rotten. She was going to do it like it was her whole entire job.

"Because you're mine," he said, looking back at her. "Because you love me."

"Because we belong to each other," Kim qualified. "The love goes both ways."

He shook his head reflexively, so used to denying that happiness was attainable for him. As he searched her face, however, his agitation slowly began to dissipate.

He sat up and faced her, growing determined. "I can fix cars," he told her.

"That's very cool."

"And I took a woodworking class a few years ago. I'm pretty good at it. Got all the tools and everything."

"Bennett, you probably shouldn't encourage me like this. I'll have you installing crown molding before you know what hit you."

"You know I'll protect you, right? I'll keep you safe forever."

"That's good," she said, "Because I'm going to protect you right back."

He blinked at her, as if that simple statement, apart from all the others, had somehow slipped between the plates of his armor and pierced him.

"Kimmie," he forced out. "How is this real? I love you so damn much."

"And I love you," she told him, "But it's not something you have to work to deserve, okay? It just is."

"Lucky me," he smiled, then leaned in to plant a soft kiss on her.

He couldn't quite meet her eyes, undoubtedly smarting over how many of his tender spots he'd just revealed. Kim knew

Bennett hated feeling exposed, but her certainly wasn't the first man to determine that all he wanted was what he'd never had.

Warrior or not, he was still human. He would force himself to wait months before he proposed, in service to some antiquated notion of propriety—and the whole time he would torture himself with doubt over whether the right time had arrived or not.

That seemed pointless. Tragically so.

Kim climbed into his lap and made Bennett look at her. "Listen Bennett, I'm no expert, but you know what they say don't you?"

"No," he frowned. "What?"

She grinned and kissed his nose. "If you like it then you better put a ring on it. Don't wait."

"Who says that?"

"Everyone, Bennett. It is conventional wisdom."

His turquoise eyes were mere slits of suspicion. "Everyone. Everyone says that."

"Everyone and Beyoncé," Kim amended.

"Oh. Well, if Beyoncé says it then it must be true."

"I mean…duh."

"Kim," he murmured, "do you mean…now?"

"Yes. Why else would I invoke Beyoncé?"

"Why indeed." Bennett lifted her off his lap and got to his feet. He looked around the room, almost crackling with nervous energy.

She couldn't tell if it was a fight response, or flight.

"What's happening?" she asked, standing slowly.

"Hop to it, girl," he said. "We got someplace to go."

He kissed Kim quickly but didn't linger. Bennett grabbed his phone off the bureau and glanced at the time, then urged, "Come on, darlin', put on your shoes. Time waits for no man."

She scrambled for her sandals, but Bennett was already in the hall. "Bennett! R-right now?" she stammered.

He clapped his hands in a short burst. "Yup. Get to steppin'."

Kim stared at his broad shoulders and tried to keep up, but the man's legs were long, and she clearly wasn't moving fast enough for him.

He marched back to her, grabbed her hand and towed her out the door and to his truck.

Twenty minutes later he'd parked downtown, and sat staring through his windshield at a lovely, Mediterranean style building across the street.

When he didn't get out, Kim wondered, "Is that where we're going?"

"I got my watch battery changed there a few weeks ago," he explained. "While I was waiting, I saw some things that made me think of you."

"Things?" Kim turned to study him. "Sparkly things?"

"Mm-hm."

Still, he didn't move.

"Bennett, I was only teasing you before. If you're not ready, or you don't want this for any reason," she told him, "We do not have to go in there. I will happily wait as long as it takes, believe me."

"*Hah.* You're even more impatient than I am. And it's not doubt…I just get a little—" He stopped and waved a hand around, declining to put a word to what he felt.

Kim took a guess. "Intimidated?"

"Places like that," he explained, "I'm always afraid that I'm going to do something wrong. Like there's an unwritten playbook that everyone knows but me. But if I ask too many questions, they'll know I don't belong."

"Bennett, you are the most capable man I know. You belong wherever you want to go."

"It's stupid, I know. I don't have this issue anywhere else. I trust my mind and my body to perform under the craziest conditions. And I know how to act around other guys," he told her.

"No complaints from the ladies either, I hear."

Bennett made a face at her. "It's just stuff like this. Rich people stuff, like buying condos and…and the sparkly things in there."

He gestured to the security guard posted beside the entrance as if to say, *See?*

Kim's heart ached for the things he'd overcome—though not quite all the way, it seemed.

"Bennett, there are no rules except to be kind," she said. "And as for the people working the counters in there, they're just regular folks. They're on their feet all day dealing with jerks like Dan, and making lousy salaries for their trouble. They're not going to hassle people like you and me because we are not going to hassle them."

"I can pay," he insisted stubbornly.

"Even better. They'll be fawning all over you for the fat commission you're going to bring them."

Bennett peeked at her, and then back at the jewelry store. After another minute, he squared his shoulders. "Alright, then. You ready?"

Kim chuckled. "I could ask the same of you."

INSIDE, THE SALESCLERK loitering near the door barely had to look twice to know what was up. "Right this way," he gestured grandly, and made for the engagement rings arrayed under glass in the far corner.

Bennett planted his feet and closed his eyes and clung to Kim's hand. She held up a finger to let the clerk know they needed a minute and gazed fondly into Bennett's handsome face.

Several weeks ago, a girl had walked into a bar. Not just any bar, though—it'd been the one Bennett Shaw had been in.

And it hadn't been just any girl, either. He'd told her she was the prettiest girl in the world, the one against whom he'd measured all others in his life.

Now, that girl was his, and he was hers. The rest was simply a formality.

After long quiet seconds, Kim framed his face with gentle hands.

"This is going to be a piece of cake," she said softly. "You'll see."

Bennett's eyes snapped open, and he took in what she hoped was utter certainty on her face. "You're it for me," he whispered. "My home. Everything it represents, all it can be—with you, it finally makes sense."

Kim could've melted into the floor right there. "I love you," she whispered against his lips. "Everything is going to be fine. I promise."

"Then let's do this." Bennett kissed her, then he pulled back, looked over at that clerk, and nodded firmly. "Let's find this girl the rock to end all rocks."

Epilogue

Wyatt

WYATT PULLED UP to the curb and double-checked the Torrey Pines address on his phone. 2943 Vista Del Mar, Unit B. This was it.

The gold star service banner hanging in the front window certainly seemed to confirm matters, though many people would not consider this a time of war.

Wyatt, and the widow inside, knew better.

He glanced at the houses nearby. There were a couple of kids riding bikes, and a neighbor mulching around his shrubs. It was a safe and painfully normal suburb.

He wondered who was helping Mrs. Burke take care of things now that Jesse was dead.

Family, he supposed, if she or her husband had grown up nearby. But was that likely, for a military couple? The Army stationed people where they were needed, not where it was convenient for them.

Mrs. Burke—Leah, he remembered—could hardly expect members of her husband's unit to rally around her, either. The few who'd survived the ambush of Nabarut had been wounded and sent home. Hell, one of them, Tate Monroe, was his new boss.

Even knowing all that, it still seemed like a stretch for Wyatt to be here.

He was about to pull away, frustrated by his inability to leave this thing alone, when the front door opened, and Leah emerged on the front step.

Damn. *Damn.*

The widow, it seemed, was absolutely gorgeous.

In all of her husband's tequila-laced ramblings, Wyatt had never dreamed Jesse was describing a woman like this.

Before he quite knew what he was doing, he'd turned off the car, opened his door, and got out.

The movement caught her eye, and her gaze snapped to his. Wyatt was caught in its spell, suspended in space and time thanks to one hell of a brown-eyed girl, when his phone rang loudly in his pocket.

Funny how, before this moment, he'd found the retro ringtone clever. Not anymore.

Wyatt wheeled away, hunching into himself as he answered. "Yeah?"

"Bro, where the fuck are you?" Joe barked, his clipped Boston accent lending his irritation an even sharper edge. "I just had to get a California king out the front door and into a moving van with no one but the kid helping me. You're fucking nuts if you think I'm gonna wrestle that shit up the freight elevator at Easy's new place without you."

Wyatt frowned. "Why isn't Buck helping?"

"Dude, are you high? He and Peyton are up in Big Bear this week. And before you ask, Easy and his girl already ran a load of boxes over in his truck—though if you ask me, the two of them are taking a lot longer to unpack than is strictly necessary."

"Shit. Sorry." He'd lost track of time. *Again.*

Wyatt ducked back behind the wheel and started his car, but he didn't glance over to see if the widow was watching. "I ran into someone I used to know, and we got to talking. I'll be there as soon as I can."

"Jesus, Mary, and Joseph," Bruiser muttered darkly. "Just meet us at the condo. We're not gonna dick around for another three hours while you chat up MILFs in the burbs."

"Would you relax? I said I'm on my way."

"Tell what's-her-name we said hello," Joe retorted, not believing Wyatt's bullshit. He paused, then added on, "You know what? Forget that. Don't say a word to her—she's been through enough. You just go through a drive-thru on your way back and bring us some grub like a good boy. And get me a coffee. I'm dying over here."

"Fine."

"Oh, and remind me to tell you about Kim's hard drive later. The boy wonder thinks he might've found something on it after all."

"Seriously?"

"No shit. Dude's a certified genius, I'm telling you."

Wyatt pulled away, but he didn't get far. There was a stop sign at the end of the block, and a pair of teenagers decided to stroll slowly across the intersection once he rolled to a halt.

He risked a glance in his rear view, to see whether Jesse Burke's goddess of a wife was still outside.

She was. In fact, Leah was standing in the middle of the road behind him, frowning and snapping a photo of his license plate with her phone.

Damn it. Beauty and *brains.*

Perhaps he'd scouted out her house a few too many times lately.

"By the way, we don't need to look for a new roommate anymore," Joe informed him.

Wyatt hadn't realized his buddy was still on the line. "Oh? Who you got?" he wondered absently.

"Noah said he'll take a room, though if you ask me, letting him have the big one seems egregious."

Noah and his baby face handled most of Black Watch's computer-related tasks, and though he staunchly claimed he was 27, Wyatt wasn't buying it.

"Seriously? He's still a student. Can he afford it?"

"With what Monroe pays? Gonna assume so. Besides, if he's being straight with us, he probably gets a few bucks from the jarhead retirement, too. He's done with school this spring, anyway, so he'll need a new place one way or another."

Wyatt shrugged, winding a few more blocks through the neighborhood before he found the exit onto the main road.

"Whatever you think. I don't care." He found the ramp for the I-5 south and merged onto it, heading for the fast lane so he could open up the throttle. "ETA twenty minutes," he told Joe.

"Twenty minutes! Christ, Stitch. There's something wrong with you. One of these days you're going to wreck that fucking car, and then where will we be?"

Something wrong? Wyatt snorted morosely. They were in the midst of hunting a powerful, corrupt senator, who was going to be breathing down their necks twice as much now that they'd gotten his asshole stepson thrown in jail.

And, instead of buckling down and seeing that mission through, Wyatt had been spending his free time gawking at a dead soldier's widow.

Joe didn't know the half of what was wrong with him.

Up Next

Brothers in Arms

(Black Watch Security, Book Three)

Wyatt Oaks had not seen Jesse Burke die, but he'd endured the same devastating skirmish, and it had deep-sixed his SEAL career. Weeks before, however, he'd spoken to the soldier for a few hours, one drunken night on leave. That connection barely made them acquaintances, and certainly not friends.

So why did he feel such an obligation to the wife and small son the Army captain had left behind? Wyatt had heard about them exactly once—he should have been able to forget them. What's more, the fact that Black Watch was in the midst of taking down a corrupt senator with a vendetta against his team, meant Wyatt *needed* to forget them.

He wasn't the forgetting type, though. And once he discovers that Leah Burke knows more than anyone could guess about that infamous ambush and what the dirty senator wrought there—he realizes he just might have to become more than another brother-in-arms Leah and her son don't need.

Wyatt might have to become their everything.

Sneak peeks and release dates will be shared in my monthly newsletter soon! Are you signed up?

FREE BOOK

Get a glimpse of Morgan, Meg, Molly and Mina—*before* their happily ever afters take place!

Sign up for the author's Reader's List and get a free copy of the Lost & Found prequel novella "Girls Night Out."

Visit Here to Get Started:

http://eepurl.com/ctGk1j

Also by Kristen Casey

The Triple Threat Series

The Titan Was Tall
The Doctor Was Dark
The Hero Was Handsome
The Triple Threat Box Set

The Lost & Found Series

Girls Night Out
Finding Home
Finding Love
Lost in Love
The Flynn Sisters Box Set
Finding a Husband
Finding Forever
Forever and a Day
The O'Connell Sisters Box Set

Acknowledgments

Bennett Shaw is my favorite kind of character to write, probably because I identify so strongly with two of his best qualities—he is petty and dogged, guys. A lethal combination.

Don't believe me? Go ahead and tell him that he can't do something, and watch what happens next. It was spite, more than anything, that no doubt got him through those earliest, hardest days on his own.

These particular traits make it into so many of my characters and I absolutely love to give them the world. But why, you may ask?

Well… guess how many times I heard things like:

"If you don't speak up, no one will ever listen to you."
"If you don't stop acting so shy, you'll never make friends."
"Good luck with that. Pisces never finish anything."
"If you change your major now, you'll never get a good job."
"If you take a leave of absence, you'll never go back and finish your degree."
"If you move in with that guy after only three months of long-distance dating, you'll live to regret it." (*)

To that, I say: Screw them. I've served up cold hard revenge for decades now, each time I've proven the naysayers wrong. I guess, like Bennett, I just won't quit. I'm petty that way.

And so, for all the folks out there who've been told you're not enough, you don't have what it takes, you can't, you won't…this book's for you.

Go out there and prove them wrong. Every day, with a smug smile on your face, stick it to the haters with the sweetest revenge of all: success, however that looks to you.

I'm rooting for you.

Thanks, as always, to my brilliant cover designer Deborah Bradseth, who brings my heroes so perfectly to life; to the most enthusiastic, supportive beta reader on the planet, Helen Snay; and to my family, who makes all the headaches worthwhile.

(*As for that guy I moved in with, our HEA is closing in on 25 years, so I guess we did alright.)

About the Author

Kristen Casey writes the kind of heartfelt, steamy books she loves to read—full of relatable characters and delicious dialogue. She lives in Maryland with her husband, two kids, and assorted cats, and in her free time enjoys all things crafty—especially projects she makes from yarn.

Sign up for her newsletter to receive exclusive content, sales, and new releases emailed right to your inbox.

Follow her on social media, for even more fun stuff!

Goodreads: Kristen_Casey

Facebook: AuthorKCasey

Twitter: AuthorKCasey

Pinterest: KristenCase0461

Instagram: Kristen.Casey.Books

BookBub: Kristen Casey

TikTok: KristenWritesRomance

Reading Order

The Lost & Found Series
Girls Night Out (Prequel exclusive to subscribers)
Finding Home (Book 1)
Finding Love (Book 2)
Lost in Love (Book 2.5 – Includes Lucky in Love)
The Flynn Sisters Box Set (Includes Christmas in Cambridge)
Finding a Husband (Book 3)
Finding Forever (Book 4)
Forever and a Day (Book 4.5 – Includes Forever Starts Now)
The O'Connell Sisters Box Set (Includes Heroes & Husbands)

The Triple Threat Series
The Titan Was Tall (Book 1)
The Doctor Was Dark (Book 2)
The Hero Was Handsome (Book 3)
The Triple Threat Box Set (Includes The Masquerade Was Magic and The Hero's Brother)

The Black Watch Security Series
False Flag (Book 1)
Heat Seeking Missile (Book 2)
Brothers in Arms (Book 3)
Fight or Flight (Book 4)
Search and Destroy (Book 5)
Squared Away (Book 6)